Walls

of

Words

Short stories inspired by travels across the world

Oliver Eade

Copyright © Oliver Eade 2018
All rights reserved.

No part of this publication may be produced or transmitted in any form or by any means without the prior written consent of the author.

All characters and events in this publication are fictitious and any resemblance to real persons, living or dead, is purely coincidental.

www.olivereade.co.uk

Cover design and artwork
Copyright © Fiona Ruiz 2018

Cover image:
walls somewhere in the city of Bologna

ISBN: 978-1-912513-51-2

Silver Quill Publishing
www.silverquillpublishing.com

Dedicated to Yvonne

'Being in love shows a person who they should be.'

Anton Pavlovich Chekhov
Doctor, short story writer and playwright
1860-1904

Acknowledgements

I am grateful to all in Silver Quill Publishing for support and advice, to my good friend David Jones for help with proofreading with some of these stories and to my dear wife, Yvonne Wei-Lun, for a love which gives me the courage to believe in myself.

The Red Chevy
The Water Girl
Fireflies
In the Heat of the Desert
C Sharp Minor
Kangaroo Dreaming
The Smile of a Samurai
The Rain in Spain
The Fragments
No Tears
A Neutralising Thought
A Cross of Sticks
Miriam
The Pringle Sisters
The Other Nathan
The Megarabbit
A Baker's Novel
The Tower of Truth
Second Chance
The Hole
One Click Away
Thomas the Rhymer
The Wave
Duck Business
Last Dance
The Old Grandmother
The Recorder Player
The Two-legged Deer
Saucers of Fire
Pink Slippers
Flatpack Wife
The Old Man in the Park
More Fish
The Christmas Dance
The Letter
Whatever Happened to
Harry Plant?
The Last Ski Station

Whispers of Death
The Fiftieth Audi
Cissy
Ryanair Aphrodite
Old Annie and her Last
  Chicken
Fallen Angel
Singularly Beautiful
Frog Therapy Ltd
Paradise Lost & The
  Helmsman
Our Lake
Automatic Door
The Girl on the Bench
The Soul Sweeper
Hawai'i
The Visitor

The Red Chevy

"Miss Mary-Anne, what is you doin' by that window? Why, you's only wearin' a nightie. Catch the death of cold, you will. Come on back into this nice, comfy bed of yours!"

The wrinkled face of the white-haired old lady glanced at the broad, smiling African-American nurse, but the face was in another place, another time.

"He was there again, so fine in his white flannel suit and those shiny shoes, just leaning against the door of that red Chevy. Oh my, I do believe he was looking right up at me with those bright, blue eyes of his."

"Miss Mary-Anne, let me help you into bed. A few easy steps, honey. There you go. You is lookin' cosy now. I'll fix you a nice cup of hot chocolate and a cookie. How about that, huh? Oh, what a lovely smile you have," Nurse Rose said as she made the old lady comfortable in bed. But the old lady's smile remained in that other time and that other place.

"He was looking at me like there was no one else in the whole wide world!" she murmured, staring at the window.

"Be right back, honey," reassured the nurse before leaving the room.

That night, the old lady dreamt again about the handsome young man who, sixty-five years back, would stop his car to wave at her peering shyly from her bedroom window. He'd done this every day since the start of the Walnut Grove High School summer recess ten days before. This time he called out as well and when he flashed his smile at her those teeth were whiter than Carmenita the maid's sparkling, bone china dishes. She knew her daddy had already left for work, so she called back to the young man, loud and clear, and he laughed. He laughed, and, oh my, he leaned back against that red Chevy convertible and he blew her a kiss waving some more. Deep inside of that pretty, pink cotton blouse she was wearing, her young heart fluttered.

What if—?

No, she could not think of that. She was only just seventeen, after all.

He climbed into the Chevy and drove off together with his smile. There was a shout from downstairs. Her younger sister, Rachel, could not keep still when Mary-Anne appeared at the foot of the stairs. Skipping from one foot to the other, she was.

"See here!" Rachel exclaimed, excitedly waving a white envelope.

"What's that?" asked Mary-Anne. No one ever sent her letters. Later, with the letter hidden under her pillow and already in her past, she wept and she wept as the walls reverberated with the thud-thud-thud of Rachel's radio. The letter was from him and he was asking her out to the movies, but she knew her daddy would never allow it.

"Rise 'n' shine!" urged Nurse Rose, pulling back the curtains and letting in the winter sunlight. "Brought you a warm cup of lemon tea. Make you feel real good, it will, Miss Mary-Anne. Now, let's have you nice and comfy in that cosy bed of yours. There you go!"

The nurse helped the old lady forwards, puffed up her pillows and gently eased her back into a more relaxed position. But she saw no joy in her patient's face. Age had carved those cheeks into sorrowful hollows, and the lady's lizard-belly skin had become contoured by the creases of times long gone.

Like the layers of an ole tree, those creases are, thought Nurse Rose. *Why, I do believe she has as many lines on that face as there are in the Holy Bible!*

Her patient's eyes revealed only pained longing whilst the nurse cheerfully chatted and fussed around her. As soon as she had left, the old lady pulled herself to the edge of the bed, eased her bent chicken-legs to the floor and shuffled across to the window. Holding the windowsill for support, she stared out from the Palm Creek Retirement Home tucked into a quietly-forgotten corner of Texas, and she watched the world outside. She had already waited a very long time, so patience was not a problem.

Perhaps it will be today, she thought. *But there's no hurry. I can wait some more if I must.*

"Oh my! There you go again, Miss Mary-Anne! Gonna get Nurse Rose into mighty big trouble. You hear me? What if you falls and hurts yourself, honey? Here, let me help you into that chair. Take it slow, now—*real* slow!"

Fall? That was it! She fell. Broke her leg. She remembered this so clearly. Wanted to do more than break a leg. Wanted to end her life. She had not dared incur the wrath of her daddy by phoning the young man, even if it were only to say she regretted she could not accept his date, so she decided to finish it all since there seemed little purpose in continuing. Already seventeen and prevented from accepting possibly the only advance a boy would ever make to her.

She slipped out of the house without telling her momma. Music blared from Rachel's open window. *Rachel!* God, how she hated her precocious little sister. She remembered feeling horribly lonely as she stood on the bridge wall looking down at the swirling, brown water. The river was high from the previous day's heavy rainfall. She was frightened—*very* frightened. She struggled with the fear that had smothered her sadness and which seemed to prevent her from jumping. Her legs trembled, shaking her body. Then someone shouted. From behind. A man. Surprised, she half-turned, lost balance and fell backwards onto the sidewalk. She landed in an awkward, twisted way and the pain in her ankle was excruciating. She recalled screaming for her momma.

"Here's a long, cool glass of milk, Miss Mary-Anne," said Nurse Rose. "And I'll bring you a good wholesome breakfast. Make those poor skinny legs of yours nice and strong, that will! So, you just sit all peaceful like in your chair."

Nurse Rose had such a friendly face the old lady had to smile.

"Oh, Miss Mary-Anne, you have the sweetest of smiles. You know that?"

Exactly what the second letter said! She had never telephoned the young man, and there she was, stuck in bed with a plaster cast on her leg, unable to get to the window without help—her ankle being broken and all. Her daddy, he was furious when he had gotten home and heard about the fall. She felt so bad in herself that she did not care what he said with all that ranting and raving and she had told him nothing about the first letter. Not a thing! So why had he gone on at her? She had not done anything wrong apart from trying to end her life. Her *own* life. Oh, how she had wished to tell her daddy it was because of him she tried to kill herself, but she did not. Not then. Something inside of her wanted to save that pleasure for another time. A time when, perhaps, *he* might be lying immobile in bed and *she* would be looming above him and telling him.

Oh my, that second letter! This time he pleaded with her. Good as told her he loved her, and he had only seen her from afar. He even mentioned her smile:

'Ain't you gotten the sweetest smile I ever saw,' he wrote. He did!

It was Rachel who had brought her the second letter and made fun of her as always.

"There now," said Nurse Rose. "Scrambled eggs and a muffin! And some fresh orange juice. *Real* fresh! Ain't you just one lucky girl, Miss Mary-Anne?"

The nurse placed the breakfast tray on a holder that rested across the arms of the old lady's chair. Her patient took a few mouthfuls of egg, a sip of orange juice, then flopped back into the chair and stared once more at that window.

I really ought to be up there looking out, thought old Miss Mary-Anne. *Just in case!*

Food was the last thing on the mind of the seventeen-year old girl as she lay back on her bed with her right leg all heavy in a cast. She was so relieved when she heard her daddy leave for work. At least her momma showed her love and she clung to that love like it was all that mattered in the world, but even this could not dispel the feeling of despair that had taken over her tender, young spirit. Her momma called in the doctor to see whether he could figure out why Mary-Anne was behaving so strangely. The doctor, he said it was the time of the month and growing pains. Nothing more.

Growing pains? she questioned. *Ain't grown for three years!*

Mary-Anne waited for the moment when she could get back to that window by herself. Waited for a third letter. Then she might find enough courage to—

But a third letter never came.

A few days after her fall, the sound of a car pulling up outside urged her to struggle out of bed by heaving her plastered leg to the floor. She heard Rachel open her door, rush downstairs and run from the house. Her sister's shrill, flirtatious voice mingled with the deeper voice of a man. *Him?* She grabbed her crutches and pulled herself up. Sunlight, mixed with laughter, filtered through the window. Laughter and the alluring giggle of a teenage girl. She reached the window just in time to see the red Chevy drive off. Rachel was standing at the head of the driveway, waving at the car. For the rest of that day, the younger girl was even more cheerful than her usual confident self.

Miss Mary-Anne felt trapped in her chair, the tray with her unfinished breakfast forming a barrier between her and the window. She called out. Her fretful cry cut through the stillness of Palm Creek Retirement Home like a conquistador's sword. Nurse Rose came running.

"Oh my, oh my, why all this fuss, Miss Mary-Anne? And you ain't even finished your breakfast! Still, it'll not be too long before lunch, so I guess that'll have to do for now. Let me take that tray from you, honey. Then you can go for a nice wash 'n' brush. We'll have you lookin' real pretty! And how about another of your lovely smiles, huh? Just for Nurse Rose. All righty?"

Rachel was gone all afternoon and evening. She told her mother she was going to see a movie with a girlfriend. Her father was beside himself with worry when he learned this, for Rachel was his darling. Always had been. Their momma said she would be fine and told him not to worry. Mary-Anne knew it was the young man with the red Chevy. She would not tell her daddy, of course. Could never do that, for one day he would grow sick of Rachel and come back for her. So, when her leg was better, she was at the window again, looking. Always looking.

From that day onwards, Rachel was a changed person. She no longer goaded her elder sister. Worse, she ignored Mary-Anne altogether as if she, Rachel, lived in a different world and could not be bothered to communicate with her sister. She was out with her 'girlfriend' several times a week and no one questioned her further. One evening she did not come home. Their momma discovered a suitcase was missing, together with some of Rachel's clothes and personal effects. The girl had simply vanished, and she was not yet sixteen.

Mary-Anne never forgot her father's anger when he found out what had happened. He called the police and they were up the whole night, waiting. Rachel did not return that night or, indeed, ever again.

They had a phone call from her the following morning. She would not say where she was. Only that she was with a friend in another state, taking 'a few days' vacation'. Days passed—days turned into weeks. Even at the start of the new semester, she had failed to reappear.

Mary-Anne returned for her final year at high school. There were occasional calls from Rachel to her mother, but she would never say more than how happy she was and not to worry. Her father, more morose than ever, forbade anyone to mention his younger daughter's name in his presence.

One day, a few months after Rachel's disappearance, Mary-Anne got home from school to find her momma in tears. Her daddy, home early from work, sat beside his wife, head in hands, face hidden. Mary-Anne was handed a letter in Rachel's handwriting by her mother. The letter revealed how the younger girl had gotten married, for she was now sixteen, to a wealthy old man who was taking her to live in Las Vegas. She also wrote that she was done with 'lover boy' since he was 'just not rich enough'. Mary-Anne knew perfectly well who 'lover boy' was, but she was not telling. However, she took to smiling again and she was back at the window each weekend—looking... hoping.

"Oh, Miss Mary-Anne, you is at it again! Know what? I'm gonna bring that chair of yours over to the window so as you can just sit there and look outside without gettin' Nurse Rose into any kind of trouble! Heaven forbid, I'd sure like to know what it is you stares at all day long. Ain't no view at all. Just a driveway and a few ole trees. That's all I can see, anyways."

Nurse Rose placed the chair beside the window, helped the old lady into it and folded a quilt around her feeble body.

"There you go, now. And how about seein' that sweet 'n' pretty smile of yours again, huh?"

He would come back. Mary-Anne knew he would. He loved her smile, he had told her that, and her smile would always be there for him. She could wait. She was good at waiting.

Mary-Anne's mother fell ill. Her father blamed the stress surrounding Rachel's disappearance. First, she would drop things. Then she began to fall about. Her speech went funny. Words became so slurred that folk could barely make out what she was saying. When she started to choke on her food they called in the doctor. Motor Neurone Disease, he said, though Mary-Anne's father knew better. He told everyone it was stress, and by letter he implored Rachel to return to her mother, but she never did. Far too caught up with the high life in Las Vegas, she said.

It fell upon Mary-Anne to look after her mother as the poor woman grew weaker. When Mary-Anne graduated from high school, she had the best grades in her year and was all set to go on to law school after college. But that fell through when she became her mother's main carer. She put her heart and soul into her new role, for she loved her mother very much. Somehow, the woman's illness brought them closer together. Day and night, Mary-Anne was with her, tending lovingly to her every need. Mary-Anne's daddy came and went like a shadow, and barely a word was exchanged between father and daughter.

"Time for your nap, Miss Mary-Anne," said the nurse, supporting the old lady as she shuffled from the chair to the bed. "Maybe after a sleep you'll feel like givin' Nurse Rose one of your nice smiles. And you know what? Fish soup for lunch. Your favourite! Fish soup and a lovely little surprise for dessert! Now you just take it easy, honey."

She was tired. Always tired, but she never complained. Folks said her mother would have died a lot sooner if Mary-Anne had not been looking after her. Somehow the strengthening bond between mother and daughter kept them both going. A bond that helped to shut out the father whose presence the girl barely tolerated.

Mary-Anne's mother died after three years of illness. She died in her elder daughter's arms. She had not seen the younger daughter since the girl disappeared, but she had come to accept this. Her husband, excluded from the love that bound Mary-Anne to her mother, never did get over the loss of his beloved Rachel.

During her mother's illness, Mary-Anne was far too busy to spend time peering out of her bedroom window, but after the woman's death, with time again on her hands, she would stand for long hours staring at the world and waiting for that red Chevy to pull up outside just one more time. She was still young. He would come back for her. She was sure of it. And she could wait.

Mary-Anne went to secretarial college to learn short-hand and typing. She was certain to get a secretarial post somewhere and everyone knew that she would make an excellent secretary. Then, with a weekly wage, she could leave her father when *he* returned for her.

"Lunch time!" Nurse Rose cheerily announced, waking the old lady by gently nudging her arm. "See here, Miss Mary-Anne. Fish soup, some nice fresh bread, orange juice, and that special surprise—fruit salad with ice cream! Ain't that awesome? Just the right formula to bring back a lovely smile for that pretty face of yours."

The nurse propped the old lady up with a back rest and some pillows. She opened the window a fraction.

"Gettin' kinda stuffy in here, Miss Mary-Anne, but mind you says if you get any kinda draught from this window."

The old lady smiled.

"There you go! Such a beautiful smile. Like I keep tellin' you!"

Three weeks after his wife's death, Mary-Anne's father had a stroke. She found him one morning, in the kitchen, sitting back and staring like a shop-fitter's dummy. She asked him why he had not gone to work but she got no reply. He could not reply for he had lost his speech and his right arm was as useless as a car without gas. His right leg went all stiff and funny like it never belonged to him no more. He was in hospital for three months during which time he slowly learned to walk again with the aid of a stick. He was even able to feed and dress himself, after a fashion, but, although he understood perfectly well what was said to him, his speech never returned.

Mary-Anne was forced, by the hospital staff, to make a difficult decision. Her father could no longer remain in hospital and she would either have to take him back or arrange for him to go into a nursing home. That would mean selling the house and using every cent of her assets to pay the fees. She knew there was no decision to make. Fate had made it for her, and, oh boy, was she bitter! When her crippled father arrived home, she felt not one flicker of the love and compassion that she'd felt for her ailing mother. She positively hated him.

The only thing that kept her going during those long, tedious years, when saddled with the speechless, irritable man who had so tormented her in childhood, was the certainty that *he* would one day come back for her. Then she could leave her daddy for *he* would take care of her. She would sell the house, use the money to put the fractious old cripple into care and live on in the knowledge that she might never have to see the horrid man again. She had it all worked out and she waited. Whenever possible, she would stand at her bedroom window and look out for the red Chevy. She so wanted to be there, at the window, when he did return. Then she would give him the brightest smile ever and wave. She would wave just as she had once done during that long, hot, high school summer recess.

Over the years that followed, she began to talk to her father. Never done that before. Now that he was unable to talk back, she quite enjoyed the experience. She told him how much she had always hated him, how he had destroyed her only chance to meet the love of her life and be happy and how like his treasured Rachel he was: selfish and uncaring. She enjoyed the look of pain on his face as he desperately tried to respond to her biting words but could only grunt. Then she would tell him all over again. That was as close as she came to unleashing the demons of her past.

"Well now, ain't that just wonderful!" said Nurse Rose. "Finished all your soup! You know, I think we could have you sittin' in that chair by the window once more after we have been to the bathroom, Miss Mary-Anne."

Her father lived on for another ten years. During that time no one visited him, for before his stroke he only had his work and his bitterness. No friends. Mary-Anne, she worked as a secretary for a group of lawyers downtown. She earned enough to get by and even bought herself a little car, but she never had enough to be fully free from her daddy. Although by no means unattractive, as a young woman she remained forever shy. Her disarming smile did catch the attention of a few would-be suitors, but she became evasive when they asked her out and, somehow, she always managed to stay quietly in the background wherever she happened to be.

She hardly noticed her father's death when it came. Only that there was less food to prepare, less washing to do and she felt happier. Otherwise she continued as before, keeping herself to herself at work and living in hope back home. She would spend more and more time staring from her bedroom window as she grew older. Hope never left her.

Nurse Rose looked in during the afternoon to check on the old lady. There she was, leaning forwards in her chair to get a better from the window.

"Well, I sure don't know what the old lady is lookin' at out there," the nurse muttered to herself. She called to the back of the white-haired head silhouetted in the window: "Hey, Miss Mary-Anne! Be back real soon, I will. With a nice cup of hot chocolate and more of your favourite cookies, honey."

Always true to her word, Nurse Rose returned with that cup of chocolate and cookies on a tray. Her hands went limp and the tray crashed to the ground, splashing hot chocolate over her feet. The chair was empty, and the window wide open—far wider than when she had left the old lady only minutes before. The nurse shrieked and ran to the window. In that fraction of a second, as she leaned out and looked down at the ground twenty feet below, her heart dropped like a brick from a high rise.

"Praise the Lord!" she exclaimed, breathing a sigh of relief when she saw only the gravel path and a few parched shrubs. She caught a glimpse of a car disappearing up the driveway. Indeed, it would have been difficult not to see the car for it was bright red—an old vintage Chevy convertible from the fifties with two people sitting in the front. The young man driving, he cut a real fine figure, he did, in his smart white flannel suit and smoothly swept-back black hair. The pretty blonde beside him, she turned around and she waved at Nurse Rose.

"Now why would she do a thing like that?" the nurse asked herself.

The girl smiled, and Nurse Rose reckoned she had never seen such a nice smile on a young girl. Briefly, she wondered whether she recognized that smile, but she merely shrugged her shoulders at the thought as the red Chevy eased itself out onto the road and disappeared. She assumed the young people had taken a wrong turning.

"Miss Mary-Anne, is you in the bathroom?" Nurse Rose called out. "You just gave me one awful big fright, you did! Hey—Miss Mary-Anne...?"

The Water Girl

"What is that child doin'?" asked Anne as she watched her six-year-old daughter struggle across the sun-parched yard with another full watering-can. With a look of determination, little Holly tipped the contents into a large puddle framed by her dolls. The child had already made trips to the tap at the back of the house to create this curious water feature.

"Drivin' all of us mad, this summer heat is," Anne said, leaving the kitchen window to sit beside her husband.

José Santos was only half-listening to his wife whilst he scanned the *Dallas Morning News*, at the same time slurping from a pint-sized mug of coffee. He wiped his mouth across his sleeve.

"Sure thing," he replied without looking up.

Holly had inherited her father's Mexican features and dark complexion, but her striking, blue eyes were her mother's. Anne, being of Swedish descent and fair, suffered during the long, hot Texan summers. Holly, like her father, thrived in the heat of the sun.

"Bye, Papa!" Holly called out whilst staggering across the yard with yet another heavy can of water before José Santos wedged his large body into the cab of the rusting Dodge truck parked in the driveway.

"Bye, honey!" responded José.

The engine spluttered into life. José swung the vehicle out onto the long, dirt road leading to the highway. As Anne watched the Dodge bump along the track, raising a coon-tail cloud of dust in its wake, she looked anxiously at the cruel disc of the morning sun already high above the horizon. José, meanwhile, breathed in the warm air with intense satisfaction. Like his little daughter, he absorbed only pleasure from the sun. He could sense himself coming to life as he squinted into its glare, casually tapping the steering wheel of the old Dodge and humming tunelessly. Anne stared at the receding dust cloud until it disappeared into the shimmer of a Texas summer. The only remaining sound was a monotonous whir from the cicadas hidden in a dried-out thicket at the back of the yard.

Holly squatted beside her artificial puddle, talking to her Barbie doll and the soft animals neatly arranged round its edge. Studying her daughter from the kitchen window, Anne so wished there were other children nearby for the girl to play with during the summer recess. They lived just too far out of town, and Anne had no transport of her own, but what concerned her most was how Holly seemed perfectly happy playing those strange games on her own beside that puddle. Close to tears, she left the window and sat at the table until she could summon enough energy to get on with the tedious routine of household chores in the Texan heat.

*****

"Hi there!" Holly said to the puddle, grinning as she peered down. Slowly, in the blueness of the reflected sky, two bright eyes appeared, their blueness even more intense than that of the sky. Feature by feature, the face of a young girl formed in the water. First, a small, slightly turned-up nose, next a chin followed by lips parted in a mischievous grin. Then the girl's cheeks showed, dimpled by her smile, and lastly her long, blonde hair which hung upwards, touching the surface of the puddle from below.

"Hi!" Only Holly could hear her. "What toys you gotten today, Holly?" the Water Girl asked.

"Look!" replied Holly excitedly, reaching for her Barbie doll which she held over the puddle for the other girl to see. "I've brought her nurse's uniform. We can play hospitals!"

Later that day, Anne once again let José know how worried she was about Holly.

"Oh, she's jus' fine! Quit worryin', Anne." The woman's husband hungrily dug his fork into a large plateful of burger, beans and fries. "See... honey—" he continued, his mouth full of food, "—See, she's just like her Mexican Grandma. Now Pa, he always said how *she* used to talk to herself. Said *she* had amazin' powers for seein' into the future, too. People used to—"

14

"I do not wanna hear this!" snapped Anne. "Holly needs friends. Long hot summers playin' out there on her own ain't no good for that child. Ain't nothin' for her in this God-forsaken desert." Tears glistened her eyelids.

"Okay, honey. I know how you feel," reassured José, looking up. "See, when them folks in management finally pays me real bucks for all the goddamn work I do for the comp'ny then I'll get us a real nice place in town." Anne turned her face away as the tears trickled down her cheeks. "Till then, we'll just have to make do."

José got up and gently kissed his wife on the forehead.

"Papa!" shrieked Holly, bursting into the kitchen. She ran to encircle her father's sturdy legs with her small arms and looked pleadingly up at him. "Papa! Can you make me another one of those paper boats?" José furrowed his forehead in mock displeasure at his daughter as she tugged at his jeans. Holly was grinning. "Um—*please*, Papa," she added.

José hesitated. A look of dismay shadowed Holly's little face.

"What colour?" José asked the child, scratching his head. He winked at her and she laughed.

"Oh, blue of course, silly!" replied Holly, giving her father a friendly slap on the arm for asking the obvious. She always wanted blue boats. He knew that. Blue like the eyes of the Water Girl.

The next day was even hotter than the previous. With José at work, Anne watched again as her young daughter played in the yard around the puddle she created afresh each day. Bordering this was her collection of dolls and toys, together with José's blue paper boat. Holly picked up the boat, held it over the puddle and waited.

"Hello!" she called out. Moments later, she saw those eyes appear in the reflected sky of a similar colour. The Water Girl smiled up at her from the puddle, her blond hair again hanging upwards to touch the surface of the water from below.

"Look!" said Holly excitedly. "Papa's made me another boat."

Carefully, Holly placed the paper craft in the centre of the puddle. It floated perfectly. The Water Girl looked up at her little friend. "May I play with it?" she asked.

"'Course you can," Holly replied, smiling at the puddle. Slowly, a child's hand reached up from the depths and touched the tip of the reflected sail. The boat on the surface wobbled and Holly giggled.

From the kitchen window, Anne watched in horror as she saw the blue paper boat propel itself across the puddle in the hot, still air. It changed direction and moved back towards Holly who was so obviously enjoying herself. Anne had had enough. *I'll have to do something,* she thought as she stepped back from the window.

After Anne and Holly had eaten a simple lunch of bread, ham and pickles, in the kitchen, the mother broached the subject of the puddle with her daughter:

"See, honey, those folks in the water comp'ny, they say it's been such a long, dry summer this year we must save every drop of water from now on. *Every* drop, honey!" She placed her hand over her daughter's. "And, well... that, I'm afraid, means no more puddles." Horror darkened the girl's face. "You do understand, don't you, Holly?"

The silence was unbearable, but Anne knew that she must not shed tears. The child looked up, those blue eyes wide and questioning. They gave her the saddest look that Anne had ever seen, and she turned away as her own eyes of identical blue moistened. Holly spoke:

"Ma—just a little water? A tiny bit? The water comp'ny'll never know. Please, Ma."

Anne was looking at the window.

"No, honey! Every drop from now on is for drinkin' and washin'," she insisted.

Suddenly, Holly grinned.

"Ma! I know what!" she said excitedly. "I don't *have* to always wash, and I really don't drink much. *She* can have *my* water!"

Anne looked at Holly as if she'd been stung.

"Who, Holly? Who are you talking about?"

"The Water Girl, of course! She can have my water."

Holly smiled sweetly, stroking her mother's arm in the hope that this might persuade her to give permission to continue making a puddle in the yard over and over.

"Holly, no!"

Holly's smile vanished. She was not a child prone to tantrums but, like all young children, she could sulk when things did not go the way she wanted. All afternoon she sat indoors drawing and looking through her books, avoiding anything more than monosyllabic communication with her mother. By the evening, the puddle was no more than a damp patch lined by Holly's soft animals, the boat keeled to one side in its centre.

The heat of the summer and the drought dragged on. As the days passed, Holly seemed to have forgotten about the puddle. Heedless of the sun, she played happily out in yard. Anne was relieved. No longer was she forever peering anxiously out of the kitchen window whilst her daughter did strange things beside that awful puddle. Anne, like Holly, appeared to have forgotten about the Water Girl until that hot and hazy evening, towards the end of the summer recess, when she found Holly sitting in front of her dressing table gazing into the mirror. Disgruntlement distorted the girl's pretty features.

"It ain't fair, Ma," Holly said, pulling at her hair, her mother's large hairbrush grasped in her small hand. "Why can't I have yellow hair like you and Phoebe?"

Anne froze. She reached out to the end of the bed for support then sat down slowly. At first. She merely stared at her little daughter whilst the child tugged crossly at her silken black hair. It was quite a while before she could speak.

"What did you just say, honey?" Anne finally asked. Her voice trembled.

Holly turned to face her mother.

"I said I want yellow hair like you and Phoebe. Will you dye it, Ma?" the girl asked.

"Who... is... Phoebe?" Anne stressed each word. Slowly. She knew the answer, but she had to hear it from Holly however painful this might be.

"Phoebe? The Water Girl of course!" came the reply that Anne so dreaded. Holly's frustration showed in her face, as though everybody surely knew that the Water Girl was called Phoebe.

Anne knew only too well who Phoebe was. Phoebe had been Anne's twin sister until she and Anne's father were killed in a car crash all those years back. Phoebe was six when she died. Same age as Holly. Anne and Phoebe were almost indistinguishable and quite inseparable. Anne, the shy one, used to follow her twin around like a little shadow. Even now, so many years later, she could still see Phoebe's lively, cheerful face in her mind, hear her constant chatter and her infectious laughter.

"How... why—?" Anne began, but she was at a loss to come out with a coherent sentence.

"Can't you dye my hair, Ma?" Holly repeated.

Anne seemed not to hear what her daughter was saying. She stood, uneasily, tears streaming her cheeks, then wrapped both arms around Holly who had her face turned towards the mirror again.

"I love you just as you are, Holly," she said quietly.

Holly's reflection smiled back at her from the mirror.

All evening, Anne tried hard to forget what Holly had said. She did not feel able to tell José in case he should go on about his Grandma's special powers. She knew she would just crack up if she heard another word about old Grandma Santos. This was different. It was about their daughter and her long-departed sister.

Best try to forget, she thought. *Anyways, Holly will be back at school in a few days.*

That night, Anne slept fitfully. In one of her many dreams, she was lost in a vast and strange city where gigantic grey buildings started to fall all around her. The collapse of each edifice caused rumbles that sent Anne running off in the opposite direction as she tried to find her way out of this nightmare city. She awoke with a start and realized that the sound of falling buildings in her dream had been caused by thunder. A violent storm was bringing a deluge of much-needed rain to their arid corner of Texas. Periodically, the bedroom was illuminated by lightning flashes, and the rain, driven hard against the window, sounded like handfuls of nails being thrown at the house. But Anne was relieved to think that the days would at last be cooler. She drifted off to sleep once more, only to awake early. José was snoring. Sunlight filtered through the half-closed blinds as the cicadas outside busily sawed away at the early morning stillness.

The storm... rain... water?

Anne sprang upright.

"Oh my God!" she muttered, quickly slipping out of bed. She ran to the kitchen without bothering to put on her dressing gown. It was just as she had feared. There were several puddles in the yard, and there, in its usual place, was that same pool around which, once more, Holly's dolls and soft animals had been placed. The woman's eyes searched the yard, but she could not see Holly. She looked again at the puddle. Holly's shoes were there, in between her Barbie doll and teddy. Shaking with dread of what she already knew, Anne rushed out into the yard.

"Holly!" she called. "Holly darling, where are you?"

The only reply came from the teasing cicadas. Anne peered into the tool shed. Empty! Overcome with panic, she glanced back at the deck outside the kitchen, willing her daughter to miraculously appear.

"Holly! Holly!"

She now shrieked her daughter's name but still there was no reply. She ran back into the house and shook José so hard he thought, in a half-awakened state, that he was being attacked and he lashed out with his large fists.

"Ow!" cried Anne, rubbing her arm. "José, get up quick! It's Holly! I can't find her anywhere. Her dolls—they're all around the puddle, but—" She waved her arms frantically. "And her shoes are there too. It's the Water Girl. Phoebe. She's taken Holly."

José rubbed his weary eyes.

"Honey," he said, "you ain't makin' no sense at all. Just what *are* you talkin' about, woman?"

He eased himself up and sat on the edge of the bed scratching his head as Anne hopped from one foot to the other, repeatedly pulling at her husband's arm.

"Oh, José! Come quick! She's not out there. Holly's gone!"

With an expression of irritated resignation, José wandered into Holly's empty room. Anne stood behind him.

"See!" she said, sobbing. "She's gone!"

José turned to face his wife.

"Honey, will you just keep calm!"

Anne followed José out into the yard. No Holly.

"There!" cried Anne, pointing at the display of dolls and much-loved cuddly animals, together with Holly's shoes, at the edge of the puddle.

José stared at Holly's little red shoes reflected in the water of the puddle, but there was something else. José walked slowly towards it. Anne held back. José tried hard not to see what he saw as he approached the watery mirror. He turned his face away, not knowing quite where to fix his gaze, then looked back at the puddle. Not only were Holly's shoes reflected in its stillness, but Holly stood there, upside down. Just her reflection. The space above the puddle was empty. Although unable to clearly see his daughter's face, he knew it was her. He watched Holly's reflection reach out towards the face of a girl with long blonde hair like Anne's. The face looked up at José and smiled. Those azure-blue eyes were Anne's eyes—Holly's eyes—the eyes of the Water Girl.

"H-H-Holly?" José stammered. Holly's reflection moved, became less distinct, and her black hair seemed to merge with the dark grey of the wet ground. "Holly!" he shouted.

The reflection turned its face up towards the blue sky. Its mouth moved and seemed to be trying to say something, but no sound emerged. The still water showed Holly's short legs, her nightgown and her beautiful hair, but the face had no eyes. The figure, its arms stretched out, continued to move towards the Water Girl whose bright blue eyes stared cheekily at José.

"Hi, Papa!" said the Water Girl. Holly's voice—Holly's eyes. "Tell Mama to—" Then the voice of the Water Girl was drowned by Anne's screams.

Fireflies

"Fireflies!"

George looked at his father who sat with his right leg pointing north, like a jammed compass needle, the left folded awkwardly. The word came out awkwardly too, as though being squeezed from an almost-empty toothpaste tube. The lop-sided mouth remained open.

"No, Dad. I want to know what you'd like for your birthday. For dinner. When I get back. Macaroni cheese? Lentils?"

George knew the old fellow's jaws would make heavy weather of steak, his one-time favourite food. But for steak, *Homo sapiens* would never have gained the strength required to leave the African plains, he had repeatedly been informed as a boy. But his father's hatred of fish, chicken and cheese, combined with his stroke, meant that every meal required precision planning. And blending. The old man's choking episodes were the last straw, Sally had happily told George the day before she left him. Later, he discovered this was just a convenient excuse to open her legs for her boss. Before the stroke, George's father had tried to warn his son about his daughter-in-law's infidelity, but the young doctor had refused to listen.

"Fireflies!" repeated Tom Bunyan.

George sighed. He briefly fussed around his father, ensuring the old man was comfortable, rearranging his book, reading glasses and a glass of water on the tray fixed to a special chair purchased at great cost (yet another of Sally's excuses to leave him) from Medi-Supplies Inc.

"Please stay put till Mrs. Perez comes in half-an-hour, Dad," George pleaded.

"Fireflies!"

George left.

*****

Old Tom Bunyan had it all planned. He wished he could have discussed it with George, but the words inside his head would have to remain there because of that goddamn stroke. For a Harvard professor of astrophysics to remain locked inside a prison of bone, that his medical son conveniently called a cranium, was indeed a cruel fate, but no way would he allow this to prevent him from seeing the fireflies again on his birthday. His imprisoned brain had worked out the logistics. Mrs. Perez would give him the opportunity. She alone understood his true needs. What did it matter what sort of a slop his son served up that evening after work, so long as he could see those fireflies?

It was a bright young Chinese post-graduate student who had given him the idea. She had been working on a thesis which, he told her, brought Einstein and Planck closer together. She had the insight to see distant galaxies and black holes obeying the same laws as subatomic particles colliding at close to the speed of light in a manmade tunnel. And when he had asked her where the fireflies fitted in, she merely smiled. He never forgot that smile. It was in his head when the stroke caused him to fall off a ladder whilst trimming a hedge.

Before the stroke, whenever he came to visit his son and daughter-in-law in Texas, Professor Bunyan made a point of taking a stroll beside the bayou after sunset. At first, it was to escape the bickering between George and Sally. If he had stayed in the house he would have sided with his son, for he already had suspicions about his daughter-in-law. This, however, might have made things worse. So, he would creep out and, after a twenty-minute walk, sit on a bench listening to the frogs and the bayou birds—alien sounds for someone from Massachusetts—until dusk had spread her grey veil over the city. Then he would wait. Wait for that first firefly. Like those exploding galaxies and particle collisions, it was all so transient (that was another thing—what thoughts did the girl have about the physics of time?) but unbelievably beautiful. A point of light that flicked on, shot sideways, hovered and then—

Once he saw a firefly suspended, infinitesimally briefly, above the mustard-grey water of the bayou in which a point of light, reflected, came and went in that dark place where black snakes curled against the fast-flowing current. He could never understand how the water flowed so fast when the city his son lived in was as flat as a breakfast pancake. Even the water in Houston seemed to disobey the laws of physics.

Sometimes he sat for up to two hours watching the darting fireflies until, in the blackness, they became distant stars to his Hubble-telescope eyes. After tutoring the Chinese girl with the face of an angel, and a brain of which his academic colleagues were supremely jealous, he saw so much more in the seemingly random movements of the fireflies. He saw a divine purpose. He saw God. Oh, if only he could have told her!

*****

Mrs. Perez, known more simply as Carmen (*did that Chinese girl also know about the opera of the same name?* wondered the professor) arrived on the dot of eight o'clock. Tom only had to wink at her, and she knew something was afoot in that brilliant, trapped brain.

"What today, mister professor?" she asked in her Mexican-Spanish accent.

"Fireflies," he answered.

"Ah, *iluciérnagas!* Yes! I understand."

Tom smiled, closed his eyes and, whilst Carmen got on with the housework, punctuated by motherly attentions to his various needs, the vast cinema screen within his skull sparkled with stars and nebulae and photons—and fireflies. Later, he overheard the telephone conversation between Mrs. Perez and his son—at least, the important part:

"No, Dr Bunyan. It would give my family great pleasure for him to eat with us on his birthday tonight. Yes, you must be busy in the hospital. Always busy, huh? And so kind to us."

"Your son, he was too good for her!" she announced for Tom's benefit after she came off the phone.

When Carmen helped him into her 4X4, he felt as guilty as a child sneaking off to play when it should have been glued to a desk doing homework. So, George would be back late from the hospital—wonderful! The Perez family were used to feeding him, on occasions, but all he could say to them that evening was 'fireflies'. They understood.

"¡Sí! ¡Luciérnagas!"

Carmen's teenage daughter, María, accompanied them to the bayou. His walker would not fit in her mother's car, so she insisted she should be a human walker for the old man. She wanted to become a doctor, like the professor's son whom she secretly worshipped. Supported by the two Hispanic women, the old professor's contorted body was helped along the same path, ending up on the same bench, the right leg pointing north, mouth lopsided and open, mind as alert as ever.

Ever? the old man thought. *What would that Chinese girl make of the concept of eternity?* he wondered. *And how will she finish her thesis without me?* His brain so wanted his mouth to ask these things.

Suddenly María gasped.

"Ahí, mamá. Una luciérnaga. ¡Mira!"

The old man looked at the girl, then at what she was looking at: a scrubby bush. To think God could show up as a transient point of light in an unappealing bush—but He did! The old professor's heart raced for those few seconds whilst his eyes trapped the fleeting image. There was no need to ask the girl now—that Chinese girl with eyes like delicious almonds—for he knew, but he felt saddened that *she* might never know. They sat for ten minutes or so, and there were other fireflies, but it was the first one that had been so supremely significant. María had seen this too. Her expression told him, so he had something to be thankful for. She could become a doctor now knowing the significance of that firefly.

*****

"So, Dad, what did you have at the Perez house? For your birthday dinner?" George asked his father after the old man was brought home by Mrs. Perez and her daughter.

"Fireflies!"

María did not giggle. She, too, knew about the fireflies. And for what they stood.

In the Heat of the Desert

She slammed the brake, causing the car to screech to a halt within feet from the large, wild-eyed man who had stepped into the road and aimed a gun at her vehicle. Her mind went blank. There she was, in the middle of the Mojave Desert, alone with an armed madman.

Jesus, why didn't I just get my head down and drive into the bastard? she thought as the man edged towards the car. The bag with her cell phone lay on the seat beside her. Wary at first, the man came closer until, on reassuring himself that she had no firearm, he opened the car door.

"Out!" he ordered. Sally, her mind blank, remained glued to her seat, trembling. The man pointed to her bag. "Hand it over, lady!" She reached sideways, grabbed the bag and gave it to the man without taking her eyes off him. He had a quick glance inside. "Now get out!" he commanded.

His voice sounded like a dustcart, dirty and mechanical. She unfastened her seat-belt, and, with jelly legs, stepped out onto the frying pan hot tarmac road. It was like entering an oven. Or Hell. With a casual swing of his gun, the man indicated where he wanted her to go... off the road and into the desert.

The bloody bastard, she thought. *He's gonna rape me!*

She had no choice. It was as if she had been sucked into a horror movie—the sort she would never watch on the telly, only this was a movie she could not switch off. Sally listened to the crunch of the man's footsteps behind her as she headed into the heat. With its clumps of bright yellow flowers and blue sky, the desert should have looked beautiful, but those garish flowers, the vastness and the loneliness of the place, turned it into a place of nightmares. Nowhere to hide, no one to hear her screams. The only sounds were his footsteps and his breathing. His awful, animal breathing.

Ahead, a clump of cacti reached up into the heat with searching, spiky arms.

"Stop!" the man called out. Sally halted and half-turned. The evil in his reptilian eyes seemed to slither all over her virtually-disrobed body. "Your dress, lady," he grunted. "This here ain't enough!" He indicated her bag.

Slowly, and with shaking hands, she reached for the buckle on the belt of her dress. *I must stay alive*, a voice in her head said. *I must stay alive—I must stay alive*—over and over, like a faulty tape.

Then she saw it. From the corner of one eye. It slid silently sideways over the bone-dust dirt of the desert, curling, uncurling—halting within inches of the man's feet. It raised its head. The man remained unaware of the closeness of death.

Sally knew about snakes. Her father, an expert, had taught her as a child to distinguish the deadly from the harmless, and, oh boy, was this one deadly!

The strike was so quick she would have missed it had she blinked. The man screamed, and the gun flew from his hands, raising a puff of dust from the desert floor. The snake slithered away amongst the cacti. Sally ran forwards, grabbed the gun and turned it on the man. He appeared not to notice her as he yelled obscenities and hopped around, twirling pirouettes in a dance of death before crashing to the ground. It was as if he just did not know what to do with the bitten leg. Kicking frantically, he clawed at it and groaned.

Shall I just shoot him? Sally asked herself.

But she could not. The man had robbed her, had been about to rape her and, in all probability, kill her, yet she could not bring herself to pull that trigger.

Leave him, then, she thought. *Let God and nature do the rest.*

She picked up her bag, spat at the man's contorted face and walked off, holding the gun. She walked back towards the highway. The screams got louder. She stopped and peered over her shoulder.

He was on his back, his bitten leg flailing the air now pierced by his screams.

Jesus Christ, woman, leave him, an inner voice told her.

"Leave him!" she muttered aloud, echoing the voice, but she walked back towards the man, repeatedly halting as a part of her fought with herself:

Don't do this, Sally, warned the voice. *Let the bastard suffer. Let him die.*

But her legs would not obey. They refused to take her back to the car and drive off and away to safety. The gun in her hand was useless. She knew she would never be able to squeeze that trigger. Slowly, she retraced her steps.

"Does it hurt?" she asked.

Stupid bloody question, woman, the voice in her head said. *The man's in agony and good luck to him. Go back to the car, you idiot!*

Sally knelt beside the man, placing the gun on the ground. After tearing a strip from her dress, she rolled up the man's trouser leg. The skin was crimson and swollen with two blood-filled puncture holes. Bending forward, she pursed her lips over the snake bite, sucked hard and repeatedly spat the foul taste of the man onto the desert dust. She wound the torn strip of material round the man's calf, tightening it until his screams turned ear-drum-splitting. She fashioned a knot then opened her bag. In it was the small bottle of painkillers she always carried around for migraines. Two of these she spilled into the palm of her hand before offering them, together with her water bottle, to the man. Taking out her cell phone, she dialled 911.

And she waited there, in the heat of the desert, listening for the whir of the helicopter and again and again she told herself—told that voice—that she could not have done anything else.

C Sharp Minor

"Not again!" He rose up from his chair, untidy and depressingly short. Standing gave him height. Not that he needed this, for even at her level his eyes fixed her like a nail in a post.

"C sharp, for God's sake! We're in C Sharp minor and you go and play C natural!"

He walked over to the window and gazed out at a rectangle of precision-cut lawn. Ornamental trees broke up the monotony of green whilst its borders were bursting with blooms of vivid hues. Like the flowers, she, too, seemed frail. And almost ornamental. But he liked that. The girl disrupted the monotony of his life. He needed a woman so badly.

"Energy," he said, quietly. "That's what's lacking here. Laziness has crept into your playing. You're all lazy, your kind!"

My kind?

The girl focused on her hands. They felt safe in her lap. On the keyboard they belonged to him. On the keyboard they exposed her soul. Once returned there, the tears would flow again.

"I need to go to the toilet," she whispered.

"What?" He glowered. Something tickled her cheek. She flicked away a long, dark curl that had escaped her hair band.

"I said I need to go to the toilet!"

"Hmm!"

Obviously somewhere else, those eyes told her nothing. They were like the tinted windows of a celebrity's E-type. Whereas he could read her like book, she saw nothing solid in him; only sensed an energy that threatened to choke her. And perhaps she already belonged to his past.

His past!

Everyone knew he had suffered. His father had been an alcoholic. With his mother dead, it was he who directed the struggling family like the conductor he always wanted to be. When, at the age of fourteen, she was told she was to have a new piano teacher considered to be the best in Vienna, she wanted to know everything there was to know about the famous man. Only then would she be able to let her spirit run free in the music.

Julia hated playing in public, particularly at school concerts, but her father was insistent:

"How will you ever become a concert pianist if you shy away from people?" he challenged. "You'll get nowhere relying on making recordings all the time. Why, even Beethoven was performing in public by the age of thirteen."

Even Beethoven? Wasn't he the best?

Luigi was not how she had imagined him to be. He looked handsome in the Wikipedia mug-shot. Close-up, in flesh and blood, he was short, his hair was a mess and he walked in a funny way as if always searching for something, but his eyes set him apart from others. Because of them, she both loved and hated the man from the first time they met.

She did not really need to 'go'—just wanted a little space because of that C natural. Of course she knew she had played a wrong note! She hardly needed reminding. But it was fear, fear of him, that caused it, and this he must never know. In the toilet, she dabbed at a single tear with a torn-off tissue, fixed the errant curl then, peering at the miserable face looking back at her, re-applied eye-shadow. Another forty minutes and he would be gone. And then she could get back to learning her lines.

Three years seemed a long time, yet she remembered that first lesson as clearly as if it were still happening. It began with hatred of the man, his manner, his choice of words and his smell. Not a dirty smell, but a male smell ludicrously out of proportion to his diminutive stature. Wikipedia made no mention of the smell. But it was the smell that turned her like a subtle change of key. By the end of the lesson she wanted it to go on forever. She wished he could take her away and make her a famous concert pianist overnight. She wanted to become 'his' instrument, yet she was no Trilby to a modern-day Svengali. This was womanly love. After all, she was fourteen!

When he took his leave after that first lesson, he was already somewhere else, and this angered her. Although desperate to know where this might be, she was too scared to ask. He left her marooned on that week-long desert isle of a posh girl's school and a millionaire's suburban residence until her next lesson the following week when the hatred and the love kicked in all over again. This charade continued for over two years until the pressure of schoolwork provided an excuse to tell her father to stop the lessons. They were getting her nowhere. Worse, even. One more lesson and she feared she would never escape from his hold over her. Or never again touch a piano key.

After telling her irate father she no longer wished to be a concert pianist, and did not want any more lessons from Luigi, her piano-playing improved. She now played for herself alone. Or so she claimed. Not entirely true. Those eyes had never left her. She was just sixteen when she would last seen them—old enough, she had told herself to...

Something that both excited and frightened her!

He was more than twice her age. A good reason for stopping the lessons. Now here she was, thirteen months later, having another lesson to get into the character of the girl for whom the immortal genius had composed a work that she had always found so challenging. It was all too bizarre. The Contessa was unlikely to have been the 'Immortal Beloved', anyway.

It was the school music teacher who suggested Julia take up acting a year after she stopped taking piano lessons. Later, the woman responded to a mass e-mailing for 'musical' girls to audition for the role of Contessa Giulietta Guicciardi ('Julia') in a Beethoven TV biopic of the doomed love affair, and she suggested Julia re-learn the Moonlight Sonata to get into the soul of the seventeen-year-old countess after landing the part.

"Drama is performing with a different face," she told the girl. By becoming someone else, Julia could learn to confront her audience. Her teacher was no fool. Maybe she understood Julia better than the girl understood herself.

Now, reduced once more to tears, something had been prized apart. Something that had sheltered her true self from reality. With this protective layer gone, she felt exposed and vulnerable—and ready to take on the role of the Contessa. She returned to the living room, to the piano and to those eyes—

*****

"Julia, what's eating into your spirit today, sweet girl?" Ludwig takes hold of his pupil's hands. They feel cold. Something is wrong. "You don't like it? Tell me! And watch out for that C sharp in the base. It's there for a purpose. C major? Yes, I do love C Major. So simple and unencumbered yet all-encompassing. But here we're in sadness and melancholy. This is about our love, Julia. In the face of that tyrant of a father of yours."

Julia feels her fingers play within his grasp. They want to escape, yet refuse to, in the same way she wishes to tell her authoritarian father about her love for the famous piano teacher but cannot.

She has loved Ludwig since her first lesson. Now seventeen, she should surely be allowed to decide her own fate. How cruel they are about poor Ludwig. He cannot help looking different. Why should respectable men have to wear wigs, anyway? Only older ones clung to the past like dead spiders hanging on to sagging cobwebs. Men like Herr Haydn. Ludwig had freed himself from all that nonsense. His soul was with the revolution spreading across Europe. He was a part of this. Men of freedom looked up to the great composer, though not her father and his like.

"Nothing," she says.

"My music's nothing? Look, just because it's not my best gives you no right to—"

She draws her hand away. He is in one of his moods.

"You asked me what's eating into my spirit today. I said 'nothing'. Why do you have to turn everything into—?"

32

"No, no! I'm sorry. Forgive me, my dearest. Just that—this thing with my hearing. And the noises. Sometimes they drive me insane. Then I lose control over the things I say. Look, you're no more in the mood to play than me to suffer your C naturals. Even if I don't hear them, I feel them when your fingers hit the wrong keys. Tell that woman over there we have to go out. To the woods. My carriage is outside. Give her something your father won't notice if it goes missing. A necklace, perhaps."

The girl grins.

"We're not wealthy. You know that."

He turns to look through the window at the neatly-trimmed lawn and the colourful flowerbeds. A stooping gardener is digging out weeds.

"Then why spend money on destroying the wilderness," he says. "Wildflowers are so much more beautiful. You aristocrats want to command everything. Even nature! But it's changing. The whole world's changing."

"Don't call me an aristocrat! We're poor. It's why—" The girl pauses then looks away, afraid of those searching eyes. "Herr Beethoven and I must take a walk," she informs her chaperone seated by the door and pretending to be absorbed in her tapestry although her ears have absorbed every word of her charge's conversation. But she, too, hates the master of the house. Contessa Giulietta links her arms around her piano teacher's elbow. Her chaperone winks as they pass out through the French windows and the girl smiles back sweetly.

They walk on down the driveway in silence. The carriage takes them to a path that snakes into the woods. She feels the tension relax in the man she loves as they breathe the moss-heavy air and she longs to tell him about the bird-song and about the distant call of the cuckoo but fears this might tip him into even deeper melancholy. He hates his growing deafness as much as he loves life and for much of their time together, when not playing music, she feels as if she is trying to pull on a rope with Ludwig dangling in a deep ditch of despair dug by his deafness, and she with only the strength of a child.

He stops.

"I apologize—" he says. She dare not ask why for fear he'll fly off the handle again.

"Thank you," she says instead.

"For not asking before. I apologize," he explains. "But you see, that father of yours. I couldn't bear it if you said 'no' because of him."

"I've known all along. And you did ask—when you dedicated the C sharp minor sonata to me. I knew then. Everyone loves it. But *'Quasi una fantasia?'* What fantasy?"

Before he can answer, she breaks free from his hold, runs to a splash of blue nestled against a rock jutting from the bank. She plucks a gentian and skips back to her piano teacher, offering him the flower. He places his hand, unusually strong for a man of his stature, over the flower and his pupil's own small hand.

"*You* know—*I* know—and this flower surely knows. I'll write to him tonight. He can't refuse me. He mustn't, my dear girl."

They kiss. He taps her forehead.

"Remember. C sharp. Always sharp in the base."

"It's so beautiful."

"No. You, my little countess, are beautiful. That's what worries me. How can a girl like you love a grumpy old man like Herr Beethoven?"

"Because!" she replies, kissing him again. "Back to my house now! Before my father returns."

"Curse him!"

"No—please not that! Don't lose your temper. Let me work on him."

That evening he wrote a letter, tore it up, wrote another, tore it up then a third emerged. Assertive and demanding, this one would leave the Count no escape from the inevitable course that his and Contessa Giulietta's love must take. She would become his wife.

*****

Julia thought she understood her character. A girl full of love who meets an older man full of despair—a man who needs her. But circumstances, society and money, or rather lack of it, get in the way.

That is, until Luigi played the C sharp minor sonata as it should be played. The melancholy, the joy and the anger of a love about which the world knew nothing were coaxed out of the piano and the girl felt small, insignificant and started to cry. And if this was her response, how would the Contessa have felt having the piece dedicated to her? Of course she could never have married the man—that wonderful, loving monster of a man!

After finishing in a frenzied fortissimo, Luigi placed a comforting arm across Julia's shoulders. She turned, held his head in her hands and kissed him. A green light for the notorious lecher? Now she knew why he had insisted he could only continue to have her as a pupil if lessons were held in his apartment. But she no longer cared what happened to Julia, the twenty-first century piano pupil. She had to be Contessa Giulietta, also known as Julia. She had to let her teacher make love to her. After all, how else could Beethoven have written such music if he had not made love to the young Countess? How could she act the part as a virgin?

*****

Ludwig throws the letter to the ground. He shouts abuse at the boy who delivered it. The boy, too often a target of the great musician's sharp tongue, takes to his heels and vanishes. The composer punches the slammed door before returning to his desk where he picks up his quill, dips it in the inkwell and composes a reply.

She'd as good as said 'yes'. He had it all planned: whom they should invite to the wedding, what he must wear and the gifts he would shower on his young bride. And now that swine of an impoverished count says 'no'. His anger flows through the hand that coaxes the voice of God from the piano, on through the quill to the untidy scrawl of words on the page. Smudges and splats of ink reinforce the anger. He does not care what insults he hurls at the father of the girl of his happiness. The man deserves nothing better than a place in Hell!

*****

Julia peered at the girl in the mirror, no longer a virgin. They wanted her on set for the first shoot in five minutes. The young man playing Beethoven was nothing like the image she had of the Promethean genius who wrote the C Sharp Minor Sonata. Thank God for Luigi. She had almost melted in his arms when he made love to her. But he freaked her out afterwards by saying he had 'only been doing his duty', and she cried, but those moments of bliss with the bastard had turned her into a more likely Contessa Giulietta Guicciardi. The actor she was playing against was far too nice and she felt sorry for him being saddled with a bitch for the series, but the Contessa had been nothing short of a bitch to lead the great man on only to dump him 'because her father said so'. But worse was to come—the final scene. How could she, a recently de-flowered schoolgirl, ever play that last scene?

*****

His friend Ries has told him of the Contessa's unhappiness. Now married to a human shrimp barely older than her, a weakling who pretends to compose music and whose promised wealth never materialised, she was victim of her father's folly. The master composer has no sympathy for her unquestioning acquiescence, for his thoughts now dwell on her beautiful cousin, Josephine, but he agrees to see her...

*****

It was not supposed to be like that. The actor playing Ludwig was good. A nonentity off-stage, he had become her master, her adorable, crazy, self-centred master who had written, for her, the most beautiful piece in her repertoire. Every note of the sonata was perfect whilst every failing of the composer cried out to be perfected.

Because of those failings he needed her, and she had mentally given herself to him (off set). Now she had to beg his forgiveness; forgiveness for wasting her body on that

36

jumped-up conductor who loved to seduce his girl pupils. Luigi was no longer Ludwig. She loved the real Ludwig. And the actor who played him turned out to be *too* good...

In a nineteenth century house in Prague, taken over by an Austrian television company, a room is set for the final scene of the biopic of one of the great composer's failed romances. Littered with manuscripts and books, the piano stands in the middle, dominating the set:
L: Curse that man Ries. Why can't he let me alone? After what she allowed her father do to us, she's the last person on earth I'd wish to meet.
Enter J.
L: Why are you here?
J: Can't you guess?
L: Let me see. You've just discovered you've been saddled with a worthless husband so you come crawling back to Ludwig for forgiveness. Trying to pretend there's still passion somewhere in that sweet breast of yours that's been so cheapened by his touch.
J: No. It's in the sonata you wrote for me. Nothing can cheapen that. It's immortal and because of your music no one can destroy our passion, Ludwig. Please try to understand—
L: Try to understand? Why—did you even for one moment give a florin's worth of thought for how I felt when rejected? Did you even care about our passion then?
J. approaches L. but he steps back, walking round to the other side of the piano. She starts to cry. Genuinely. Because of what that bastard of a conductor had done. She no longer has what would have been the most precious gift she could give to him; the young actor. He turns away from her, in disgust.
J: But the C Sharp Minor Sonata! It has to mean something, Ludwig. There has to be—
L: That? Did I really write that music? I can't believe I ever wrote anything so bad. Shame on me! Yes, shame on you, Ludwig.

J—the *real* Julia—burst into tears and left the room. The director, red with rage, called after her but it seemed that, like Beethoven, she had grown deaf. She ran to the changing room, slipped out of her period dress and into her jeans and blouse. L—no, that actor pretending to be the master—was there outside her door when she opened it.

"Go away!" she said.

"Not until you give some explanation. You're not the only one in this stupid movie, you know."

She stared in horror.

"Stupid?"

"Yeah! But I need the money. *You* need the money. So get back into that ridiculous costume and play the little tart who dumps me after leading me up the garden path."

"No—you don't understand. That music's for real. I was going to be a concert pianist before—"

"Shut up and get back out there before we all lose our jobs!"

The girl obeyed. She would do anything to escape from the cheap little tart who yielded up her body to a lecherous conductor who only gave piano lessons to rich young girls. *Pretty* ones. But back on the set she felt confused, uncertain about who she really was, or to whom she belonged; Ludwig, Luigi or the actor she had spurned but was growing to love? The only thing that seemed certain was the music that flowed through her head, like an eternal stream, belonging not to Man but to God.

Do they not say God is Love?

Kangaroo Dreaming

Kar the Spider heard it from the Great Kangaroo. He must bite the White Man, he was told. It was time for the White Man to go for he was destroying the land and all would become darkness again if the White Man did not leave. The plants of the land and the animals were slowly disappearing and being replaced by things that did not belong. In time, they too would be gone and then the land would become empty. The light would fade, and darkness would return. Kar and the other animal people knew what had to be done...

Billy Lismore awoke with a start. Such a vivid dream! *Perhaps it's important*, he thought. At breakfast-time he recounted it to his father. Joe Lismore, after hearing his son's dream, stared at the boy through deep-set eyes.

"And you were Kar?" he asked.

"Yes, Dad. I think so. But it was so strange. Not like a proper dream. Sort of real."

Bill's father remained silent as they ate breakfast together. He looked troubled. When they were finished, Joe Lismore put together pieces of food and bottles of water then, after squeezing these into a small backpack, addressed his son:

"Bill, we're going walkabout."

"But what about school, Dad?"

Joe Lismore shook his head. "No school today, son. Or ever again."

Father and son left the concrete apartment block at the edge of town and headed for the bush. Joe walked with a purpose. He knew where they must go. They walked for hours, heedless of the scorching sun. Bill never once questioned his father about where they were going. He knew this was because of his dream and that his father was doing the right thing.

The sun was already sinking towards the horizon when father and son reached a wide clearing in the bush. There was a cluster of red rocks in the clearing. Bill had never seen such rocks before, yet he knew at once how important they must be. There were markings on some of these, and upon one sat an old Aboriginal man. His hair was as untamed as the bush and white like the belly of a cloud. Bill's father approached the man in a manner that displayed profound respect. The old fellow looked at father and son through eyes in which Billy also saw the invisible gorge that had been cut through the land by the Great Serpent. Understanding flowed between the two men. Joe Lismore spoke:

"Bill had this dream," he said. "I think he should tell you about it himself."

At first Bill felt nervous, but when he looked into the old man's eyes he felt at peace with everything, including the plants and the land around him. Those same eyes drew forth his dream, word by word. When Bill had finished, his father spoke again to the old Aborigine:

"Do you think we should call a meeting of the tribe?" he asked.

"No need, Joe," replied the man. "Others have already come to me. It is perfectly clear what we must do. Through the animal people, the Great Kangaroo has spoken to many in his dreaming. Our folks have seen this in different ways, but all are saying the same thing. That White Man's time has come to an end. It has to be if we are to save the land. In fact, it's already started."

The older man's stare settled on Joe Lismore's eyes and the two became one.

'We must leave behind all White Man's things—all his ways. They don't belong to the land. White Man is finished and so are we if we don't listen to the Great Kangaroo through the animal people. The land has to be saved, Joe.' Joe Lismore read this in the old fellow's eyes. Not a word was spoken. Quietly, Bill and his father slipped back into the bush. The sun was setting, so they spent the night in the open and reached the town as the sun rose above the lifeless buildings. Some families had already gone. They had discarded their clothes, left behind vehicles, television sets,

washing machines, soundlessly disappearing into the bush. Joe spoke with his wife and daughters, but they knew without being told. Food and water, enough to last the family for one day, no more, had been prepared. Like other families, they left without clothes and other artefacts from White Man's world. All they had, apart from one day's worth of sustenance, were a few simple tools that they would need to live with the land. They passed rusting cars, bicycles and abandoned skateboards, once the pride of the youth of the community, and kept on going until they reached the big road, the highway that linked the great cities of Sydney to the east and Melbourne to the south-west. By now the sun was high above the town, but there was brightness in the land beyond the horizon to the east; a strange light that was not the sun and which hung over the point where the big road vanished into the band of blue hills that separated land from sky.

"Yes, I can see that it's started," said Bill's father, facing east.

Normally, at this time in the morning, the road was alive with cars. Bill had never seen it completely empty. Not a single vehicle destroyed the silence. The family was about to cross when Joe Lismore raised a hand to stop them. He must have heard it before Bill did, but after a few moments of standing there, at the edge of the road, the boy also heard the sound: a deep-throated rumble like a far-away animal in distress. The noise became gradually louder, until, to the east, Bill saw an approaching truck. At first it was barely visible and seemed to be moving very slowly, but as it drew closer, in a crescendo of sound, the boy realized it was travelling at a considerable speed. Not only that. He saw that the immense road-train truck was careering along in a wild, zigzag fashion like a wounded beast in its final throes.

Joe Lismore pulled his family back from the verge. The mighty truck, its engine roaring, hurtled towards the Aboriginal family as they stood as still as gum trees. Suddenly the truck swerved in the opposite direction before jack-knifing and thundering off the other side the road. The vehicle and its first trailer rolled sideways, skidding over rocks and snapping trees before coming to rest in a cloud of dust. The engine spurted out dying grunts, then went silent. Its silence merged with the silence of the land. As the road-train left the road, Bill caught a brief glimpse of the driver. A large white man, his face a deep purple, slumped lifeless across the steering wheel.

"Must've got bit by a spider," explained Joe.

Bill looked up at his father. "Kar?" he asked.

There was no reply. Joe's eyes were focused on the road beyond, whence the road-train had come. Bill also looked. Father and son both saw it. A vast kangaroo, the same colour as the red soil, staring back at them.

"You have nothing to fear, son," Joe said, turning to Bill. "The land can breathe again. Come!"

Bill, his father, mother and two sisters crossed the highway and vanished into the bush.

The Smile of a Samurai

At long last she would become his wife.

Ishiro Hashimoto stood in front of the mirror in the registry office staring at an anxious, reflected figure in a morning suit. Somehow it had all been too easy. Not what he had expected. Only a token donation to the registrar for the paperwork to be in order.

He pictured Yumi whilst he studied his own features. Her eyes were huge, but for a nose she merely had two dots. He hated girls with large noses. And what lips! Parted in that perpetual smile, from now on they would always await his passionate kisses. Those eyes, lips and that nose would be there for him every evening, and after telling Yumi about his troubles at work, and the news from Tokyo and the rest of world, their lips would come together, and they would make love. Then he could fall into a deep sleep and dream— dream about Yumi. In the flesh.

He only ever saw her out of her frilly little pale pink or blue girlie dresses when dreaming. How he loved those dresses that revealed ninety-nine percent of her curvaceous legs, but that day he wondered whether, at her wedding, she might be dressed more demurely. A kimono perhaps? At least something more befitting a woman. After all, she had a womanly bosom—certainly not young girl breasts—and whatever else his father said about Yumi, she *was* a woman.

Ishiro had never seen the man so angry as the day he announced his engagement to the manga girl. He totally flipped, threatening his son with psychiatrists, lawyers and a long line of Samurai ancestors as far back as the great Akira Hashimoto himself.

"Men in our family can have any woman they want! And you tell me you're marrying a two-dimensional cartoon drawing with an over-sized head and who shows off her panties to the world!"

Panties? Those were the best pages! He had a drawer full of them.

Red with rage, Mr Hashimoto senior warned his son that the boy would be disinherited if he were to go through with the crazy plan.

"I don't care, *Otosan*. I love Yumi and that's the end of it. We're to become man and wife. It's all arranged."

Man and wife? That is all that Ishiro could think about. A wife without a single unsightly mark or blemish, perfect lines for her shapely legs and undefiled by other men. He knew he could never be sure about those innocent-looking girls he saw on the Tokyo metro. Most of all, though, she would be temper-free. It was a placid Yumi who filled his mind as he took a step back from the mirror to wait for Seiki, his old college friend.

All his childhood, he had seen his mother nag and let fly at his tough, business-tycoon father, a modern-day Samurai in a suit. Of course, out in the streets, or at public functions, she would become the man's silent shadow, an ever-dutiful Japanese wife, but encapsulated in their home the same man would cower and hide his shame against the onslaught of sword-sharp words. Behind closed doors, a serpent emerged from the gentle doe wife, striking out at her husband's pride. It would be so very different between Yumi and himself. Always submissive, she would forever greet him with those large, loving eyes and that eternal smile.

Seiki, the best man, had arranged for a projected image of Yumi to appear on a screen in front of the registrar's desk. Ishiro now stood waiting beside the screen, his head bowed. The registrar was busy typing on his laptop. The projector rested on the desk beside this, softly humming. Soon Yumi would emerge from it—but what would she look like?

"A surprise!" Seiki had informed him. His old college friends clubbed together to pay for a wedding gift that he would "never forget".

He knew they were all taking the piss, but he did not care. Like his father, none of them understood. And in twenty years' time he would be the one laughing, for Yumi would still be young, fresh and beautiful in her little frilly dresses whilst they would be saddled with ageing, bullying wives. He only prayed that they would not make him look a complete fool on his wedding day. That is all he asked. Why they had insisted on informing the press, he had no idea. Although Yumi was the most popular manga girl in Japan, their wedding was a private thing—about the two of them starting a life together for all time.

"But this is a first!" Seiki had insisted. "A first for Tokyo and a first for the World. You'll be famous, Ishiro. The very first man to have a two-dimensional bride. Got to get decent press coverage. You could start a whole new trend. Get all those other gorgeous little manga girls married off, huh?"

A serious American guy at work had taken him aside and had tried to dissuade him:

"Don't do this stupid thing! You can't marry a drawing. You do know they're all making fun of you, don't you?"

But he was in love with Yumi and now there was no turning back. Soon, he prayed, his sweet, his cute, his very own adorable manga girl would be up on the screen beside him.

Seiki arrived ten minutes late.

Damn him! Typical!

As he breezed into the office, the registrar looked up, glanced at his watch and tapped it a couple of times.

"You've only five minutes left," he announced. "Then I want you two blockheads out of here!"

Blockheads? The biggest event of his life and he was being called a 'blockhead'! Ishiro wanted to kick the man all the way to Hokkaido, but he realized that only a registrar had the power to sign that piece of paper that would join him and Yumi in legal matrimony.

"What kept you?" he whispered to Seiki.

"The press—outside—photographers fighting for the best positions."

"And Yumi?"

Seiki winked at the registrar. He offered the man a CD.

"At least this has got a—erm—you know—" he whispered, tapping the hole at the centre of the disc.

Ishiro stayed calm. If he were to lose his temper now he could lose Yumi forever. The man loaded the CD into his laptop and clicked the mouse. The projector shot an image onto the screen.

"The bride!" exclaimed Seiki. Ishiro turned to look.

"Can't see her sideways on, my friend. Stand in front of her."

He stepped out in front of the screen and stared at his shadow. Seiki laughed.

"She's on your back now! Move to the side a little."

Would it be a monkey, a penguin or a crocodile instead of his beloved Yumi? Holding his breath, he moved to one side.

Thank the Lord Buddha!

Never before had she looked so beautiful. Her melon-sized eyes stared at him, eager for his love. In her hair, she wore a gold and pink tiara and she had on a Western-style wedding dress. He'd half-expected her to be standing legs astride, in a micro-skirt, peering at him from between those shapely legs, with her pony-tailed hair hanging down to the ground and revealing her intimates to the registrar. But here she was in a wedding dress drawn just for him.

"Thanks, Seiki," he whispered.

"Oh, don't thank me! The artist was delighted. Great publicity. He's been a little worried about her rival, Akiko, recently. Akiko's manga comics have been doing well, but this should nail it for Yumi, huh? He did the drawing for free! Think what we've all saved marrying you off to her. A real wedding dress would've cost a fortune!"

"But—?" Something had just occurred to Ishiro and it worried him.

"But what?"

"I can't see her knees."

It was the first time he had seen a full-length image of Yumi without her knees, and most of her thighs, showing. Was something wrong with her knees?

"Knees? No man worries about his bride's goddamn knees on his wedding day! Now, just stand there beside her,

Ishiro, and answer the registrar's questions. I'll speak up for Yumi, all right?"

Speak up for her? What were you two up to before she got put onto that CD? I heard what you whispered about the CD. You've done it, haven't you? You've taken her virginity, covered up her knees, because others can always tell from the knees, Mother Nature's protectors of innocence, and then put her on the CD! Pff! Some friend you are!

He had already promised Yumi his undying love. At least *he* would not disappear for golfing weekends with company colleagues like his father did. Little wonder his mother nagged the man. Or was it the other way around? Did his father golf and enjoy the curvy comforts of Shinjuku because of all that nagging? He and Yumi would never be caught up in such a loveless cycle of deceit and distrust. He would love her forever. And Yumi would never have to bear children, dye her hair or wear false teeth.

Ishiro tried to forget about the knees as the registrar rushed through the marriage formalities. The manga image was switched off, the screen dismantled. He was handed a marriage certificate and CD.

"Your bride!" the registrar said, tetchily. "Now hop it!"

"Ready for the crowd, then?" asked Seiki, grinning.

With his wife in his pocket, Ishiro stepped out into the street. A sea of faces and banners was accompanied by roars, shouts, jeers and laughter that drowned the chuckles of Seiki standing behind him. He turned around, hoping for comfort from his friend.

"But—?" he began.

"Smile!" insisted Seiki. "Smile for the cameras. For the newspapers, for the TV—for Yumi!"

He looked back at the screaming crowd, focused on one of the banners and saw an image of Yumi in a micro-skirt, her long legs dancing in the breeze. Across the banner was written:

'We all love you Yumi!'

His Yumi, *his* girl, *his* bride? *Their* wedding—or Yumi's publicity stunt?

He forced a smile for the cameras. The same smile he had seen so many times on his father's face whenever the man was accompanied by his mother at official functions: the smile of a samurai.

(In 2010, a South Korean man married a pillow that bore the image of a well-known anime girl.)

The Rain in Spain

I remember running from the silence of the village to the silence of the fields. A small child running for help. Running away from what he had seen in the village. I remember stopping in the fields, held back by the smell of death. The smell, etched into my nostrils, is still there and it came from the rain that fell during that night, blending with death in the blood-soaked ground...

*****

"Alfonso, say *hola* to the man!" Mama came out from behind the bar, the evening before, to shake hands with the gaunt, young man with wild, red hair who had recently arrived in the village. "His name's Jock and he's from Scotland. He's come to help us beat the fascists."

"*¡Hola!*"

I was used to those rough foreign men who came to Spain to fight for a dream and left their bodies, broken and bullet-ridden, in her streets. Few spoke my language.

"Hello," said the Scotsman peering down at me without smiling.

No one smiled in our village back then. War does that to a village. Stops the smiles and the laughter. My mama *did* smile at Jock, though, and her smile shone like the sun in all that darkness. As a child I had never thought of Mama as a beauty, but seeing her now, in my mind, I know she was ravishing. My father had been killed early on in the war fighting for the Republicans. Mama and I lived together in a small room above the bar, and when men came to that room I would have to leave.

"Mama has to make plans with these men," she would say.

But I saw the hurt in her eyes. I knew 'making plans' was what helped us to survive and I never questioned her further.

But Jock was different.

I found out more about Jock from his sister who came to visit our village years later. Their father worked on an estate in the Scottish Highlands. They were not poor, but Jock, a serious lad with a head full of dreams and communist promises, was determined to champion the cause of the 'poor people'. Spain gave him that opportunity.

"The girls back home all loved him," his sister said, fighting back the tears. "*I* worshipped him—my stupid, pig-headed, big brother!"

Yes, Mama smiled at Jock, and when they shook hands he stared at her face as if he had just seen the Holy Virgin herself. I sensed the anger amongst our own boys sitting around in the bar, their rough, brown hands impotently clasping glasses of cheap, red wine.

"You any good with a gun, Jock?" grunted Carlos, a heavy brute who often 'made plans' with Mama.

Frowning, Mama translated for the Scot. She was the only one in the village who spoke the harsh languages of those foreign men. Jock looked embarrassed. His sister told me later that he had never fired a gun in his life.

"Anna-Maria, put a cabbage up there on the bar counter!"

"Carlos, you don't have to," Mama said. "He's only here to help us." I still remember her very words.

"A cabbage!" insisted Carlos.

Mama could not afford to upset our men. She fetched a cabbage and placed it on the counter.

"Now blindfold me!" commanded the bully.

With trembling hands, Mama tied a cloth around Carlos's broad face. We all knew what was coming, and I covered my ears. I saw the confusion in Jock's eyes as he stood there, watching. The cabbage exploded into a thousand fragments and Carlos laughed. The first laugh I had heard in our village for a very long time.

"Waste of a cabbage," someone complained as Carlos pulled the cloth from his face. But Carlos ignored the man. He had stopped laughing. His eyes narrowed. He stared at Jock and there was a coldness in that stare.

"If you can't do that you're a dead man, *¡Escocés!*"

I remember the anger in the eyes of Carlos and his compatriots as Mama talked to Jock, later, over a glass of wine. They talked in his language, and Mama ignored the others' taunts for there was something going on between her and Jock. Now I understand, after what the red-haired Scot's sister told me. Girls are full of love, even those used and abused like Mama was, and there are men who seem to draw out that love without even knowing it. Jock was one of these, and I looked on not realizing then that I was looking at two people caught in a nightmare: Mama, a young widow thrown into a war that she had never asked for, and Jock, the idealist living a dream that he refused to accept as a nightmare.

It had not rained for months. The land was parched, the crops had failed and the whole area was sealed off by General Franco's troops. Jock must have been the last in from the outside world. We were beginning to starve, there was little water left and we all prayed for rain. Prayed that clouds, not armies, would come our way.

That exploding cabbage was indeed a careless loss caused by a man driven crazy by a combo of war and lust. Now I hate Carlos more than ever for destroying not only the cabbage, but also my mother's purity. Jock must have sensed that purity. I am sure of it. And his sister told me he always respected girls who loved him.

That night it rained with a rain I had never known before. Droplets from Hell hammered onto the roof. There was lightning and thunder and I clung to Mama. For the last time.

I was awoken by a different sort of thunder. This thunder shook the house when it exploded. My mother was already up. She grabbed me and carried me outside where people were running about, screaming. The church was on fire, its roof gone. She ran with me to the edge of town. She splashed and stumbled, holding me in her arms, through a rain-soaked pig-pen, then pushed me, half-asleep, into the pig-sty.

"The pigs are all dead," she whispered as if this should reassure me. "You can hide here till it's over."

Then she left, and I crouched there alone with my fear.

I never saw Mama alive again. Nor Jock. The screams died down and were replaced by silence. The sun came up, strong and hot, as always, but the ground was still wet from the rain.

Now I understand why they attacked that night. The rain would have brought hope to our soldiers, and much-needed drinking water. Water for the animals and for the plants in the fields. For the cabbages. Our men would have become stronger and an enemy must be destroyed before he gets strong. It was rain that killed our village. The Devil's rain.

I ran from the pig-sty to the bar. Most of the houses had been burst apart by shells, their inhabitants littering the narrow streets in shrapnel-peppered pieces. The bar, alone, stood intact.

"Mama! Mama!" I cried out, rushing into the bar. "Mama!"

She was lying there, on the ground. But she could not hear me, with her skirt pulled up, her throat cut. A stream of dried blood curled like a red snake from her opened neck. I knew she, too, was dead. I pulled her skirt down before wiping my tears with bloodied hands. I had never seen that part of her before. Now, looking back, I feel only fury with Franco's men for leaving her so exposed after raping and killing her.

May they all rot in Hell!

I ran from her spoilt body. I wanted help for her. *Even dead people need help*, I thought. I ran through the rain-sodden, death-littered streets, through the puddles, screaming, "*¡Ayuda! ¡Ayuda!*" I ran past the smouldering, roofless church where men and women once prayed for God's cruel rain, on and out into the wet fields. And there I stopped.

The fields were strewn with the mud-spattered bodies of men. Men I hated, like Carlos, and men I loved and who played with us children, like Xavier and Pedro. Then I saw *him*. Jock the Scot. Face-down, legs blown off, with the red of his hair mixed with the red of his blood. The stench of death hung heavy in the morning air and flies danced and hummed around the bodies—the only sound in that field of corpses.

Ever since, I have always hated the rain. The rain that killed my Mama and never allowed that young, red-haired Scot to find out how much she could have loved him. Never allowed him to discover how pointless was the war in which he had got mixed-up.

Years later, I moved back to our rebuilt village. That is when I met Jock's sister. And I told her about the rain that fell during the night when a different village, her brother and my childhood died together. It was so long ago, and now I am a very old man, alone with my memories, but I often wonder whether she, Jock's sister, was also unable to ever forget the rain in Spain that so changed both our lives.

The Fragments

They came in their billions. Soft blue bubbles. Inside each were more bubbles. These both saw and spoke as they rolled over the curved, hot surface of the world, gathering up the fragments, their multiple tiny hands grabbing, pulling, turning over and piecing together. Sometimes they would bump into each other, for they only had eight pairs of eyes.

"Excuse me!" one would exclaim. "The bit you're holding is mine!"

The fragments floated on water, too. Even the larger pieces. And the smaller bubbles, each the size of a soccer pitch, would sometimes fight over these if their eyes reckoned the colour was right.

Yes, the colour. So important! 11.7 billion colour shades. Not surprising that there were arguments, despite the spectral precision of the bubbles' globular eyes. Sadly, whenever this happened. the fragment became a coruscation of rainbow-flecked dust, the owner lost in the Transfer Process. But there was no other way, and, gradually, sufficient numbers of fragments were collected, grouped, pasted together and shaped inside larger city-sized bubbles.

Gradually?

The process took less than a trillionth of a second. Faster than the previous transfers, but the bubbles knew that they had to be speedy this time. These fragments were special. Any delays, and the Universe on the other side of the Bang might never happen. It could only happen if the refashioned life could see, hear, smell and feel its existence. Only then could time become real.

*****

Jonathan Wright hesitated for a split second, staring at the face in the mirror. He observed a hand reach up, his hand, and rub a chin, his chin.

Could swear I wasn't here a moment ago, he told himself.

His thoughts trawled through his life to date. Fifty-five years of it. It was all there, complete with a job, marriage, divorce and a near-fatal car crash. So why that curious question mark in his mind? Why had he wondered what he was doing looking at his face in the mirror if, in that split second, his life had only just begun?

Or had it?

He shrugged his shoulders, slapped on more after-shave and went to make himself a coffee. A ginormous coffee that would kick-start his brain into action for the day, for he knew it would be a bugger of a day. Like every other day in his pint-sized life.

"Hi, honey!"

A loving arm encircled his waist from behind. The fingers at the end of it played a silent tune on the blubber of his belly.

Too much blubber! Why doesn't she just give me up?

He turned and drank in the love in those blue eyes before kissing their owner's love-hungry lips.

"Helen—" he began, smoothing his plump hand over the fine-haired skin of the woman's cheek.

"Yes. I'm Helen. Weren't expecting me to be anyone else, were you?"

She broke away from him. She, too, had a lot of blubber on board. It made them equal, perhaps. Well-balanced, at least. But, in another split second of uncertainty, why did he suddenly wonder who *she* was? He felt certain his boss's wife had been in bed with him the night before.

My boss?

A brief moment of panic was followed by sudden recall. The guy was on a business trip in Australia.

Where the heck is that? flashed across his nerve cells like a Times Square neon advert.

"He's far enough away," Jonathan reassured himself. "And not expected back till tonight. So, you and me—it being Saturday—"

"What? That's tomorrow, honey! Better get that coffee into you, my lovely man! I'll still be here when you get back this evening. Here for more of you. All tonight and half of tomorrow."

"Are you sure it's Friday?"

"Sure as you're Jonathan Wright!"

But moments earlier, whilst looking in that mirror, he hadn't been so sure who the heck he was.

He gulped the coffee into his gullet, dressed, kissed his boss's wife and left for work. *Everything is for the best and the best of all possible worlds,* a philosopher once said. This had to be right, for he knew exactly where to go. Which street to walk down, which subway train to take and where to get off. The office building downtown was wonderfully familiar but, after passing through the automatic door, with his name on a label attached to his lapel, he stepped into a shit of a day. His one consolation: the boss's wife would be there for him when the shitty part was over.

Or will she? How can I be certain of anything?

In the rest room, he peered again at his face. His fingers felt for joins in the skin where the fragments may have been pieced together.

Fragments?

"Won't find 'em!" a voice said.

Of course I won't. I'm me and always have been.

Always?

"You're too old," the voice continued.

Jonathan turned, relieved to see his project manager standing there. For a moment, he thought—

"What do you mean, I'm too old?" he asked.

"For pimples! Acne. A teenage thing."

"Oh, no, I was—" *What the heck <u>was</u> I doing? And was I ever a teenager?* He looked down at his blubber-bloated belly. "Just checking that I hadn't cut myself shaving. Boss back tomorrow night, right?"

"Right or wrong, due back tomorrow, Jonathan. Why?"

"Oh—nothing."

"Donut? I have a couple on my desk if you're hungry."

Jonathan peered at his belly again.

"Better not. Bugger of a day ahead, you know."

"Shouldn't be telling your project manager that, man."

"No. Lovely project. A great day. Really!"

It *was* a bugger of a day, but that seemed normal, so Jonathan no longer worried about his place in the Universe. He and the boss's wife shared their blubber in his bed that night, and the following morning into the late afternoon when Helen left for the airport. Then, as if scripted, his existence returned to the solitude that his brain told him had to happen, for he was Jonathan Wright, divorced survivor of a terrible car crash who was enjoying a secret affair with his boss's wife.

*****

The Transfer went to plan, the bubbles melted then faded into the intergalactic dust as stars, galaxies and planets were formed. Time slipped through 13.8 billion years and the fragments, all joined up as perfect colour matches, got on with their programmed lives. On Sunday morning, Jonathan Wright sat alone at the kitchen table in his pyjamas with his hands clasped around a mug of coffee. He enjoyed the warmth of the mug, for it reminded him of the warmth of her body. And as he sat, quite reassured that she was for real, he wondered about Venezuela.

"He might be going to Venezuela next week," he had overheard someone in the office say.

Jonathan knew nothing about Venezuela but if the boss had to go there it would, hopefully, be for real. As real as his love for Helen.

He looked at his hand on the mug. The right one. He raised this up close to his face. *Real* close. He turned it around. Part of his hand was a different colour. *Never noticed that before! Maybe I'm getting vitiligo*, he told himself, before returning to the bed and remembering Saturday.

"Helen is *so* for real!" he said aloud. To reassure himself.

No Tears

Professor Hans Lehrenholler sat at his favourite table in the old coffee house around the corner from the university administrative building. It was a quiet spot, separated from the main area by an oak panel with a dimpled glass window.

He could sit there for hours on end and no one would bother him. With his laptop on the table, and a constant supply of black coffee to fuel his agile mind, he could work away at ideas and thoughts without constant interruptions concerning faculty business. He knew that he had one of the most brilliant minds in the university and, because of this, they tolerated his eccentricities and disdain for protocol, for his worldwide reputation meant big money. The professor also knew that he was one of the world's greatest lovers.

A sexual athlete irresistible to nubile, young female students, he took every opportunity to admire his handsomely-chiselled features whenever these were reflected in a shop window, a well-polished car or a conveniently-placed mirror. No wonder those girls swooned. They adored his soft Edinburgh Morningside accent, and the greying hair at his temples gave him the edge over young lecturers. It spoke of a maturity and confidence of technique that could bring the most anxious of his female conquests slowly but surely to the boil until the hapless girl found herself in such an incandescence of orgasmic passion that the image of Hans Lehrenholler would be indelibly etched upon her mind for the rest of her days.

Or so he thought.

Of course, he had no qualms about abandoning these girls when he had tired of them. Being a busy man, he would sometimes 'accommodate' a female student on only one or two occasions. As far as he was concerned, she should feel only gratitude for being chosen and bedded by him. Besides, he had a wife. Until Daniella, there had been no space in his life for lasting, sentimental relationships.

Professor Hans Lehrenholler looked away from his laptop, yawned and stretched back, with hands clasped behind his neck, whilst turning over, in that vast cauldron of his mind, his latest research project: the neuro-physiology of tear production. And he thought about the luscious young psychology student who was using the project for her PhD thesis.

Although he had been involved in several collaborative projects with the Department of Psychology, his opinion of psychology as a discipline, and of psychologists in general, was damning. 'A load of hogwash' is how he once described the academic effluent from that department. Daniela, half-Italian, soon bridged this interdepartmental rift with her large brown eyes. Undressed, her Canova figure, with its soft-though-firm white breasts replacing the marble versions, refused to leave his mind.

Within a fortnight they had become lovers. She responded so completely to his caresses that he felt certain they were made for each other. This had never happened with any of his previous student lovers. His long-suffering wife had always been there, waiting dutifully somewhere in the background of his life, for they both understood that his affairs were a sexual necessity, a physiological requirement for such an amazing dopamine-driven brain. As for those silly little girls, he reasoned it was all a part of their extended education to experience a sexual virtuoso in bed.

But Daniela?

The Italian girl was different. For three whole months, she was the only student with whom he made love. Things had changed. Whereas, before, he reckoned it was a female's privilege to end up in bed with him, now it was he who had become demanding of Daniela's time. He arranged 'meetings', his term for those little interludes of carnal lust, as often as possible. Sometimes thrice a week. Initially, Daniela showed no resistance to his advances. In fact, she led him on. However, of late she had become more remote and it was Daniela who set the agenda. There was none of the timid submissiveness he got from his other female student bed-mates.

Daniela, a Botticelli beauty in her late twenties, achieved a first-class honours degree as a matter of course. She had already distinguished herself with several academic awards and came to him with glowing references. She took over the 'Tear Project' with an enthusiasm that even he was unable to match. Their first combined paper, based on *his* data through which *she* had sifted, had already been accepted for publication and hers was to be the first name on the list of authors.

For some weeks, something had been eating away at the back of Professor Lehrenholler's mind, and that morning he had made his decision. He wanted Daniela so much that he would now leave his wife, Suzanne, and move into a flat in town with the girl. He argued to himself that his wife had been incredibly lucky to have had him for all the years during which they had been together, and why shouldn't another woman now enjoy his awesome company on a more full-time basis? Of course, he would care for Suzanne. He was a good man. His colleagues and un-bedded students could vouch for that. He had gone over all the pros and cons of such a move with his analytical mind and reached the conclusion that the sooner he and Daniela were to set up something together the better. Only the previous day, he had looked at an apartment close to the old coffee house that would suit perfectly. Later that afternoon, he would be seeing Daniela, and he planned to then give her the good news. He expected no problems with the university. It was his private life, and if Daniela were to stay on, what an asset she would be for the psychology department. As for Suzanne—well...

Returning to his laptop, Professor Lehrenholler looked through Daniela's latest dynamic brain scan images from the Tear Project, images of the brains of volunteers whom, somehow, the girl had persuaded to cry. The scans showed the changes in their brains before, during and after tear production. How fascinating it all was.

He remembered how Daniela had once teased him for being unable to produce tears of his own. It was for this reason he could never be a subject in their study, and it was partly because of this physiological deficiency that he had become so curious about tear production as a response to human sadness. What was the point of tears, he had frequently asked himself? Surely his life-long state of 'alachrymosity', as he called his tearlessness, was a strength, not a weakness, he told the girl? Daniela said this was rubbish. Every physiological process must have a purpose, she argued.

Throughout his childhood, Hans Lehrenholler never cried. His father, a reluctant young soldier in the German Army during World War 2, had, after release from POW captivity in Scotland, stayed on and married a Scots lass. Hans was the last of her eight children. His older brothers and sisters doted on their bright, young brother, as did both parents. He knew he was thoroughly spoilt, and protected from serious mental trauma, but even knocks and falls failed to extract a single tear from the young Hans. It was very odd. He became known as 'Dry Eyes' at school.

The professor casually mentioned his fascination with the physiological nonsense of tears when the psychology head of department approached him. She had 'this bright young student seeking a PhD topic', and 'what did he think?' He was evasive until he heard the student's name. Female and Italian-sounding. Partial to Mediterranean women, he automatically responded with "delighted to help out!"

It was not just the electrifying orgasms that he and Daniela experienced together; he enjoyed being with her, looking at her and sharing opinions with her. Although he had no doubts about the young woman saying 'yes' to moving into that flat with him, he obviously needed her verbal agreement before taking it on. He would wait to tell Suzanne until the very last moment.

Hans Lehrenholler clicked through more images on his laptop, flabbergasted by the amount of data Daniela had accumulated. He knew that the girl was mad about him.

This was why she worked so hard. Now he had to find out more about her—had to *be* with her. Thank God, they would soon be living together!

He had already learned that she was an only child and that her father owned Italian restaurants across Britain. How funny that girl could be when describing some of the mishaps behind the scenes in these restaurants. Funnier still when she related the goings-on in her extended family in Italy.

Hans Lehrenholler continued to study the digital brains of Daniela's volunteers, marvelling at the colourful patterns produced in response to thoughts about their deepest and saddest secrets. Which were the brains of his own female students, he wondered, and which of these were crying because of memories of his heavenly prick? All data were coded, so he would never know, but he had witnessed many a young female dissolve into tears after being dumped—something that he found both embarrassing and annoying.

As the professor was examining a particularly colourful image, a familiar voice started up behind him from the other side of the partition. He turned his head slightly to confirm its owner was who she sounded like. Although distorted by the dimpled glass, there was no doubt. Dear Daniela! Across the table from her was another woman, but he was unable to clearly make out her features. He was about to get up and join them when he changed his mind. Instead, he thought he would have a bit of fun listening in on their conversation. He would be able to tease Daniela about it later, plus perhaps he might learn more about this most gorgeous of girls. All ears, he withdrew into the corner on his side of wooden partition, away from the window.

"So," said Daniela's companion, "how goes it with old Leatherbollocks?"

Hans flinched as though he had been stung. He had often heard that derogatory nickname used by certain small-minded academic staff but had always disregarded it with Olympian detachment. Only jealousy on their part, for sure. To hear the same term used in front of Daniela was awful. He barely managed to restrain the urge to get up and give the trollop a piece of his mind. Instead, he waited to hear Daniela speak out, loud and strong, in his defence.

But Daniela only laughed. The professor shrank. *How could she?*

"Oh, he's not really such a bad old fart!" It was Daniela talking. He tried to pretend it wasn't, but the voice was unmistakable.

"Is it true what they say about you and him? I mean, old Leatherbollocks, of all people!"

Professor Lehrenholler held his breath during the awful silence that followed. Daniela seemed to spend an age thinking what to say. *Now she'll tell the truth, tell that bitch how much she loves me*, he thought. His eyes remained tightly shut as he waited for his girl to speak up for him.

"It's nothing!" scoffed Daniela. "Nothing at all!" Hans Lehrenholler breathed a sigh of relief. *Pretending—and protecting me! Now she's gonna stand up for me.* With ears pricked like a rabbit's, he listened on. "You see," Daniela continued, "he does have some brilliant ideas."

Yeah, you tell her! Put a stop to that Leatherbollocks nonsense, my dear, dear girl. There was a pause before Daniela resumed her 'accolade'. *Take your time, but please don't be too hard on her.*

"Of course, it's so easy to flatter old Leatherbollocks, he's that conceited!" Hans Lehrenholler's face twitched. "You see," explained Daniela, "this PhD is important to me. Not only that. There'll be papers. Lots of them. In fact, one's been accepted already. Should be out in a couple of months!" Daniela's voice reduced to a whisper. The professor could barely make out what she was saying: "He put my name first. And with the right amount of attention from me, I'm sure the old fart will agree to do the same with all those other papers. The next is gonna be a seminal paper linking emotional distress with some of Leatherbollock's neuro-physiological findings. Really important stuff, and with my name out there—in front of his—well! Understand now? Just think of the implications for my career. Old Leatherbollocks is only the first rung of my ladder. I've always told you I've got ambition, Chris. Like my Dad!"

The other girl spoke, quietly:

"But Daniela, there's more to life than making a name for yourself. For God's sake, don't waste yourself on Leatherbollocks. Don't do it, Daniela! And what about Mike? Does he know what's going on?"

Mike? Who the heck—?

Daniela was swift to reply, and her voice sharp and clear:

"Don't you *dare* tell Mike! Not one word!"

She sounded angry. He'd never known her to be angry. It frightened him. And she had never mentioned anyone called 'Mike'.

Hans Lehrenholler suddenly felt very weak. He trembled. Why? What physiological response was forcing his body to shake?

Daniela, tell her, for pity's sake! Now! That you're gonna break off that thing with Mike, whoever the bugger is. You don't have to hold back any longer. No need to pretend.

Daniela continued:

"Mike mentioned marriage, you see. Not official yet, so keep it quiet, but we're agreed that when my PhD is out of the way in two years, we'll marry. Meanwhile, we've found a great flat just around the corner from here. Thanks to Leatherbollocks! Found a slip of paper with the address on it in his Tears Project folder. Can't imagine what it was doing there. The flat's above the bookseller's. We're moving in together next week. But not a word about the other thing, Chris. I told you, it's nothing!"

That flat? The one I had chosen for her? Hans Lehrenholler felt physically sick as Daniela's sweet voice talked on:

"I know what you're thinking, Chris. About Leatherbollocks. But my career is *everything* to me. I'm gonna make the grade, whatever it takes. That's me, I'm afraid! Once I'm getting somewhere, I'll wind the old bugger down, and he'll move on to some other pretty little piece. Actually, I really didn't expect him to get so intense. A bit awkward really, but I'll work on it when I've got those papers under my belt. As for Mike and me—we honestly *are* in love."

The words sank into Hans Lehrenholler like a knife driven into a naked belly. Chris resumed the conversation:

"But Daniela, I still don't understand. I know how close you and Mike are. How could you—you know—with old Leatherbollocks? Yuk!"

Daniela replied in a low voice:

"Chris, I can tell you it's like being made love to by a cordless drill with a flat battery!" Both girls giggled. Professor Hans Lehrenholler had never known such pain.

"No wonder his wife got herself a new drill with a decent battery!" Chris said loudly. The ensuing feminine sniggers played with the professor's pained brain. Shock contorted his face as unwanted thoughts pieced together like a mental jigsaw:

My wife? Suzanne? What did that impudent girl just say? No, I can't have heard correctly. But—that is what she meant. Suzanne has a lover. He remained slumped sideways staring into space. The young waiter at the counter noticed something was wrong with the professor.

"Are you all right, professor? Would you care for a refill?" he asked.

Refill? Suzanne getting refills on the side? Hans Lehrenholler shook his head. If he were to reply verbally, Daniela would recognize his voice. She spoke again:

"Well, can you blame her? Willie Stevenson must be the answer to most women's dreams. I can tell you, I certainly wouldn't mind swapping old Leatherbollocks for Willie. Wouldn't have to fake those orgasms—but then Mike really *would* have reason to worry. Unfortunately, bedding Willie wouldn't take me far. Professionally... if you get my meaning!"

"Daniela, you are incorrigible!" scolded Chris. Professor Hans Lehrenholler blinked. Something felt wrong with his eyes. "I promise I won't say a thing to Mike. Besides, I like you both too much. But be careful! Please! Heavens, look at the time. I must hurry. Have to see my own supervisor in twenty minutes. And I can thank my lucky stars she's nothing like Leatherbollocks. There *are* advantages in having a woman, you know."

Daniela spoke again as they left their table: "Advantages in having a man, too, if you play your cards right, Chris."

Hans Lehrenholler heard the door close with a thud. Crumpled in front of the frozen image of a brain which seemed to mock him, he blinked again. The image had captured a moment in time when its owner was about to cry for a past pain; a pain reduced to a collection of digital pixels decorating the cortex of her brain.

'So, *you* can't cry, then?' teased the brain.

Willie Stevenson? Suzanne and Willie? Surely not! A lecturer nearly half her age? Suzanne is my wife, for God's sake. How could she? She loves me! And I'm a great lover. The greatest! Suzanne, please don't believe what that stupid girl was saying! Oh Suzanne... oh Daniela!'

Hans Lehrenholler became aware of a coldness on his face. He raised a trembling hand to one cheek, looked at the moistened tips of his fingers, then touched the other cheek as tears trickled freely from the corners of both eyes.

He realized, then, that it was not the tears but the pain that mattered.

A Neutralising Thought

"Fifty feet! Fifty bloody feet! Awesome, Seb! Come in!"

I hesitated, held back by guilt. My old friend's eyes seemed like lasers, so different from those bright, mischievous eyes that egged me on when we were students together in the Southeast Division College of Technology in London. I was always the cautious one, the studious nerd who won all the prizes whilst Griff somehow scraped through, but we had fun until the bastard stole her from me. We lost contact after that, and I tried to forget about her by incarcerating myself as a post-grad in the Government Communications Research Laboratory outside Reading, England. Later, as project leader, I had free rein. They left me alone, though, in truth, she was the driving force behind the work that brought me into contact with Griff again after all those years. I wanted to know 'why?' Why leave me for my best friend whom we all knew was a bastard where women are concerned.

"Don't look so surprised! It's your invention, after all. Come on in! This calls for a celebration. For old time's sake."

Against my better judgement, I followed him into the house. One befitting the Minister of Information. Not only did he get her, but he also ended up with a top Government post and a mansion that must have belonged to royalty before the monarchy was dissolved. Nevertheless, I felt almost overwhelmed by guilt as I entered that palace of the past. My gaze remained firmly fixed on my feet for fear of catching sight of anything that might remind me of her.

One careless remark and I could lose my job at the very least, and maybe my liberty. But why the fake camaraderie? I wondered. *And how much does he know?*

I should have stayed on the doorstep. Instead, I soon found myself in a drawing room where the past was preserved, like an amber insect, in the rich bastard's ill-gotten glory. Griff headed for the drinks cabinet. Did it house a gun? I quickly took in my surroundings when his back was turned.

"Got the full range, Seb, my friend!"

Friend? What's he bloody playing at?

"Glenlivet, Glenmorangie—all the best Strathspey single malts. Here—try this. Fifteen years in an oak cask, Seb. Think of that. Just like you. Fifteen years in the laboratory that my department set up, and what do you come up with? A miracle!"

He turned to face me, a bottle of whisky in one hand and two crystal glasses held together, like reluctant friends, by the stubby fingers of his other hand. I used to have nightmares about what those hands and fingers would be doing with *her* body whilst I slept alone in my tiny student cell. Even then, he had influence not only in student politics but in Politics with an upper case 'P'. I reckon that was how he scraped through college. Now, of course, no one would dare to close the doors of opportunity on the second most powerful man in the country.

I quickly scanned the walls, mantelpiece and laden bookcase for pictures of her. Nothing! Maybe these were all in their bedroom. I felt pain on thinking about the two of them there together whilst the guilt of our recent shared past swelled like an inflating balloon. But the whisky? Was this to be the equivalent of the last cigarette they used to offer to a condemned man?

"Like this whisky, Seb, (he lifts up the bottle) you're the best! Never thought you could do it, but fifty feet—wow! So, what's it to be, then?"

"What?"

I summoned the courage to look him in the eye. Did he really not know the truth? Those laser eyes gave nothing away. How ironical that I should be in this position after what I'd created. A veritable monster, indeed! My second name should surely be 'Frankenstein'. *Seb Frankenstein! Has a good ring to it, right?*

"Neat? On the rocks? Your choice, Seb!"

On the rocks? My choice? I chose her, you fucker! In bed!

"Oh—anything! As it comes. Nothing special," I said.

That was it. For me, she *was* special. For Griff, she was just any girl he could lay his filthy hands on.

"Glenmorangie. As it comes, Seb. Sit down!"

Maybe it's poison that he's about to give me. And it'll be easier to pull a body out of a chair than to scoop it up off the floor.

I looked for somewhere to sit that would befit a commoner like me.

"There! In one of my armchairs, mate. Designer armchairs. Like the whisky, one of the perks of being Top Minister, see. Bet you've not sat in anything like that since the old days. Relax—and let's see you smile again. Not done that for quite a while, right?"

Because of you!

I sat down, tense and far from relaxed. And I didn't smile. He knew why, the bastard. He handed me a neat double whisky and I sat forwards, perched on that ridiculously-comfortable chair as if balanced on the edge of a cliff.

"At least let me try to make you smile, Seb. What do you earn, now, as project leader? Thirty thousand a week?"

"Twenty-five."

He bloody-well knew! After all, he paid me. To rub salt into the wound, the guy I'd once thought of as my best friend, and who used to rely on me to bail him out with those science assignments and who took from me the only woman I've ever loved, was now my paymaster.

"Double it! As from today. Because you've exceeded all expectations—even those of the minority in our cabinet who proposed you for the task. Oh—you didn't know? The results came through yesterday. It's why you're here, mate! So, drink up and smile and join me for a meal out."

'Me', not 'us'? Thank God! I'd never have coped with 'us', and neither would she.

"Fratelli's. Just around the corner. Best Italian in the country. A change from all that genetically-engineered crap you commoners have to put up with. And we'll share a bottle of Galestro. My favourite Italian white."

It was a relief to get out of that house, although I had seen nothing that reminded me of her. Even the décor was all clearly his, his... *his!* The fear that she might suddenly appear had twisted my smile into a vapid grin. I felt more comfortable in Fratelli's. The pride of what I'd achieved had nudged aside the horror of my creation. Plus a doubling of my pay? Two reasons to smile.

Wine on top of whisky befuddled my brain and I enjoyed the food if not the company. Not since I was a boy, before they killed the King and all those who reminded them of the past, and when my parents lived in a sizeable semi-detached in a London suburb, and we had roast chicken or roast beef every Sunday, not since then had I tasted such delicious food. As Griff prattled on about the past—his, not mine—I thought about the times Sal and I had together. Whenever he was abroad doing political battle with countries that 'still live in the past', as our present Government would put it, we made up for lost time in my tiny room using a bed just big enough to accommodate our writhing bodies.

I know now that she's always loved me. One reason I got into Thought Transference Technology, or TTT, was a masochistic desire to learn why she exchanged me for him back then. But even after meeting up again, not through Griff's high-ranking position, but because of a chance encounter in the street, I've not dared to ask her that vital question: why did she leave me for the bastard? When we make love now, it's as if all those years apart, because of him, never existed. Being an Eeyore to the very core of my soul, wherever that is (are scientists allowed to hold such beliefs?), the only way I can find happiness nowadays is to erase those fifteen years during which that whisky was trapped, like my soul, in a cask. Neverthless, although Sal was the inspiration behind my research, she is the last person on earth whose secret thoughts I would wish to see spilt across a computer screen.

"Thanks to your success, Seb, we can install your little gizmo into buses, trains, planes—all public spaces and places. There'll be no escape from our watchful eyes. All secret thoughts uncovered at the click of a mouse. We're already linked up with the Ministry of Security. We supply the information, they act. Within minutes, they'll have their officers making arrests. Places of worship—churches, mosques and other hotbeds of dissidents—will get raided. Maybe closed down. As you know, the Government has had a hard job suppressing these buggers, but now, by using what you've come up with, it'll all be so easy. More wine?"

Griff picked up the wine bottle, reached across the table and refilled my glass. I stared stupidly at it through alcohol-laden eyes, wishing I could dismantle my Frankenstein cell by wretched cell. Then I thought of *her* and her warm body in my embrace. I felt so shy when we made love again for the first time in fifteen years, and so very happy—almost ecstatic. I remember thinking, *if God and heaven exist, this must be what it's all about.*

As Griff wittered on, I undressed her in my mind, fondled her soft white breasts (whose owner had never conceived children, a small comfort to me), and whilst Griff's ugly mouth opened and closed around words that spell death for democracy and became, at the same time, a portal of entry for forkfuls of food only enjoyed by the privileged, I countered my guilt by mentally caressing the woman who should have been mine. On leaving, with my body unable to walk in a straight line, she filled my mind and I failed to register the exchange of looks between Griff and Guido Fratelli.

*****

I twist and turn, wriggle and squirm, but the pain won't go away. Being naked makes it a thousand times worse. Perhaps humiliation alters the pain threshold. Pulls it downwards till mere light pressure becomes agony.

Each of those pads in contact with my bare flesh is armed with thousands of tiny metal spikes which intermittently and unpredictably discharge fifty thousand volts. Curious how the scream, *my* scream, comes later when, after the initial muscle spasms, those electronic bursts cause my jaw muscles to spring open in a hollow-sounding howl. Encircling that part of me meant for Sal is a metal ring attached to a simple rheostat. Nineteenth century technology to torture a twenty-first century super-scientist. Bloody effective! Whenever Griff slides it to the right, the pain leaps beyond the unbearable. I want to die. I'll say anything to stop it from happening again.

"Always were too damn clever, you cheat," he says. "Read our thoughts, ay? Gain favour with us whilst you get inside our heads."

"Where is she?" I ask. "What have you done with Sal?"

"Nothing to do with you!"

"You shit—Ow!"

My teeth chatter like castanets as the electricity does its job.

"Do you think I didn't guess what that bitch of a wife of mine and you got up to whilst I worked my guts out to keep this country afloat?" I take in a series of deep breaths when the pain of the shocks is replaced by the pricking of a thousand needles that seem to be specially designed to seek out the most sensitive of my nerve cells. "Thanks to Guido and *your* thought detector he set up in his restaurant, I got proof. I already suspected your little game from the sensor in our bedroom. What appeared on the computer screen wasn't what a husband should expect from his wife."

"Damn you!"

"Oh, but we gave up talking a long time ago. In fact, I only married her because her father was a revolutionary leader and I needed to use him. *He* was the one who stopped her from seeing you. Too much of a risk, he told her. And she needed comforting. I gave her that, but never thought she'd hang on to you in that silly little head of hers. Lost a use for her when we eliminated her beloved daddy and his cronies after we came into power. Had to keep up the 'good appearance' thing going, though. Because of our 'morality drive'. To pull the carpet from under the rebels' feet, so to speak. You see, *we* were working for the people. As far as the people were concerned, anyway. Family values. Abolition of divorce."

"Bastard!"

"'Survivor' is a better term, Seb my old friend. There's brains and there's brains that control brains. That's the difference between us. I used you as a friend, used your girl and now I'm using the fruit of your brain: Thought Transference Technology! Boy, what a weapon this is gonna be. I'm really sorry you'll never reap the rewards of fifteen years' challenging work, but when I saw you fondling my wife's tits in that head of yours, well—it not only confirmed what spilled out of her own silly little head, but it bloody hurt. So, it's your turn to feel pain!"

A quick left-to-right flick on the rheostat and I yell like a banshee.

Griff comes up close. *Horribly* close. I can still smell the alcohol from the night before on his breath and it's mixed with a foul smell of decay that must have surely percolated from Hell. A smell that he imposes across the whole of our country.

"But Sal's not what this fun little electrical game is really about, is it?" he says.

"Dunno what you mean!"

"Oh yes you do. And we'll get it out of you. You see, when I checked the thought sensor hidden in that ornament in my drawing room, there was nothing. Like the head of the brainiest scientist in the country was empty. Not quite right for my clever little friend. But at Guido's, when you were pissed as a newt and off your guard, it was a different matter. Your filthy hands were all over my wife. And I do believe you'd not listened to one word I said. So, what is it then?"

"What's what? Ow!"

"I'm a patient man, Seb. You know that. Guido's one of ours and he's an expert. Should be here any minute. And see there? Where my pretty little assistant is standing?"

It's a small room with bare, white-washed walls, a single chair on which I sit and a table in one corner with a black box on it. So far, I've not focused on the young woman in ministry uniform—a tight-fitting grey trouser suit—no doubt included to satisfy Griff's warped sense of humour. Even *he* might have more sex appeal than a naked human light bulb. Beside her is a camera on a tripod.

"We'll record it all for her to watch. As he shortens your limbs one by one till you spill the beans. Or you tell me first and I'll make it quick. For her too."

"Guido? I don't—" The door opens.

"He's here!" a voice informs us.

Moments later, the large man enters. I recognize Guido Fratelli from the previous evening. He looks like an opera singer past his prime, dressed in an immaculate dark suit and tie.

"He's all yours, Guido my chum," says Griff. "Get it from him. The neutralizing thought that bloody blocks the sensors. And find out who else he's told. Otherwise his little gift to the Government will be useless. And you, my pretty one (he turns towards the girl), I think you should leave. What you've seen so far is like a kid's movie compared with what Guido's gonna hand out to my old friend."

The girl leaves and closes the door. Just the three of us now. Griff walks across to the table and opens the box. Guido winks at me. *Another bastard*, I'm thinking. *Apart from Sal and me, are there any non-bastards left?* I grit my teeth when I see what Griff extracts from that box: a broad-bladed, curved knife, so shiny that it lights up his face, and a pair of pliers the size of chain-cutters. Then, without a word, Guido pulls a gun, swivels and takes aim at Griff.

What the Hell?

Griff gawps as if the Italian has suddenly transformed into a pink, three-headed sheep. Guido lowers his aim and fires. Silent, Griff crumples to his knees. His hands flap helplessly, the instruments of torture clatter to the polished wooden floorboards, then the rat who stole Sal from me clutches at the crotch of his trousers, red with blood. Even if Guido turns and shoots me too, I can go to Hell a happy man.

"So, you think you can get away with it because of who you are, *stronzo!* I saw it all on my computer. And she's not yet sixteen. My own daughter, huh? She was helping out last night. You didn't even notice her, but she saw you. I thought it was just her age making her so unhappy—so *silenziosa!* But you'd raped her! My lovely daughter! And she never dared say. But I saw the terror in her thoughts all recorded by your little machine!"

Griff's lips open and close like those of a deep-sea fish as Guido re-aims the gun at his head and edges slowly towards his prey.

"You raped my *carinissima!* And she means nothing to you. Well, you know what? You mean nothing to me."

Griff shakes his head, but not for long.

BANG!

A black hole appears in the middle of the bastard's forehead. His eyes turn blank, he seems to rock slightly then, like a felled tree, he crashes forward onto his face. Guido turns to me. I expect to be his next victim.

"That man's enemy is Guido's friend *per tutta la sua vita!*" he says with a grin that shows teeth whiter than a plate of spaghetti.

Whilst he undoes my bonds, I start to laugh. At first in little bursts of giggles then, as the irony sinks in, I lapse into uncontrollable guffaws. My clothes lie in a heap in one corner and my frantic struggles to get into them in haste merely increase my mirth. "Thank you," I say, as I pull up my trousers. "And the food last night was great! The best!"

In the foyer, ministry officials stare at me, dumbfounded.

"He's not to be disturbed," I inform them, trying to come to terms with the hilarity of the situation. "He's got what he needed and is sorting things out with a higher authority."

Then I run. Run like hell. Back home, for that's where she'll be. I've figured it out. His plan was to have her bound like a trussed chicken on my bed whilst forcing her to watch me being dismembered, limb by limb, by the Italian, to uncover the neutralizing thought. As soon as I'd uttered the words, he would have had her killed. Even I reckoned she wouldn't be safe with the words—back then. But now?

Only one guard outside my front door? I always knew Griff was stupid. A brick to the head sorts out the stooge. Inside, Sal is alone and (God, what a predictable fool the man was!) lying bound and gagged on my bed. Her mouth remains hidden, but I see the delight in her eyes as I enter. On a monitor screen, I see ministry officials gawping at Griff's body. Guido's gone.

"You're gonna find this so funny!" I tell her as I remove her bonds and the gag. She sits up and rubs her wrists and ankles. "So very funny! Remember how I explained there had to a neutralizing thought that would inactivate the sensor of my monster as I used to call it."

She looks at me wide-eyed. I kiss her long and hard.

"Remember?" I repeat, taking hold of her hands. She nods. "And I said no one but me must know or the whole thing would become useless?" She nods again. I detect a hint of a smile. We're that close I have no need for TTT to guess her thoughts. She already knows.

"I don't believe it!" she says slowly.

"Sure is. 'Kill Griff!' Had to be. Couldn't be anything else. And you know, he could only tell there had to be a neutralizing thought because the sensor he fitted in your house failed to pick up anything from me yesterday evening. Reckoned I was actively trying to block it. And the joke is it never occurred to me he'd do that. All the thoughts I had on entering your home were for real."

Sal smiles, she chuckles then laughs and we hold each other till we're helpless with amusement.

"How?" she asks when we finally pull apart.

"An Italian bloke. His ministerial torturer in fact, only Griff had been silly enough to rape the man's underage daughter."

"Well that figures! Only interested in little girls, the swine! Was he made to suffer?"

I recall my old friend's face as he clutched his blasted privates whilst kneeling before a subordinate.

"Yes. But—" I start to chuckle again. "Think of this. If they go ahead and use my monster after the neutralising thought goes viral, everyone in the country will be thinking, 'Kill Griff!'—in every public space, church, mosque or synagogue. Imagine the sound of it crossing over to where the bastard is now. For him, the music of Hell."

"Seb?"

"Yeah?"

"Your monster. Bring them down, will it, when the people know the truth? So that we can all start over again? Without Griff?"

"As long as we always have a neutralizing thought!"

Then, in the certain knowledge that Griff is struggling in a place run by Satan, we make love on my bed.

A Cross of Sticks

A cross was made from two sticks, one longer than the other. Someone came up with the idea of using sticks broken from the hazel bush in the front garden. Who this was, no one remembers, but it seems appropriate to place this on the altar every time. As Hazel (was this why?) is helped into her dress, the tall man carefully balances the cross behind two candles.

It takes three to dress Hazel; two to support her, whilst the third eases her into the long white dress. It smells fresh and clean and Anna detects a hint of a smile from her patient. She and Tom care, however much bother the routine causes. Then there's the hair and the make-up. These things take forever, which is why the tall man goes out for a smoke to await his arrival. Someone different each time.

The hair's a problem because there isn't much of it. The scarring accounts for that, and scarring is about all you see, even after make-up has been applied—thick daubs of it, like the oils on a Van Gogh painting though the result is a far cry from the sublime beauty of the post-impressionist's masterpieces. It's grotesque, but she appears to look pleased and this, after all, is what matters.

"Are you ready?" Tom calls out from the open window. The tall man looks at his watch.

"He's late," he replies. "Are you sure he understood what it's about?"

"A free lager six-pack? That much he understood. He'll be here, don't you worry."

They carry Hazel through into the other room and lower her gently onto the high stool, with Tom supporting her back. Anna re-arranges the folds of her dress then peers at Hazel. Something's wrong. She can tell from an expression that struggles through the puckered constraints of the scars and the layers of make-up. Suddenly, Anna grins.

"The veil!" she exclaims. "We nearly forgot! Harry, fetch the veil!"

Harry, an obedient helper who never asks 'why?', disappears then reappears clutching a white filigree veil which Anna uses to carefully conceal what could not be restored. Hazel's hands, useless claws, lie motionless on her lap. She must be happy otherwise they'd be on the move, trying to do things they'd not done for years.

Once a local beauty queen at the age of twenty-two, Hazel remains stuck in a past that will forever be secure. A picture of her taken at the time of her engagement stands next to the cross, a reminder of what the present might have been but for the accident. One thing is certain. When whoever is hired to earn that six-pack sees the picture, he will be willing to go ahead with the charade. Some shed tears.

Tom hates it when they have to wait, for he knows how this must hurt Hazel, so he talks to her; talks about the pageant when the girl's beauty raised her to royal status, and about the young men who flocked for her approval... and the one who won the prize. They were to be married exactly five years, seven months and eighteen days ago.

Tom returns to the window. Cigarette stubs lie scattered around the tall man's feet, and Tom cannot help thinking that if Mother Nature had had her way the tall man would be confined to bed long term as a nicotine-cripple and Hazel free to blossom and burst from her scars like a butterfly emerging from a chrysalis. He and Anna feel anger. Not with the tall man for his addiction but with Nature for not insisting that in her game with Fate, the cards of DNA dealt to Hazel were properly played.

Both of the girl's parents were killed in the accident. They were the lucky ones. Hazel was pulled, unconscious, from the burning wreck with third degree burns. Someone trained in cardiac resuscitation got her heart going again. *Would that they had never done that*, Tom believes. The pain in her disfigured face when her fiancé visited just once, briefly, never lifted. Tom had often wondered whether, if the young man had loved the girl rather than the beauty queen, that sublime loveliness captured in camera might have miraculously returned.

But fairy stories never happen. The charade of a mock-up wedding was Anna's idea after Hazel was transferred from the hospital. Although the young woman could only grunt, the pretence of a marriage ceremony conducted by a tall man (Anna's brother) with a cardboard dog-collar, and a pseudo-groom eager for a free six-pack, appeared to please her. Anna was so convinced of this that the exercise was repeated after a month, then again at two months, three months—becoming a routine for five years and seven months. Since she was the owner of the long-stay nursing home, no questions were asked.

"He's arrived!" announces Tom. "Pissed as a newt, as always!"

Anna scowls. Tom returns from the window to make last minute preparations, placing the ring on the chair beside Hazel and the Bible on the altar. Inside the Bible is a folded sheet of paper with the order of ceremony and the words, in big, bold font, to be uttered by the priest and the groom. Many a groom stares blankly at the words as if chewing these over in his mind before getting his beer-sodden tongue round them. Some giggle.

The door opens. The tall man enters (Anna assumes Hazel cannot recall names, and to call him a priest feels wrong, so her brother is always referred to as 'the tall man'), hastily adjusting his cardboard dog collar, followed by a drunken 'groom'. The 'groom' reaches for the six-pack beside the door, but the tall man slaps his hand and pulls him towards the 'altar'.

"Don't look," he whispers. "Not a pretty sight. Just stand in front of that chair over there and say, 'I do' when I tell you to. I'll do the ring thing."

Hazel cannot stand. Each leg is folded and fixed like the blade of an unused penknife. The inebriate 'groom' is taken through the mock marriage ceremony by the tall man, slurs "I do" at the appropriate time, loses interest after the tall man slips a ring over Hazel's bent finger, grabs the lager pack on his way out and is gone.

"They're getting harder to find," says Tom under his breath. "And they never return!"

"Shhh!" rebukes Anna. "Help me take her back to bed and out of this confounded costume."

"But it's true!" Tom insists. "Why don't *I* do it?"

Anna shakes her head.

"Wouldn't be the same. She'd know," she whispers. "Look into her eyes. Surely you can see how happy she is."

Tom sees only emptiness, but he accepts that his boss is a remarkable woman who sees things invisible to him, so he sets about lifting Hazel, with Harry's help, from the stool before carrying her to bed. The tall man removes his dog collar, dismantles the altar and returns the cross to its resting place: a hook beside Hazel's bed.

*****

Something white flaps over her face like the wing of a swan. She feels only light pressure, no swan-wing scrapes, since the scars numb all fine feelings. Then come the voices. She understands every word, and she knows, but gave up a long time ago trying to tell people... knows that the tall man, the false priest, is Anna's brother; knows that the 'grooms' have nothing to do with who she once was and only come because of the beer, and she knows the cross is a fake.

But the cross reminds her. When she attempts to smile for Helen, and Helen is a truly remarkable woman, it's because of that cross, not the nonsense of a fancy white dress and being perched like a broken ornament on a stool beside a swaying stranger reeking of alcohol. Religion meant so much to her as a girl. They called her an 'angel' when she sang solo at mass. Entering the beauty contest— her mother's idea—seemed like a thank you to God for the good fortune of a Botticelli face and a voice to match.

She felt no anger when the engagement was broken off. What else could he have done? The accident was God's will, not *his* fault. Someone had defied God and brought her back from the dead, and all she could now do was to wait. Two things, only, seemed to give her purpose: Anna's smile, whenever the woman's gentle face came into her line of vision, and that cross of sticks.

She so wanted to ask Anna whose idea this was, so that they might be thanked, but her tongue and lips had become disconnected from her brain and mere guttural sounds emerged. She wanted the monthly charade to stop, but, for the same reason, it didn't. She wanted to die but couldn't. Months and years passed. They fed, watered and turned her, frequently changing her oversized nappies. Her life became her penance, and in her overactive head she would count the days till the next time they washed her in preparation, plastered her pink, corduroyed face and reddened her puckered lips, covering their failure with a fine white veil before carrying her to the stool. Then she would feed on the memories that the cross, lit by candles, evoked: the stolen exchanges of smiles with the young trainee priest from Ireland, the racing of her teenage heart before mass, the heaviness of disappointment if he was not there, the soaring rapture of singing for him, not God... and the kiss.

It only happened once. *She* was underage and *he* was a priest sworn to celibacy but she couldn't stop herself for she'd heard he was leaving to take on a parish himself and she would never see him again and surely there was no harm in it, she thought, so when it was just her and him left in the church, for her parents had left early, she ran up and kissed him full on the lips and on tip-toes, for he was quite tall, and the kiss seemed to continue forever for she wouldn't let go and he didn't appear to want her to. But there is no forever. It's an illusion. She ran sobbing from the church to await God's wrath.

She could never understand why it hadn't come sooner. When she first saw the cross of sticks, enrobed as she was like a dying swan, she expected a quick end as punishment for her past wickedness as a young temptress, despite the normality of life between kiss and accident. Was it a sacrificial altar? But Mendelssohn's Wedding March, the ring and the drunken pseudo-groom told a different story. Plus, with time, words that were spoken began to have meaning again. Her true punishment was to be trapped in a scar shell as an eternally hideous bride-to-be until the cross of sticks had done its trick and purified her guilt.

*****

"I do believe—" begins Anna whilst removing the layers of make-up, "I really *do* believe she was a religious kind of girl before—I mean *is*—now—still. Something about the way she looks at this cross. It's as if—"

"I remember!" blurts Harry.

"What?" Tom and Anna ask together.

"The cross. Who made it for her. He only came once. Soon after she arrived from the hospital."

"Why didn't you say before?"

"No one asked me. I'm only Harry the helper, after all!"

"Who then?"

"A tall young Irish priest. She was asleep at the time. He said not to wake her up but left the cross. I forgot to tell you at the time."

"A tall young priest, huh? So, I did the right thing in choosing my brother then. I—" Something in her patient's eyes urges Anna to hold back. "Well—thank you for owning up at last. The mystery of the cross of sticks is no longer. And we can look forward to your wedding next month, Hazel. What an occasion it'll be, huh?"

The lips attempt to speak in response to what was said but can't. The once-beautiful eyes try to cry, but no tears emerge. Instead, the hands jerk and twitch. Not even Anna knows why.

83

Miriam

Miriam was different. How and why was unimportant. She was different, and that was enough for her peers at school to use the girl as target practice for their jibes and cat-spit cruelty. Not a day went by when Miriam was not surrounded by a circle of hormone-laden, adolescent girls hell-bent on making her existence at school a total nightmare. All verbal, of course. Not once did any of them lay a finger on her, but their words were razor sharp. Those girls had no need to resort to physical violence.

For a start Miriam was pretty yet never flaunted her looks. When the boys found themselves cold-shouldered by her, they labelled her a snob, moving off to find easier game, allowing the female cat-pack to close in with its claws and canine teeth of gossip and innuendo. Miriam was also brilliant (she could hardly be blamed for coming top in all subjects) but what really did it was that Miriam was kind. She had befriended a stammering, overweight girl called Mandy, and in doing so had defied the pack's unwritten rules on how the class pariah should be treated. The two girls got called the M&Ms and Miriam herself now bore the full brunt of the pack's vicious verbal attacks.

But those girls knew nothing about Miriam. All they saw was their own mirrored jealousy framing an image of the girl created from the spite that frothed in feline female brains. It was not Miriam. And the cat-pack had no idea what Miriam did after school.

Every evening, she took a detour via a ruined manor house at the edge of town. Some said it was haunted, and no one except for Miriam went there. He was only seven when a five-year-old Miriam first wandered into the porch at the side of the derelict building to discover what lay beyond that entrance overhung by trailing ivy. Together they would play and talk in the porch whilst her parents cuddled on the overgrown lawn outside, but she never went on through the doorway into the house, and he, Edgar, never emerged with her into her own world outside the curtain of ivy. Both knew they could not, for they sensed that the porch was special and only for them. It was their secret time-space wormhole into which no other soul might enter, but from which neither could escape into the other's life.

Now he was seventeen.

"I thought you weren't coming," he said that evening, stepping aside for Miriam as she entered the porch. They sat together with their backs against the wall peering through the open door at a world forever denied to Miriam: a reception room where women in wide crinoline dresses would small-talk incessantly about nothing, and beyond that an oak-panelled dining-room where the large family would sometimes be seated downstream of Edgar's walrus-moustached, patriarchal father with his side-burns and his long, dapper dinner jacket. And they would grin whenever the man roared out:

"Edgar, you intolerable youth, where are you?"

She knew they were invisible in that timeless porch when Edgar's father sent the boy's brothers and sisters to search for him. They would sit and giggle, neither in one world nor the other, as they listened to shouts of "Edgar, where the devil are you?"

Miriam had always accepted that her friend came from a past world, but he was no ghost. It was merely a time thing—a mysterious phenomenon to do with the old porch which only they could enter. Of late, she had realized it was love that preserved this phenomenon. She felt no need to question this until that day when he told her:

"Miriam, he's sending me off to London to stay with my uncle to get started in the family business, and then—oh Miriam, he plans to marry me off to a girl with a face like the backside of a cart horse but who'll bring wealth into the company. I can't bear it! I beg you, Miriam, come across the threshold into my world and we'll escape together. Build a life here."

Miriam squeezed Edgar's hand and held him close. For some while their relationship had changed. They were no longer children.

"I can't," she said, looking away. "You know I can't. It's my father. There's only the two of us since Mum died, and he'd be heart-broken. Why, if I became another of those missing kids—" Her eyes moistened, for she no more wanted to lose Edgar than he her. "The other way around?" she suggested, looking up at him. For a few moments, her wide brown eyes held him motionless.

"Miriam, how is it possible anyone could be as lovely as you?"

"That's not an answer," she replied.

"In your world I'd be a nothing. It's different for a boy, don't you see?"

"Why?" the girl queried.

"Because I'd be laughed at. Called names. They'd say I'm stupid." Miriam was unimpressed. "Those things you tell me about, Miriam. Machines that fly about in the sky with people in them. Horseless carriages that travel at amazing speeds. It'd all be so strange to me. I'd be labelled an ignoramus."

"I don't mind."

Edgar took hold of Miriam. She was on the brink of tears.

"I want to look after you. I *know* my own world. I'll overcome that father of mine. Just explain it to your father, then come with me. Surely he'll understand? Perhaps we'll discover a way for you to come back and visit him."

For a long while, they had decided that if one of them were to cross over into the other's world, the porch would disappear and there'd be no return. Something told them the porch was only there to enable their love to span different worlds.

Miriam was crying.

"My dad could never understand. He'd get hurt. I can't leave him."

"Miriam, I have to go to London tomorrow. I've no idea when or even *if* I shall return. Father is only too pleased to see the back of me."

Miriam held onto Edgar and sobbed. She had been able to put up with all the torment at school only because she always knew that Edgar would be there, waiting for her. Being with Edgar was the real world and the rest was a total nightmare. Now that world was about to vanish.

"Please don't go. Pretend you're ill. Anything!" she pleaded.

"You don't know my father. He'd pack me off to London in a coffin if he had to! Just speak with your father, Miriam. Beg him to let you go. I'll be back here later. And wait all night if I have to!"

They kissed.

"There's another thing," Miriam said, looking away from Edgar. "We don't really know what would happen if one of us were to cross over. If I went back a hundred and fifty years, would I no longer exist? And you might suddenly become a hundred and sixty-seven if you come with me. It's got to be good-bye, Edgar. I'm so sorry!"

Miriam turned and ran, weeping, from porch.

She could not imagine a life without Edgar. Although they had only met for brief periods in the blissful space of that porch, Edgar was Miriam's life. She had no idea how she would now cope with the cat-pack at school.

Miriam came close to telling her father. She even packed a rucksack with the intention of returning to the old manor house that night. But when she opened her mouth to tell the man she couldn't. She loved him too much.

"What is it, Miriam?" he asked as his daughter stood open-mouthed and wordless.

"Oh—nothing, Dad!" Most of that night she wept in her bed thinking only of Edgar waiting alone in the porch, his hope fading.

The following day at school was the worst Miriam had ever experienced. She was teased mercilessly when the pack discovered her trying to help Mandy with the other girl's homework. Even the boys joined in:

"Hey, boys. The M&Ms are looking particularly ugly today, don't you think? Which one would you go with, guys, if they were the last two girls left on earth?"

Mandy, who really was unattractive, became upset. Miriam gave her a comforting hug and led her away. Mandy never could understand why all the others were so cruel to her; even less, why Miriam stood for her.

"Come round to my place this evening, Mandy. I'd like you to meet my father."

Mandy was over the moon. She couldn't stop smiling. But Miriam? Suddenly there was a huge gaping hole in her life. She had to do something to fill it.

The bell sounded. Miriam dreaded being seen going home with Mandy, and the wolf-whistles and cutting remarks. Just because she tried to be kind to Mandy, the cat-pack accused her of having no interest in boys. She could imagine their taunts:

'Oh, look at those two love birds! Aren't they cute? Hey, tweetie pies, what do you get up to together, huh? How do you do it?' If only they knew the truth.

"Wow, take a look look at *him!*"

Miriam turned, whilst packing her school bag, to see Vanessa, the ring-leader of the cat-pack, staring out of the window. The girl must have seen someone at the school gate. Vanessa's side-kick peered over her shoulder.

"Funny clothes he's wearing!"

"Oh, you know nothing about designer stuff! He is gorgeous!"

It was as if a light inside Miriam had been turned on. She grinned from ear to ear, quickly stuffing the remaining books into her backpack.

"Hurry!" she said impatiently to a surprised Mandy before pulling the girl by the arm out of the classroom.

"Look at the M&Ms!" exclaimed Vanessa. "Let's follow them! See what they get up to tonight, for a laugh!" She cackled like a witch. *She is a witch*, thought Miriam, *but what do I care now?* She grinned as if the whole world belonged to her, and Mandy, confused and frowning, struggled to keep up with her friend. Out in the playground, Miriam let go of Mandy, threw her backpack to the ground and ran to the gate. She leapt into his arms, allowing him to swing her round and round as he kissed her over and over.

"Do I look a hundred and sixty-seven?"

Miriam laughed.

"One of the girls said 'wow!' when she saw you. That means you look great, Edgar."

"I couldn't leave without you. Spent all night in the porch just thinking. Knew you wouldn't be able to leave your father. I was selfish to suggest it. Forgive me?"

Miriam gave him a gentle slap on the wrist.

"Of course I do! And now I guess somehow I'm gonna have to explain you to Dad."

Miriam turned to look for Mandy. The girl had held back, a frightened rabbit standing alone half-way across the playground, staring in disbelief. Closer, a semi-circle of girls gaped like inquisitive cows. A few acne-studded boys had grouped timidly behind the girls as though emasculated by the manly presence of Edgar. One, secretly in love with Miriam, stepped forward, picked up her backpack and handed it to her.

"Thank you," said Miriam, grinning.

"Are those the girls who were bothering you, Miriam?" Edgar asked, glowering at the cat-pack.

"Oh, they don't bother me, Edgar. Here! Come and meet my friend Mandy."

Miriam took Edgar's hand and led him straight through the pack, forcing her would-be tormentors to stand back and make way for them. Edgar took Mandy's hand and kissed it. The poor girl almost fainted.

"I am delighted to meet you, Mandy. Miriam has told me so much about you. From now on, count me as your friend too." Edgar put one arm around Miriam, the other around Mandy, and escorted the two girls from the school playground, to a collective of stupefied stares, whilst Miriam chattered away about nothing in particular.

The Pringle Sisters

Violet was sitting at the kitchen table, absorbed in a novel of intrigue and romance. Before her was a cold cup of tea and a half-eaten biscuit fringed with crumbs. Her sister called out from her arm-chair throne in the sitting-room:

"Violet, are you going to just sit around all day long or will you at least think about getting my lunch? All my life I've slaved away for both of us, and here I am, at my age, having to beg for a little help from my younger sister! Beg! And if..."

For a while, Violet continued to read against the verbal outpouring from the sitting-room. Then, without replying, she folded the corner of the page, closed her book, stood up and went quietly over to the cupboard. The telephone in the kitchen rang just as she opened the cupboard door. She picked it up and put it to her ear.

At ninety-two, Daphne, the elder of the two sisters, still had a razor-sharp mind and kept as close an eye upon her younger sister's comings and goings about the house as she had always done:

"Violet, why are you taking so long in the bathroom?" "Violet, those books on the floor! What are they doing there? Why should I always have to tidy up after you?" Or, "Violet, what are you up to in that kitchen all this time?"

Violet would retreat into the kitchen for long periods. Daphne never entered this part of the house. It had too much to do with household chores, Violet's duty.

The younger Pringle sister now only rarely replied. An invisible wall had developed between her and the elder one many years back. It had been a gradual process. At first, after their mother died, and Violet was compelled to live with Daphne, she had found it exceedingly difficult to put up with the woman's constant nagging. She would even stand up for herself and answer back. Slowly and painfully, she discovered this approach to be pointless for it only intensified Daphne's verbal attacks. Violet learned that if she remained quietly submissive, then her sister's anger would, sooner or later, transform into low-grade muttering about the burdens and responsibilities that she, Daphne, had to bear.

Violet loved books. As a young girl, she had been a regular at the library and she abandoned the idea of teaching when offered the position of assistant librarian at the local public library. She had no ambition to further her career and remained in the same poorly-paid post until she retired at sixty. She loved her work and never raised the question of promotion with her employers. Instead, she got on with the job in her own quietly efficient way. Whenever the opportunity arose, she would lose herself in a book. Like her mother, Violet was one of life's dreamers and, in this respect, she could not have been more different from her big sister.

Daphne resembled her father both in appearance and character. Major Pringle had been killed in action early on during the Second World War. He had always doted on Daphne but was forever criticizing and castigating the younger of the two girls. Violet would cling to her mother when their father was at home, carefully watching his every move through fearful large brown eyes. Even this seemed to irritate the man. Daphne was only too eager to team up with her father against her little sister should the opportunity arise. Consequently, the bond between Violet and her mother became strong. They understood each other perfectly. When a twelve-year-old Violet heard the news of her father's death, she skipped around the house happily waving the telegram. She received no reprimand from Mrs. Pringle who knew precisely how her daughter felt. By then, Daphne had already left home after accepting a junior placement with the Ministry of Defence in London.

Unlike Violet, Daphne was always bursting with ambition. She successfully climbed the career ladder of the Civil Service and soon ended up with quite a senior position in the Ministry. Repeatedly, she reminded Violet how secret her job was, not that Violet had the remotest interest in what her elder sister got up to at work. Daphne's retirement pension well exceeded Violet's salary when the younger woman was still in employment, and Violet's own final pension was meagre indeed. The house, together with all other assets, had been left to Daphne in her father's will. There was nothing that Mrs. Pringle could have done to change this, and Violet remained forever dependent on her sibling.

It was a great comfort to Violet's mother to have the younger child at home with her during her last few years of life. She was a lovely girl, and Mrs. Pringle was always on the lookout for a young man who might someday propose to her. The woman never told Daphne about allowing Violet to go to the RAF dances, frequented by American servicemen, with her friends. The censorious elder sister, who only returned home once every month or two, would never have approved.

Daphne moved back to the family home after Mrs. Pringle died, and she commuted daily by train to London. At first, Violet thought that she would never get over the death, from tuberculosis, of her mother, but she did. In fact, she somehow became stronger and she learned how to deal with her sister's moods and tempers. Of course, her circumstances meant that she would be forever beholden to her sister for financial support.

*****

"What's the rush for?" Daphne would ask. "The postman's not going to take it away again once he's put it in the letter box."

One morning, a particularly fat envelope arrived. Violet knew this was it. It had a blue airmail label. She looked at the unfamiliar stamp. On this was written *'U.S Post'*. Her fingers trembled with excitement as she held the envelope before turning it over to see the sender's hand-written address, then the other way again to look at the stamp once more. She escaped into the privacy of the kitchen where she knew she would be completely safe from Daphne's hawk eyes, despite the fact that Daphne was still in bed upstairs having another of her 'off days'.

Violet carefully opened the envelope with a knife and shook out its contents onto the kitchen table. She read the letter—all three pages—several times. Staring at the hand-writing, with tears confusing her eyes, she gently stroked the dried ink script with the tips of her fingers as if this might bring her closer to the writer, then she picked up the photograph that had fallen out with the letter.

"So like Alan," she whispered as a tear trickled down one cheek. "So like him," she repeated, stroking the photograph.

The younger Pringle sister returned the letter and its other contents to the envelope before concealing this in the book she had been reading. Daphne never touched Violet's books. She hated books.

I'll wait until the last possible moment before telling her, thought Violet before she set about the day's chores.

She had six weeks to sort out affairs. First, she would have to renew her passport. The Pringle sisters' last trip abroad had been almost twenty years before—a visit to Tuscany that proved to be a disaster. Ten days of nagging from Daphne, Violet ran out of books and, to complete the picture, Daphne fell ill with diarrhoea. This, it turned out, was Violet's fault for insisting that they ate at a romantic little restaurant in a hill-top village near Bagni di Lucca. Violet had endless earfuls about her 'ridiculous little fancy' for years to come and they never went abroad again.

There was also the question of money. Violet had a small amount in her bank account, which she withdrew and converted to US dollars. However, he did say, in a later telephone call, that she really would not need to bring anything at all. She would be met at the airport in Boston and he had arranged for a friend of his in London to take her to Heathrow Airport early on the morning of the flight. As the day approached, she felt more and more excited and nothing that Daphne said seemed to irritate any longer. She would just smile back at her grumpy sister and say, "Yes,

Daphne," or "No, Daphne." Of course, she had done her best to make arrangements to ensure her sister would be cared for: Mrs. Williams would drop in daily, clean the house twice a week and do the laundry; groceries would continue to be delivered to the door and, whether she liked it or not, Daphne Pringle would be getting meals-on-wheels every day. She could then direct complaints about her food to the council rather than Violet. Most of all, Violet could reassure Daphne that she would no longer have the financial burden of a younger sister. Surely that should please her?

On the eve of her departure, Violet had set her alarm clock for six in the morning. The pick-up for the airport was to be at seven. Daphne never got up before eight-thirty, so Violet entered her sister's bedroom the preceding evening just before Daphne would normally turn out her light.

"Violet, you really should knock before coming into my room, you know." It had been another off day.

"Don't worry, sister. I won't do that again. In fact, after tomorrow you'll see no more of me. Isn't that wonderful? I'm flying to Boston to stay with my son. He invited me over and sent the air tickets, but the last time we spoke he said to throw away the return ticket because he and his wife now want me to stay with them. It's all arranged."

Violet had spoken in her usual gentle matter-of-fact sort of way whilst her sister stared up at her from her pink, floral-patterned pillow. The older woman's mouth hung open and, with her stone-grey eyes, she suddenly resembled a fishmonger's cod. Violet thought Daphne's bed cap was uncommonly like a tea cosy.

A cod with a tea cosy for a hat? Her hand covered an unstoppable smile that appeared on her face. Daphne remained speechless.

"You'll find plenty of food in the fridge," continued Violet. "Mr Freeman will deliver the groceries as usual. Mrs. Williams will see to most things and I'm sure you'll enjoy the meals-on-wheels."

The elder sister's cod-fish face went through a series of Rowlandson cartoon contortions as she struggled to make sense of what she'd heard.

"Violet!" Daphne finally found her tongue. "Violet, I don't think I heard you properly. I thought you said—"

"Yes," Violet calmly affirmed, "I'm off to live with my son in America. I have three grand-children and four great grand-children, and I can't wait to see them. It's so exciting, don't you think?"

Daphne was not used to having questions put to her, but this one was simply preposterous. The cod-fish mouth opened and closed, offering little in the way of sound beyond a meaningless squeak. It wasn't until Violet had left the room, and closed the bedroom door, that the fireworks really started:

"Violet, come back in here at once!"

Violet re-entered.

"Violet, what on earth were you saying? If this is one of your dreamy little fantasies, I think it's in bad taste. Very bad indeed! And what do you think Father would have said had he heard you talk like that? Shameful! A thoroughly distasteful joke, Violet!"

Violet took the liberty of sitting down on the edge of her sister's bed whilst she gave Daphne the whole story. She told her how she had become pregnant towards the end of the Second World War, when just seventeen, explaining, in response to Daphne's expression of bewilderment, that those months away supposedly doing teacher training were spent with a close friend of their mother prior to the baby's birth. Mrs. Pringle had made the adoption arrangements, despite her poor state of health, when it became clear that Violet would not be able to keep the child. The pain of having her own baby taken from her was, said Violet, indescribable, but her mother helped her through it all. Violet paused. Daphne's mouth had remained agape whilst she listened, its owner obviously unable to either believe a word of what she had heard or formulate any comprehensible speech. Violet continued her story:

"And yes," she said, "I do know who the father was. We were going to marry when the war was over, but he never even got the chance to know that I was pregnant. He was killed a month before the end of the war. What do you think of that, Daphne?" Daphne visibly flinched at the word 'pregnant'. "David traced me after his adoptive mother died at the end of last year. There were papers from our mother which his adoptive mother had kept from him all these years. Thankfully, the old lady hadn't destroyed these. So that's about it. In a nutshell, so to speak!"

Daphne found her voice again. It was loud and clear: "Disgusting!" she shrieked. "True or not, it's all too disgusting! I don't want to hear about it again. Our father would have been appalled!"

Daphne pulled the bed clothes up to her pimpled chin as if this action would somehow settle the matter for good.

"*Your* father, Daphne!" remarked Violet quietly, leaving her half-sister to her mutterings after she'd closed the door behind her.

That was the last time Violet saw Daphne. As she sat in the airplane bound for Boston, a smile lit up her face when she mused over the previous evening's confrontation with her half-sister. She was happy—*really* happy—for the first time since Alan got killed and David was taken from her. Her son sounded so nice from their talks over the telephone. She pulled out the envelope from her bag and extracted his photograph. Every bit as handsome as Alan, the American airman she should have married. How ironic that David ended up in America after his adoptive parents emigrated in the early fifties. Alan had promised her such a wonderful life in America. Their love was so intense that she always knew there could never be anyone else, particularly as a part of Alan, their son David, was alive somewhere in the world. Until then, Violet never knew that her mother had sent details about herself to the adoption agency for forwarding to the baby's adoptive parents. She took, from the envelope, the family tree that her mother had drawn to accompany the baby boy to his new home. It showed that a certain Joseph

Barrington, who died from tuberculosis at the age of thirty-four in nineteen twenty-nine, a year after Violet was born, was her true father. She was ecstatic to know that she was not a true Pringle, after all.

The Other Nathan

"Something terrible is going to happen. I feel it in my bones." Nathan's heart sank. A regular occurrence of late. Because of Aunt Beth.

He was the only surviving relative of the slowly-dementing old woman who insisted she could cope on her own "with just a little bit of help"—which sometimes meant hourly telephone calls. Often, these continued into the night and the effect was an intolerable strain on his already troubled marriage. The fact that Aunt Beth lived four hundred miles away in Devon used to be a blessing. No longer. Sara had just left him again ("this time, for good," she said) when the telephone rang.

"Aunt Beth, that'll be your arthritis. Not your bones. Stop worrying about it. Take the pills the doctor prescribed. On the bathroom shelf. In a brown bottle."

"Brown bottle, blue bottle! What do you know about my bottles? You never come to see me."

"I was down two weeks ago. Remember? I made arrangements for them to check on you twice a day."

"Them? The police? But that was all so long ago!?"

"No, Aunt Beth. The carers. From Social Services."

"Sent that lot away, the good-for-nothings! Always asking questions, they were! Anyway, it's not my arthritis. It's Bill! What if he finds out?"

"Uncle Bill?"

"Don't know any other Bills. Apart from the telephone bill."

A sigh emerged from Nathan. He took the phone to the kitchen window to see whether his wife might have had second thoughts, but her car was gone. He returned to the table whilst Aunt Beth explained:

"Yes, your uncle. I'm really worried. Do you think he knows? He's not been himself."

"Not been himself? Can say that again!" whispered Nathan, aside.

"What's that? You think he's at it again?"

"Aunt Beth, Uncle Bill is dead."

"Oh, I wouldn't put it like that. Boring, yes, but dead is far too strong a word."

"The accident, Aunt Beth. Twelve years ago. He fell downstairs. I'm sorry, but there's only you and me now. Nathan. Your nephew."

"What about the other Nathan? You always forget about him. Was here a fortnight ago. And so good to me."

"That was *me*. I just told you. I was down two weeks ago."

"So you keep saying. But the other Nathan's a different kettle of fish altogether. So kind. Nothing's too much trouble for him. Puts up with Bill, too. You should've heard them laughing together. Full of fun, the other Nathan. But that's what's worrying me. You see, I might have told him. And suppose he told Bill. Or those social people. I'm sure I told someone."

Aunt Beth and Uncle Bill had no children of their own. When Beth's brother committed suicide, Nathan was but ten years old. After his mother took ill and passed away two years later, the boy's uncle and aunt, who looked after him, were like second parents. Now, as a hospital doctor, he had little free time to travel from Newcastle to Devon to see his aunt, but following his uncle's death, he had made the journey whenever possible, much to the annoyance of his wife, Sara. This was not helped by Beth taking against Sara. When Nathan informed his wife that they would have to cancel a long-planned holiday in Italy because he would be too concerned about his aunt to enjoy it, they had a blazing row.

"She doesn't even appreciate what you do for her! Just bangs on about the 'other Nathan' all the time! I'm telling you, it's either her or me!"

"The other Nathan is me, poor old thing. Only she's too confused to realize."

"Huh! I wouldn't be so sure. She'll be the death of you!"

Taking the phone with him, he filled the kettle at the sink then switched it on. Drinking endless cups of coffee kept him going. Sara would eventually return. Threatening to leave was her way of making a point, but such behaviour was far from helpful.

"I'm starving!" the phone said. Nathan picked it up.

"Just help yourself to something out of the fridge, Aunt Beth. They promised there'd always be something for you to eat."

"And how am I supposed to get to the fridge, huh? I'm on the floor and can't get up. My hip's agony—so don't you fob me off with that 'it's my arthritis' nonsense!"

"On the floor? Why didn't you say, Aunt Beth?"

"Why didn't you ask?"

"Did you fall?"

"I don't normally crawl around on my hands and knees. I am a biped, you know!"

"Call an ambulance. Dial 999. You might've broken your hip."

"Oh, if only the other Nathan could come here. He'd sort things out."

"Will you call an ambulance, or shall I do it?"

"The other Nathan cares!"

"That's me!"

"No! The airline pilot Nathan."

"What?"

Nathan could not prevent a grin from appearing despite Sara having gone off in a huff. Uncle Bill had run a small travel company, and, as a child, Nathan used to pretend he was an airline pilot. He would run around the sitting room with arms outspread, stop off beside Uncle Bill, seated on the sofa, to pick up a passenger (a teddy or an action man) then take off for some obscure destination in the kitchen (hot country) or bathroom (cold country). It intrigued him how the past and present had become merged for his aunt.

"He's a pilot. Surely you knew?" she questioned.

"Then I became a doctor, Aunt Beth. Look, I'm off this weekend. I'll phone for an ambulance right now and come down by train on Saturday."

"You'll come down by ambulance? Harry always said you might be a doctor one day. You should think about it."

Nathan made another cup of coffee and drank it in one continuous motion.

"I'll do that, Aunt Beth. Now promise me you won't do anything silly before they arrive."

"You are coming, then? What about that wife of yours? What's her name—Sally or something?"

"Sara. No, she won't be coming."

"Good!"

Nathan gritted his teeth. Suppose this time was for real with Sara?

"I'll let you know about the ambulance. Stay by the phone."

He rang off. There was no reply when he called again after contacting the Southwestern Ambulance Service. An hour later, he got an earful from their operator to say that the old lady he'd phoned about had been perfectly well when she answered the door and denied any knowledge of a fall or pain in the hip.

Sara returned and begged Nathan not to go down to Devon. They struck a deal. She'd stay if arrangements could be made to get Aunt Beth into some sort of residential care.

"Just stop messing around! It's what she needs!"

*****

Tired after the long journey and worrying both about Aunt Beth and about his marriage, Nathan rang the doorbell. His aunt answered the door, looking fit and well.

"Oh, it's you! I hoped it would be the other Nathan."

"Aunt Beth, we have to talk. May I come in—please?"

"If you must!"

The bungalow was clean and tidy. Perhaps what she'd said about sending the carers away was no truer than the 'other Nathan' business. He sat at the table whilst Aunt Beth occupied her favourite armchair facing the television—switched on. Soccer! He knew how she loved a good game.

"Which teams are playing?" he asked.

"The other Nathan's team, Spurs. Against Man United."

The ancient television fizzled then went blank. Were the gods on his side after all?

"Look, your telly's gone bust now. And my marriage is going the same way if I don't sort this out. Do you remember me talking to you about an old folks' home a fortnight ago? We looked at the brochure together?"

"The other Nathan wouldn't have it."

"Does he really care about you, this other Nathan? Flying around in his airplane?"

"Not all the time, he isn't. Sometimes he lands. I told you, he was here two weeks ago."

"That was me."

"Wasn't!"

"What's he look like, this other Nathan?"

"His father."

"Your brother?"

"No need to rub it in!"

"Never thought I looked much like Dad. More like Mum. Look, let's turn off the telly. It's still making a funny noise. We really should talk."

"Oh, do let's play the game before your Uncle Bill gets back."

"Game?"

"*His* game. Airplanes."

"Okay. if it's the only way I can get you to see sense about that care home." Nathan stood up and spread his arms wide. "I'm taking off, Aunt Beth. Tell me when I've permission to land."

Nathan began to glide round the living room making an engine noise last heard fifty years back in the company of his uncle, spiralling back in time until he giggled like the child he once was. After several circuits, Aunt Beth called out, "Stop! You're in Paris!"

The human plane halted beside a cabinet. Next to a small china corgi, firmly lodged in Nathan's memory cortex, was a photo he'd never before seen. A pretty, teenage girl grinned at him from within the silver frame, wearing the expression of a National Lottery winner. With one arm around her waist was Nathan's Dad from a long-gone era, sporting long hair. Nathan turned towards his aunt, his smile gone.

"You?" he asked.

"Of course! Not bad looking, ay? The other Nathan had it framed."

"But—you and Dad? It looks like you were both—"

"Paris nineteen fifty-five. I was fifteen. You've no idea how wonderful it was. Just the two of us. You see—I'll let you into a little secret. Come over here."

Communicating with Aunt Beth called for lateral thinking. Playing along with her fantasies formed part of Nathan's plan to persuade her to go into care, the old folks' home being the ultimate paradise holiday destination for her, but the photo disturbed him. His plane had gone off course. He sat on the sofa, beside the old lady, playing the ever-dutiful nephew, only to learn things that shone disturbing lights on dark corners of unspoken family history:

"Our father, your grandfather, was a bully. You knew that, didn't you?" Nathan only knew what his father had told him: that the man had left a dying wife, his grandmother, when his father was at university and Aunt Beth still at high school. "With mother dying, he thought he'd try it out on me, only Harry came home just in time. Wasn't expected back. Maybe he knew something might happen. We'd always been close, see, Harry and me. Anyway, Harry went ballistic when he found us. I screamed at him to stop hitting father. I knew he'd kill him if I didn't intervene. Mother was upstairs. She told Harry to take me away. Somewhere he'd not find us. She gave Harry some money. 'Go to Paris', she said. So, we did! Like a pair of newlyweds, we were, in that little pension in Montmartre. I can't tell you how much fun we had."

Nathan looked from the photo to Aunt Beth and back at the photo. There was something about the expressions of those young people that was more than would be expected of brother and sister.

"You shared a room?" he asked naïvely. Aunt Beth beckoned him to come closer. He moved up against her. She whispered proudly against his ear:

"A bed!"

Confusion tinged with disgust overwhelmed Nathan. His father and—and her being underage? He tried to change the subject:

"I really think that the home we talked about two weeks ago would suit you. You'll get your own room. I can afford it. And they were so nice there."

"So now you can see why Bill must never know."

"Know what?"

"About the other Nathan."

"Aunt Beth, for the hundredth time there's only one me and I'm struggling. Struggling to look after you from four hundred miles away. Struggling to keep my marriage together with all that's going on. And now—"

Oh my God!

His father and his father's sister in bed together? No way! But he'd never been told why his father left his mother. Or why the man later killed himself.

"The point is, Bill must never know," continued Aunt Beth.

"What?"

"About the fishing line."

Nathan breathed a sigh of relief.

"Fishing line?"

"I had to do it. To save all those children."

"Aunt Beth, you really will like it there. The food's good too."

"Food? Yes, he used to lure them with sweets. I've never felt the slightest bit guilty, you know."

"About what?"

"The fishing line, of course! Across the top of the stairs. It was invisible. Fish don't see it and neither did he. Neck broken. They said he'd not have felt a thing. So, quite humane. But the other Nathan might tell them. I had to confide in someone. I remember doing that. But was it Nathan or one those other people? The social people."

Uncle Bill—saving children—a fishing line?

"Save them from what? The children, I mean."

"From Uncle Bill. Didn't it ever occur to you with those games you and he used to play? Didn't you ever realize there was something—something unpleasant about him?"

Nathan wanted this to stop, but he could no more escape from an unfolding, hitherto-unknown, past than from the nightmare of his collapsing marriage. It all seemed horribly unreal. His beloved Uncle Bill a paedophile, murdered by his beloved Aunt Beth? And Paris? What really happened in Paris?

"Tell me about Paris, Aunt Beth?"

"Paris, my foot! Why should I tell you about Paris?"

"Because—because I've a feeling it's important."

"Of course it's important. But nothing to do with you. Only the other Nathan."

"Yes, but I need to know."

"But you're not the airline pilot. You want to become a doctor, heaven forbid."

"Am, Aunt Beth. *Am* a doctor. Which is already a strain on our marriage, but the added stress of phone call after phone call has caused a humungous gap between me and Sara. Plus this other Nathan business is the last flipping straw. So tell me about Paris."

"You won't tell the police?"

"Why on earth should I?"

"He'll end up in jail if you do."

"Uncle Bill?"

"Don't be silly. He's dead." *We're getting somewhere at last.*

"Your father. Posthumously, of course."

"Your brother?"

Nathan looked at the photo. In a flash he understood. Panic hurtled through his mind like a vehicle out of control. His father and Aunt Beth, brother and under-age sister in post-war Paris together, sharing a bed. The doorbell rang.

"That'll be the other Nathan."

Nathan looked around the room for somewhere to hide. Nothing. No cupboards.

"Somehow he tracked me down after all those years. Your half-brother. You might as well meet him now that you're here."

Aunt Beth got up and went to the door. Nathan's mobile phone rang. One of his ears heard a deep man's voice talking to his aunt in the hallway. Into his other, Sara asked Nathan whether the old lady had agreed to go into a home.

"I'm here at Aunt Beth's," he replied. "Trying to make her see reason. But quite possibly a solution to our problem is about to walk through the door. Wait—"

He covered the phone as the door opened. Aunt Beth entered first.

"Tell him the truth. That I was adopted," she whispered. "Your father *always* knew. And don't mention the fishing line."

Nathan's jaw dropped when a large plain-clothed police officer appeared.

"Her nephew, I believe?" the man questioned. Nathan nodded. "Don't mind if I ask you a few questions, do you, sir? About your family? Seems your aunt has been saying a few things to her carers."

Questions? He felt he knew less about his family than anyone. Most importantly, this old lady he had always called 'Aunt Beth' wasn't even a true relative.

"Nephew? No. I'm the other Nathan," he replied.

The Megarabbit

Megan screamed when a giant rabbit, the size of a double-decker bus, appeared from around the corner and bounded up the road towards her. She barely had time to leap out of the way and crouch down behind a hedge, hoping she would not be spotted. But she was. The rabbit stopped where she had been standing a moment earlier. His head was bigger than that of an elephant, his ears were enormous and his giant, air-hungry, flabby nostrils twitched as they sniffed at her.

Normally, Megan was fond of animals, but this was different. And it was not a *proper* rabbit, although it was a *sort* of a rabbit. As she stared at those big nostrils and dinner-plate sized eyes, she kept repeating to herself:

"Rabbits don't eat little girls, rabbits don't eat little girls—"

"Off course they don't!" agreed the rabbit in a gruff voice, "but, all the same, I'm *very* hungry!"

A talking rabbit? Megan began to feel braver. She stood up and approached the creature.

"Why are you so large?" she asked. "You must be as big as a whale!"

The rabbit cocked his head sideways so as to take in, with one eye, the whole of the little schoolgirl.

"Don't know anything about whales. I'm just a megarabbit," he said. "And not a particularly big one at that!"

"What's a megarabbit?"

"Silly question when you're looking at one."

"What *do* you eat, then?" She wanted to be absolutely certain that megarabbits did not eat little girls.

"Another silly question! What do rabbits *usually* eat?" The megarabbit seemed horribly grumpy. Megan thought it wise not to ask more silly questions.

"Erm—carrots? Grass?"

"And you know it hasn't rained for six weeks and all the grass has turned brown?"

"Daddy says it's called a drought."

"Never mind what it's called. I'm starving! That's why I've come here."

"You want food?"

"What do you think?"

Megan reckoned the enormous rabbit really did need food, and pretty quickly... judging by his bad temper.

"I'll see what I can get you," she replied. "Mummy always has some vegetables in the fridge."

"No potatoes! I don't eat potatoes. They're bad for my digestion."

"All right, Mr Megarabbit. No potatoes. Stay here. I'll be right back."

Feeling sorry for the hungry megarabbit, Megan ran home as fast as she could.

"What *are* you doing?" her mother asked when she ran straight into the kitchen, opened the fridge, and took out a cabbage, two lettuces, a bunch of carrots and a few tomatoes.

"There's this enormous rabbit, Mummy. It's very hungry and it's in the middle of the road. I don't think it'll move until it's had something to eat. All because of the drought, you see."

"Megan, what *are* you talking about? There's enough food there to feed ten rabbits for a whole week."

"Not this one! I'll show you."

Megan's mother followed the girl up the road, carrying two bulging bags and muttering crossly about the cost of vegetables. She dropped the bags when she saw the megarabbit. Her mouth remained open and soundless.

"He's a *mega*rabbit, Mummy. He's okay, really. Just a bit irritable because he's so hungry."

"Oh my gosh!" Her mother had finally re-found her tongue.

Megan took a cabbage up to the megarabbit. His nostrils went into overdrive as he sniffed at it. Leaf by leaf, he gobbled it up then went on to eat the two lettuces, all the carrots and a bagful of tomatoes.

"Thank you," he said politely. "That was very nice—but—"

"You're still hungry?"

"Uh-huh!"

"Megan?" Megan looked at her mother. "Megan, that—erm—that rabbit thing—"

"He's a *mega*rabbit, Mummy."

"Did it just—erm—talk—like?"

"Yes. Why?"

"Nothing. Nothing at all. A talking giant rabbit. Perfectly normal." Megan's mother looked vacantly into the distance.

"Do you have any money, Mummy. I think we'd better buy some more vegetables at the supermarket for the megarabbit."

"Sounds like a good idea," said the megarabbit.

Megan took her dazed mother to the supermarket where they filled a box with all sorts of vegetables, except potatoes, and returned to the megarabbit. He munched through everything, then finished off with a loud cabbagey burp.

"Thank you," he said, "but I think I—"

"More?" asked Megan. She'd spent all her mother's money on the vegetables.

"No—erm—" He made a funny face and began to strain. "The other end," he grunted.

"Mummy, I think he's going to—you know—"

BOING!

Something large fell out from the back end of the megarabbit and onto the road. Megan knew it must be a poo, and she went to take a look.

"Mummy!" she yelled excitedly.

Her mother, with the expression of someone still in a dream, joined her.

"Oh my gosh!" she exclaimed again.

There, rolling towards the side of the road, was a huge ball of gold. It came to a standstill in the grass. Megan, laughing, skipped across the road and stroked the smooth, shiny surface of the golden dropping.

"Can we keep your poo, Mr Megarabbit?" she called out.

The megarabbit turned his head and looked at her.

"Why would you want my poo?" he asked.

Megan thought for a while. She did not want to say the wrong thing.

"Well—if it's made of gold, we could use the money to buy more vegetables for you."

"I've no idea what it's made of—but I am beginning to feel hungry again," replied the megarabbit.

Megan and her mother rolled the giant gold rabbit dropping all the way home. Megan's father put the dropping in the garage and said he would look after it. When Megan suggested she take it to the bank and exchange it for lots of money, he said:

"Nonsense! Gold is only for grown-ups. Here! Take this money and buy some vegetables for the—erm—"

"Megarabbit!"

"Sure! I'll clear space in the garage for more gold droppings."

Megan and her mother returned to the supermarket to buy vegetables, only to discover the shop crowded with people, the shelves empty.

"What's happening?" the girl asked the shop assistant.

"It's that giant rabbit. A megarabbit. Blocking the road. They're all out there feeding it. Emptied our shelves of everything!"

Megan took her mother's hand and together they ran back to the megarabbit now surrounded by a horde of excited villagers. He was happily munching his way through the pile of food laid out in front of him. Not just green vegetables. There was fruit, bread, sausages and—potatoes.

"You mustn't give him potatoes," Megan pleaded. "They're bad for his digestion!"

No one listened. They were too busy squabbling over the gold droppings that kept emerging from the megarabbit's bottom. The girl went up to the megarabbit and spoke to him:

"Why are you eating all this stuff? Sausages and—and potatoes. They're bad for you, Mr Megarabbit! You know they are."

But all he said between mouthfuls was:

"Hungry! More food!"

Megan went home with her mother, feeling sad.

"Why no more gold droppings?" her father asked.

"They've rolled them all away," replied Megan. "*And* they're giving him sausages and potatoes. It'll be bad for his digestion!"

"But I've cleared space in the garage! For more gold poos! Come on! Let's join the others."

Megan refused to go with her father. She ran, crying, to her room.

All night the villagers, including the girl's father, fed the megarabbit with food and rolled the gold droppings back to their homes. People were talking about building bigger and better houses with all that gold, changing their cars from grubby little Fiats to posh Lexuses and sporty Alpha Romeos and going on fabulous holidays. By morning, there was no food left in any of the villagers' fridges. Except for Megan and her mother, everyone slept on, their garages full of gold megarabbit droppings and securely locked.

"I'm going to see if he's all right," Megan said to her mother. "They should never have given him potatoes. Or sausages!"

"I'll come with you, Megan."

The streets were deserted, even for a Sunday. Ahead of them, in the road, was the giant furry hump of the megarabbit. He was on his side, his ears flopped back. His eyes were shut. Megan ran to him.

"Are you asleep, Mr Megarabbit?" she asked.

There was no reply. Not even his nostrils moved.

"Mummy!"

Her mother came over and put an arm around her.

"Megan, I think he's—"

Megan burst into tears.

"I know, Mummy. He's dead! They killed him with those potatoes and sausages and all that other rubbish from tins. Just to get his gold poos! And all I wanted was to be his friend!"

That day, the delivery lorry could not get to the supermarket because the road was blocked by the body of the megarabbit. The villagers were furious because they had no food in their fridges. Some went looking food in the nearby town, but because of the drought there was none to spare there. And the next day, when the megarabbit's body had been removed, the delivery lorry never came. The lady at the supermarket said the suppliers had run out of food and were waiting for shiploads to come from abroad.

There was no food at all in the village, and the petrol pumps had run dry, so people could not drive further afield to find any.

"But we're rich!" they said. "We shouldn't starve when we've so much gold!"

But they did. Many fell ill, they were that hungry.

Megan went out into the field where they had buried the megarabbit in an enormous pit. She had overheard someone saying that they should dig him up and eat him, and she thought that was very wrong. When the girl got there, she saw a little old lady dressed in a tatty brown shawl. She had never seen the woman before. The pit had indeed been dug again and was empty.

"Did they take him away?" Megan anxiously asked the woman.

"No, my child" she replied. "He was already gone when they came."

"What are we going to do?" Megan asked. "They gave him all our food to get those gold poos, and now, because of the drought, we've nothing."

"The pit!" the woman answered. "Return all the gold droppings to the pit."

Megan ran home and shook her parents awake.

"Mummy! Daddy! An old woman says we must put the gold poos in the pit where they buried the megarabbit. Hurry!"

"Bury our gold? Nonsense!" mumbled her father before rolling over in bed.

Megan begged her parents to give her the key to the garage, but her father just went on about the things he would buy with the gold, and her mother was too weak to talk. So, she went back to the field, thankful to see the old woman was still there.

"My Daddy won't give me the garage key, and Mummy's too weak to do anything. Please help me!" she begged.

The old woman smiled. She pulled something from her straggly grey hair and handed it to Megan.

"A hairpin?" queried the child.

The old woman laughed.

"Every good burglar has one. Pick the lock. Do as I say."

Megan took the hairpin. She turned to leave but stopped and looked back at the woman.

"Who *are* you?" she asked.

"Does it matter?"

"Are you also—you know—?"

"The megarabbit?"

Megan nodded.

"I'll leave you to figure that out," the woman replied.

Grinning, the girl hurried back home, poked the hairpin into the garage key-hole, gave it a twist and opened the door. Rolling a gold poo, she retraced her steps to the field. The old woman had gone. She pushed the golden ball down the slope into the pit and kicked and scraped at the dry earth until it was completely covered. She went back home to fetch her precious bottle of water. The taps had run dry the night before, and each person in her family had only one bottle of water. She emptied hers onto the dusty mound overlying the megarabbit's poo, watched the water seep quickly into the parched ground, then sat down and sobbed.

She sobbed for the megarabbit who had been killed by potatoes and sausages, for her parents who were too weak to get out of bed and for all the villagers who were now starving despite having garages full of gold.

A strange rumbling noise made her look up. It came from the pit. She wiped her eyes and stared at the ground where the noise came from. A thick green shoot sprang from the damp earth, then another and another. Soon, plant shoots were sprouting up from all over the pit, their leaves unfurling. Some quickly turned into cabbages and lettuces whilst others grew huge pods of peas and beans. A large tomato plant, hung with plump ripe fruit, reached for the sky. Megan lifted her dress and filled it with as much as she could, then ran home. She fed her mother first, then her father.

"Come quickly!" she urged, pulling them out of bed.

When she was sure that they were strong enough to walk, she led them to the megarabbit's pit, now filled with vegetables.

"I planted the gold poo like the old lady said."

Her father looked at her mother.

"Old lady? What old lady?"

"Does it matter?"

Megan's father stared at the colourful mass of vegetables where the megarabbit had been buried and said:

"No! Hurry now. Tell the whole village." And to Megan's mother: "We should have listened to Megan."

One by one, starving people crawled slowly from their houses and began rolling gold rabbit droppings back towards the field where the megarabbit had been buried. Megan helped those who were too weak to bury their own gold. The more droppings they planted, the cloudier the sky became, until, soon, Megan felt drops of rain.

That afternoon it poured. By the evening, the field was producing every sort of vegetable imaginable. But when someone asked Megan whether he could now dig up his gold dropping, for surely there was enough food to last them a month already, the little girl shook her head.

"No!" she said emphatically. "It all belongs to the megarabbit!"

She never told anyone about the old lady. Or that the megarabbit and Gaia, or 'Mother Earth', were one and the same.

A Baker's Novel

For seventy years, Old Tom Deane had promised himself that one day he would write a novel. Being a baker, he knew exactly what was required. The characters would be the ingredients: the flour, salt, honey and oil. And the yeast? Ah, the smell of it! The yeast was the inspiration from within. The fire that would give the characters lives, a plot to follow, and make the dough rise—whilst his soul would be the oven. It is where the novel would be cooked, where the dough would magically become bread. It had taken all those years for his oven to reach the correct heat, but at last the temperature was right. Wait another year and it might get overheated, the novel burnt. As all bakers know, correct timing is essential. The characters had already waited for seventy of his eighty-seven years and were eager to be set free—free to live their lives, at last.

The old man sat at the table by the window overlooking the very meadow where the story would begin. His daughter knew nothing about the novel. Neither did his two grandsons nor his three great grandchildren. They only knew not to disturb him that day. Or the next, or the one after that. Indeed, for as long as it would take, he had said, but no one else had the faintest idea what 'it' was. He would, of course, write in long hand. Bakers cannot type—at least, not old bakers who know nothing about computers.

He looked up from the blank page and out of the window...

He was there, just where he was supposed to be, sitting on an upturned bucket at the edge of the meadow. A lad of seventeen. He had not changed one bit in all those years. Old Tom smiled to himself. To think if the lad had been put into the oven straight away he would now be eighty-seven. The same age as himself.

Young Tom (the flour—same name, and why not?), was lithe and quick-witted, and through his veins flowed pure testosterone. Sent by his mother to pick field mushrooms for a stew, the boy knew there were none to be found in that particular field, but it was where a certain young Priscilla Braithwaite (the honey) always rode her pony at the same time every evening.

Old Tom began to write in careful copperplate that they had taught him at school seventy-nine years back. He wrote about the young Tom's frustrations with life, about his widowed mother, who knew nothing about Priscilla, and about his old grandma (the oil) who knew more than she wanted to know about her grandson and the pretty sixteen-year-old daughter of the local squire.

He scratched his head. *Do they still have squires here in England*, he asked himself? *What the hell—land-owner, squire—same thing—that bastard on the other side of the divide!* He wrote 'squire' and took three pages to describe Priscilla when she showed up for she was even more ravishing than he had remembered her. Oh, and that girlish giggle of hers when she and young Tom swapped places and she stood and watched whilst he did his circus riding trick cantering around the field, one foot in the stirrup and the other leg extended like a sturdy branch behind him, his arms hugging the neck of the animal.

Priscilla adored young Tom as he loved her, and Old Tom took great pains to make this absolutely clear. When he came to the bit about the girl's father, the squire (the salt), he took equal pains to paint the man as black as death itself, for, like death would, one day, the man was determined to separate the teenage sweethearts. The boy's granny knew about Priscilla because she worked below stairs at the big mansion where gossip bubbled and boiled; gossip about the blazing row between Priscilla and her father after he forbade her to speak, ever again, to that 'common urchin' from the village.

Outside it was getting dark, but Old Tom continued writing without even taking a break for supper. He used up more than ten pages over the row, for it was not only about Priscilla and her father. There was the girl's dead mother, too. When the man suggested that Priscilla's mother in heaven would be horrified to see her daughter consorting with a lowly baker's assistant, Priscilla flew into a rage.

There had been a closeness between mother and daughter that the squire would never understand, and the girl told her father this. Then she told him it was because of him that her mother had killed herself. In his fury, the squire struck his daughter across the face and she ran crying to her room. Below stairs, the following day, ears strained as they listened to murmured embellishments to the story of which several versions had circulated. The old granny sent word to young Tom to visit her at once and Old Tom allowed the woman several pages to give vent to her anger: their family would become the laughingstock if he did not stop seeing the girl and heaven forbid his poor mum should find out for she had a world of worries to cope with already.

It was late at night when Old Tom finally added the yeast to the bread mix, and as the bread rose in the oven of his soul he lived in his novel:

In a disused barn, with the pony safely tied up outside, young Tom and Priscilla are lying folded in each other's arms on a bed of straw and the smell of the straw reminds the boy of freedom and of the freshness of spring. Priscilla tells him what her father said: that he's sending her to a finishing school in Switzerland (Old Tom scratched his head again—*do they still send posh English girls to finishing schools in Switzerland*, he asked himself?), and young Tom says, "no, no, I won't let it happen," and they kiss—then they kiss some more and remove their clothes (Old Tom blushed) and make love and it's pure, heavenly bliss and they make love again and together they weep, each for the sheer joy of discovering the other.

With the back of his hand moistened by tears, Old Tom grinned to himself. Ready for the oven, huh? It was past midnight. No one had called, thank God, and he set his alarm for six the following morning.

Young Tom and Priscilla are up at six as well. He in his dead father's old suit, Priscilla in her white confirmation dress (*do teenage girls still do that 'confirmation' thing*, the old man wondered?). It is the closest she has to a wedding dress. She arrives at the old barn riding side-saddle on her pony. He wants to make love to her again, there and then, but the sun's already up, and they have a long journey ahead.

All the folk downstairs at the mansion clubbed together on getting wind of the girl's plan—all except the old granny who was too upset to know what to do. One hundred and fifty pounds in notes were secretly handed to Priscilla the previous night because, like the girl, they had loved her mother and none of them wants to see the pretty young thing go the same way.

"And hurry!" they said to her. "Before his granny tells his mum and his mum tells your dad."

Young Tom leaps up behind her, and together they gallop to the nearest town.

Old Tom rubbed the back of his head. One saddle?

Yes, only one saddle, I am sure! And she was side-saddle. So young Tom would be—no, it wasn't like that. Of course it wasn't!

He lifted her down, gently, because he was that sort of person, then he got up into the saddle and she sat sideways across his lap. And off they galloped.

It'll be the yeast, Old Tom thought looking at what he had just written. *All this galloping about! The yeast must be doing something.*

Of course, the elopement to Gretna Green in Scotland does not go smoothly. There is a train strike. The station's closed. The boy realizes the police will be out in full force as soon as her father discovers that his daughter is missing. For several chapters the young couple play hide-and-seek with the authorities as they lie low wherever they can, travelling only under the cover of darkness, zigzagging northwards, meeting many characters—friends and fiends—some who help them on their way and others who block their paths and threaten to turn them in. And in quiet places, in dark places, they make love until they know every square inch of each other, every sweet hillock, every curve and every eager fibre of their inner souls and still they yearn for more—for a life together.

Too much yeast, Old Tom wondered? *Need to prove a bit longer?*

No time. They reach Liverpool. It is raining and they find a room for the night. The landlady, an over-sympathetic woman, already knows about them. The whole country does. They are splashed all over the newspapers and Priscilla's photograph is posted everywhere.

"Gretna Green? It's just too far away!" the landlady says. "You'll never make it. All the stations will be blocked. And the roads. No way, my little love-birds!"

Priscilla would be in tears. Old Tom spent much time writing about the young girl's tears for he could think of nothing sadder. You see, Priscilla, by now, is sure she is pregnant. So far, she has kept it from Young Tom.

"There's a cargo boat leaving for Panama in the morning," the landlady suggests. Rather, she tells the couple it's their only way out. If Priscilla were to give her fifty pounds (this is all that is left of their money after paying for the room), then she can fix it for them. Young Tom is uncertain. He is a canny lad and has little trust for a world that treats him like dirt because his mother is poor and treats Priscilla like dirt because she dared to fall in love with him.

Then Priscilla tells him about the baby.

"Are you certain?" he asks.

She nods, and they fall into each other's arms and weep. *Are they weeping too much*, Old Tom asked himself? *No, they're not—because that's how it was.*

"Three of us, now! We'll have to get as far away as possible," Young Tom says.

They give the landlady the money. The tip of her tongue pokes out between her thick lips as she carefully counts every note and it's arranged that the young lovers meet the cargo boat skipper down by the dockside that very evening.

On waking up the following day, Old Tom still felt exhausted. He had hardly slept the whole night as the bread of his novel baked in the oven of his soul. And now, as he sat once more at that table, tears streaming down his age-hollowed cheeks, he just wondered how he could ever write the next chapter. He picked up his pen and stared at it. If only the pen could do the job itself, he thought. *Bread-making is so much easier.*

There are three men at the dockside, not one. Three brutes the size of cart horses. Two have thick sticks, like clubs, and the third a knife.

"Bet she'll earn us a pretty penny, Bill," one of the men with sticks says, a leer stretched across his ugly face.

"We're going to Panama by boat," insists young Tom. "That's what this is about. Our landlady arranged it. We gave her all our money."

Bill, the man with the knife, laughs. Young Tom has never before heard such a cruel laugh.

"Panama? Ha-ha-ha! Too far away, I'm afraid! Manchester more likely. For her, any road!"

Bill is clearly the boss. He grabs Priscilla by the arm. She screams. Young Tom lunges a punch, but one of the other thugs, cackling like a devil from hell, swings his stick. It cracks across Tom's skull, sending him sprawling onto the filthy wharf. He lies concussed for nearly half an hour. When he comes to and looks up, Priscilla and the three men are gone.

Old Tom wiped away the tears. This was not how it was supposed to be with his novel. This time, he was supposed to have control. He had meant young Tom to take Priscilla to Panama, and thence on to South America where he would look after her and their unborn child; where he would grow rich and one day own a ranch with a thousand head of cattle. He stared at the tear-stained sheets of paper—all that remained of his bread—then mopped the damp patches with his hanky. He felt shattered. Maybe a change in the story would come after another sleep for he suddenly felt an overwhelming desire to close his eyes. Yes, he would create a new life for Tom and Priscilla when he had woken up.

Folding his arms across the table, he rested his head on his hands.

After three days without an answer to her phone calls, she decided to pay her father a visit. Okay, he had said he did not want to be disturbed, but this was ridiculous. After all, she only wished to check that he was all right. She got one of her sons to drive her down.

She rang the bell. No reply. She banged on the door. Nothing.

"There's only one thing we can do! Are you up to it?" she asked her son.

The large man hurled himself at the door several times, crashing against it with his shoulder until it finally burst open. They ran on into the house. The old man's head rested, sideways, on the table by the window, his eyes closed. She touched his hand. As she feared, the skin was cold. She felt for a pulse. There was none.

"Call the doctor," she said quietly.

Whilst her son was on the phone, she pulled crumpled sheets of paper from under her father's stiff hands.

"So, this is what he was up to!" she murmured. "Writing a novel, of all things. At his age!"

Then she noticed, at the foot of the top page, what must have been the last words he wrote. Strangely, it was in a different script. Neat, rounded, feminine writing, like that of a young girl:

'Please don't blame yourself, my darling. I love you forever. Priscilla. XXX'

The Tower of Truth

Like the Tower of Truth, the gravestone was bone white, but the stark, sharply-carved gold lettering could not have been more different from the colourful, flowing words that had adorned the high walls of the tower.

'Unbelievable!', *'Experience of a Lifetime!'*, *'Amazing!'* they had proclaimed in purple, red and blue.

Malcolm remembered standing there with his ten-year-old grandson, Chris, looking up at that tower all those years ago. Every summer the same fair came to town, but never before had he seen that tower, so garishly decorated with weird zodiac creatures. The battlements on its summit gave it the appearance of a peripatetic Studio Ghibli castle and a huge banner dangled from up there beckoning the public to enter the *'Tower of Truth'*. More eye-catching exclamations vied for space with the zodiac creatures on the walls of the tower. Malcolm learned that *'The Tower Never Lies'* and that in it you would see *'All the Truth of Your Life—Past, Present and Future—Before Your Very Eyes'*. In front of the entrance stood a freckled, curly-haired man in a black tee-shirt emblazoned with *'The Tower of Truth'* in red and gold. He called out:

"Roll up, roll up, boys and girls! Ladies and gents! Come and visit The Tower of Truth. Only two pounds, children half-price. Once in a life-time! Roll up, roll up!"

The man saw Malcolm and Chris staring up at the tower.

"You, sir! Come and experience the Tower of Truth. You'll want to come back and bring your missus, you will. *And* tell your friends! You won't believe it!"

Those animals—so odd, thought Malcolm. Each teased his uncertainty, goading him to go on in. He turned to Chris. "Fancy that tower?" he asked, grinning like a child himself.

Chris stepped back, wide-eyed.

"No, Granddad. I don't want to. Can I go on the dodgems then have a go at the shooting gallery?"

"Of course, Chris. Look, why don't we separate? You go and have fun on the dodgems and I'll just pop into this tower."

Chris looked up at his grandfather. He was frowning. "In there?"

"Yes," replied Malcolm. "We could meet up in an hour. Right here." Chris said nothing; Malcolm couldn't understand the fear in the boy's eyes. "Okay then! We'll meet up over there. By the candy floss. Take this money. Should be enough. And don't lose it!"

He gave the boy a handful of coins.

Chris ran off quickly as Malcolm approached the man in the black tee-shirt.

"Good decision, sir. Only two pounds! Through there. The girl will take your money."

Malcolm heard the man call out again after he had passed through the unlit entrance. A bored, gum-chewing girl took his money and, without a word, casually pointed to an open doorway which led to a spiral staircase. In the silence of the tower, Malcolm started to climb the stairs. It grew darker and darker. No lights, no windows. He had to feel his way, up and round, using a hand-rail. Just when he began to reckon he had been done, and that there was nothing in the tower after all, a pale light illuminated a landing ahead, highlighting a door decorated with more zodiac images. One word was written across the door in golden flowing copperplate: *Past*.

Now nervous, Malcolm opened the door. It was surprisingly heavy, and he had to use the weight of his whole body to pull it free. What he discovered after opening it was not quite what he expected to see.

He was in a street. One that he recognized from his childhood. It was like stepping into an old photograph, and yet this was no photograph. It was for real. He walked up the street. Slowly. He saw a house. One that he knew so well. His family home—the small yard in the front, the clipped bushes, the boot-scraper by the red front door. His eyes filled with tears as he rang the bell. One of those old-fashioned doorbells. The sound of it was so familiar to him that it seemed perfectly natural when his mother, long dead, opened the door.

"Malcolm dear," she said. "Why are you so late? We were worrying about you, your father and me. Please come on in."

A bent figure appeared in the hallway behind her. It was his father, older and frailer than he remembered him, but his father all the same.

"Hello, son," his father said.

Tears streamed Malcolm's cheeks. He knew it had to be some sort of illusion. As he had read on that tower, it was amazing, but also cruel. Nevertheless, he felt compelled to follow his parents through into the living-room; compelled to perpetuate the illusion. Even the smell of the house was just as he remembered it: a smell-mix of carpets, on which feet from the past had imprinted faded memories of a home that was once his, and of his mother's cooking that used to so tantalise his young nostrils—and which here seemed so normal. In the living-room, a small boy played with a train set on the carpeted floor. Malcolm remembered the train set but it was the boy that caused him to stop and stare. He steadied himself by holding onto the back of the worn settee. How could they know all these things? The boy had been Malcolm's small brother, Derek. They had played together with the same train set over fifty years back. The two boys had been inseparable. Malcolm now remembered, so vividly, those warm summer days when he and Derek ran wild in the park. He recalled a day when they explored the mysteries of space, their space-ship a battered cardboard box that had brought, to their home, the shiny, veneered radiogram which still occupied its proud position in the living room in which he now stood—right there, adjacent to the glass-fronted cabinet of trinkets and family photos. On other days, Malcolm and Derek would be detectives, complete with pocket torches and imaginary handcuffs, seeking out desperate criminals, or explorers in a jungle about to come across a long-forgotten city of gold.

Derek looked up at Malcolm and smiled. A smile of trust and of love for his elder brother whom he worshipped. Tears blurred Malcolm's vision. He wanted to hug his little brother and say 'sorry'. His parents had told Malcolm over and over that it was not his fault—he was not to know that the branch would break—but, deep down, Malcolm could never forgive himself. A nagging guilt told him he should have warned Derek. He was Derek's elder brother, for God's sake, and he should have shown that responsibility which is a part of being an elder brother. That is what Malcolm continued to tell himself for all those fifty or more years gone by. So many times had he wished that Derek would suddenly reappear and come back into his life. Now Derek was there, playing on the floor. And it pained him even more.

Malcolm felt a desire to stay, an overpowering pull from the past, but he had to leave. He could not face his parents telling him yet again that it was not his fault. Also, he knew that if he spent another few minutes there, he might never return to the present. The past was trying to take hold of him, to force him to get down onto the floor with Derek and play with their old train set. Its pull was becoming almost too strong to resist.

He turned and headed for the door. His family remained silent. There were no farewells now, and there had been none when they had died. He ran back along the familiar street, looking for the door through which he had entered this film set from his childhood. One building stood out. It did not belong to his memory. On its walls were strangely-painted zodiac creatures. On its door, in curly copperplate, was written *'This Way'*. Malcolm turned the handle and pushed hard. It opened slowly. Just enough for him to slip through and escape from the torment of his past into the dark.

He was back in the tower. When the door had swung shut, blackness enveloped him once more, but he had seen enough to locate the spiral staircase. After several turns, it became lighter and Malcolm was able to make out another door inscribed: *'Present'*. He opened it. Like the first door, it was heavy, as if fashioned from tempered steel. Its hinges squeaked, breaking the silence as he eased it open.

"You're back early, Malcolm," Catherine, his wife, said, looking up. He had walked straight into the kitchen back home. "Where's Chris?" she asked.

"Chris?" Malcolm echoed. "Why, he's at the fair."

"I know that," said Catherine. "But why aren't you there with him?"

Malcolm looked around the kitchen. It was exactly as it had been when he had left his house earlier. The kettle in the same place, the still unwashed breakfast things, the open cupboard door. *How can they possibly know?* he asked himself as his wife waited for an answer. Of course, it was not real, but all the same it was unsettling. And his wife still needed an answer even though she was not his real wife. She could not possibly be. He knew the Tower of Truth would not be able to physically transport him into his home without leading him along the street. Without actually taking him there. At least he thought he knew this.

"Malcolm, where is Chris?"

"Chris is on the dodgems. He'll be fine. I'm meeting him by the candyfloss in—" Malcolm looked at his watch. "In forty minutes. So—" He nodded at the pile of plates and the cups in the sink. "So, I came back to do the washing-up for you, dear."

"Oh, you're impossible!" his wife exclaimed, laughing.

Funny, that's just what Catherine would have said, thought Malcolm as he started to wash the dishes. "I'll dry them later," he announced when finished.

Catherine looked up from her book, the very one that was on the kitchen table at breakfast time. "That's all right, Malcolm. I'll do it. You get back to Chris."

As soon as Malcolm had left the kitchen, he found himself in an unfamiliar hallway, once again looking at a door, painted with colourful zodiac animals, on which a notice instructed him to go *'This Way'*. He went through the door, making his way up the spiral staircase until he reached another dimly-lit landing and another painted door:

'Future'.

Malcolm did not want to pass through this door. He wondered why he had entered the Tower of Truth. But when he looked back he saw only darkness. It was greater than any darkness he had ever seen before. There was nothing in that darkness—no stairs to take him back down to Chris and the fair—and beyond the landing ahead, a gaping emptiness. He opened the door. It was so heavy that he had to use both hands and pull with all the strength he could muster. Finally, it gave way.

Malcolm now found himself in a hospital corridor. Catherine was by his side. This he could scarcely believe. He had passed through that door alone and now he was walking alongside his wife in a brightly-lit corridor, a distinct hospital smell filling the air. His wife was silent. He too. They walked together through a pair of doors on which was written *'Paediatric Unit'*. Their son and daughter-in-law were standing in the ward by the nurses' station. There was an intense sadness about the place. His daughter-in-law was crying.

"How is he?" Catherine asked, anxiously.

Malcolm was aware that they both knew the painful answer to her question. It was in the faces of his son and his daughter-in- law. His son's voice was shaky:

"They don't expect him to pull through, but they say they can never be absolutely certain. They've done everything they possibly can."

"Can I see him?" Catherine asked.

"Come with me," Malcolm's son said to his mother.

Catherine walked a few paces up the ward. Then she stopped and turned towards Malcolm.

"You?" she asked.

Malcolm was standing beside his daughter-in-law, his arm around her shoulders as he tried to comfort her.

"Later," Malcolm said.

He spoke to his daughter-in-law. He had wanted to tell her it wasn't her fault. She was not to know that the headache that Chris mentioned when he went to bed that night was the start of a lethal form of meningitis and that by the morning his brain would have become damaged beyond repair. Instead, Malcolm told her he would fetch a cup of tea. The nurses were extremely busy, so he helped his daughter-in-law down onto a chair and headed back through the swing doors into the corridor and towards the lift that would take him to the canteen in the concourse. Although he had never been in that hospital before, he knew exactly where the canteen was. He was about to enter the lift when he remembered. There was a door beside the lift. A door decorated with zodiac creatures. *'This Way'*, it said.

Of course—the Tower of Truth! He had almost forgotten. *No, none of this can be true*, he thought with relief as he pushed on the ton-weight door. He pushed and pushed until finally a crack opened, through which he just managed to squeeze. The door slammed behind him.

The fairground! There it was, as though he had never left it. Behind him was the tall castle-like structure sporting a large banner from its battlements:

'Enter the Tower of Truth!'

Truth?

Malcolm walked hurriedly away from the tower. He didn't look back. He spotted Chris taking aim at a moving row of cut-out ducks in the shooting gallery. The gun made a popping sound and one of the ducks fell backwards. Malcolm approached Chris and called out. Chris turned, looked at his grandfather, glanced anxiously at something behind Malcolm then looked back at him.

"Won't be long!" the boy shouted, taking aim again at the ducks. Another one went down. Chris swivelled round, his face alight with pride.

"Did you see that, Granddad?"

"Yes, Chris. Look, I think we should get back to your granny now. She'll be getting worried."

"Worried about what, Granddad?"

"Oh, this and that! You know what women are!"

"Yes," said Chris with a sigh, as he retrieved his prize of a black and white football. "Dad's always telling Mum not to worry!"

Malcolm and Chris made their way home. Chris chattered non-stop and Malcolm just listened, for the sound of the child's voice was sweeter to his ears than the most lyrical music in the world could ever be. All he wanted was to hear his grandson's childish talk about nothing in particular, and he wanted it to go on and on forever. And that tower? Just an illusion! No *truth* in it! No more than in the act of a stage magician able to mysteriously produce a rabbit, a white dove and a string of brightly-coloured handkerchiefs from a hat that he has just removed from his head. Clever, but all illusion.

On returning home, Malcolm found Catherine in the kitchen. She was sitting at the table reading a book.

"Back for good this time?" she asked, looking up. "Thanks for coming home to wash up the breakfast things, Malcolm. As you see, I'm still stuck in my book, lazy old me!"

She glanced guiltily at the crockery and cutlery piled up on the drying rack beside the sink, exactly as Malcolm had left them in that tower—the Tower of Truth.

A few years later, Malcolm, now alone, knelt down and gently laid half of the flowers by the grave. He stood, supporting himself on the white headstone with gold lettering then walked over to Catherine's resting place. Her final wish was to be buried next to her grandson. He stooped down to leave the remaining flowers beside a grey stone with simple black lettering.

The Urn

Jamie was tired. He had been driving down from Glasgow since the early morning and it had taken longer than expected. He had driven cautiously because of the passenger beside him. His mother. In an urn.

Twenty miles from Brighton, dusk encouraged him to pull into a roadside café as he resigned himself to waiting until the next day. With the urn on a chair next to him, Jamie sat at a table by the window where he was able to keep an eye on his car. He saw himself and the urn mirrored in the window and, behind him, a group of young men seated at the next table. Their faces were trained on him.

"Oy, mate! What yer got in that thing there?" taunted the nearest man. Jamie turned to take in the group. They were dressed scruffily, perhaps labourers on a late shift having a meal break. Each had a large mug of tea and a plateful of chips. "Mother-in-law is it, mate?" the young man continued. The others guffawed at their companion's wit.

"No, my mother," Jamie replied quietly. The labourers switched off their laughter and looked at each other.

"Wanker!" one exclaimed. The men did not stay much longer and most of their plates were decorated with uneaten chips when they left. Jamie ordered a meal and ate in solitude, repeatedly glancing at the urn.

He had to do this for his mother. It was, after all, her last wish. He realized how eccentric she had become in her old age with her heavy makeup, orange-dyed hair and all that muttering when she went about the locality in long, flamboyant dresses; an ex-pre-Raphaelite beauty gone to seed after losing the battle against time. In truth, this is very much what she had been doing for the greater part of her long life. Fighting a losing battle. After she died, he had gone through all her belongings. They smelt of sadness and a long-forgotten past, not madness as the family tried to have him believe.

Jamie took his time to look through the stack of old photograph albums and portfolios of newspaper cuttings. His mother had often told him how beautiful she had once been and when he looked at the sepia images of the young woman staring back at him he saw how true this was. A young actress from Glasgow, whose ethereal beauty had enthralled the critics. *This* is what he found out from all those press cuttings. Now, looking at the unimpressive urn containing all that remained of her, he wondered why fate had been so cruel. This, her last journey, would be a way of getting back at Old Father Time; *her* way of posthumously raising two fingers at the black-cloaked skeleton figure whose sweeping scythe had cut away her painted-doll life.

Jamie finished his meal. The café had become busier and he was again aware of pairs of eyes staring at him and the urn. He ignored them, paid up and took the urn back to his car. He drove on to Brighton and pulled up outside a reasonable-looking bed-and-breakfast establishment. He stood at the door holding a small case with one hand and cradling the urn in his other arm. A grumpy, middle-aged woman answered the door. She looked at Jamie then at the urn.

"Sorry, I'm not interested!" she said abruptly.

"Bed-and-breakfast?" enquired Jamie before she could close the door on him. "It says bed-and-breakfast outside. Vacancies. I'm just looking for a room for the night."

"Oh!" responded the woman, eyeing the urn with suspicion. "I thought you were one of those—you, know— those religious people. Wanting to save my soul. Yes, I do have a single room. Just the night, you say?"

"Yes, please," replied Jamie. They discussed rates before the woman stood back, frowning, as Jamie brushed past with his urn.

It was a clean, well-lit room with en-suite facilities. Just what Jamie needed after his long drive down from Glasgow. He carefully placed the urn on a small dresser then threw himself back onto the bed.

His mind filled with images of his mother: the beautiful and promising young actress of the photographs and the press cuttings; the young, unmarried woman of his childhood, always on the move as she searched for lucrative acting parts, but who was given ever smaller and less significant roles until she was finally reduced to just the occasional walk-on; the flamboyant, middle-aged, fading beauty still desperately trying to impress agents and film studios but in ways that became increasingly bizarre and counter-productive; finally, the eccentric old recluse, shunned by the rest of her family, well-known for reciting Rabbie Burns to the birds in Kelvin Park where she would make little arthritic skips on the grass. An ancient Isadore Duncan in a Barbie doll outfit. He could not blame his family. No wonder they gave the poor old thing such a wide berth. But what went wrong, he would ask himself? And why? Over the previous few days, he had painfully put together the jig-saw pieces of his mother's life. The picture he saw was so obvious he felt ashamed for not seeing it before. It was as clear to his mind now as the grey urn on the dresser was to his eyes...

He, Jamie, had been the problem.

His mother's slow descent into a world of lost dreams and half-crazed fantasy was all due to him. It was nothing that he had done. Just the fact that he existed. That he had come into her world. And despite all that happened, she had never once rejected or blamed him. Instead, she had turned in on herself, thereby protecting Jamie from her sense of loss and failure. Now, as he stared at the urn, the weight of guilt bore down on him very heavily. She had held onto, and loved him, as a mother should, but in so doing had sacrificed what might have been a monumentally-successful stage career. It had been for his sake, all that sadness.

Jamie finally got off to sleep. In a dream that seemed more real than reality, his young mother was reading him a story in her soothing Glaswegian accent, stroking his hair as his eyelids grew heavy. He became aware that she was changing into a large and beautiful white bird with wings which, when outstretched, seemed to fill the room, fluttering like waving shrouds. The room turned into a cliff top and the grass reaching to the edge of the cliff sparkled from the sun reflected in the morning dew. He could smell the sea. The beautiful bird called out to him from the sky above the cliff. There were no words, but Jamie knew the bird sang of freedom from the sadness of her past. He awoke just as she flew away over the shimmering water beyond the cliff.

Jamie glanced at his watch, got out of bed and went to the window. The sky was brightening. It would be a fine day. She would have liked that. She was always happier when the sun shone. He showered, dressed and went downstairs for breakfast. The irritably worn-out landlady appeared no less tired after a night's rest. There was no sign of a man about the house and Jamie wondered whether the woman was single, as his mother had been.

Funny how death makes one think about life, he pondered as he ate what was put before him. *What burden does this woman carry through life?* he wondered, for judging from the look on her face she must surely have borne some sort of burden. He thought about his own small burden upstairs: the urn that carried his mother on her final journey. And he thought of his mother's burden throughout her long life: himself.

Jamie finished his breakfast, settled up with the landlady. then took the urn and his case out to the car. He paid special attention to securing the urn for the last lap of his mother's journey. He headed for Brighton, found a car park in town, and, leaving his case in the car, walked on to the Royal Pier, carefully holding the urn in both hands. Many stopped to stare as he went out to the end of the pier. He passed by the clatter and the electronic noise of the amusement arcade, the screams of terror from the Ghost Ride and the shrieks of pleasure from the Tower of Fun. He passed the fishermen, silent and still over their bending rods. All of this now seemed so temporary and fleeting compared with the mission he had to complete. He looked at the brightly-painted pier buildings where, for a brief period, many years back, a promising young actress from Glasgow had played a lead in performances at the quaint little theatre at the end of the pier; where a handsome young reporter was bowled over by her beauty and went on to seduce the virgin actress, enjoying the delights of her heavenly body until she fell pregnant. Ashamed, and unable to face the predicament in which he found himself, the reporter had left the actress's life as quickly as he had entered it. He disappeared the day after she told him about the baby. *Their* baby.

Jamie's mother's letters to the reporter had all been returned. Jamie found these, tied carefully into a little bundle with a pink ribbon. The letters showed Jamie how his mother had never stopped loving the young man as she had never stopped loving her son. *His* son. Jamie understood perfectly why his mother had asked him to do what he was about to do.

At the end of the pier, he made sure that there was no one watching. No one who might be offended by his performance. When certain that he was quite alone, he opened the urn and gave his mother's ashes freedom in the wind. A haze that sparkled in the sunlight, they spread out, sank, then faded until his mother was no more. Jamie looked out to sea. A large white bird flew slowly and gracefully, just above the white-flecked waves. It seemed to fly with gentle determination and with purpose. Then it made a sudden turn and allowed itself to be lifted up into the sky by the same wind that had taken his mother into its care and which flicked the waves white. High in the sky where the whiteness of the bird merged with the whiteness of a cloud and was gone.

Second Chance

Open-mouthed, three CERN scientists stared at the three silver-bodysuited figures who had appeared in the tunnel, out of thin air, moments after the last proton burst from the Large Hadron Collider. None of them had believed the mumbo jumbo about time-space wormholes forming in mini black holes. Least of all Yvette, the crabbily-brilliant young French physicist.

"C'est incroyable, ça!" she exclaimed.

The figures spoke to each other in a curious mix of known languages before one of them, a grey-haired man, and the eldest of the three, approached the scientists.

"English all right?" he asked.

"Merde! Pourquoi toujours l'anglais?" muttered Yvette, clearly irritated.

"Hey, that's so cool, guys! You speak American!" observed Benny-the-Yank on rediscovering the power of speech.

"Américain—anglais—c'est la même chose!"

"We bring you glad tidings from the future," continued the grey-haired time traveller, the oldest of the three. "Glad... but also sad. And we've no time to explain. The wormhole we used is as unstable as the time we come from. We bring three gifts—"

"Ah so! Gifts from future!" Tatsu, a Japanese particle specialist, was unable to contain his excitement at the mention of 'gifts'. Gifts meant so much to him. He often bored the pants of Benny by going on about the gifts he bought for friends and family back in Japan prior to his six-monthly return visits to Tokyo.

"Gifts that we were supposed to deliver personally but I'm afraid I'm going to have to call on your assistance now," continued the time-traveller. "Please take them as soon as possible to 5218 Red Willow Drive, Houston, Texas. And give them to *her*. No one else. Three gifts. Three chances to get it right this time."

"*Her?* Who the heck is 'her'?" Benny, too, sounded irritated.

"A poor, illegal Mexican immigrant. The most I can say, and even that's giving away too much. It doesn't matter. Just do it. For the world of the future. For mankind."

"Jesus, man, this is the greatest scientific event of all time and you go on about a chili-chewing, immigrant Mexican leaf-blower. Look, guys—"

The grey-haired man, whose eyebrows rose up at the mention of 'Jesus', cut Benny short: "You," he said, pointing to Yvette.

"*Moi?*" Yvette was not used to being told what to do. After all, she was French.

"The first gift. A blue pill. Take it to her as soon as you can. Before it's too late."

One of the other time-travellers, a blonde much the same age as Yvette, stepped forwards and opened out the palm of her hand for the Frenchwoman, revealing a solitary, tiny blue pill.

"Remember! 5218 Red Willow Drive," repeated the grey-haired man.

Yvette took the pill, turning it over to see whether there was anything to distinguish it from any other little blue pill.

"A cure-all pill," explained the oldest time-traveller. "Contains a million nano-computers. Particle technology way beyond anything anyone here could dream of. Came about after they discovered the Higgs boson. Each less than a billionth the size of any computer you've ever worked with." He glanced sideways at a frowning Tatsu. The Japanese was a world expert on particle physics. Was the visitor from the future forcing him to lose face? "Each nano-computer is so minute it can pass through spaces between the cells lining the intestinal tract, and from there they're carried on throughout the whole body. Programmed to receive data from all living cells and scan for anomalies of function. It's a one-off, but any cellular disturbance caused by overwhelming infection, cancer or degenerative disease will be picked up and the malfunction corrected. She'll know whether to use it. And when."

"Formidable! Mais pour une pauvresse du Mexique? C'est idiot, ça! Il faut—"

Compounding Yvette's annoyance, the visitor interrupted her flow of anger: "And *you*—I want you to take this peach to her." The grey-haired man was now addressing Benny.

"Take a peach to Texas? You've gotta be joking, dude!"

"She'll know when to use it. Genetically modified to alter the status of pheromone receptors in the brain." Benny looked quizzically at the vacuum-packed peach offered to him by the third time-traveller, a dark-skinned, middle-aged man of mixed race. "In simple language, the person who eats it will develop a positive response for the very next person he or she sees. Again, a one-off."

"Like in Midsummer's Night's Dream?"

Benny, a New Yorker, was proud of his cultured background. In the Big Apple, he had been a frequent visitor to The Met and would often take a girl to Broadway, to impress her afterwards (he always hoped) with his detailed analysis of the play they'd just seen. His girlfriends never remained such for long.

"Take it, and as quickly as possible. You've little time left."

"But suppose—you know—just *imagine* a bite went missing... somehow?" Like Yvette with the pill, he had his own thoughts for the peach—thoughts far from Houston, Texas. But the time-traveller, growing less distinct, semi-transparent, was already offering the third gift to Tatsu: a small lozenge-shaped case covered with tiny crystal 'eyes' that sparkled, even in the low light.

"Time spectacles," he explained. "Will only work once. Backwards in time. And for one person. Should the other gifts fail, they could give the world its only chance to get it right this time. If you know anything about intercellular communication via nano-tubules, then you should understand the technology. Using clustered nano-tubules combined with mini-black holes, the wearer can reconnect with his- or herself in the past. Relive a life and change the present. And therefore the future. *She* will know if and when the spectacles should be used."

But Tatsu, taking the spectacles case from the time-traveller, thought only of his father who, a few years back, had been CEO of Tanakawa Motors, and who, because of an error of judgement, had been sacked and now lived in poverty, his family disgraced.

Already the young woman and the dark-skinned man had become so indistinct that they were little more that faint outlines in the dim tunnel.

"Each of you must take a different route. In case of disaster. An air crash, perhaps? Just believe me, and believe in *her*, for the sake of our world of the future and what's left of our species."

The word 'species' was a fading whisper in the cool air, for the third time-traveller had already vanished.

"Wow! You dudes gonna help me write this up?" an excited Benny asked his colleagues.

"*Quoi? Je n'ai rien vu, moi! Toi aussi?*" She gave the particle specialist a challenging glance. Tatsu, not a good liar, avoided her gaze.

"Not Father's fault," he insisted under his breath.

"Suit yourselves, guys, but for me this is gonna be my big fat chance. Write a report for Nature, Science—Scientific American. And tomorrow I'm off to Texas. To deliver a peach. I'll have all the media boys there on the doorstep of that place he mentioned and—now hear this: I'll be onto the White House and have the President himself hand over the peach! Then I'm gonna leave this hole. Get me a TV science channel back home in God's country, huh?"

"*Le Président Américain? Lui? Pff! Aussi un imbécile!*" Yvette returned, alone, to her office, placed the tiny pill beside her laptop and pondered over her encounter with three visitors from the future. She felt disappointed, despite having witnessed their remarkable sudden appearance and disappearance. There had been no explanation and not a single word of French. But that little pill—just suppose it *was* a 'cure-all' pill? Did she not have as much right to its potential as some ignorant Hispanic woman in Texas? Of all people, she could not afford to let a chance like this slip through her fingers. What if the grey-haired man was correct? She reached down for her bottle of Evian water in the bag beside her chair, placed the pill on the tip of her tongue then swallowed it in one gulp. She avoided Benny and Tatsu for the rest of the day, and the following day continued to deny any knowledge of the strange event in the LHC tunnel.

Two weeks later, the oncologist in Geneva could not believe the scan. The breast cancer that had spread throughout Yvette's liver and lungs, and had failed to respond to chemotherapy, had simply vanished.

"La Sainte Vierge, ç'est un miracle!" the man exclaimed.

Yvette did not believe in miracles. Only in science, in data and proven hypotheses.

"Une rémission spontanée. Ç'est tout!" protested Yvette—but she could not stop smiling. That is, until two weeks later when she had a massive heart attack.

"Mais je ne comprends rien!" she angrily complained to the doctor. *"Le cancer est guéri, enfin!"*

The doctors were puzzled as well, for she failed to respond to any of the treatments. They told her it was as if natural defences had been uninstalled from her body and that nothing would cooperate with her medications. Clotbusting thrombolysis failed and none of the usual drugs had any effect on the dangerous disturbances of her heart rhythm. The following day she had another heart attack. Her funeral was a week later.

Benny was at the funeral. Hoping to find out more about the missing blue pill. Hoping to use that instead. But there *was* no pill. As for the peach, the day after the event at CERN, and when he had planned to fly out to Houston, all that was left was a stone, and of his pretty Swiss partner, a few dirty underclothes in the washing basket.

"Not hungry," she had said when he told her to take a bite from the peach. "Tomorrow lunch-time when I'm back from work, then?" he had suggested. "Have to fly to Houston, Texas, in the afternoon. Have a bite before I leave. Please. It's a most incredible peach, I promise you. But only one bite!"

Benny, aware that her affection had waned of late, did not know the girl had the hots for the handsome young Polish postman with blue eyes. She was forever trying to gain the lad's attention by giving him little gifts. A Swiss cake here, a CD of German pop music there. Why not let him have that peach? It certainly looked appetizing and she could tell Benny at lunch that it was so delicious she could not resist eating the whole thing.

"What do you think of it?" she asked the Polish postman afterwards.

But it was not what he thought of the peach that concerned him. He began looking at Benny's partner in a most extraordinary way. An hour later, as they disentangled themselves from an amazing session of love-making on her and Benny's bed, both exhausted, she wondered how one man could have so much passion. She left an explanatory note for her ex-partner, weighted down by the peach stone.

And Tatsu? He simply vanished. "Gone back to Japan," someone said. "Couldn't take the strain of international competition at CERN." The investigating police officer found a strange spectacles case on his bedside table. Covered with thousands of twinkling crystal eyes, it was empty.

"Odd, the things they make in Japan," he remarked.

Odd, too, was the fact that the cupboards in his apartment were empty, the fridge too. They could not find his passport, so people assumed he had returned to his home country. Strangely, his father, the CEO of Tanakawa Motors, insisted his son had been killed in a car crash five years back. He was most upset to have been approached by Interpol.

Meanwhile a small boy was fighting for his life in intensive care in a Houston hospital. He had pneumonia and they said he had been brought in too late and was showing no response to medications. The local Hispanic community had clubbed together to raise enough money for his medical treatment since his immigrant Mexican parents were penniless, but by the time there were sufficient funds it was too late.

"Only a miracle could cure him," the doctor told his distraught young mother, María Salvador. She could not understand why those three visitors had not come as promised, for that dream, a year back, had been no ordinary dream. The visitors who appeared to her said that there would be a boy child. She and José had no children, and she had grown to accept their barren marriage, unable to afford fertility treatment. Nine months later she had a boy child. And somehow, because it was nothing short of a miracle, she knew that he was a special child as one of the visitors told her he would be. "To give the world another chance," he had said.

"But do I have to call him that?" she asked.

The visitor chuckled.

"It's a good Hispanic name," he replied.

Neither she nor the world ever discovered whether a second chance would have made a difference. The boy died. She and her husband were hunted down by the FBI, alerted by the hospital authorities, and deported to Mexico. Not even a bribe would have changed the mind of the hard-faced immigration-enforcement officer on their case—and nothing short of a miracle could have bent him in their favour. María never did find out what the promised gifts might have been, for her bullet-ridden body, with that of her husband, was discovered on waste ground outside Nuevo Laredo. The price they paid for standing up to the local drug cartel before fleeing across the border into Texas.

It was the new residents of 5218 Red Willow Drive who found the child's death certificate hidden in a drawer.

"How sad!" exclaimed the wife after her husband told her it belonged to a small child. "What was its name?"

"Jesus Salvador," he replied. "Funny first name to give a child, huh? Have heard it's quite common amongst Hispanics, though."

"Not funny! Stupid!" she scoffed. "Stupid and... and wrong! Sacrilegious, I call it. How could any ordinary child ever be given that name again?"

The husband, an agnostic, laughed.

"So, you don't believe in the second coming, then?"

"They were illegal immigrants!" replied his wife as if this answered a question that was so clearly a dig at her religion. "A neighbour told me!"

And in the future, the world, and what remained of mankind, never got that second chance. It died in the wake of an all-out nuclear war, together with the last surviving humans.

The Hole

His wife called it a 'hole' but for Alex it was something quite different. An old shepherd had given him the idea. Alex had met the man one Sunday whilst walking on the hills in the Scottish Borders. A misty drizzle had turned into a downpour and Alex ran to join the wizened fellow who stood taking shelter under a tree. The tree and the shepherd seemed well matched, both bent and gnarled by time, frail-looking and yet somehow indestructible against the elements. The rain dripped from the branches as Alex bade the shepherd "good day". They got into conversation about many things, including the weather, the Borders landscape and the solitude of being alone on the high hills. Alex told the man how he loved to find peace, just by walking alone on those hills, but stressed how frustrated he was to have to rely on the vagaries of the Scottish weather. Often, he felt imprisoned indoors because of the rain. The shepherd, whose forbears had come to the Borders from the Highlands in the north, told him about an old Celtic custom of making an underground cavern—a retreat where someone could escape from everything for a period. A place where his or her worries might just melt away. The idea struck a chord with Alex. His personal cave where he might hide himself away with nothing more than his secret thoughts to trouble him?

"Mind you," the shepherd added, "you might need a notice at the entrance saying, '*do not disturb*'."

"How right you are," chuckled Alex with one person in mind.

At the time, Alex thought no more about this, but over the weeks that followed, whenever he wished to go walking, it always rained, and the idea kept on coming back. One day his wife found him staring at an area near the wall of their garden where there were no trees or shrubs.

"Why are you always just standing here looking at nothing in particular?" she asked.

He had made a decision, he told her. He would create an underground cavern there.

"Like a retreat," he explained. "An old Celtic custom," he added proudly. It would be somewhere where he could meditate and get rid of all his worries.

"Worries?" his wife scoffed. "What worries? Seems to me you'll be giving both of us a whole load more worries. And what am I supposed to do when you go and sit in your hole?"

"It won't be a hole!" insisted Alex, irritated.

"Sounds awfully like a hole to me," snapped his wife before disappearing back into the house when the rain started up yet again.

Every weekend, Alex worked at his underground cavern. He bought a large, heavy pick, and with it loosened the soil and the stones. He scraped and stabbed at the rocks with his garden fork and dug away with a spade, creating a rising mound of earth and rubble as the hole grew steadily deeper. Soon, he required the use of a step-ladder to get down into the hole. His wife shook her own head in despair whenever she saw her husband's disappear below the rim, only to re-emerge, hours later, his face blackened like a coalminer's.

Alex ordered a batch of ten-foot posts, together with several thick, weathered planks. To his wife's annoyance on her return from the supermarket one day, she discovered these blocking the driveway. She observed Alex struggling with a huge piece of wood. He reminded her of an ant pulling a leaf many times its size.

"Don't expect any sympathy from me if you break your back moving this stuff," she muttered as she picked her way around the planks to get to the front door.

Slowly, a large pit was formed at the back of the garden. The posts were cemented in at the four corners and at strategic points along the edges of the pit. Planks were laid lengthwise over the posts at the edges, then crossways, supported on each side by the longer flanking planks. A step-way was cut to lead down into the cavern, then the huge mound of earth was shovelled, pushed and raked over the planks, creating what looked like a giant mole hill complete with an entrance tunnel. Alex stood back to admire his handiwork.

"What a bloody eyesore!" exclaimed his wife in despair, theatrically flapping her hands.

"Don't worry," reassured Alex. He held up a packet of wildflower seeds. "It'll soon look like a natural meadow."

"Looks pretty unnatural to me!"

Alex furnished his underground cavern with a wooden chair, a small table and a cabinet which he filled with books. An old piece of linoleum, dormant for years in the garage, made a perfect floor, and a discarded mattress was ideal for planned periods of more prolonged meditation. The cavern was illuminated by multiple torches, although Alex had it in mind to bring in electricity using an extension cable. That, he thought, as he stretched himself out on his mattress for the first time, might require some prior discussion with his wife.

Alex was lying, proudly staring at his planked ceiling, when the peace was rudely disturbed by loud thuds. He sat up. Was there a water or drainage pipe nearby? It did not quite sound like water. He scrambled up the steps and peered outside. Nothing. He looked over the wall into Mrs. Kerr's garden. As always, a horticultural catalogue perfection of colourful blooms and neatly-trimmed bushes with not a soul in sight. Alex returned to his retreat. The regular thuds got louder and louder until, suddenly, whilst he stood staring blankly ahead, a great metal point struck out at him from an earthen wall causing a fall of soil and stones onto his linoleum floor.

He jumped back in alarm before slowly edging away, speechless, as the metal pick disappeared then reappeared with another forceful blow which left a gaping hole in the underground wall. Alex was about to bolt for the steps when a head popped through the hole. He remained rooted to the spot whilst the head, long-haired and bearded, spoke. He could not make out a single word of the curious, sing-song speech. The head's owner smiled at him and Alex attempted a return smile.

"Who the hell are you?" he asked the man. The man raised his eyebrows as if to say *'sorry, but I can't understand what you're saying'*. For a few seconds, the two faces studied each other with shared concern.

'What are you doing here?' something finally asked inside his head. Not speech. Just a thought. His natural reaction was to think back:

'I was going to ask you exactly the same question.'

'If you must know, I was trying to make myself a place to escape from—well, from the likes of you, I suppose,' the thought told him, accompanied by a corresponding expression of annoyance distorting the face of the bearded head.

'Have you just burrowed along from Mrs. Kerr's place?' Alex thought with irritation.

'No idea who or what you're thinking about,' entered his head. The two heads stared at each other.

'Where are you from?' thought Alex.

'I have exactly the same question for you,' replied the thought voice. The head's forehead frowned. *'You're not one of those Scots from the island in the west, are you?'*

'Actually,' thought Alex, *'I am a Scot. And what of it? We're in Scotland now, aren't we? Or is this your personal way of taking over our country by tunnelling your way from the other side of Hadrian's wall?'*

'I don't know about any wall. And who's Hadrian anyway?' asked the thought in Alex's head. The head sticking out from the hole offered Alex a countenance that said, without words, *'haven't a clue what you're thinking about.'*

'Look, we're not getting far with these thoughts, are we? I've just built an underground cavern. My wife calls it a hole, but she doesn't understand. It's a retreat to get away from all the stresses and the worries of my life, then suddenly you appear, invading my privacy and giving me

a load more stress. Now please, where on earth—or under earth, so to speak—have you come from?'

After this silent verbal offering, Alex folded his arms in a gesture of defiance. The head looked forlornly down at the earth wall below it, clearly missing its own arms to make a similar point. The head looked up again at Alex.

'Actually, I made this cavern,' with which the head jerked itself upwards and rolled its eyes to indicate a space, blocked from Alex's view, behind it. *'I made my cavern to get away from all the arguments and skirmishes in the village. It started when you Scots began attacking us and going off with our women. Back in the village, some of them want to head out west. Others say we should stand our ground and fight you lot. But all I want is just a bit of peace and quiet.'*

'I've no idea what you're thinking about,' Alex thought. *'You're obviously a foreigner, but don't you speak any English at all? Most people in the world can speak some English.'*

Immediately, another word-thought entered his head:

'What do you mean by English? And, excuse me, but you lot are the foreigners. We Celts and Picts got along just fine until your thieving bunch arrived.'

The two heads looked at one another again, clearly bewildered. A querying thought appeared in Alex's head. He chased it away and came up with his own questions:

'What century do you live in? Do you know anything about cars and televisions and computers?'

He allowed the other thoughts back in:

'These things mean nothing at all to me. As I said, you Scots are giving us all a big headache and are ruining our village life. I just want a little place to think things over by myself.'

Alex thought for himself:

'It so happens that's all I'm looking for. Are you thinking what I'm thinking?'

An outside thought appeared:

'*Close this hole here?*' it suggested. The head's eyes traced a circle round the rim of the hole in the wall through which it had so rudely appeared.

'*Close the hole,*' Alex agreed. The head popped backwards after Alex thought, '*shake hands on it?*' It was replaced by a grimy, hairy arm. Alex offered his hand to shake the arm's hand, but his fingers closed around air and he ended up with a tight fist.

'*Can't feel your hand there,*' came into his head.

'*Well,*' thought Alex, '*I can see your hand, but I can't feel a thing. Do you really exist, or are you some sort of a ghost?*'

'*My thought about you!*'

'Well, I know I'm real,' affirmed Alex.

'*Not for me you aren't,*' thought the thought. The hand's fingers wiggled as if to demonstrate that there was no one there on Alex's side of the earthen wall.

'*Close the hole?*' he repeated.

'*Close the hole!*' came the agreed response.

The hole was carefully refilled with earth and stones from both sides. No more extraneous thoughts entered Alex's head and he was able to enjoy the peace of his underground cavern. Apart from an occasional muffled sound from the other side of the wall through which the head had shown itself, it remained quiet. When he went back into the house later that afternoon, his wife asked him about his hole.

"Filled it in," replied Alex.

His wife looked out of the window.

"That's funny," she said, "because to me it still seems to be there."

"I keep telling you," said Alex, "*that* is not a hole. It's a cavern. We filled in the real hole down there together. Both of us!"

Alex's wife looked uneasily at her husband and decided to get on with preparing supper in silence.

(The Celtic use of caves and subterranean caverns remains a mystery. One of the largest of these complexes, in Friuli-Venezia Giulia in Northern Italy, The Celtic Hypogeum, has a series of underground passages and six chambers.)

151

One Click Away

Humphrey turned on the computer. He felt a much-needed sense of relief for there was simply nothing else in the large, white, plastic bubble of a pod in which he found himself. Only a computer on a desk and the chair upon which he sat.

Wonderful, he thought! *This is going to be so easy. Be there in no time.*

Humphrey scanned the icons on the screen, but none appeared to be particularly helpful. He clicked on *'My Computer.'* Just the usual list. How about *'Control Panel'?* No! *'All Programs'?* Worth a try? No! Waste of time.

Time?

Humphrey scratched his head. *Files,* he thought. *Must be a 'search for files' somewhere. But where?* He clicked back to the control panel as panic threatened to engulf him. *Click on the wrong bloody thing and the entire system might crash,* he told himself. Then he saw what looked like a router underneath the desk.

"Of course!" he exclaimed aloud. "The internet! That's how you're supposed to do it!" A broad grin changed Humphrey's face. He had spent hours each day connected to the internet, an incorrigible surfer bouncing his way around a universe of electronic knowledge, from search engine to website, to links, to website, to links again then on to another search engine. He gleefully rubbed his hands. *This is gonna be really easy. Won't take long now!*

"We'll try my usual search engine for starters," he mumbled to himself after switching on the router. "Now... type in 'heaven', click on 'enter' and—"

The screen filled with a list of 'heaven' websites. Two hundred and thirty-six million of them, but that did not worry Humphrey too much. He remembered once hearing the phrase 'you're a long time dead', so he was in no hurry. *How about trying the first site?*

'Heaven' it read. Pure and simple. 'Heaven'.

'Heaven... derived from Anglo-Saxon, Heofan.'

Never knew that, thought Humphrey.

'Himin-S, *Gothic; like the German,* Himil. *Latin,* Coelum, *from which the Italian,* cielo, *and the French,* ciel. *Location of heaven: everywhere.*'

Humphrey looked around at the smooth, bare, white wall of his pod.

Here?

He scrolled the page down and up and down again, then returned to the search engine's list of websites.

'Vegetarian Heaven?'

Why should vegetarians have to go to a different heaven, he wondered? *Perhaps there are lots of fruit trees there!* But he was not—or rather, *had* not been—a vegetarian.

'Dog heaven?'

Interesting! So, dogs go to heaven too. But why shouldn't they if they've been good enough?

Old Mr Cranshaw's dog, though, tried to bite Humphrey once. He could not see it getting into dog heaven.

'Monkey heaven?'

Monkeys too? And why not? Closer to us than dogs are.

He clicked on *'Monkey Heaven'.* Up came a page about a Japanese movie back on earth.

"Wouldn't bloody help a monkey trying to get into heaven!" he muttered irritably. He returned to the search list.

'Kingdom of Heaven?'

Looked good, until Humphrey found out that it was a website for yet another movie back on the old place.

'Bunny heaven?'

Rabbits too? Oh no! Surely not! Looking at the website he saw that it was about rabbit jewellery, fluffy, stuffed bunnies and other rabbit-lovers' items.

'Hardcore heaven?'

Oops, thought Humphrey. Surely a 'no-no' for where he was heading!

'Bollywood heaven?'

Movies again, he realized, browsing through images of beautiful Indian women dressed in flowing saris. He hoped that they would be just as good-looking at his final destination.

'Entry to Heaven?

At last, thought Humphrey! *This is it and it really hasn't taken long.*

He proudly clicked on *'Entry to Heaven'* but it turned out to be someone's idea of a joke concerning a guy telling St. Peter about his good deed of rescuing a little old lady who had been attacked by a gang of thugs and on being asked at the Pearly Gate when this had happened the guy replied, "ten minutes ago".

Disgruntled, Humphrey went back to the search list.

How the heck is one supposed to get to heaven? he agonized, breaking into a cold sweat. Another website looked marginally more promising. *Surely this must be it...*

Click...

'Page cannot be displayed.'

He had seen that appear on his computer screen countless times before the accident. Often, he had wondered why a page could not be displayed if still somewhere out there in the digital ether but being stuck in this white pod with zero technical support, he could do nothing about it.

Humphrey narrowed his search. He typed in *'Instructions for Entry into Heaven'* then clicked on *'go'.* Only slightly fewer websites.

'What happens after death?'

Click...

'Request a free booklet.'

A bit late for that! Anyway, Humphrey no longer had a postal address. Not one that he could access. So, back to the search list...

Then, finally he saw it. He felt certain this was the right website. It promised detailed step by step instructions on how to get into heaven. He clicked himself onto the site.

'Personal ID? Password?'

These were essential if he were to get any further, after which he would be just one click away from entering heaven.

First, he tried his own name for ID. Lower case, upper case, lower and upper case, space between Christian name and surname, no space. He tried all possibilities. For password, he tried 'Boris', the name of his long-defunct dog (did *he* manage to reach dog heaven?). No good. Had to be a minimum of six letters with at least one number. He thought and thought, then typed in a few random words and numbers. Each time the response was *'password invalid, please try another password'*.

Suddenly, a window flashed up:

'Forgotten your password?'

He had indeed!

Humphrey clicked on this and typed in his personal ID (they seemed happy with capitals for the first letters of his Christian name and his surname although on the screen he saw just a row of dense black dots). He was informed that they (in heaven) would e-mail a temporary password within minutes. *Not too bad when you're hoping for an eternity in heaven,* he thought. He did wonder whether they (on earth) had kept his old e-mail address. He never told them he had died. Well, how could he have? It was so sudden; one moment, happily driving along the motorway, listening to John Denver, then—BANG! Nevertheless, he felt sure his e-mail address would still be there, in the old place, and it was.

"Heaven forbid, look at all that junk mail!" Humphrey complained after a lengthy list of spam flashed up.

No, I do not want a free holiday to the Bahamas, he protested. *'Viagra?' No! Not what I need just at the moment. 'Earn lots of money!' No need for that any longer. Ah! There it is:*

'Password for entry into the Kingdom of Heaven.'

A string of meaningless letters and numbers—not a word at all! With neither pen nor paper handy, he repeated the 'password' to himself many times. When certain he had it off pat, he returned to the website and typed it in.

'*Congratulations! You have reached the Entry into the Kingdom of Heaven website!*'

Humphrey was overjoyed. His gaze fixed on the '*ENTER*' button.

One click away!

With his right hand back on the mouse, he paused before that final click. His forefinger trembled as he took in one last deep breath. Then...

'*SYSTEM SHUTDOWN. Encountered a problem—error code 059CD00XFS. Unsaved files will be lost...*' A small window displaying a countdown of numbers appeared.

'*30...*'

Humphrey started to sweat.

'*26...*'

He tapped randomly at the keys.

'*22...*'

Try different keys?

'*20...*'

"Let me think—what would I have done down there? Got it—"

'*18...*'

"*Ctrl, Alt, Delete, all at once—thus—*"

'*16...*'

An hour-glass appeared, the hope held within it draining fast.

'*14...*'

Hour-glass vanished. '*Not responding*'.

"*Shit!*"

'*12...*'

"Why? Why 'not responding'?"

'*10,9,8...*'

Humphrey gripped the edge of his seat.

'*6,5,4,3,2,1...*'

The screen flickered then turned blue. *Heaven?* An instant later it was black. The computer gave a polite little click and shut itself off, a reminder to Humphrey that his time had expired. Apart from the sound of his own breathing, all was quiet, all still, in the globular white pod.

Thomas the Rhymer

"Wake up, Tommy boy! Get your arse moving, will you. Cannae stand it when you hang aboot and gawp like that."

"Thomas," corrected the young man, moodily. "Thomas from *Ercildoune*," he added pointedly when out of earshot of the grumpy head-waitress. "That's Earlston to you, hen!"

Thomas filled a toast rack, a jug of coffee, backed against the swing doors and entered the hotel dining room. A red-faced American smiled at him. The man's fat wife frowned.

"I asked for tea," the woman grumbled.

"Give the poor boy a break, honey," her husband said, still grinning at Thomas.

"Tea, m'am. Aye! We have Typhoo, Lapsang, Earl Grey—"

"Would that be a *real* Earl?" she asked, her frown fading.

"Not sure what—"

"Honey, jus' make up your mind!"

"Well, I only wanted to know, Walt. We have 'Earls' back home. Quite a regular name is Earl, but they ain't *real* earls, see. Jus' wanted to know!"

"Aye! A *real* earl," Thomas assured her.

"I think I'll just go for that, then. See, Walt? If you don't ask you don't know, and you'd better believe that."

"Actually, a lot of things roond here are for real and people dinnae ken. Or they dinnae *want* tae believe."

"Like what?" the husband asked amiably. "Ghosts—spooks? I sure wanted to try that 'Haunted Edinburgh' tour yesterday, but my good lady here, she said it's all a waste of money, that kinda stuff."

"Na! Nae ghosts. Jus' things. In the Eildon Hills oot there—and roond aboot. They're true, these things, ken?"

The American grinned again.

"What's your name, laddie?" he asked. "I *can* call you that, can't I? Laddie? Here in Scotland?"

"Thomas," replied Thomas. "Thomas the Rhymer."

"Strange name! You an' I, we must have a talk sometime, Thomas. I'd like that."

"And I'd like a cup of Earl-whatever-it-is-tea, thank you very much!" snorted his tight-lipped wife.

"Your eggs, m'am? How'd you like 'em done?"

"Properly!"

"Aye, but—?"

"'Scuse my wife," interposed the red-faced American. "She means scrambled. Me too, Thomas. Suit us both fine, that will."

Thomas returned to the kitchen. Slowly enough to catch a continuing, verbal dog-fight.

"Well, did *you* hear me say 'scrambled eggs', huh? Did you honestly *hear* me say that?"

"Predictions," Thomas muttered under his breath. "I'm famous for predictions. Yer marriage, it'll nae last another year!"

In the kitchen, he halted. There was a girl he hadn't seen before. Her long golden hair, in ringlets, was tied into a ponytail and she wore the waitress's uniform of a skirt of unspecified tartan and a crisp white blouse. She smiled at Thomas.

"Françoise from France," explained the head waitress. "With us for the summer months. Oh, Tommy, for pity sake stop staring at the girl and do a bit of work can't you. Just take no notice of him, Françoise."

Thomas wasn't *just* staring at the girl. He was thinking...

'A French Queen shall bear a son, Shall rule all Britain to the sea—'

Soon—it has to be soon, he thought.

Jan, the other waiter on for the breakfast shift, dug an elbow into Thomas's ribs as he swung past him holding two steaming plates of full Scottish breakfast.

"She's mine!" the man whispered in his Polish accent. "You look at her like that again and I gonna damn kill you."

Back in the dining room, Thomas served the bickering Americans their scrambled eggs, sausage, black pudding, tomatoes and mushrooms. He overheard Françoise talking to a young couple from down south:

"*Pardon, mais* I speak so little zee English. *Oui, un jour* I wish to become an *actrice. Mais, pour* zee French, 'Ollywood, eet is not good. Important I learn zee English." Then: "Lovely girl—absolutely charming—" as Françoise disappeared back into the kitchen.

They became lovers, Françoise and Jan. Or so Jan boasted:

"Tits like ripe fruit," he said to Charlie-frae-Hawick one day when Françoise had the morning off. "I tell you, she can't get enough of it. Us Poles—they say we live to our name!"

"Live to your name?" queried Charlie.

Charlie was dim. Something to do with coming 'frae Hawick', Stan, who fried the sausages, reckoned. 'Keeps his brains in his Hawick balls,' was Stan's explanation. Stan came from Selkirk, eleven miles north of Hawick.

"Live *up* to your name, Jan," corrected Stan. "You Poles live *up* to your name."

Charlie still looked puzzled.

"Pole—*pole*?" prompted Stan, winking at Jan as he scooped the sausages from the pan onto a tray. "Oh, forget it, Charlie! Take care, Jan. Pretty girls, they have a nasty habit of becoming pretty mums, ken?"

Jan caught Thomas's eye.

"Watch it, Tommy boy! You might get erection with us talking about pretty girls, eh?" He chuckled. "And you wouldn't know what to do with it! Right?"

A mum? The Queen of France? But that other queen— the *Faerie* Queen, the Queen of Elfland—when, oh *when* would she come for him?

Thomas would go there every day, to the large stone off the Melrose-by-pass that marked the spot where the Eildon Tree once stood. No, where it *still* stood, because he, Thomas the Rhymer, knew it was there. He could feel the shade of its branches, hear the wind in its leaves. And here, one day, he would kiss those *'rosy lips'*, he would climb up on the *'milk-white steed'*, embracing her fair *bodie*, and, together, he and the *Faerie* Queen would ride *'swifter than the wind'*, on and on until they *'reach'd a desart (sic) wide, living land—left behind'*.

"Aye, it's got tae happen soon," he would reassure himself whenever he rested against the stone with not a single tree within thirty feet. "That earthquake in Pakistan. I predicted that. Told my mum I'd predicted it, but she did nae want tae ken. They're all like that. But they'll ken when I'm gone. Seven years I'll be gone! Seven long years, 'cause I'll tak that road to fair elfland where I *'maun gae wi' her!'*"

Jan was right. Thomas had never 'had' a girl. All those girls at Earlston High School, they'd avoided him like the weirdo he was. Thomas-the-Prick, the lads called him. Came top in English, and bottom in everything else, and the system just couldn't make him out.

'Brilliant,' his English teacher wrote. 'A genius! Such an imagination!'

'Hopeless dreamer', 'Bone idle', 'Cannot apply himself to anything,' other teachers complained. He translated *'Lord of the Rings'* into Scots verse—mostly during maths, history and geography lessons. As for the *'tree'*—he was forever going on about the 'Eildon Tree'. 'There is no flaming Eildon tree, you arsehole,' derided those testosterone-filled rugby buffs.

> *'True Thomas lay on Huntlie bank;*
> *A ferlie he spied wi' his ee;*
> *And there he saw a ladye bright,*
> *Come riding down by the Eildon Tree.'*
"Wanker!" the other boys snarled.

Melrose seemed to Thomas the ideal location when he saw that advert for a waiter in a well-known local hotel. So close to the *'tree'*, it was. Every day he would be able to go there, stand in its shade and wait. Feel the closeness of that cavern hidden in the Eildon Hills where King Arthur's knights lay in *'solemne slumber'*.

'He heard the trampling of a steed,
He saw the flash of armour flee,
And he beheld a gallant knight
Come riding down by the Eildon-tree.'

"That's it!" Thomas said one fine August day. "I've had enough! Enough of the English and the Americans and the Poles and... and—" He was standing in the kitchen and glanced at Françoise as she entered. "No—not enough of the French," he whispered.

She was the only one who never sneered at him. Jan had spent most of the morning taking the piss out of Thomas, and even Charlie-frae-Hawick had put in his ha'pence-worth of fun before Françoise came back to collect her bag for her morning break:

"What does Tommy see when a girl takes her clothes off?" he asked Jan and Stan, deliberately within earshot of Thomas. "Come on now! Guess, guys!"

"Dinnae ken, Charlie. What *does* Tommy see?" asked Stan.

"Jus' two birds!"

Charlie guffawed. Jan too. They winked at each other when Françoise entered the kitchen. After Tommy said he had had enough, the Pole sidled up to him and whispered in his ear, glancing at the French girl:

"Françoise, she can *never* have enough. More... more!" he squeaked, imitating a female voice, mockingly. "Please, Mr Pole, more!"

Françoise ignored Jan.

"The Eildon Tree!" announced Thomas. "You lot know nothing! I've waited long enough! Seven years, I'll be gone. Seven long years!"

"Tommy boy, dinnae tak it tae heart! The lads are only having a wee bittie o' fun," said Stan, trying to smooth things over.

Françoise left.

"Don't you get it, Tommy? Two birds! *Birds? Tits?*"

All three men laughed at Thomas until the head-waitress appeared and lashed them with her sharp tongue.

"I'm off the noo," said Thomas when she had done.

"What? You're going nowhere, Tommy boy! You've customers to serve, in case you hadn't noticed," the woman snapped.

"She'll come for me today, I know it, and I'm off. For seven years, or—" His eyes narrowed as he looked at the others gawping in disbelief.

"Tommy, we're far too busy for bampots in this place. Get out there and take orders!"

"—Or maybe for ever!" Thomas added.

She, that *'fiend frae Helle'*, shouted after him, but nothing could stop the lad. Still dressed in his waiter's shirt and his waist-coat and tie, he headed off up the Melrose-by-pass for the stone that marked the spot. The place where then, as now, the Eildon Tree stood, tall and proud, a beacon to all those who wander astray from Elfland.

He hardly had to wait at all. She did not have a horse. No *'white steed'*, no *'shirt o' grass green silk'* or *'mantle o' velvet fine'*. But when her rosy lips touched his he knew it was her. Her long golden curls fell about her shoulders as he held her close.

"My *Faerie* Queen," he whispered, their cheeks brushing lightly.

"Zey are so 'orrible. I cannot stand eet."

Gently, he stroked away her tears, the tears of the *Faerie* Queen.

"Do you—?" he began. She took his hand and kissed it. "The tree? The *Eildon* Tree?" he questioned, his shyness melting in the warmth of her smile. "You hear its whispers? And the wind in its leaves?"

She nodded, still smiling.

"*Oui!* I 'ear what you want me to 'ear."

"Which way, my Faerie Queen?"

"Yes, I know zee way. Eet is not far."

The cars sped past as Thomas-the-Rhymer retraced his steps along the by-pass, hand-in-hand with his *Faerie* Queen. They entered 'Elfland', unseen, through the hotel side entrance. And there, up aloft in a flower-scented *elfin grotte*, Thomas found heaven with his *Faerie* Queen. So loving they were with each other compared with the meaningless matings of mortals going on in the rest of the hotel. He spoke to her as he caressed her sweet body, for he knew that by speaking there, in Elfland, he would never need to return to that other world; never again have to hear the jibes of Jan and Charlie-frae-Hawick. He, Thomas the Rhymer, would simply disappear forever with his *Faerie* Queen.

"Where's Tommy today?" asked the head-waitress the following morning. "He's bloody late! I'll kill that boy! And the French girl. Where the hell's *she* got to."

Stan, Jan and Charlie-frae-Hawick shrugged shoulders in unison.

"Damned if I know," said Stan. "But naebody tells me a thing, onie road, so what's new, hen?"

Jan remained silent all morning.

"Maybe he foond oot the truth," said Charlie later. "Took the clothes off the girl and foond oot, eh?" He chuckled, but Jan just glowered at him.

No one at that hotel in Melrose ever saw Thomas again. And Françoise, the young would-be actress, so keen to learn English, also vanished. Rumours abounded. Some said they made a nest for themselves in Edinburgh. Started up a French restaurant. Others said they had been seen in Glasgow at the Film House. On the screen. Someone suggested they were both in Los Angeles, destined for great careers in the movies. Said he had read about it on the internet. But there were those who knew the truth but never said. Knew about the Eildon Tree. Those who had heard the soft hoof-tread of a magical white steed in the twilight world of the shade of that great tree that only few could see; heard the sounds of the *'fifty siller bells and nine'*, and who had

seen the wind-blown, golden locks of the Elfin Queen as she
and her lover from the land of mortal men swept by.

*(Acknowledgement to Sir Walter Scott for extracts from
'Thomas the Rhymer'.)*

The Wave

How come time never healed the pain?

Dr Chalong Sarit stood on the very same beach, wondering, as he gazed at the sapphire glass sea. Barely a ripple troubled its smooth surface. Along the horizon a laden container ship followed the coastline like a nautical snail as it headed for the Chao Praya River and the bustle of Bangkok where the doctor worked.

He closed his eyes, breathing in the ancient smell of the ocean, listening for reassurance in the soft slap of water against rocks. The primordial power of the sea that had caused the pain was surely hidden there, somewhere. Unlike *her*, he got no comfort from the sea. Only fear. And he remembered the same feeling of uneasy fear whilst standing at the same spot as a city boy of fifteen shortly after his parents bought a large house at the edge of what was then a tiny fishing village, now a thriving tourist town.

The Sarit family would escape the smells and the noise of Bangkok and retreat to their seaside house as often as commitments would allow. The young Chalong became well-acquainted with the locals, all of whom looked up to his father, 'the doctor'. He used to tell them about the big city and his father's work in the hospital. Even boasted that he too would one day become a doctor. Indeed, for the hardworking schoolboy nothing else seemed of importance, but always, on that beach, he would stop and talk to the friendly fisherman's wife whose family lived in a tumbledown wooden shack close to where he now stood. He remembered how the shack leaned drunkenly seawards, propped up with brine-washed driftwood. Several of its planks were patterned with peeling paint whilst others, bare, resembled blackened bones stripped of flesh. A tattered grey curtain flapped like a shroud across the single open window. But what distressed Chalong the boy more than anything else was how he and his parents owned a spacious apartment in Bangkok *and* a large house by the sea whilst that tiny ramshackle wooden dwelling had been the only home for two adults and a child.

Yes, the fisherman had but one child. A bright, young girl of thirteen called Pranee. She would chatter non-stop to Chalong, plying him with questions about life in Bangkok, about its temples and what the women wore. Chalong rarely saw the child's father, a dour, wiry man with strong gnarled hands the fingers of which reminded him of tree roots. Sometimes the fisherman's wife would give the boy fresh fish to take home to his mother. Once, after taking home generous hunks of a large barramundi, together with a bag filled with fat prawns, he suggested to his mother that the fisherman and his family might use their house when they were in Bangkok—which was most of the time. The woman saw red and Chalong never got to taste the prawns or the barramundi at dinner that evening.

Not only did the house become the boy's second home, but the whole village, including the fisherman's shack, was like a magnet to the metal of his soul. He grew to love the smell of the sea, the ceaseless unrolling of the waves and, more than anything else, the villagers' open friendliness.

And he found peace there. A peace which helped him to study. In the city it was difficult to escape the noise, and the stink of diesel and rotting vegetables invaded his brain when he most needed to work. He hated the crushing morning rush of the ferry to school. It was his mother who had persuaded his father to buy a place by the sea to help her son with his studies, and often mother and son would spend a long weekend there together before school exams.

Mrs. Sarit was proud of her studious son. Her belief that Chalong would also become a doctor was confirmed when he was awarded a scholarship to study medicine at Bangkok University. Chalong was eighteen. He had grown into a handsome and confident young man. With only a few weeks to spare before starting medical studies, he and his mother decided to spend this time at their seaside home.

The villagers, too, were delighted for Chalong when they learned of his success but told him how they prayed that he would not forget them when he became a top doctor in the big city. The boy laughed and promised that could never happen. Instead, he would buy them all big houses like the one his parents occupied, servants included. Of course, there was one dwelling on his mind when he said that: the fisherman's shack.

One evening, as Chalong strolled along the beach towards the shack, lost in thoughts of how radically university was about change his life, he suddenly stopped as if he had struck an invisible wall. There in the doorway of the fisherman's shack stood the prettiest girl he had ever seen. She smiled anxiously and gave a tentative wave. In her sleek, black hair, which hung down to her waist, she wore a purple orchid above the left ear. Draped in a blue sarong, her young figure was both lithe and shapely.

For a while, Chalong could only gape at the wonderful creature. He knew this to be Pranee, but how could he have been so blind as not to have noticed how lovely she had grown over the previous three years? The lively, talkative child had transformed into a shy and beautiful young woman.

Pranee looked worried. Spellbound by her beauty and rooted to the spot, Chalong had failed to acknowledge her. He simply stared stupidly at the vision of such sublime beauty. Disappointed, she turned to re-enter the shack before the boy at last found the courage to call out: "Pranee! Good evening! How are you and your family today?"

The girl spun around and faced him again, her smile reappearing. She pressed her hands together in a traditional *wai* greeting. Chalong did the same, but his confidence plummeted as he looked at her, feeling inadequate in the face of such loveliness, unable to believe this was the bubbly child to whom he had always listened so politely but who had never been more than just the 'fisherman's daughter'.

To Chalong's profound disappointment, the girl turned her face away again, but, thank the Buddha, only to close the door of the shack.

"It's Father," Pranee said, quietly. "He's sleeping." She paused, looking shyly down. "Is it true you're going to be a doctor?" she asked. "I think that's so wonderful! Mother says you'll be the best doctor in the world."

The girl's eyes lifted. There was something warm and liquid about their beauty that almost melted his insides as she gazed at him so proudly. All that study had blinded him to the allure of those amazing eyes. Now, as he stood looking at the girl, becoming a doctor suddenly seemed of little importance.

"Well—first I have to study to be a doctor!" replied Chalong, his confidence slowly returning. "If I become even half as good as my father—" He stopped. A frown clouded Pranee's face and this troubled him. "You see, Father is— he's like—um—"

The girl's presence had robbed him of sensible speech. Her lips curved a shy smile.

"No! Mother's right," she insisted. "You'll be the best doctor in the world. I know it!"

"Look, would you—um—like to—?" began Chalong, struggling to find the right words.

"Yes," replied the girl before the question could properly form itself. She giggled.

"Yes? So... you *would* care to join me for a walk along the beach?"

"I said 'yes'," repeated Pranee grinning. Her expression of sheer delight caused Chalong's confidence to soar like seagull. "It's such a wonderful evening. And I get so lonely by myself, you know. What with Mother being ill and Father either out at sea or asleep!"

They walked and talked in the privacy of an otherwise deserted beach. Pranee was no longer a child. She spoke with such wisdom and maturity that Chalong was quite taken aback, but he loved her all the more for it. He learned that the girl's mother had recently fallen gravely ill and that her poor father was sick with worry. She, Pranee, could no longer attend school as she had become her mother's carer since her father was out fishing all night and all morning and asleep for the rest of the day. She had to wash her mother, do the cooking, laundering, cleaning and housekeeping.

The girl forgave her father his bad temper. She understood, but all the same tried to keep out of his way. Twice a week, a teacher from the school came to give her tuition for she had been one of the top students in his class. Every evening, when the day's work had been done, and both her parents were asleep, Pranee would sit down with her books and study. She wanted to become a nurse.

"My mother would love to see you, Chalong," she said as they stood together looking out to sea. "Would you visit early tomorrow morning when Father's still out fishing? Because—" She hesitated, then added: "You see, if he knew I'd asked you in he'd beat me for sure."

Chalong felt angered. He could not bear the thought of anyone harming her. She must have read the fire in his eyes and his hardening features.

"He relies upon me now as he used to rely upon Mother," she explained. "He's a good man, but Mother won't tell if you visit us tomorrow. She talks about you so much."

"Of course I'll come! Tomorrow morning without fail!"

Their eyes met, and for a fleeting moment they became as one in an eternity that lies outside the dominion of time and place. As the sea joins separated lands, this same eternity seemed to link them together.

Chalong returned to the fisherman's shack early the following morning. He had told his mother, curious about his eagerness to get down to the beach so soon after sunrise, that he needed to find out more about the sea connecting all lands on earth. She told him to stop talking in riddles or they might have second thoughts about paying for him to become a doctor.

Pranee opened the door. A wave of happiness engulfed him on seeing her again. He grinned, but his smile quickly vanished when he spied Pranee's mother. Inside the shack, everything appeared dim after the glare of the beach, and in a corner, lying propped up on an old mattress that spewed stuffing from holes at all four corners, was the fisherman's wife, a mere ghost of her former self: shrunken, with cheeks hollowed out and eyes and mouth disproportionately large. The woman's face, all teeth and eyes, greeted him from a tatty, torn pillow, but despite that corpse-like countenance those teeth shone the boy a smile. He knelt beside the mattress.

"Such a clever young man!" Pranee's mother said, looking up at him. "I wish my doctor was as clever as you!"

Chalong expressed his concern for her poor health, making polite enquiries about the nature of the problem. He truly wished he had the medical knowledge to help the poor woman. It appeared the doctor thought she had stomach cancer but the family had no money for her to have tests.

"—And if I do have stomach cancer he says there's nothing that can be done anyway."

"Oh Mother!" exclaimed Pranee, standing at the foot of the mattress, but the woman's expression was one of total acceptance. The boy had seen that look so often amongst the destitute of Bangkok. Whenever he saw this he knew the beggar bearing it would no longer be around the following month.

"Perhaps—" began Chalong thoughtfully, "—perhaps if I were to have a word with my mother she could help by paying for the tests. You really don't know what they might be able to do. An operation, maybe? My father says they can work miracles nowadays."

Pranee's mother nodded, still smiling.

"No one can alter what must be," she said. Then, changing the subject: "But what a fine young man you are! We're all so proud of you here."

She glanced at her daughter but Pranee turned her face away as if her mother had been implying something that should kept hidden from Chalong. The girl headed for the open door.

"Father's other nets, Mother—" she began, pausing before glancing over her shoulder. "I must check them for tomorrow."

"Pranee! We have a guest!" scolded the woman. "Please prepare something for him to eat at once!"

Embarrassed to hear Pranee being admonished because of him, Chalong merely scratched his head. The girl looked mortified and he was not even hungry.

"No, please don't trouble yourself," he begged. "I know how busy you are and I'm taking up your time. I really must get going!"

Too late! Ignoring his protestations, the girl disappeared behind a tatty curtain that partly separated off the cooking area from where her mother lay, and the sounds that soon emanated from that space informed him that she was preparing food.

"She's such a good girl," asserted Pranee's mother. "I just don't know what we would do without her. Clever, too. That teacher from the school is so kind—though, mind you, she was his best student. You know, she wants to become a nurse. My daughter a nurse! I can hardly believe it."

She paused then, leaning towards Chalong, whispered:

"Please watch over her—when—" She nodded, her oversized eyes fixed on his. The boy, staring death in the face, felt out of his depth. He looked down. For a few moments he remained silent, drawing circles in the dusty floor with his finger, not knowing what to say.

"I will speak with Mother," he finally announced. "Today. As soon as I get back. I'll tell her to phone my father at the hospital. He'll get something done, for sure!"

"That's not what I want," replied the woman. "Just watch over my dear child. It's all I ask for."

Chalong and the fisherman's wife talked on. About how his life would change and about what would be required of Pranee to become a nurse. The girl eventually re-appeared carrying a bowl of rice and a small dish of fish and vegetables. Handing these to Chalong, she offered such a lengthy apology he reckoned she'd been worrying all that time about her apparent oversight. The boy marvelled at the grace of the girl's small hands as he took the bowls from her and he so ached to take hold of those hands and tell her how lovely she was. Instead he quietly thanked her.

Chalong ate in silence whilst Pranee slipped out to check her father's nets.

"Why don't you two young people go for a swim?" the girl's mother suggested after he'd finished eating. Chalong glanced up but said nothing. He could only hope the girl would agree. Pranee returned.

"What?" she asked on seeing her mother grinning at her. "Have I done something else wrong, Mama?"

"No, child! A swim? You and Chalong? A break would do you good."

Pranee glanced at Chalong, both uncertain what to say. There was nothing on earth the boy more desired than to go with her for a swim.

"It is a fine day—but I've no swimsuit to wear!" he said, meaning *'yes, and I don't care what I wear—not when I'm with one so beautiful!'*

"Oh, we can just swim in our clothes," the girl replied. "They'll dry quickly in the sun."

She became her old self again, the child he had always known. After she'd cleared away and washed the food bowls and chopsticks, they left Pranee's mother, emerging from the dull, dirty shack out onto the sun-blazed beach. Childlike, the girl pulled her sarong up above her knees and ran, laughing, towards the sea. Chalong followed. She stopped at the water's edge. The sea was calm, the water crystal clear. The girl looked back at Chalong, her face radiant, before running on, splashing and giggling then diving below the surface.

Chalong's heart stood still during those awful seconds when she was gone, gripped by an irrational but terrible fear that he might never see her again. Had the sea simply swallowed her up? Holding his breath, he stared at the spreading ripples and waited and waited for what seemed a life-time but in truth must have been a matter of seconds.

Only when she resurfaced and swam swiftly back to where Chalong stood thigh-deep in water could his happiness return. The girl was laughing.

"It's so wonderful! Do come on in!"

She pulled playfully at his arm but Chalong remained motionless, captivated by the child. Her clinging top revealed her nubile breasts whilst her wet sarong showed up the womanly shapes of her hips and thighs. Chalong beheld a creature balanced between childhood and adulthood, between fragility and strength; a beautiful creature bursting with the joy of her innocence.

"Please! You must join me!" she begged.

Pranee swam off, and this time, eager not to lose the girl again for one second, Chalong dived in after her. As a swimmer he was simply not in her league. He observed with awe the ease and power of her movement through the water as they played and splashed together like children until, breathless and laughing, they returned to the beach. They ran in spirals and circles, on the warm sand, to dry themselves. Here, on land, he, the young man, was faster and stronger. He recalled the words of the mother and swore he would use every ounce of that strength to 'watch over' and care for the girl. Later, as they sat panting on a rock, hips touching, feet dangling in the warm water, Chalong could not remember ever before having felt so free and so happy. Together they gazed out at the jewel-sparkled sea.

"Every morning I sit here to see the sun rise," Pranee told him, her eyes focused on the horizon. "I have to get up to prepare Father's food and help him get ready for work when it's still dark, and when he's gone I just sit on this rock and I watch the sun wake up."

When she turned towards Chalong he saw her pretty face troubled by worry.

"Is it bad of me to feel proud for waking up before the sun does?" she asked.

Chalong chuckled to hear her revert back to childish questioning.

"Of course not! It's me who should feel ashamed for sleeping on till everyone in Thailand is awake!"

"Nonsense!" exclaimed Pranee. Both laughed. "Chalong—I'm not sure how to say this, but—" the girl began, from the tone of her voice woman again. "Chalong, I cannot let you go to your mother to ask for help. I do appreciate your kindness, really I do, but, you see—"

Pranee paused, clearly having difficulty deciding on the correct words as if she didn't wish to risk making yet another mistake that morning. The boy looked intensely at her, his concern almost caressing her confusion. He so wanted to hold her close in his arms, but he had too much respect for the girl. Even to have taken hold of the hand that lay limp on her lap, the other fingering her long wet hair, would have been a breach of her trust. But how disturbed she now looked compared with only moments earlier.

"I wouldn't wish your family—" she continued, then halted before trying again: "I would not wish *you* to think I was only being friendly to get help for my mother because it's not like that. Not at all. People in the village would talk, too. They'd say, 'look how she gets money for her mother!' And then there's my father! I know he wouldn't have it. He'd think I was just trying to show him up and he works so hard for so little."

Tears welled in Pranee's almond eyes. She began to cry and Chalong could no longer stop himself from softly stroking the small hand on her lap. She offered no resistance.

"People in the village would be wrong, Pranee. You must have the courage to see that. Please let me do what I can for your mother. Even if you and I weren't friends, I'd still want to help her."

Pranee withdrew her hand—slowly. Chalong felt her warm, smooth skin as it slid underneath his fingertips. The girl touched his lips with two fingers, telling him to say no more. Tears trickled down her cheeks and she once again turned her face to the sea.

"I always feel I'm with the Buddha when I look at the sea. Even more so when I see the sun rise in the morning. But that also makes me cry because everything seems so big, and me, I'm so small. So insignificant. Is it wrong of me to have these thoughts, Chalong?"

The child in her looked back at Chalong, her wet cheeks glistening in the sun.

"If you feel that way then it must be right. Only you would know, Pranee."

He was overjoyed when her smile reappeared, but she troubled him with what she said next:

"My father will never let me marry. I know it. He needs me too much."

Chalong, startled and saddened by what she said, had no idea why she should have come out with the remark.

"Rubbish!" he insisted. "Your father will arrange a fine marriage for you one day. Why, maybe when you become a nurse—"

He never finished the sentence. The boy had barely begun to understand this complex girl sitting beside him and yet he found the thought of Pranee ever marrying anyone else very painful indeed. He had meant to say, 'when you become a nurse and I'm a doctor we'll meet up and—' his mind completing the story by having them sumptuously and blissfully married. Secretly, he hoped Pranee's father would not arrange a marriage for her. When he became a doctor, able to support her, he would approach the man himself. Only a silly dream that entered his head because the girl had spoken of marriage, but occasionally dreams, even silly ones, come true.

"Besides," Chalong continued, "when you get old, who would take care of you then? Your father's sure to think of that." Pranee just stared at the sea.

"I shall never be old," she responded with disturbing certainty.

Chalong glanced at her. Her beauty was such that he could not imagine her being old, but he was concerned that there might be another meaning behind what she was saying. Was there something she had not told him? About her own health, perhaps?

"Time changes everything, Pranee," he affirmed, but immediately feared he might have said the wrong thing because time would soon remove Pranee's mother from the child's life. He had such difficulty fathoming the depth of this girl. In many ways she appeared to be so much wiser than him. Even so, her answer surprised him:

"I only wish I could alter time," Pranee said, wiping away tears with the back of her hand. Suddenly she smiled and jumped down. "I must go back and check on Mother now," she declared as if reading his thoughts. "Then I have to take the washing to the river, and then—oh, then I must get some more vegetables from the market." She winked at Chalong who chuckled.

"Because I've eaten them all up! Tell me, Pranee, is there anything you don't have to do?" Without replying, the girl walked quickly yet gracefully back to the rickety shack. When she reached the door she turned and, hands pressed together, acknowledged their parting.

"Shall I see you again?" she asked. "Tomorrow, perhaps?"

"Every day until I return to Bangkok!" answered Chalong, praying that particular day might never happen. Pranee's face, child-like again, lit up, and it was then that he realized there had always been a special closeness between them. He'd simply not seen it before.

"Tomorrow I'll cook for you without having to be reminded!" Pranee added, beaming like a freshly-opened flower.

"Oh, you have enough to do!" the boy protested.

After Pranee had disappeared back into the shack, Chalong stood alone on the beach. An image of her lovely face still seemed to hover above the warm blue sea.

Over the next three weeks, Chalong visited the fisherman's beach shack every day. He and Pranee would swim and play in the sea, then sit and talk for hours on end. Chalong never ceased to wonder at the girl's agility of mind and the depth of her spirit. He loved her not only for her beauty. He loved the very fabric of her soul.

Chalong made his annoyance with his mother quite clear when she told him, with less than one day's warning, that they would be returning to Bangkok early because her sister had fallen ill and needed help with her young family.

"I can stay on by myself," he said irritably.

"No, Chalong!" his mother insisted. "We return together. Your father wouldn't hear of you being here alone." Of course, she knew all about Pranee and had begun to worry that things were getting far too serious between her son and the fisherman's daughter. After all, they were no longer innocent children.

Angered, Chalong sat gloomily with his mother on the bus to Bangkok the following day. He had been prevented from saying good-bye to Pranee as he would have wished, for she was out when he had called at the shack early that morning. He worried that Pranee might think him rude, so he decided to write to her but was concerned that her father would intercept the letter.

Perhaps write, instead, to the schoolteacher who visits Pranee at home? Surely he'll pass on a message to the girl?

The boy stared glumly out of the bus window as his mind turned these things over. Of one thing he was certain: he *would* marry Pranee.

It was whilst thoughts of a future with Pranee were coursing through Chalong's consciousness that his mother spoke to him:

"Chalong, your father would never allow you to marry that girl!" she said bluntly. "From such a poor family? It would be unthinkable!"

Chalong was furious. It seemed as if his privacy had been invaded and his dream dashed in one blow, but what really flipped him was the insult to Pranee being labelled 'that girl'.

"I don't know what you're talking about, Mother! By 'that girl' I assume you mean Pranee? Well, you may be interested to hear that she'll never marry anyway. She told me so!"

Chalong turned his face away and glared angrily from the window at the passing countryside. Mrs. Sarit sat stunned to hear how her son had already discussed marriage with the impoverished village girl without first informing her. Each brooded in seething silence.

Over thirty years had passed and Dr Chalong Sarit still remembered every minute of that miserable bus journey. Even now, he felt a curious pain as he looked out to sea from the same beach where he and Pranee last talked together so freely. The pain came from recalling the nightmare that followed after the bus ride back to Bangkok. Something he had never been able to speak about to anyone, especially not to his wife and family. Time had not lessened the pain one iota.

One week after the bus ride back to Bangkok, Chalong-the-boy came home after a visit to the temple, where he had hoped for divine help with his dilemma, to find his parents in a state of shock.

"The house—we don't know for sure, but it must've been severely damaged, even destroyed," his father was saying as he entered the room. "I should've thought! The price was far too low! The insurance company showed no interest whatsoever when I called them. Some clause about 'acts of God'—and 'too close to the shore', they told me."

Chalong stared at his father. He had no idea what the man was talking about. Just an uneasy feeling. His mother looked up.

"He hasn't heard yet," she said.

"Heard what?" cried Chalong. Mounting alarm muddled his mind, but somehow the boy already expected what came next:

"The house!" his father explained. "We think it must have been damaged beyond repair by the Tsunami that struck the east coast this morning. You see, the village was one of those listed as having been wiped out. It was on the news only an hour ago. I was onto the insurance company straightaway—"

Chalong was no longer listening. His only thought was for Pranee.

Wiped out? What's he mean? Pranee's a strong swimmer. She'll be all right. She has to be. Nothing bad must ever happen to Pranee. I've just been at the temple praying for our destiny together. Of course she'll be all right.

But already he knew that she was dead and as the glimmers of hope were extinguished one by one, the pain of this knowledge became ever more unbearable.

"—And although they don't have a death toll yet they said they expect few if any survivors in the worst hit areas," he heard his father say.

From that moment on the nightmare never stopped. The vision of Pranee's face, her smile, her tears, refused to leave his mind as he struggled to find out whether or not she was still alive. Slowly the truth emerged, the painful jigsaw forming piece by piece. Up and down the coast, a giant tsunami had caused incalculable destruction and Pranee's village was in the centre of the worst hit area. There were no reported survivors. Pictures of the devastation appeared on the television and in the newspapers. They showed crushed vehicles, houses reduced to rubble, uprooted trees and pitiful remnants of human habitation chaotically strewn about. Chalong made enquiries at the police station. To his shame, he did not even know Pranee's family name. The officer, when asked whether the body of a girl called Pranee had been found, responded with exasperated sarcasm.

"If it's dead it can't tell us, can it?"

Chalong sank to the depths of despair and remained there. He had not even said goodbye to the girl, alive or dead. Now, as Chalong-the-man stared out to sea, he wondered why time had never healed that pain. Maybe this was because he'd been prevented from saying goodbye and Pranee had died without knowing how much he loved her.

He remembered Pranee's words so clearly: "I wish I could alter time." He could still see her face as plainly as if she were there beside him and had only just spoken. In addition to her death, a large chunk of his life now separated them: a successful medical career, a caring wife and two sons all of whom he loved. But that love was so different from the love he still held for Pranee and which he could not shake off. She had filled his mind for a part of every day of his life since their last meeting on the beach.

There was something more than her beauty which had brought them together and which still bound him to her. Pranee, in her wisdom, would have called it destiny. It was for this reason that he chose to revisit the girl's village for the first time since her death. Perhaps there had also been an element of fantasy in that he almost expected to see the young Pranee, as she was then, running from the little fisherman's shack across the sand towards him. The fantasy quickly dispersed when he saw the place so utterly changed, apart from the sand, the rocks and the sea.

Chalong decided to return to the beach before sunrise the following morning. He had never seen the sun 'wake up', as Pranee had put it, and he thought this was one way of getting close to her in her re-incarnated state wherever she might be. Perhaps he, too, might feel 'as one with the Buddha'.

It was still dark when the doctor got there shortly before dawn. The beach seemed more familiar in the dark, apart from the shore-line being further out than he remembered. An off-shore lighthouse picked out the rocks upon which he and Pranee used to sit and talk. He lowered himself onto one of these and squinted at the horizon. A breeze had built up overnight, the waves now curling with impatience to reach the shore. He listened to their reassuring rhythmic trawl across the sand as, slowly, a faint rim of brightening sky appeared above the horizon. The crested waves moving towards him changed from black to pale grey where the dawn light touched their foam. It had started. At first, an arc of pink that grew until it opened the whole of the eastern sky with a rose glow. A sliver of gold seemed to rest on the horizon before slowly expanding into a rising dome. Majestically, the golden disc of the Sun God slipped up and out of his nocturnal resting place beyond the farthest reaches of the sea.

"I've seen the sun wake up now, Pranee," whispered Chalong.

He felt an inner warmth such as he had never before experienced. He was smiling as he had not smiled for a very long time. The sun unrolled a carpet of vivid orange across the sea, from the distant horizon to the waves breaking shore before him. A carpet that would lead him to Pranee, 'at one with the Buddha'.

Then he saw something. At first the doctor was not sure what it was. He stood up to get a better view. A slight disturbance? A sort of shadow in the water? As the sun brightened the sky, things became clearer. It grew larger and was moving extremely fast. A wave of immense size, still far out to sea, but travelling at an incredible speed and bearing a huge crest of white foam that glistened proudly in the dawn sunlight. Chalong, already standing outside time and space, felt no fear. Because of this, he had no doubt that Pranee's spirit had not been destroyed and that the tsunami that had killed her had been meant for him as well, their shared destiny, but circumstances had changed this. He knew, also, that Pranee's spirit could alter time, for the girl was there, beside him, but he did not look round since he had no wish for her to see how his face had aged. He was still standing on that same beach where they had last been together as one, so many years before, when the enormous wave, the height of a tall building and roaring like thousand express trains, broke over the land dragging behind it a wall of black water that smashed everything in its path until all was reduced to a swirling wash of bobbing cars and boats, torn-up trees, upturned tables, empty chairs and a myriad pieces of wooden and plastic artefacts from the lives of those people who were now no more than lifeless bodies floating and turning in the filthy water a mile inland from the shore.

Many bodies were later identified. Their loved ones saw them and claimed them, as with the body of Dr Chalong Sarit. Other bodies remained unknown, nameless and unclaimed, like the body of a young girl in a blue sarong found floating beside the body of the doctor. Named or nameless, the bodies were gradually removed and buried or cremated. Thousands upon thousands of bodies that had once known the joys and the fears of life. Bodies of people, named and nameless, who had loved and those who had been loved.

(In memory of over two hundred and thirty thousand souls who lost their lives in the 2004 December 26th tsunami that struck the coast-lines of South-East Asia, and the thousands who died in the Japanese tsunami of March 11th, 2011.)

Duck Business

She was not there.

Clutching the photo, he scanned every table of the Dick Whittington, the London pub where they had arranged to meet. No females! Disappointed, Harry walked up to the bar. There was an empty table near the door. He ordered a half-pint—nothing too heady—and went to sit down whilst awaiting her arrival. Of course she would come! Boy, what passion she showed in those e-mails. Plus understanding. For years he had struggled with the fear that he would *never* find a woman who might understand that he could only 'do it' dressed as a duck.

He blamed his mother all those years back. They were staging a pantomime to commemorate the fiftieth anniversary of their local pub, and had aptly chosen 'Dick Whittington', the same name as the pub.

"You *must* be in it," she had insisted.

How much torture can a thirteen-year-old suffer? he had asked himself, grumbling all the way to the audition. He stopped grumbling on seeing Donna Fairley there. Donna with her golden angel-curls and eyes that turned his insides to jelly. He then wanted nothing more than to have a part in the pantomime. Perhaps if he were to play Dick, and Donna the female lead, he might have a chance with her.

Sadly, thirteen-year-olds only get rubbish parts. He was to be a duck. Donna played a fairy. It was all so long ago, he could not remember why a pantomime about Dick Whittington should have a duck and a fairy in it, but he remembered his first duck costume. It smelt of sweat and mould and after climbing into it he began to bake, but Donna looked gorgeous in her pink tutu which revealed as much of her legs as was allowed in Little Brampton at the time. Because of Donna, he decided to suffer the heat of the costume and, whenever he shuffled up close to her delectable pantomime fairy, he felt dangerously turned on peering at those lovely legs through little holes in the duck's eyes.

Harry soon discovered things happen to a pubescent boy inside a duck costume in the proximity of a pretty girl. Changes in certain parts of his anatomy about which the audience were thankfully unaware. Each evening, after the show, he would hang around, as a duck, until the girl had changed, for fear that she would notice the tenting of his jeans and disapprove. That was as close as he got to declaring his adolescent love for Donna Fairley, but when the pantomime was over he started to save up his pocket money for a duck suit.

Twenty years later, he had got through several duck suits and one wife. They were seriously linked. At first, Kathy giggled when cuddled by a husband dressed as a duck, but the novelty was short-lived. Harry tried ducks of different colours, various bill sizes, and both with and without tails, but after a disastrous decline in lovemaking they ended up in separate beds. Harry would lie awake, in his duck suit, wondering how he could turn things around.

"How about a chicken?" he asked her. "Might really turn you on. Then I could—"

"No more ducks or chickens, for God's sake!" she snapped. "I've had enough! I need a *real* man!"

After finding one at work, she cast aside the impotent duck. That was when Harry began to search the web for like-minded women who might not only tolerate but also get excited by going to bed with a duck. His search took him to dodgy websites—digital niches of peculiar goings on in hidden places—and finally he found one that seemed to suit his purpose, and in the list of respondents a woman who perfectly matched what he was looking for. A true kindred spirit who had already done fantasy time with a rabbit and was looking for a bed-mate who would not hop away at the first opportunity. Duck, she wrote, was just what she was looking for.

Progressively more explicit e-mails appeared in in-boxes until nothing was held back. Harry promised the lady his duck would light her up like a Piccadilly Circus neon hoarding in a way that might cause even Eros to blush crimson. A meeting was arranged, and photos exchanged. Harry could not believe his luck. The woman tolerant of ducks was ravishing. Auburn-haired with tantalisingly high cheek bones, a fine nose and large liquid eyes that even rivalled those of Donna the Fairy.

Harry gazed greedily into those eyes peering at him out of the photo as he sipped his beer, glancing up every time he heard the door open. Not a sign of the duck-loving Venus. One woman entered with her man—or rather, *a* man. Wearing enough eye shadow and lipstick to decorate a Romany caravan, and a skirt small enough to fit a child, her profession was spelt out in her plunging neckline and hip wobble. Although it had been an exceedingly long time, Harry swore he would never be reduced to making use of the services of a sex worker. Besides, they would probably laugh at him as he struggled into his duck costume, ruining everything.

Half-an-hour passed and still she had not shown up. He got himself another half-pint and that is when he noticed a balding man in a smart suit staring at him. He waved the photo at the man. "Meeting someone. A woman," he explained, to make his sexual orientation perfectly clear. "Wife left me, you see."

The man shrugged his shoulders, said nothing but continued to study him. Harry felt uncomfortable. After three-quarters of an hour and three half-pints, he went up to the bar and showed the photo to the barman.

"Have you seen this lady?" he asked. "We were supposed to meet here only she hasn't shown up. Just thought—well, perhaps she came early and got called away. You can never tell." The barman took one look at the photo and burst out laughing.

"If she came into the Dick Whittington, I'd have a queue a mile long out there. You know who that is, don't you?"

"Yeah—well, we sort of got together on the internet. Kindred spirits, you see."

The man behind the bar guffawed so much that he had to hold onto the beer pull.

"Kindred spirits? Oh, that's a good one," he chuckled. "Give me great mileage with the lads, this will. You really don't know who the lady is?"

"Sharon?" offered Harry, his knees beginning to feel wobbly.

"Sharon, my foot! That's—oh God, what's her name—that bird on the telly? That soap opera. You know. Not Emmerdale. The other one—"

"On the telly?"

"Yeah. That soap thing."

"Coro—?"

"Bill!" the barman interrupted. "Here, take a look at this floozie. It's what's-her-name. You know the one! Name's gone clean out of my head." He snatched the photo from Harry and slapped it down in a pool of beer on the bar in front of a rotund, stubble-chinned man who sat perched on his stool like a football on a golf tee. Bill looked at the photo, scratched his chin, burped then nodded.

"Her—on the telly. You know!" asked the barman again.

"Yeah! But buggered if I know what she's called in real life," replied Bill.

The barman retrieved the soggy photo and gave it back to Harry who never watched TV soaps.

"Not an audition then?" he goaded.

Ignoring him, Harry turned and caught the expression of the inquisitive fellow in the suit. A curious mix of disgust and smugness similar to what he saw written across Kathy's face before she ditched him for that gorilla at work. After wiping the photo on his sleeve, he returned it to his pocket and left the pub.

A painted Dick Whittington, jauntily sporting breeches, a hat with a feather and a bundle-laden pole resting across one shoulder, taunted Harry with his permanent wink whilst hanging from the safety of the pub sign. Accompanied by a painted black and white cat, the double of the one in that pantomime all those years back, he was clearly teasing Harry for not having had it in him to play the cat. Donna Fairley had put her arms lovingly around the cat and tickled his chin. Oh, if only he had been that cat!

*****

A few minutes later, the balding man in a suit also left the pub, his anger temporarily quenched; a man whose wife could only get turned on by men in duck suits. The very thought of being a Donald Duck Romeo had sickened him. His marriage in ruins, he vowed revenge on any freak who promised women duck-filled pleasure. A computer-wise friend had helped him by uncovering all the websites his wife had visited. *'Kindred Spirits in Unusual Love'* gave him the opportunity. As he drove home, he consoled himself with the thought that he had perhaps helped save someone else's marriage from duck-filled nonsense.

Back home, Harry pinned the photo to his kitchen door. He Googled the TV soap, found out the name of the actress concerned and drafted a letter:

Dear—

A fan of yours to my dying day, I wondered whether you would allow me a few moments of your time to tell you in person how wonderful you are. I could come to the recording studio if you wish.

Yours respectfully

Harry Albright

P.S. Do you like ducks?

The letter got no further than Harry's computer. He went up to his bedroom, removed the duck suit from the cupboard, lay back on his bed with one arm around the suit whilst his mind started to fill with cat thoughts. Dick Whittington was right. Cats are more assertive than ducks. Cats are predators. Girls like Donna Fairley stroke and hug and generally make a fuss of cats, not ducks.

Cats... cats... cats...

Last Dance

Forty-five minutes late!

Carmen Ruiz had just glanced at her watch for the hundredth time. Within the bounds of punctuality for most Spanish men, but not Pedro. He was never late. Something was wrong. An accident? No—impossible! Pedro was the safest driver in Andalusia. How she loved to be driven home by him, for she knew no harm could come to her with Pedro at the wheel.

And she felt safe in his arms when they danced. Life had become hollow after all those years living alone. She used to be haunted by the thought that something terrifying would leap out of the hollowness and destroy her, but after befriending Pedro at the *Salón de Baile* one Saturday evening, this feeling, and the fear of it, left her. Life had a new purpose: to dance.

They say true dancing partnerships are born out of a yearning of two souls to move together as one, not a forcing together of separate beings who act in opposition. So it was with Carmen and Pedro. They danced as one all that first evening—and the week after and the week after that.

Pedro, inordinately shy off the dance floor, was an organic farmer. One week he gave Carmen a bag full of organic vegetables, for she had owned up to being an excellent cook. He handed her the vegetables with a nod and almost a smile, but when she told him she couldn't possibly carry the bag home on the bus, for her back would give her hell if she tried, his face lit up. His expression told her everything. The vegetable offering was his way of saying that their relationship should shift upwards a notch or two. Her response, a covert request that he drive her home. Thereafter, he drove her home every week and she would invite him in for tapas and a glass of Málaga.

The conversation was always one way. Pedro would sit at a respectful distance and listen intently to Carmen's life history delivered in widow-sized instalments. Some evenings, he would be sitting for two or more hours. He never changed his position and one glass of wine was his limit. He prided himself on not once having been drunk in all his sixty-eight years.

Carmen's husband, Pablo, had died from alcohol poisoning of the liver some ten years before. Their last fifteen years, as husband and wife, had been spent living apart in the same house, Pablo upstairs and Carmen downstairs—the only way she could tolerate him—and they communicated through their son in Seville eighty kilometres away. Occasionally, they would pass each other in the entrance hall as one came in and the other went out, but not a word was exchanged.

And Pablo never danced.

Ten years a widow and fifteen years in the same house with the estranged Pablo—that was twenty-five years of loneliness to make up with Pedro, and she savoured every second of their time together, especially on the dance floor. There was no dance they could not master; waltz, foxtrot, jive, paso doble, quickstep—anything—and he told her it was truly remarkable that she had never danced before and that she must be a natural. His shyness seemed to melt away when he held her close, but she often wondered how many other women he had held like this, for one thing was certain: he had been an expert dancer long before they first tripped the light fantastic together.

Curiously, Carmen had no idea whether he was a bachelor or a widower. She never asked, and he never said. She only knew that he lived by himself, like her, and that he must be very wealthy judging by the extent of his lands.

She began to cook for him. Offering tapas was merely a starter to tempt him. Later, she served up *pollo* and *patatas a lo pobre*—and he loved her cakes. He would turn up mid-afternoon, every Saturday, and they would eat together, no wine, as she spilled out her heart, and then he would drive her to the dance hall and they would dance and dance and dance and he would drive her home and she would give him more tapas and a glass of Málaga and talk until the early hours when he would leave and she would hold on to the memory of him and, once asleep, would dream again of dancing.

Perhaps if Pablo had danced things would have turned out differently. Unlike Pedro, the man jabbered incessantly and drank. At first, as a young woman, she felt sorry for him. A child in Franco's dark and sorrowful Spain, all opportunities for success had been denied him because his family happened to be on the wrong side of the divide. He was skilful with his hands and should have been a cabinet maker, like his father before Franco's thugs killed him, but the authorities saw to it that Pablo got nowhere when he attempted to set up a business. He ended up as a labourer on the roads; a labourer who could recite Lorca, and who crafted small animals out of bits of old wood for children. Probably she did love him then, perhaps to mother him and turn him into what he should have been, but, gradually, as their son grew up and diverted that love away from her husband, the alcohol thing progressed from habit to addiction. Initially, it was shame that caused her to banish the drunken Pablo upstairs. Shame that she had failed him in some way and that the neighbours would blame her for the rows. But the shame turned to disgust, and the disgust remained with her till Pablo's death, his body rotted by alcohol.

At seventy-two years of age she should have known that happiness is an illusion, that it could not last, and that loneliness would return, its bleakness reinforced by that brief illusion. At the very least, she should have read the warning signs the week before when they danced their last dance together.

It was a waltz. Pedro kept looking over her right shoulder, steering her purposively around other gliding couples to keep a certain person within his sights: an elegant, dyed brunette not a day over sixty, with legs that could have belonged to a woman half her age. Carmen noticed the exchange of smiles between them after that dance. She tried to persuade herself that they were already acquainted, and that these were no more than smiles of recognition, and she promised him her special *Estofado de Coejo con Pasta* the following week. It should have been obvious when he phoned to say that he was busy that afternoon and he would collect her later, on the way to the *salón de baile*. But her mind refused to accept the pain of deceit. She had had enough of this in the past. Enough of pain.

After an hour had passed, she could deny the pain no longer. She returned her dance shoes to their box in her shoe cupboard, slipped out of her dance dress, hung it at the far end of her wardrobe, never to be worn again, and prepared for herself some tapas. Perhaps, she thought, she should allow herself two glasses of Málaga to soften the pain. Then she could pray, with the fading embers of hope fanned by Málaga, that one day that woman's legs would grow old and misshapen and that he would realize what a rare and wonderful thing a true dancing partnership can be.

Marcel's Head

They said it was the hole in his head that made Marcel dance. Before the accident he was a perfectly normal, hard-working young man, but after a steel rod fell and bored a tunnel into his brain he began to dance. Anywhere and everywhere. He lost his job, of course, for what use is a dancing postman? Madame Lapierre, a widow, gave him a room and fed him, but all day he would be out in the streets, in the village square, dancing. At church on Sundays, the priest allowed him space behind the crowded pews where he would dance away during mass. He did not even stop for the homilies. The children of the little Swiss Alpine village loved Marcel. They would run, laughing, from school to join him in his dance and he would wink and grin and pull funny faces for them, and they would laugh all the more. The children grew up, became adults and stopped dancing, but Marcel danced on and more children were born to join him. He lived for another twenty-five years and not a day went by when he did not dance.

His last dance was on a level crossing in front of the cog-train that travelled up and down the mountain twenty-four times a day. It was snowing heavily, the ground was iced over, and he slipped. Madame Lapierre could not understand why he never came back and the children remained glum for the rest of the winter, always searching the quiet streets for Marcel the dancer, calling out: "*Marcel—ou tu es, Marcel?*" The train driver had not seen him, and his body emerged beside the train track when the snow melted in the spring, a smile still frozen onto his face.

Madame Lapierre was the only one who knew the true reason for that smile and all the dancing. Hidden in a large envelope under Marcel's mattress, she found two hundred thousand Swiss francs and a letter from the construction company whose steel rod made the hole in the postman's head. He had not spent a single centime for she had taken care of all his needs, and the villagers had always stuffed money into his pockets as he danced. She could think of no reason to mention the stash to anyone else, though the other villagers did wonder why the straight-mouthed widow now smiled.

"She no longer has to put up with the noise of Marcel dancing all night long," they joked.

The smile never left Madame Lapierre.

There *is* Life on Mars!

The sun had baked the land into a barren biscuit. Dried sticks, once plants, stuck out from the biscuit crust and dangled pitiful impressions of leaves. 'This is all we have now', they seemed to say. *But does the world care?* Janet wondered as she looked out from the Jeep at the tiny village in a remote corner of Niger.

Many people back home had not even heard of the country she was in, let alone the name of the village. The previous season, the same village would have been bursting with life—children running around and screaming, mothers washing, cooking and doing what mothers do the world over—yet here she was, a visitor to a ghost place, come to seek out living survivors. For three successive months the rains had failed in this little-known part of Africa. No rain meant no water, no food, and ultimately no life. Janet Ziegler, an experienced American aid worker, and her African driver, Jean-Baptiste, devoted their lives to fellow humans who, through no fault of their own, had been born into a world harsher than anything Janet could have imagined as a doctor's daughter in New Jersey.

Their Jeep trailed a fan of dust as they bumped along the dirt track towards the village. They parked and followed a short path into the compound. After separating, they began to search the huts, repeatedly calling out in the local tongue: "is there anyone here?" No answer. They checked every hut. No sign of life, apart from the mummified corpse of a dog now home to a colony of flies. Janet could almost imagine herself transported to a dead and distant planet in the far reaches of the universe, confronted with the remains of a long-extinct civilization.

The two aid workers met up again in the centre of the village. Janet shook her head.

"No one here," she said, flicking flies off her face.

Jean-Baptiste stayed silent. He held up his hand. Janet heard nothing. She studied the man's dark frown and the concentration in his deep-set eyes.

"*Là-bas!*" Jean-Baptiste announced before heading off towards the huts she had just checked.

"*J'ai déjà—*" Janet began but stopped. She, too, could now hear something from beyond the huts. A barely-audible whimper but distinctly human. They pushed their way through the scrub behind the huts before coming across a makeshift tent camouflaged by a covering of dust. The dried-out bushes surrounding it afforded little shade from the blistering sun. Jean-Baptiste, followed by Janet, crawled inside. The stench of disease, a smell surely from Hell, hit her. For a few moments, whilst her eyes became accustomed to the dim light, she could not make out much at all. Then an outline of the whimper's owner emerged in the gloom, curled up on a straw mat.

At first, all Janet could see with any clarity were the woman's teeth and the whites of her large eyes. Closer, she saw a skeletal frame draped in a garish, loose-fitting garment. Nestled up against the woman's body was that of a child with a head and belly grossly out of proportion to its stick-like limbs. The child's eyes were wide open like the mother's, but blank. Janet assumed the child was dead until a frail little arm jerked. A fly-covered mouth gasped. Janet, crouching beside the mother and child, reached forward and gently touched them. The child was a young girl.

"We're here to help you," she whispered in the woman's language.

They would have to work quickly if they were to save the child whose head, helpless as a ball on a string, flopped backwards. Janet gently lifted the head back into the cradle of the mother's arm. Its face was neither truly alive nor properly dead.

Janet recalled Kurt's latest e-mail as she gazed upon the mother and daughter. She had read it that morning before leaving with Jean-Baptiste:

Wonderful news. NASA mission has found life on the red planet. There is life on Mars! Tiny lichen-like plant on rock near polar region. Awaiting DNA analysis. Will send image later—they may not show it on TV in Africa. All those years of work paid off. God Bless! Love—Kurt.

Janet and her husband, Kurt, had grown apart over the previous several years and now lived entirely separate lives. They had started off as university students together, both majoring in biology. Slowly their career paths diverged. Kurt, forever the pure scientist, became a senior biotechnologist working for NASA. Janet took more and more field trips to developing countries in South America, Asia then Africa. In Africa, her interest in natural history became replaced by an intense humanitarian desire to do something about the appalling poverty and suffering she saw amongst people whom she had grown to love so much— love with a fervour that Kurt gave up trying to comprehend. Equally, Janet failed to see what sense of fulfilment her husband could ever derive from searching for molecules of life in space. At first, this yawning gap caused feelings of irritation in both parties and, later, frank rows. But there came a time when Janet no longer felt anger. Her work had become so demanding that she was too tired for argument. They continued to communicate by e-mail and occasionally over the phone.

So different had they become that each gave up trying to understand the other, for neither could really figure out what the motivating force was that drove their partner. Passion had long gone from the marriage. Strangely, living apart had strengthened their mutual respect as friends. Neither bothered, nor wanted, to legalize the separation with a divorce. Both were far too busy. Besides, Janet quite liked having Kurt there as someone against whose life she could measure her own. She signed on as an aid worker for three years and soon she could not imagine herself doing anything else.

The child's eyes blinked. Briefly, they looked up at Janet when she gently rested the little head up against the mother. Seeing that small face with vacant white and brown eyes filled Janet with so much anger. A child's face should show life, wonder and hope, not that awful blankness of the shadow of death. This, Kurt would simply not understand, despite his religion.

Kurt's religion! At least he no longer added quotations from the Holy Bible at the ends of his e-mails. How odd that he was an atheist with Jewish ancestry and she the lapsed Catholic when they first met. He once told her that his search for life out there in the universe was a continuation of the search that brought him to God. 'Born Again Christian' is how he described himself after the first meeting he attended. Then the quotations started. When they were sitting, relaxing, or at mealtimes and even in bed. Many of these Janet knew by heart from her days as a Catholic schoolgirl. Not only did the inappropriateness of Kurt's Bible quotes annoy Janet, but somewhere, deep down, she felt they were blasphemous. Although Janet had not been inside a church for many years, something that remained a part of her shuddered as her husband tried to 're-educate her in the ways of the Lord', as he put it.

Janet could not feel a pulse in the child's skinny wrist and the mother's was barely detectable. When she told Jean-Baptiste, he ran back to the Jeep whilst she tipped water from her bottle over the woman's parched lips. Her co-worker returned with the first-aid bag and stretcher, but they had to resuscitate the woman and child before returning to their base in town as quickly as possible.

She had been formally trained in first-aid and resuscitation. Also, the hard-pressed nurses and medics had passed on to her many of their skills. She managed to insert an intravenous line into the woman. However, Janet could not find anything that resembled a vein on the little daughter's desiccated body. She tried soaking her handkerchief with water and squeezing drops of fluid into a fly-fringed mouth, but the child showed no response.

Resorting to the last-ditch option, she slipped an intravenous needle under the skin of the girl's bloated belly, to which she attached a plastic line from a giving set and a bag of intravenous fluid. The fluid dripped into the girl raising a soft, boggy mound where a strip of tape held the needle in place. Whether or not that brown mound would be sufficient to give the child her life back Janet did not know. She could only hope. Hope and, together with Jean-Baptiste, act fast to get her to the medics at their base.

As soon as the woman's pulse had become stronger, they cautiously lifted mother and daughter onto the stretcher and, between them, bore the pitiful pair to the Jeep. Janet stayed with mother and daughter in the back of the vehicle as Jean-Baptiste drove carefully, though as quickly as possible, on the dusty, bumpy road to town. During the three-hour journey, the mother became stronger. She found the strength to smile at Janet and could drink more than just sips. She murmured a few words in her native tongue, although all that Janet made out was "thank you", and she gently touched Janet's arm to show her gratitude. The touch went some way towards undoing the hurt Janet felt inside from the suffering she had witnessed over the previous few weeks. That single touch meant much more than all Kurt's Bible quotes put together.

They arrived at their base on the edge of town. Jean-Baptiste opened the back of the Jeep and Janet leapt out and ran to the medical hut to fetch a nurse. When she left the Jeep, the woman was lovingly stroking her daughter's crinkled hair. On her return, with the nurse, the woman's head was bent over the face of the child. Tears had produced a damp patch on the child's hollowed cheek. The nurse lifted back the woman's head. The little girl's eyes were empty. There was simply nothing there in those tiny portholes of death. Only blankness.

Despite what she had done to try to save the girl, Janet felt excluded from the grim scene, as if merely a spectator of some macabre and meaningless drama. After the nurse had taken the dead child from the weeping mother's arms, Janet knelt down and held the grieving woman close.

No, Kurt, she thought to herself, *I have no faith, but I love these people all the same.*

She helped to carry the woman to the medical hut where the medics took over. There, the nurse placed the little corpse on a white sheet and closed the child's eyes for the last time. Yet another wrapped bundle to be buried in a graveyard of drought victims. Yet another paper statistic for a world that had no eyes for Africa. Having lost her faith, Janet had given up asking God why such a thing should happen to a small child.

Weary, she returned to her hut for a rest, a wash and maybe some food, although eating was the last thing on her mind. Before lying down on her mattress, she switched on her laptop. A few clicks, and up came a list of e-mails, including one from Kurt. She opened it:

'Hi Janet! Here it is. Three billion dollars' worth of life on Mars. Ain't it just cute! Keep in touch, Love—Kurt.'

Janet clicked on the attachment. A window appeared, flickered, and there 'it' was. A patch of dark square pixels on a red background. Nothing else.

"So that's 'it'?" Janet whispered to herself. She clicked on 'reply' then typed a message:

'Thanks... and guess what Kurt... there's death here in Africa. Love—Janet.'

Janet was about to click on 'send' but stopped and added a P.S.:

'And now abideth faith, hope, love, these three; but the greatest of these is love'—Corinthians 1, 13'.

She sent the message, turned off her laptop and stretched out on her mattress. With her eyes closed, she saw the face of the dead child and the look of hopeless despair on the face of the mother. She, Janet, had no hope, no faith, but she still had love. Love for the beautiful people of Africa. Nobody could take that from her. Not even God.

The Old Grandmother

What, I wonder, is my wife? Second generation Chinese, she was born in London, England, and now lives in Scotland. Sino-British, Anglo-Chinese or, in a country that may one day may no longer belong to the United Kingdom of Great Britain and Northern Ireland, a second generation Asian-Scottish double immigrant?

It really doesn't matter, for she has an amazing pedigree linked with a civilization that stretches back over five thousand years to long before those living in these parts north of a then un-built Hadrian's Wall could fashion quality ceramics. And do not even try to compare Hadrian's efforts with those of Qin Shi Huang, China's First Emperor and the man who began construction of the Great Wall. Every time we visit my wife's family in China—she has half-sisters there whom we see every few years—I feel I'm entering a land not of communist cadres, corrupt officials and MAGLEV super-trains, but of restless ghosts (the *guǐ*), of mighty rain-breathing dragons and of eight immortals who will wander the face of Planet Earth till her last lights are finally extinguished.

One of my sisters-in-law lives at the foot of Tai Shan, the holiest of China's five holy mountains and the one up which the great Qin Shi Huang climbed in the hope of escaping mortality. The mountain's nickname is 'The Old Grandmother' (of China). Even in winter, when her hair turns white, pilgrims trail up her forested skirt to the Buddhist temple perched on her head. My wife and I took the cable car, instead, to the five-thousand-foot summit where, in the summer, the temple precinct teems with a mix of tourists and pilgrims, but we did walk down through the deciduous forest unchanged since Shi Huang last walked up the same path before mercury pills, with which his physician plied him, turned him into a raving idiot. Some folk we passed were obviously pilgrims, not tourists, bare-footing their way up, periodically prostrating themselves out of respect for the old lady, but I could not be sure about one old man and a girl of thirteen or maybe fourteen.

This, perhaps, is their story:

Old Cheng is hardly fit enough to walk down to the market, let alone scale the Old Grandmother, but he promised his granddaughter, Jiao, he would do the pilgrimage with her to the very top of the mountain by the time she was fourteen. It's her fourteenth birthday. He promised nothing could stop him. Not age, not infirmity—nothing! He made that promise when she first looked up at him with those eager, searching eyes. Even if the most violent of storms swept inland by the sea dragons were to tear at the head of the old woman, he would take her up the ten thousand steps to the Ming temple so that they could look down at the world from heaven and pray together. Pray for her other grandmother. This, he promised the child over and over.

Jiao, his only grandchild, lives in Sichuan in the far west of China. His son works in an agricultural university there and every year the girl and her parents travel across the country to Taian for the May festival which happily coincides with her birthday. They stay in a stark hotel near the old Buddhist temple, but it's sufficient. And this year should not be any different but for the weather—and that other thing.

Every year it rains, but on her fourteenth birthday the weather promises to be perfect. No storm warning. The sun is still low in the sky but already warm. The sky is as blue as the Dragon of the East and wisps of white, dragon-breath clouds lick the mountain about its peak. There's no rain in these clouds but Jiao will bring water. She promised. Many times, she told him, *she* should carry the water for at fourteen she's no longer a child and he's getting old. The forest, Old Grandmother's green skirt, will offer shade on their way up the steep-stepped slope.

Cheng meets up with Jiao under the arch at the foot of the steps where pilgrims begin their journey. The Old Grandmother should feel honoured to see the girl, for she has grown into such a beautiful young woman. *'So like my dear dead wife,'* he says to himself when he sees her standing alone—waiting. An entire year has passed since they last stood together, in the rain, and when he last repeated his promise to her.

He glows with pride to have Jiao by his side as they set off. Periodically they stop and sip water, for the girl tells her grandfather how important this is, and they listen to the haunting song of a cuckoo calling from another bird's nest, unseen, somewhere amongst the still trees. They pay their respects to the Buddha, and to the Old Grandmother, at the many shrines along the path.

The sun has brought out both tourists and pilgrims, all of whom carry secret cares and hidden worries up the mountain, all hoping that the Old Grandmother might relieve them of some of this burden. Cheng thinks that if they could see how beautiful Jiao has become this would surely make their burdens seem lighter, particularly if they were to see her smile. But all look straight through her. *Why is it we never see what's there in front of us before it's too late?* the old man puzzles.

"Grandfather, stop and rest a while on that wall over there," Jiao suggests after they've climbed for about two hours. Cheng sits on the wall with his granddaughter beside him.

"Here—have some more water," suggests the girl, smiling that captivating smile of hers. Her smile means so much more than the decaying wooden and stone relics clinging to China's Old Grandmother. Jiao's smile shines bright against the darkness that gnaws at the souls of the Grandmother's aged children who trail up her side; the darkness that dulls their faces and urges them, blind to the girl's beauty, to seek strength from a secretive and stubborn old woman. Each longs for a small rock of her strength to fight that darkness and yet, with head down in silent self-conversation, he or she fails to see the girl's smile that might make it all go away.

"Come," says Old Cheng when well rested, "we must keep going, my child."

Jiao helps the old man up from the low wall, for age has made him stiff, and they resume their long trek.

"Grandfather," the girl says as they set off again, "I wish I had known my own grandmother. What was she like? I was so young when she died. There's only emptiness inside me where she should be. Was she strong for you, like Mama is for Baba?"

"Jiao, I will show you your grandmother. At a small shrine further up. There you will set eyes on her."

Jiao smiles again. Old Cheng sees it, but others don't.

Further up the slope, they stop at the shrine. The girl gives her grandfather more water then he takes her to a small garden behind the shrine. The path leads to a stone-lined pool, dark in the shade of the forest. The pine-scent mingles in the still air with the warm whir of the crickets, and again they hear the cuckoo, now far-off.

"Grandfather, that bird makes me feel both sad and happy," says Jiao. "She seems to be calling from another world, and that makes me sad, but she also sings of happiness."

"Like your grandmother." Old Cheng nods his head. "Thinking of her brings me sadness and happiness as does that cuckoo. But come. I must show you something."

Jiao's face lights up.

"Look!" says the old man, pointing to the pool. "There. In the water."

The girl peers into the liquid mirror and sees a face smiling up at her.

"My grandmother?" she asks, excited.

"Who else, Jiao?"

Grinning like young children, they walk on. They pass more tourists and pilgrims, more faces worn by grief or made ugly by greed and disappointment, and they pass 'stick-men' (pole-bearing porters) whose spring-steps sweep them on up the steep-stepped path, their balanced burdens bouncing on bamboo poles to the rhythm of their running. Again, grandfather and granddaughter stop to rest, and she gives him water. She gives it to him knowing how important this is for an old man at altitude.

"Always drink, grandfather," she insists. "Never get thirsty!"

How wise, Old Cheng thinks. *So like her grandmother.*

Slowly, they scale the mountain. The air grows thin and they leave behind the large trees and the dream-song of the cuckoo, the crickets and the smell of pine, and the trees give way to scrubby bushes and rocks and bare ground. There are more shrines and temples and high up on the mountain are stalls and small shops selling food and drink and all manner of colourful tourist trinkets, but Old Cheng and Jiao pass by such things, walking on through the crowds disgorged from the cable car station near the summit of Tai Shan. They pass under the white marble arch to the Street of Heaven, and on to the temple at the top. There, Old Cheng and his granddaughter kneel and bow three times. They bow for the Buddha who has known their lives as they now know death, for death is why they're there. And from the temple Old Cheng and Jiao walk on to a rock where pilgrims and tourists alike stand proud to beam away and have their photos taken. They sit on the rock, unseen, and look down at Old Grandmother's forest-skirt and across to her sister mountains and to the lands beyond.

"Jiao, you and your grandmother, you were the same. The real sadness for me is that she never knew this. But here, with the Old Grandmother of China, you two can be as one at last—and this gives me great happiness, child. Very great happiness!"

But he could not bear to look upon the girl's last smile.

*****

Cheng Liuping, his mouth parched, knew that he was dying. Unable to afford a nurse who might bring him water, his only comfort in that bleak hospital where no one told him the truth was a photo beside the bed—a picture of Jiao in her school uniform, smiling that unforgettable smile, taken the day before she was killed. If his son had not been forced to work that last May holiday it might never have happened. And if all the money allocated for building the new school had been used to buy strong materials able to withstand an earthquake of such magnitude, Jiao would now be just fifteen (*Chinese counting) the age when, of old, a Chinese girl would pin up her long hair and cross over to womanhood.

The only water Old Cheng received, he produced himself. It streaked his cheeks as he drank in his granddaughter's smile. The anger, so pointless in Modern China, had gone. Only sorrow remained. Sorrow and hope that his son, forced into shame when Jiao's mother was shut away in a 'black jail' for blaming her daughter's death on the local party leader, would be allowed time to visit before the cancer finished him off. Hope, also, that the Old Grandmother might forgive him for never fulfilling his promise to Jiao.

(In the 2008 Sichuan Earthquake, over seventy thousand were killed, of whom at least five thousand were children. Seven hundred shoddily-built schools across the province had collapsed. The writer was there.)

Traditionally, Chinese count age in years from 'one' at birth.

The Recorder Player

That underpass. Marble Arch in London, England. On the way to Speakers' Corner before it got turned into a car park. You must have seen him there. and you would have been extremely doubtful about his ability to utter anything that resembles human speech. And if you passed him, you would have surely felt sadness for that is all that was left of him. A dirty, silent sadness, curled up sideways in a sleeping bag full of sorrow.

He would probably have had his face turned to the grimy wall—that is, what could be seen of his face for, apart from eyes and nose, it was mostly hidden behind a feral tangle of hair, beard and moustache. Not only did this gaunt and motionless figure exude sadness, but just looking at his pitiful possessions would bring tears to most eyes: that scruffy Sainsbury's polythene bag barely concealing a half-eaten crust; discarded orange peel and an abandoned crisp packet; the frayed *Daily Telegraph*, six months out of date; the filthy jacket and dirt-greyed shoes. Plus the tin with never more than half-a-dozen small coins. These were all that he owned. These and the desolation of the undefined space around his huddled body. Surely you would have at least noticed him, and in doing so you must have felt something of that sadness? But, you know, he was not always like that. Oh no!

"Proper toff, that one," the one-time residents of the Marble Arch underpass would say as, daily, he used to stride through the tunnel, proud in his dark pin-stripe suit, his white-collared shirt with gold-linked cuffs and his shiny, black, Italian leather shoes, nonchalantly swinging his rolled umbrella with the air of a lord and carrying a laptop that quite possibly stored all the electronic secrets of the business universe imprinted upon its hard drive. And the 'proper toff' never once stopped to throw a coin into the waiting tins and hats of those underpass residents. He was far too proud.

Every morning, he would make the journey from Marble Arch Station through the underpass and across the green expanse of Hyde Park, past the Serpentine Lake, to his office in Knightsbridge, and every evening he would retrace his steps. He had done this for three years, whatever the weather. Many a time, those in his office asked, "Why? Change lines, get off at Knightsbridge," they would suggest.

If only he had taken their advice.

"No!" he always replied, for he needed that brief encounter with the grass, the trees, and the space without cars and faces full of sadness. Perhaps it was some sort of premonition, but he hated those sad faces on the London Underground, in the streets and, most of all, in that underpass. How free he used to feel on emerging from the tunnel into the brightness that was Hyde Park, and how he dreaded the approach to that underpass on his journey home each evening. He would try to switch off and think about life with his wife and his two children as it should have been. And they, the residents of Marble Arch underpass, only thought of him as a toff as he swept past swinging his brolly. They always knew when he was coming. They had learned to recognize the confident step of his Italian shoes on the pavement even before he appeared from around the corner.

Deirdre, his *Homes and Gardens* magazine wife, was every bit as proper as he appeared to be. Perfect posture, always smartly dressed, and everything in their elegant, 'just so', detached, suburban house was, in an inanimate way, a copy of the mistress of the house. Beautiful, but untouchable. Their two children had been packed off to boarding school at the earliest possible age, and at times he had to remind himself that they had children. This was why he resisted any attempt to cut out the twice daily promenade across Hyde Park, the one pleasure in his otherwise barren life. In the comfortable capsule of his mind, those interludes of freedom allowed him to dream another life and run free with his children across the green expanse of Hyde Park.

Then it all changed...

He heard her before first seeing her. A soulful melody played out on a recorder. He heard it even before he had entered the underpass, that evening, on his way back to Marble Arch Station. There was something about the haunting music that caused him to stop in his tracks, to stand and listen. It was only a recorder, but he was amazed at how such a humble instrument could sound so beautiful. And from that moment on it was as if he had stepped into another life. Even the swings of his brolly and the steps of his polished shoes seemed to have lost their confidence as he walked on into the underpass. When he saw her, he halted. Never, before, had he stopped in that underpass.

At first glance she looked quite scruffy. Not his type at all. She had on pale, shabby jeans, holed at the knees, a large woollen jumper so frayed at the cuffs that unravelled wool hung in straggled strands as she held the recorder to her lips. But the music that came from the girl and her recorder was something out of this world. He was utterly transfixed and, as happens at such times when the mind is focused like a microscope on some miniscule object, he looked and saw so much more than other mere passers-by would have done. In that shabby waif of a girl he saw a creature more beautiful than he imagined possible. The music had ensnared him, but it was the vision of the girl that held him captive.

Her hair, the colour of ripened corn, hung in cascading ringlets about her shoulders. She had so much of it that her face and her fragile body seemed disproportionately small, although she was perfectly proportioned: her figure, her facial features, with a gently turned-up nose, soft peach cheeks and sensuous lips, engaged with her recorder, hinting at every possible nook and cranny of love. All perfect. But it was those eyes that doomed him. The same hue as Meconopsis, the Himalayan Blue Poppy, they seemed to light up his life when he first saw them. If he had turned and fled perhaps he might have been saved but this was the last thing on his mind. Looking at the girl from a short distance away, he stood mesmerized. As soon as she had stopped playing, turned her face towards him and smiled, it was too late. The hourglass of his life opened and the sand passing through it no longer trickled but started to pour.

She was still smiling with those hauntingly-beautiful eyes as he fumbled in his jacket pocket, pulled out a wallet and extracted a ten-pound note. Red-faced with embarrassment, he reached forward and dropped the note into the girl's pink woollen hat lying on the ground in front of her. Until then, this had contained only a few copper coins.

"Oh, sir!" she exclaimed in astonishment. "You shouldn't!"

He had so wanted to hear her voice. It, too, was beautiful. Soft and warm with a hint of an Irish accent. The man braved a smile.

"You deserve it," he said. "You play that thing so beautifully. I—well, I just couldn't believe it."

He had to stay and talk with this beautiful creature. He could not leave her. Not now. She smiled again, her furrowed brow exposing genuine concern for his ridiculous generosity.

"Really, don't feel you have to." She even laughed as she gracefully bent down to retrieve the ten-pound note and attempted to hand this back to the man. He held up his hand.

"No," he protested. "Please. I want you to have it. Your playing has made my day."

They froze for a few moments, the ten-pound note still in her outstretched hand. Then she shrugged her shoulders and returned it to her pink hat.

"Thank you so much, sir," the girl said.

"Tell me, are you a music student?" he asked, thinking she must be about twenty or so.

She laughed again. *Such a pretty laugh*, he thought.

"No, not yet," she replied in her gentle Irish voice, "but I hope to be. One day."

"You've real talent," he continued, knowing nothing about music. Her deceptively waif-like appearance made him feel bold and strong. "Look, would you like a little break from playing? On that bench up there? I'm in no hurry. And I'm quite safe, you know."

She grinned. "I'm sure you are," she said, quietly. "Okay then!"

The girl seemed almost cheerful as she picked up her pink hat and her recorder box then followed him out of the underpass to an empty park bench. The sun was already low and trees cast long shadows across the short grass. A group of grey geese, motionless as decoy ducks, squatted in the middle distance. A squirrel played with something in the grass, ran towards them, stopped, stood up on its hind legs, looked, shrank down then darted off in the opposite direction. The girl giggled. The shadows of the trees, the geese and the squirrel, these were the things he loved to see and watch in that old life, but now there was just himself and the girl on that bench, and now he saw nothing else but her.

"Tell me, what's a girl like you doing begging in that underpass? It can't be safe. Do your parents know?"

The girl's pale blue eyes appeared pained. He should never have asked her. He was about to apologize for being so crass when she spoke: "I have no parents," she explained. "No parents and no home." The quivering of lips found his heart and the look she gave him penetrated his very soul. "I only wish I did have. Parents and a home, that is."

"But where do you—you know—stay? Live?"

She laughed.

"Oh, here, there and everywhere!"

He simply could not escape from the girl's eyes. Her gaze seemed to melt him inside. He took out his wallet and offered her a twenty-pound note.

"No, no. Please, no pity," she pleaded, but he insisted and, reluctantly, she took the money.

"I do so wish I could help you some more. Will you be here tomorrow?" the man asked. She laughed that laugh again.

"If you say so," she replied.

"I say so," he said, held by those eyes.

The following morning. she was not there in the tunnel and he felt a slight panic, but in the evening, as he approached the underpass, he heard that haunting music again—and there she was. This time he took her to a food bar in Oxford Street and fed her. He had never seen anyone eat so quickly. She must have been ravenous, he told himself.

And they talked. She said little about her parents' death, about her family or her home back in Ireland, if, indeed, she still had one, but she did talk about her music and about her love for nature and the park. He spoke about his wife, his children, his work and his boredom with these things and she listened, looking at him all the time with those blue poppy eyes and inside he continued to melt like an iceberg as it slowly, and imperceptibly, starts to disappear.

That day, he gave her two twenty-pound notes, and the next, two fifty-pound notes. Each time she would protest at his generosity, saying she could not possibly accept such large amounts of money, and yet each day his money found its way from the girl's pink hat to a pocket hidden somewhere under the overhang of her large grey woollen jumper. He began to spend even more time with the girl, taking her to small Italian restaurants off Oxford Street, and giving her small bundles of banknotes rolled up and secured with rubber bands. That way it somehow seemed less. The same protests and the same rejected protests, but soon the girl was passing sums of four or five hundred pounds from her pink hat into her hidden pocket.

He was fully aware that the need to be with this girl, to talk with her and to look into those eyes, had become an addiction, but, as with all addictions, he was powerless to overcome it. The twice daily walk across Hyde Park no longer meant anything to him. The smell of the grass after the rain, the rustle of wind in the trees, the bird song, these things no longer held sway, and the walk, that one pleasure in his life, was merely a necessary chore until he could hear that music, until he could sit with her and until he was able to see those eyes again.

Deirdre suspected something for several weeks. Why should he suddenly have to work late every single day? She called the office at six p.m. He had already left. So why did it take him so long, she asked, when he arrived home at nine-thirty? And why was he withdrawing so much cash, she wanted to know? She needed answers, but he was not giving her any and they had a blazing row. Years of pent-up resentment and niggling grudges on both sides erupted like a volcano of anger. He left there and then, still dressed in a pin-stripe suit and shiny black shoes, with a sleeping bag and a pillow and some rolled-up bank notes that he had withdrawn from the cash-line after saying good-bye to the girl. He took the tube train back to Marble Arch. The girl had gone, but he reassured himself she would be there the next day. Then they would go away somewhere together. To the country, even Ireland, anywhere to escape from the boredom of his old life. She would become his new life.

He did not go to the office the following day. Or the next, or the day after that. In fact, he never returned to his office and he never returned to his wife. All that first day he waited for the girl with the recorder, but she did not show up. Or the next day or the one after that. He stood around in the underpass, already transformed by a growth of beard with a covering of dirt and park mud on his shoes. He sat and ate on the park bench. Days merged with days merged with weeks. Still she did not show. He took to sleeping in the underpass as the days grew shorter and the night air cooler, but apart from toffs in smart, striped suits swinging their brollies, women with bags full of shopping and a scattering of other down-and-out residents of the Marble Arch underpass, there was now nobody else; no one to whom he could talk. No blue poppy eyes to look at and give him new life. She had simply disappeared. Gone was his old life of lies and self-deceit. Gone with the dream that should have replaced it.

A dream?

Never more than that!

Perhaps the girl had accumulated enough cash to go to music school. Who knows? Others had different thoughts. Now that he had grown to resemble the long-standing residents of the Marble Arch underpass, he did at least occasionally pass the time of day with them.

"What girl with blue eyes who played the recorder? No idea who you're talking about," one of them said. "And I've been here for years. That's my patch, over there. Look!" the man added, pointing to a tatty cardboard box, a sleeping bag and a two-year-old *Daily Mirror*.

And the man who had once walked proud and erect, and who would swing his brolly like a lord, this man looked, and he remembered how he used to pass by such things in his old life, and he remembered thinking back then, '*how sad, how very sad*'.

The Two-Legged Deer

He and his sister sank to the ground whilst their mother slunk silently through the undergrowth ahead, freezing every few feet. Beyond, on the jungle path, was a two-legged deer. Their mother had warned them about the dangers of this beast—the deer who cannot run fast and yet is more feared than a rampaging elephant. The deer that can kill from a distance. She had warned them, yet now, driven by hunger and the need to find food for her two growing cubs, she stalked the two-legged deer, preparing for a kill.

She had no other choice for they were on the brink of starvation and death. The jungle was shrinking and their mother, once queen of her territory, who could take four-legged deer and pig as and when she needed to, was forced to feed upon the strange beasts that lived beyond the reach of her ever-shrinking territory and upon the two legged-deer that roamed with these beasts. Overwhelmed by hunger, no longer could she afford to avoid the two-legged deer. If she were quick, and lucky, they would be easy prey, for not all two-legged deer could kill from afar. And her chances seemed better with a solitary two-legged deer—the opposite way around with four-legged deer when a herd provided a certain chance of a kill.

The two-legged deer stopped. Their mother froze, crouching close to the ground. He saw the white spots on the backs of her ears, the slight flick of her tail—a sign to him and his sister to remain motionless as rocks. The creature moved slowly forwards. Unlike the four-legged deer, it had just one horn which moved about in front of its tall body. He feared for his mother, for she had told him how easily the horned two-legged deer can kill from afar. He watched her sink down, those muscles that kept the family alive tensed. The two-legged deer also froze, but not its horn. Now he was no longer sure who was doing the stalking. His mother or the deer?

He was aware of the feelings his mother would have had at that moment for he had once experienced these moments before leaping onto a small pig. Each sharply-honed sense had been on full alert, informing him of every sound, every scent and every hint of movement as his gaze remained fixed on his prey. His mother had taught him to be guided by his senses for they alone would tell him when to make that lethal leap. Too soon, or too late, and the prey would be lost, and he would go hungry.

The two-legged deer's horn pointed at his mother. Briefly, she appeared to stop breathing and he felt the tension coiled in her. Knowing the deadly power of that tension when released, he hoped for all their sakes that this power would be deadlier than the horn of the two-legged deer.

When the two-legged deer moved backwards, his mother sprang. He recalled leaping onto that pig and trying to imitate the noise she made. A noise so terrifying that the animal, on hearing it, seemed unable to move before being hit by the weight of his body, and his clawed paws had held his prey powerless whilst he sank his teeth into its neck.

But the two-legged deer was different. In that fraction of a second, before his mother smashed into the deer, and when it should have been frozen in terror, it continued to move and its horn exploded. The jungle resounded with the bang of the deer's horn. His mother, a mass of hard muscle, of tearing claws and of razor-sharp teeth slammed into the deer, slashing and ripping at the animal which fell under the force of her strike. But something was wrong. When her powerful jaws should have been firmly closed around the throat of the deer, and when the deer should have been limp and lifeless, it was still thrashing about and his mother, clawing at the creature, was behaving strangely. She could not seem to do anything with those jaws of hers. Slowly that great mass of power went limp. Her head moved helplessly up and down as she lay slumped across her writhing prey. The deer even managed to crawl free from under her body.

He and his sister had always lived and acted as one. There was, as yet, no rivalry between them. When one jumped the other did the same, and, as one, they shot forwards from the undergrowth and pounced on the gasping, two-legged deer. Its horn, severed from the creature by their mother, lay motionless on the ground beside her useless body. Together, they tore what life remained from the deer and dragged its carcass off the path into the undergrowth. Then they stopped.

Something was wrong. They looked back along the path at their mother. Slumped sideways, she growled in distress and scraped at the side of her face with a large paw. He and his sister leapt over the still body of the two-legged deer and approached her. Her face had changed. Where an eye should have been there was a hole, and from that hole oozed blood and fluid flesh. He placed his paw on her neck and licked her face. His mother responded. Her growl told him to go quickly and leave the body of the two-legged deer. Urged him to escape from death. Her single seeing eye closed as her great head sank down onto the dust of the jungle floor.

"Go!" she growled, faintly, before the shallow movements of her chest ceased and the majesty of a life that had been his mother was reduced to a corpse. From this flowed the smell of death.

Along the path, he heard more two-legged deer. An excited collection of noises that that could only mean one thing: a whole herd of them. might possess lethal horns. In a flash, he and his sister vanished into the jungle.

Their mother's death had been her final lesson. Without her to guide them, they searched the jungle for food. It was now their territory. They searched all day, and all the territory yielded up was the fly-ridden, half-eaten, corpse of a fox. Together, weak from hunger, they picked what little flesh they could off its bones. They returned to the place where their mother had taken them that morning. They returned to the only source of food: *the two-legged deer.*

The body of their mother had gone. That of the dead two-legged deer, too. But the scent of blood and the smell of death lingered. He walked with his sister along that path of death. They walked to the far edge of the jungle and looked out at the open space where a herd of two-legged deer roamed. They crouched, and they waited, for waiting was all that they could now do. Waiting for their senses to tell them when to strike as their mother had taught them. Sooner or later, a young two-legged deer, one that had not yet grown a lethal horn, was certain to come strolling along the path...

*****

Following the discovery this morning of the partly-eaten body of a young girl from the village of Barandhapur, marksmen are combing the surrounding jungle for two young tigers believed to have turned man-eaters. The girl had disappeared from the village yesterday evening and the gruesome discovery was made by a search party at first light. Earlier yesterday, a farmer from the same village had been fatally mauled by a large tigress which he had shot and killed when she attacked him. Pug marks around the girl's body suggested that the girl was killed by two young tigers believed to be the cubs of the tigress, and authorization has been granted to the villagers to have the tigers shot.

Saucers of Fire

Two saucers of fire, two demonic eyes, threw searching beams as they swept towards her in an unearthly roar. Terrified beyond screaming, she stared into the blinding light, but the expected moment of death never happened. The beast's gaze was deflected, its ear-splitting shriek cut short by a noise resembling that of a discharging cannon. She turned and fled, for surely this must have been Satan's beast sent to deliver her to Hell for what she had done.

Silence. Darkness returned. Had something stopped the beast with blazing eyes? As her mother had promised, a guardian angel? Or was the 'thing' still there waiting to seize her in that darkness?

When she was cast out by her furious father for being with child by the squire's dandy of a son, the woman hugged her and promised that God and his angels would protect the girl, cursing the squire for allowing his lecherous heir anywhere near the milkmaids. The sordid affair occupied every corner of her young mind—the man's hurried embraces, his threats and the pungent, perfumed smell of him—and now her father and God were exacting their punishment.

She heard angry voices from where the beast lay slain—doubtless devils who had come to reclaim the loathsome creature. But was her angel there, too? Would he protect her?

The girl ran on.

*****

"'Course I'm sure this is the bloody Ambleside road. Don't believe me, do you? Oh... my God!"

Her husband slammed the brake as the vehicle swerved, spinning the steering wheel. Tyre-screech blended with frantic female screams, then a metallic bang as the Ford Fiesta hit the stone dyke. The headlights flickered and went out and the couple sat for a few seconds in shocked disbelief, propped up by inflated air bags.

"It's her!" he said. "Those eyes. Most definitely her."

"For heaven's sake! Have you gone mad? What's her? One minute you're moaning I've taken you on the wrong road, then bang! You decide to drive into this damned wall! I mean—"

"That woman standing in the road. It was the young actress. The one who—" He paused.

"That tart who took her bloody clothes off?"

"Not a tart. A hard-working actress, and—"

"Oh yes?"

"And she didn't take all her clothes off. Only down to her—"

"You saw her bottom! Don't think I didn't notice you ogling. Actress or not, she showed off her bottom in public. That spells 'Tart' to me. With a capital bloody 'T'!"

"No! It was all because of the boss's son who deceived her. And her flipping father went and chucked her out when she came clean and said she was pregnant. What a bastard! I could've—"

"Oh, why did I agree to seeing that blessed play? You knew from the reviews the tart would be taking her clothes off, didn't you?"

"Stop calling the poor girl a tart! She was lovely. And it *was* her. I could tell from the eyes."

"You weren't looking at her eyes on the stage. Just her bum. Look, stop wittering on and help me out of the car. I can't bloody breathe with all that dust from the air bag!"

He eased himself out of the car and peered into the darkness ahead. For a brief moment he persuaded himself that there was movement there, but perhaps his wife was right. Had his brain simply refused to erase the image of the pretty young actress? He had felt for both her, the actress, and for the woman she played. Why had the writer allowed that bastard to get off scot-free whilst forcing her to lose her job and having her turned out onto the street by a bullish father?

"I said bloody get me outa here!" yelled his wife.

He opened the passenger door and helped her out onto the road where she paced up and down muttering about bad plays, broken headlights and bottoms. She stopped when she realized her husband was still staring vacantly at the empty road ahead.

"Well?" she asked. "Are you gonna call the AA or would you prefer me to thumb a lift like that tart in your head? Oh—and if you do happen to see that bottom again, give it a kick from me, will you?"

He ignored his wife whilst removing the deflated air bags. Back in the driving seat, he started up the engine.

"Get in," he called out. Shaking her head, his wife stubbornly refused to join him. "Bloody get in!" he shouted.

Muttering murderously, she returned to the passenger seat and slammed the door.

"No headlights!" she reminded him as he edged the vehicle away from the wall. "Can't drive without headlights. We'll never get back to Ambleside in the dark."

He saw little point in continuing the conversation. The young actress had been standing solid as a statue in the middle of the road and wearing a long brown period dress and shawl. She was as real as the stone wall they crashed into. How she had got there from Keswick Theatre, when they had been the first to leave the car park, he had no idea, but further argument with his wife would serve no purpose. Besides, he felt proud of himself. His swift avoidance action had saved the life of a struggling young actress.

The life of a young woman for the price of two headlamps—not bad, huh?

As he drove his pride, his wife's anger, and a mental image of the young actress, at twenty miles per hour along the A591, a twenty-first century tarmac tentacle that teased its way round the timeless twists and curves of the English Lake District, a young woman tossed aside by Victorian hypocrisy ran on in the opposite direction. Ran to escape from her demons in a desperate bid to find comfort in a cruel world—desperate for that angel of whom her mother had spoken.

Pink Slippers

Someone crying? A child? Under my bed?

Jason wondered whether he had left his Play Station on after shoving a load of toys there before turning off the light. He scrambled out of bed, flicked on his torch and shone it at the jumble littering the space between bed and floor. The crying stopped.

The Play Station was turned off. Nothing to explain the sound of a child crying. He checked the TV. Switched off. His computer as well. He looked in the cupboard, the best hiding-place. Only layers of clean-smelling clothes put there by his mum.

Jason shrugged his shoulders and went back to bed. As he started to drift off, the crying started up again. Definitely from under his bed. Grabbing the torch, he slipped out of bed, knelt down, and there she was...

Being a boy, he did not scream. Not when he saw her face. It was the prettiest he had ever seen, with bright, blue eyes and long golden ringlets down to where the shoulders should have been—only she did not have any shoulders. Just a head. A crying one.

"What are you doing under my bed?" asked Jason. He did not mean to sound rude, but he felt tired, confused and the following morning he had to get up early for a game of rugby.

"It's *my* bed," insisted the girl's head, "only they won't let me sleep in it anymore."

Perhaps I'm dreaming? the boy wondered.

"You don't need a whole bed if you're only a head, do you? Find a space in the cupboard if you've gotta sleep in my room."

Oh my God, those eyes. I've offended her.

"What do you mean I'm 'only a head'? Look!"

The Play Station moved forwards on its own—then a torpedo-firing submarine, a half-built space station and a book about dangerous spiders.

"See!" the head announced crossly.

"Well, if the rest of you is invisible it comes to the same thing. Are you a ghost or have you escaped from a Harry Potter movie?"

"I have no idea what you're talking about! Look, if you were the son of a gentleman you would help me out from under here!"

Jason's Dad was always on at him about trying to act 'a gentleman' where ladies were concerned. He was not convinced the head of a girl about his age could be classed as a 'lady', but he didn't want to let the side down. He offered his hand, and was surprised to feel a small, warm hand take hold of his. Three pulls and the girl's head was in the middle of the dark bedroom. It rose up, suspended above him. The boy shone his torch at it.

"Are you standing?" Jason asked.

"What do you think?" replied the head curtly. Jason, too, stood up. The head was a few inches shorter than him.

"Well, *I* think you're a ghost. What's your name?" The face stared at him, those large blue eyes moistening. "I-I'm sorry," he said, realizing that he had truly upset her. "Maybe it's me that's the ghost and you who's real. Either way, you must have a name."

"Gertrude."

"What?"

"Gertrude! Gertie for short. Have you not heard of it? It's a very popular name for girls!"

"I suppose I've sort of heard of it—but no one's really called Gertrude. Not nowadays."

"What's *your* name, then?"

"Jason!" Jason was proud of his name. He was the only one in his school.

"Well, that *is* a silly name. Jason was a Greek hero who set off in a boat called the Argo to find the Golden Fleece that would help him to become king of a place called Thessaly. I think *you* must be the ghost if you're an ancient Greek!" Jason pinched himself and it hurt. He was sure ghosts would not feel pain.

"Pinch yourself, Gertie!" he suggested. She did. "Ouch!" she cried. Perhaps he was wrong.

"How old are you?" Jason asked.

"Eleven!"

"Actually, *I'm* twelve."

"Well, you're not very clever at Greek mythology, are you?"

"We don't do Greek mythology at school. Look—just out of interest, what… you know, what year is it? With you?"

Gertie sighed. "What a ridiculous question! Eighteen fifty-six, of course."

"Erm—I don't want to upset you again, Gertie, really I don't, but—you see, it's actually two thousand and seventeen. Here. Where I'm standing right now. I'm sorry, but are you sure you didn't die? I mean, like having some horrible illness or getting run over or something?"

"Run over? I don't know what you mean. But I do remember—" Gertie frowned, as if trying to remember something. Once more, tears welled in her eyes.

"I'm sorry again!" apologized Jason. "It's not important. Look, if you're tired you can have my bed. I don't mind. I'll sleep on the floor. There's a spare duvet in the cupboard."

"I do remember Mother saying I wouldn't sleep in my bed anymore. She was holding my hand, and I can't remember anything else. It was as if everything went blank." Jason retrieved a hanky from under his pillow. He held it out for Gertie and an invisible hand took it and dabbed at those large blue eyes. "Except—" Gertie continued, "well, I wasn't feeling well. My head was most terribly sore and spinning—and—"

"It doesn't matter," interrupted Jason. "Honestly!"

"What?"

"If you're a ghost. I don't mind. You can sleep in my bed. And we can still be friends."

"But I don't believe in ghosts. Besides, if one is dead, one should—you know—go somewhere else."

"Like heaven?"

The tears trailing down Gertie's cheeks made Jason feel bad. He wished he would not keep saying things that upset the girl and he tried to imagine what he would feel like if he were to suddenly discover that he was dead. "Perhaps this is a sort of half-way place for you. Like an airport waiting lounge." He was desperate to cheer her up.

"A what?"

Oh dear, he thought. *Airplanes in eighteen fifty-six? I don't think so!*

"Well—as though you're nearly there. Heaven, I mean. Just waiting for something to take you that bit further. Like an invisible airplane, maybe?"

"I have no idea what an airplane is, and I truly do not want to go anywhere else. This is my home. It's where I live. And you're in my bedroom, although it—well, it does look rather different."

"No problem! We can share my room. *Our* room. But there's one thing I don't understand, Gertie."

"What?"

"How come I can see your face but the rest of you is invisible?"

"I don't know. I'm not invisible to me. It must be that purple medicine. I thought it had been put out for me because I was feeling so fearfully cold and unwell. I started to drink it and straightaway my lips and face felt warm. I was certain it was beneficial for my health—but—" Gertie paused then frowned at Jason. He was grinning. "What?" she asked.

"'Beneficial for my health'? You do talk funny!"

"I do not! Funny's an adjective, anyway," Gertie pouted. "Not an adverb!"

"Sorry!"

"I heard you coming up the stairs, so I hid under the bed because of what Mother said about not sleeping in my bed any longer and—and everything seeming so strange."

"What purple medicine?"

"Over there! By the window."

Jason shone his torch at the space in front of the window. His chemistry set was strewn about on the floor where he had been playing with it. In the centre of the mess was a beaker half-full of a purple fluid. Earlier on, he had mixed together various chemicals in that beaker in the hopes of producing something that would fizz and go bang. It had not worked but he had been far too busy to tidy up the mess. It must have turned purple afterwards.

"*That* mixture?" he queried. "The stuff I made this afternoon?"

"It is medicine, isn't it?" Gertie now looked worried.

"Well—erm—of course! Sort of!"

"I think you must be so very clever! May I have some more, please?"

Jason felt himself on the horns of a dilemma. If taking a small amount had made Gertie's face become visible, perhaps the rest of the girl would be made solid if she were to finish it. But he knew that most chemicals are poisonous. Another drop could kill her. There again, if she was already a ghost, did that matter?

"I felt so good after a taking only a little of it, but the rest of me still feels so horribly cold."

Jason picked up the beaker. He could not remember which chemicals he had used. Handing it to an unseen hand, he wondered whether things that were poisonous to live people might have the reverse effect upon those who were dead. He watched as the beaker was raised, as if by magic, until its edge reached the girl's lips. Tilted up by an unseen hand, its purple contents disappeared into Gertie's mouth. Jason watched anxiously. He quite expected that pretty face to turn an odd colour and go into spasms. Thankfully, this did not happen. First the girl's small hands appeared, semi-transparent, then solid, followed by her arms, her upper body, her long, wide, frilly pink dress, and finally her pantalooned legs and dainty pink slippers.

"Wow!" exclaimed Jason. "You're—"

"Can you see me sufficiently well now?" Gertie asked eagerly. He turned the light on to get a better look at the girl.

"You're—you're Victorian and—and *very* pretty."

"Do I look whole?"

"Yeah! Cool!"

"But I don't feel cold any longer!"

"An expression. Cool. Means good—nice—beautiful!"

"Does this mean... am I—well—alive? Have I been cured?"

Please God, make her be alive, Jason thought.

"I am pretty good at chemistry. First time I've done that, mind you. Made a medicine that can bring a ghost back to life," he said.

Gertie skipped up to the boy and kissed him on the cheek. Her lips felt so warm and soft. He touched the place where they had been, and he blushed.

"You can still sleep on my bed," he insisted. "But I don't know what we're gonna do tomorrow."

"Never mind tomorrow," Gertie said excitedly. "Surely there's something I can do for you in return. Your medicine's made me feel so much better."

Jason looked guiltily at his school bag lying on the floor. It was full of unfinished homework to be handed in on Monday. Gertie seemed pretty switched on about Greek mythology. Perhaps she was good at other subjects, too.

"What's your maths like? And English—and, erm, French?"

"My governess informs me that I am the best pupil she has ever had."

"It's not that I'm bad at these subjects, you see. It's just that I'm better at other things. Like science and stuff. And rugby. I'm pretty good at that."

"Is rugby a language?" The girl looked puzzled and Jason chuckled.

"Not exactly! Look, if I take out my homework, could you just look at it? You don't have to actually *finish* it. That would be asking too much. Just sort of—"

"I do so love my lessons! Show me, please!"

Gertie sat at his desk, Jason placed his maths homework in front of her and handed her a ball point.

"What's this?" she asked, holding up the pen.

"A pen!"

"Where's the ink?"

"Inside."

Gertie made a line on the paper. "Quite magical!" she exclaimed.

"Another of my inventions! Look, if the maths is too hard—"

"Hard? But this is easy!"

Jason watched in awe as the girl quickly worked out all his complicated maths questions, without a pause, in beautiful curvy, flowing figures.

"Yes—well—erm—I didn't want to trouble you with the difficult ones. Now for the French. Erm—translation from English into French, actually. Quite tricky."

He handed the girl his French textbook and his jotter. Once again, in lovely, neat copperplate, she raced through two pages of work that would have had him struggling for more than half-an-hour, and without using a dictionary.

"So—erm—what about English? You must be good at that, too."

Gertie giggled. "I do speak it most of the time."

"There's this essay I have to do, see. An essay about 'anger'. Anything that makes you angry, our teacher said."

"Cruelty to animals! I saw a farmer beating a horse once and it made me so very angry."

"Great! I'll leave you to it!"

Jason sat on the edge of his bed and pretended to read his book but he could not stop looking at the girl as she wrote his essay on anger, her concentration showing in her angel-like face. It did not take her long. Soon, she came over and sat beside him, handing him her completed essay. He stared in wonder at the beautiful writing.

"I wish I could write like that," he said.

"Well, you can't be good at everything!" replied Gertie, "And you are exceptionally good at bringing ghosts back to life—if that's what I am."

"Perhaps you're not properly dead. You might have fallen into a time-space wormhole."

Gertie looked puzzled. "What's that?" she asked. Jason had no idea, but he did not want to display his ignorance. At least, not to Gertie.

"It's—it's a sort of black hole and—and kind of bends time. Or something."

"Oh!"

"Look, tell me more about yourself. And this house when you were alive. I mean back in the eighteen fifties. I knew it was old but didn't know it was that old."

Jason and Gertie sat on the bed and talked away about all manner of things until the early hours of the morning. The boy learned more about life in the nineteenth century than he had ever got from books or the movies, and he tried to update the girl about everything from television, computers and parking meters to rugby, space travel and Coca Cola. He was wondering how she was going to cope in the modern world with her beautiful copperplate writing, her lovely ringlets and her pink dress with its layers of petticoats. Perhaps his mum would buy her new clothes. Finally, their eyelids became heavy and they decided it was time to go to sleep. Gertie removed her pink slippers and climbed into his bed whilst Jason lay curled up on his duvet on the floor. It took him some time to drift off for he kept craning his neck to make sure the girl was still there. What if she were to become invisible again? He really had no idea which chemicals he had put into her 'medicine'.

*****

"Do wake up, Jason! What on earth are you doing on the floor?"

He opened his eyes. His mum was looming over him, her hands on her hips. He glanced up at the bed. It was empty. When his mother went over to the window to draw back the curtains, he spied a small pair of old-fashioned girls' pink slippers placed neatly together beside the bed. Hurriedly, he pushed these away.

"I thought you and your friends were supposed to be playing rugby in the park this morning."

Rugby now seemed unimportant to the boy as he stared at the pink slippers.

"Done your homework already, I see? Hmm! Glad they've got you to write legibly at last." His mum was inspecting his workbooks carefully laid out on the desk. "*And* you've tidied up your room! Never thought I believed in miracles!"

Jason sat up. His chemistry set and other things, including clothes that had been scattered about all over the floor, were now in neat, orderly piles.

"You'd better get a move on. Dad's ready and waiting."

Jason's mum left the room. It seemed so quiet and still.

"Gertie?" he whispered.

No response. He looked under the bed. Nothing! He got up and went over to the cupboard and the wardrobe, checking every corner, every possible niche. The bathroom? Empty! Back in his bedroom, he whispered again, more loudly:

"Gertie, have you gone back to being invisible? If you have, I'll forget rugby. I'll have another go at making that medicine for you."

Silence.

Could she have left the house? Gone out without any shoes on? He went over to the window and peered outside, hoping to see a girl with long golden ringlets and a pink dress playing in the garden. No such luck. He returned to his desk and looked at the beautifully written homework. Then he saw it. Thankfully his mother had not noticed. On a separate sheet of paper, underneath the essay on 'anger', was a note in perfect copperplate:

'As you said it would, the airplane arrived for me. Never have I met such a sweet boy as you. I do so hope that one day we'll meet again when your own airplane comes for you. Love—Gertie XXX.'

Flatpack Wife

An advertisement caught his eye.

Norman was sitting comfortably in his armchair, browsing through the weekend newspaper colour supplement. A young blonde stopped him from turning the page. She had a Marilyn Monroe face and figure and wore a pretty pink apron, an ecstatic smile and pink, high-heeled shoes. In her right hand she held an iron.

'New for all unmarried Men!' was stretched across the advert above the blonde's fair head. *'You too can have a lovely wife for just £499.99 (VAT incl.). Easy to assemble, available in five different racial types and three hair colours. Adjustable figure. Breathes, sleeps, eats and drinks just like a real live woman. Programmable speech in forty-two languages with dialect options. Guaranteed temper-free. Ten percent discount before June 30th if you buy online. Hurry whilst the offer lasts. Visit www.flatpackwife.com.'*

Norman flicked through a few more pages then turned back to the one with the blonde. He looked around the living room, at the tray with his half-eaten breakfast of burnt toast and unscrambled eggs on the table, the full laundry basket in the corner then he looked again at the Marilyn Monroe lookalike. He stood up, hunted for the scissors and, failing to find any, used a kitchen knife to cut out the advertisement from the newspaper supplement. Later that morning, he logged onto the internet and typed in the website address.

Why not, he thought as he scrutinised the webpage?

Norman was an exceedingly shy bachelor of forty-two years who had never managed to woo a woman into anything resembling a close relationship. Nevertheless, he thought a lot about the opposite sex. Most of time, in fact. That was why the Marilyn Monroe lookalike had caught his eye. So far, this had never gone beyond *thinking* about a woman. What an opportunity this advert would provide.

What possibilities! Perhaps even 'that'. And it would not even matter if he had never before slept with a woman.

He started to fill in the details. He chose blonde, as in the advertisement, and medium height. He noticed that the offer did not include clothing or jewellery. That was something he would have to consider later, but he had a full fortnight until the promised delivery date to ponder over accessories.

The next few days saw Norman busying himself about the house, making things tidy, polishing the furniture and hoovering the floor. Everything had to be exactly right when his wife arrived. He soon realized that his bed was not going to be large enough for the two of them, so he ordered a double bed from a furniture store. At the supermarket he sneaked some items of women's clothing, medium size, outer and under, amongst the bread, the cornflakes and the vegetables. He also purchased a few pieces of acceptably-cheap jewellery at a shop in the High Street.

I do hope she likes them, he thought as he left the shop. He felt aggrieved that all this was costing him more than his wife, but he still reckoned that he was getting a bargain with the overall package.

When the doorbell rang in the afternoon of the date of delivery, Norman bubbled with excitement. He had taken the day off work and had been running around with the hoover all morning. He grinned eagerly as he signed for the delivery.

"That's my wife," he said proudly to the dour young man at the door, pointing to a large flat box which rested up against the wall whilst they tackled the paperwork. The man looked at the box, looked at Norman, hurriedly obtained a signature and quickly departed, leaving Norman staring at the box. This proved to be heavier than expected as he struggled with it into the house.

I suppose it would be heavy, he reckoned. *It is, after all, a wife!*

He could not stop grinning as he carefully opened the box. In it he found a booklet of instructions, a CD full of software, a USB cable, an activation pack with rechargeable batteries and all the necessary body parts neatly packaged and labelled in separate polythene bags. She was all there, just waiting to be assembled. There was also a full twelve-month warranty. Norman took out the instruction manual and sat reading it for some time. It was important that no mistakes were mad, and there were several things of note under 'cautions'. Although the product was self-washing, under no account was it to be fully immersed in water.

It took Norman the whole afternoon to fit all the parts together and to charge the batteries of the activation pack. This, he later slotted into a neatly-concealed space in the back of the female form lying face down on the floor. He looked with pride at his wife as he attached her, via the USB cable, to his computer. This would be the part most demanding of his concentration. He waited anxiously whilst the soft-ware was installed. At last a window appeared on the monitor screen.

'Language?' English of course. And no special dialect.

'Temperament?' He looked at the options and went for *'mild natured'*.

'Interests?' He saw to it that his wife would be literate, musical (he loved his two classical CDs), a good cook, keen on gardening, a hill walker and into ball-room dancing. He did not dance himself, but now that he had a wife, Norman rather fancied the idea of gliding around floor with her in his arms.

'Scrabble?' 'Yes,' he thought, *'great for cold winter evenings.'*

'Name?' There were no suggested options given with this one, so he typed in 'Jane'. At least he thought he did, but the space remained blank and he could not see the cursor. How annoying! In frustration, he tapped randomly at the keys. Suddenly NHPOOMPH appeared in the name space. He tried to delete this, but nothing happened. So, his wife was called 'Nhpoomph'. Norman realized there was nothing he could about it and uttered a deep throated "Ugh!" Immediately, his computer spoke:

"I will respond to the name of *Ugh!*", imitating Norman's grunt.

In his excitement, Norman had failed to see that as well as uploading the written name for his wife, the soft-ware had programmed her to respond to his voice when he spoke her name, which turned out to be a deep-throated grunt. At least, as far as his wife was concerned. It would have been far too complicated to uninstall everything and start all over again. He might have been left with a useless, non-functioning wife, so he continued the process. When completed, he felt a curious thrill as he clicked on 'finish'. He now had a fully-programmed, functioning wife with a full range of domestic skills and a Marilyn Monroe figure and looks to boot.

Jane looked at Norman and smiled. Such a sweet smile. He felt truly happy, though he was a shy man and his immediate reaction was to ask her to put on some clothes. Her nakedness took on a whole new meaning once she was electronically 'alive'.

"Jane, please put on some clothes," Norman said timidly. But Jane remained seated, smiling benignly. *Of course,* he thought. *How stupid of me. I'm going to have to grunt as well when I address her.*

"Jane—*grunt*—would you care to come and get dressed? Please." Norman knew that you should be ultra-polite to a woman.

"Certainly, Norman," Jane replied.

What a lovely voice! Such perfect diction. Just like a BBC newscaster. Quite different from his Yorkshire drawl. So nice to have a wife with a posh accent. Norman led her into the bedroom and showed her the clothes he had bought, and which lay in readiness on their newly-delivered double bed. He told her there were some more clothes for her in the wardrobe, and if she needed anything else she only had to ask. Although he really did like looking at her without clothes on, he reckoned it was not the right thing to do. An invasion of her privacy. So, he left her in the bedroom by herself.

Jane seemed to take forever to get dressed, but Norman had heard that some women are like that. When she finally emerged to join him in the living room, Norman's eyes nearly popped out of his head. She was stunning! He gave three little claps to show his delight. What impressed him most was that she had also put on the necklace and the bracelet he had bought. She obviously liked his taste in jewellery. How well this was going.

As they sat together on the settee, Norman spoke to Jane, telling her all about herself: who her parents were, where she had gone to school and where she worked before they were married. All this had been carefully made up in case visitors, whom he could now expect to entertain, should ask. *What fun this will be,* he thought.

"Jane (*grunt*) would you care to make the tea now, dear?" Norman asked.

"Yes, Norman darling," she replied, getting up. He was glad he had programmed her to call him 'darling'. It sounded perfect. He also admired the high-heeled shoes he got for her as she tripped along into the kitchen. *Perfect again,* he thought. *Pink, like in the advert.*

Ten minutes later, Jane reappeared, and they had a nice cup of tea together. *How amazing,* mused Norman. *Just two weeks ago I could never have imagined myself sitting like this, having a cup of tea with a wife.*

Norman took to life with a wife as a duck takes to water. He remembered to grunt whenever he called for her or asked her to do something. She also answered him if he grunted accidentally, or for no real reason, so he learned to avoid grunting unless addressing Jane. They went shopping together. Jane loved shopping, but she had been programmed to ask permission from Norman if she wished to make a purchase of over one hundred pounds. She cooked nice meals, far better that he was used to, and they even had a game of scrabble. Norman did not enjoy that too much because Jane easily beat him. He put it at the back of his mind to see if there was some way of overriding the programme to make her not quite so good at scrabble.

His friends were astounded. "Norman, you are a dark horse," commented one. "We had no idea you were married. But no wonder you kept it a secret all this time. What a lovely woman she is. Perfect in every respect!" Norman was so pleased, and Jane was such a delightfully witty hostess.

They did ask him, on occasions, whether his throat was all right since he repeatedly made an odd grunting sound whenever he spoke to his wife. Norman's mother, now confined to a nursing home, was very puzzled about it all. "Oh, you must have just forgotten about Jane, Mother dear," he said to her. Before this, his mother really did not think she was demented, but now she began to wonder.

Norman especially liked to take Jane on little trips. It made him feel proud to go into a pub and say, "—And my wife would like a Martini please. On the rocks." He even wondered about giving Jane driving lessons because he was a particularly nervous driver. Now that he had a wife, so many new horizons were opening up.

There were a few hiccups, but these were not in the least serious. One morning, Norman asked for scrambled eggs. Jane seemed to be spending an inordinately long time preparing them. When Norman finally went down to check on things in the kitchen, he found a row of ten platefuls of scrambled eggs and Jane searching for more eggs to scramble.

"Jane (*grunt*) I think that's quite enough," he suggested, "and we seem to have run out of eggs anyway."

"Norman, darling, would you like more scrambled eggs?" was Jane's reply. Then on another occasion she left to go shopping on her own, wearing her panties on the top of her head like a hat with large holes in it. "Jane (*grunt*)," he said, "not on your head, dear."

Such occasions were rare. Mostly, Jane proved to be the perfect wife. The main problem was washing her. Norman was aware that Jane should not be fully immersed. At first, there was no difficulty about this. Jane would stand at the bathroom sink and give herself a good wash. The problem started when Norman fancied having Jane scrub his back whilst he was in the bath. He loved feeling her searching fingers massaging him. Jane appeared to enjoy this as well. Then one morning she removed her own clothes and attempted to climb into the bath with Norman.

"Jane (*grunt*) dear," he exclaimed in alarm, "you can't come in. Sorry, but that's how it is." Jane was clearly disappointed.

"But Norman," she said, "Nhpoomph (*grunted*) would love to join you in there. It looks such fun!"

"No, Jane (*grunt*), it's simply not possible."

Possible and impossible were not words that Jane understood. Several times, she repeated her attempt to climb into the bath with Norman and, more worryingly, Norman would sometimes catch her trying to run in a bath on her own. Norman stopped having baths and even hid the bath plug to make sure the bath could never be filled when he was at work. He thought that he had cracked it, but one day he found a wet bread-scone stuffed into the plug hole of the bath. Jane had obviously been seeking a plug substitute. Finally, Norman took to turning off the water mains before going out to work and leaving Jane enough water in jugs, and in the kettle, for her cooking, and to make herself some tea.

One day, Norman returned home to discover that Jane was missing. He phoned the police.

"What did you say her name was?" the woman at the other end of the phone asked.

"Well," he said, "Her real name is Jane, but she answers to..." and he grunted, "And you spell that N-H-P-O-O-M-P-H." There was a period of silence. Norman thought this understandable, so he repeated what he had just said.

"We'll let you know if we get any information, sir," she replied. She seemed to be in a hurry to put the phone down. Norman knew that the police were busy people.

He felt desperate. Jane had not taken any money with her, so she could not have gone far. He put on a jacket and left the house to search for his wife. He walked up and down the streets, but there was no sign of her. He knocked on neighbours' doors and made enquiries. Some were less than helpful when he said he was looking for a blonde woman with the name of—then grunt. Norman returned home devastated. He picked up the phone with the intention of calling friends who knew Jane. *Perhaps,* he thought, *she got in touch with one of them.* He even fantasised that she might be having an affair. Then he noticed that there was an answer-phone message. It instructed him to call the police station. Norman was relieved. He felt a tense excitement as he dialled the number, reassured that they had found Jane and that he would be reunited with his wife.

"Yes, sir," they said. "Someone found the body of a woman answering the description you gave us. It was face down in the duck pond in the park just down the road from you. I'm afraid they were too late to save her, but we would be very grateful if you could come to the hospital mortuary for identification purposes. There are also a few questions they would like to ask you. Seems there is something rather unusual about the matter."

Before going, with a heavy heart, to the mortuary, Norman took out the Flatpack Wife two-year warranty and examined it carefully. As he feared, damage due to total immersion in water was not covered.

The Old Man in the Park

That afternoon, the old man was sitting on the same park bench, all alone. The two children simply called him 'The Old Man'.

"I think he's lost," said the girl. "I think he went out and couldn't find his way back home so now he lives in the park. Like the rabbits and the blackbirds."

"Don't be silly," scoffed the boy. "Where would he get his food from?"

"Where do rabbits and blackbirds get their food from, then?" the girl pouted, offended at being called 'silly'.

"They're little," observed the boy. "So, they can eat anything. Even crumbs."

"Perhaps we should bring crumbs for the Old Man," suggested the girl, staring at the still figure on the bench.

"Tell you what. Let's ask him!"

The girl made an 'I'm-not-sure' sort of a face. "You do it!" she said at last.

"*You* brought it up," the boy pointed out. The girl frowned at her friend until a sparkle brightened her eyes.

"We'll ask him together. Let's—" She looked pensive. "Let's ask him where we could buy an ice cream. I've got some money. See!" she reached into her dress pocket and took out three small coins. "Might be enough."

"He may not like ice cream."

"Well, *I* think he does," pouted his little friend. She skipped on ahead and the boy followed, uncertain. The girl addressed the Old Man:

"Hello!" The boy came and stood by her side. The Old Man smiled at the children. The girl continued, for his smile made her feel brave: "Do you know where we could buy an ice cream near here?" she asked. Frowning again, she added: "You do like ice cream, don't you?"

The Old Man chuckled.

"Yes and no," he replied with a grin. The girl looked puzzled. The boy raised his eyebrows and released a sigh of exasperation. "Yes, I do like ice cream," the Old Man explained, "and no, I don't know of anywhere near here where you could buy one."

The girl seemed disappointed. The boy nudged her, meaningfully, but she ignored him. "Where, then?" she asked the Old Man.

"When I was your age we got our ice creams from the kiosk on the sea front, Cathy and me."

"There isn't a sea front here," the boy observed knowledgably. "We're fifty miles from the sea. My Dad told me."

"But we weren't far from the sea back then," said the Old Man. "We used to practically live on the beach, Cathy and me."

"Who's Cathy?" the girl asked. "My name's Cathy too."

"I know," said the Old Man. "And Cathy was my wife as well."

"Is she dead then?" the boy enquired.

"Yes!" The Old Man answered, nodding and staring ahead—at nothing. "There's only me now and not much of me at that!" He held out a skinny arm to emphasise the point. "You know, once I was the fastest runner in our school!"

"I can run fast," exclaimed the boy. "Look!" He shot off up the path, did an abrupt turn at the far end of the park and ran back.

"Always showing off!" complained Cathy.

"So was I," said the Old Man.

The boy returned, panting.

"As fast as that?" he asked, in between breaths.

"Just the same!" the Old Man chuckled.

"Was that as fast as a rabbit, do you think?" the boy asked.

"Faster!" insisted the Old Man, wearing a suitably serious expression.

"Do you eat rabbit food then, if there isn't anywhere near here where you can buy ice cream?"

"No," the Old Man laughed. "They don't give me rabbit food, though I might do better if they did."

"Who are *they*?" asked Cathy.

"The people in the old folks' home where I stay."

"So, you do have a home! You don't just live in the park then?"

"Yes, Cathy, there is a home for me, but I can't call it *my* own. There are many other old people there. Some are like me and can get out for a little while. Others just stay in their rooms all day."

"Yuk," exclaimed Cathy. "Imagine staying in your room all day!"

"Why don't you like the food in your home?" asked the boy.

"Well," replied the Old Man, "my Cathy, she was the best cook in the world."

"I like cooking," said Cathy. She turned to look at the boy. "Do you remember that chocolate cake you had the other day? *I* made it. Really, I did."

"You never!" said the boy in disbelief.

"I did so!" The girl pouted again.

"My name's Peter!" the boy proudly told the Old Man.

"I know," said the Old Man. "Mine too."

"Why did Cathy die?" the girl asked.

The Old Man said nothing at first. For a few moments he seemed lost in thought. Then he looked back at the girl and nodded.

"She couldn't grow old," he finally responded.

"That's not an answer!" observed the boy.

"It's an answer and it's a fact. She couldn't grow old."

"I don't think I ever want to be old," said Cathy, frowning again. "You go all wrinkly and your teeth fall out."

"Well," said the Old Man, "some grow old, and some don't. I did. Cathy didn't."

"I'm going to grow as old as the hills. No, even older. As old as the oldest person in the whole world!" said Peter, stretching his arms wide to demonstrate the size of the world.

"You look very sad!" remarked Cathy. "Do you miss *your* Cathy a lot?"

"Yes and no again!" replied the Old Man. "Yes, I miss Cathy very much. No, I'm no longer sad."

"Is it just because of the bad food at your home that you miss her?" the girl asked, as if needing reassurance that the other Cathy had been more than a provider of good food for the Old Man. He laughed.

"Not just the food," he admitted. "We loved each other. She was my soul mate and I like to believe I was hers."

"Well, *I* think you were," proclaimed the girl. "Did you still buy her ice creams when you were grown up?"

"Yes, always!" replied the Old Man.

"What's a soul mate?" asked Peter.

"Well," said the Old Man, "just imagine losing everything you have. *Absolutely* everything. Your clothes, your toys, your home—even your parents."

The boy's face strained as he tried to imagine losing all these things.

"*And* my Nintendo DS?"

"And your Nintendo DS."

"Ooph!"

"Now imagine all that," continued the Old Man, "*but* you have your soul mate. Do you know, you would still be happy!"

"Wow! Cool!" exclaimed the boy.

"Are you and your Cathy still soul mates?" asked the girl. "Even though she's dead?"

"Are you and Peter soul mates?"

The girl looked at Peter and bit her lower lip. "That's not an answer!" she said. "That's a question."

"Well," said the Old Man, "if I say 'yes' will you say 'yes'?"

The girl glanced again at the boy and he blushed. She stepped forward and whispered something in the Old Man's ear. She stepped back then peered anxiously at the boy. The Old Man merely nodded and smiled.

"We could bring you some ice cream from my home," the girl said, "but it might melt before we get here. Why don't you ask for ice cream at your old folks' home?"

"Yes," agreed the Old Man. "I should do that."

"We have to go now," the girl told him. "Will you be here tomorrow? And the next day?"

"Yes," answered the Old Man. "Every day until I'm as old as the hills and as old as the oldest person in the whole world!"

"We will see you again, then?" she asked.

"If they give me enough ice cream to keep me going!" chuckled the Old Man.

The children left the Old Man sitting on the park bench.

"What did you whisper to him?" the boy asked, turning to face the girl.

"I said, 'I'll say "yes" if you say "yes"'."

The children ran off together. Quite suddenly, the girl stopped and glanced over her shoulder at the park bench. The boy stopped too.

"Was there really an old man on that bench?" she asked. The boy turned around, briefly, to take a look. The bench was empty. He shrugged his shoulders.

"My dad's getting a new job by the sea-side," he said. "D'you think yours could get one there too seeing he's out of work? My dad might help him," he added. He suddenly grinned at the girl. "Quick, Cathy—race you back to your house for an ice cream."

*****

The Old Man felt himself slipping away. Beside his bed was a photo of his beloved Cathy, but he was too weak to turn over and look at it. When he opened his eyes for the last time, she was up there on the ceiling… running. Running, as she used to when they were children. He ran from the bed to ceiling, ran to catch up with her. Always, she liked to be ahead of him. Like dying first…

More Fish?

When the doorbell rang, Alicia quickly retreated into the kitchen. The fish, covered with aluminium foil and ready for baking, had to be put into the pre-heated oven. The vegetables, sliced and diced, were awaiting their terminal stir-fry, and the soup, warm in the saucepan on a low-burning gas-ring, needed additional thermal energy. Then there were the potatoes, the bread and all those other things to see to, but most of all Alicia worried about *herself*, her own appearance, for she knew she was mousy.

At least she thought she was mousy and that was enough. Enough to send her scuttling into the kitchen, where she smoothed down her skirt, patted out the creases in her low-cut blouse (Tayler had said nothing about the cut of her blouse) and brushed her hair again, several times, whilst attending to the soup, the potatoes, the fish, the bread and the vegetables. She glanced at the small mirror held in her left hand as she stirred the soup with her right hand. *More lipstick?* She reached for her lipstick. The soup smelled good, so, reminded, she dabbed a little perfume here—on her neck—and some more Eau de Cologne there—on her arms and cheeks. More eye shadow, perhaps? Then she heard voices. Tayler's and the guests'. Tayler called out:

"Our guests have arrived, darling. Come and meet John and Greta."

Strange how most of us have usually formed a mental image of someone we are about to see for the first time, then seem so surprised when the real person bears no resemblance to the mentally-imaged one. Alicia had heard so much about Tayler's old college chum, John Wrexford-Smith, recently returned from several years in the United States. She saw, in her mind, images of both John and his German wife, and *there*, in those hidden grey cells, John Wrexford-Smith was very dull and nerdy-looking, for what other appearance could he possibly have? After all he was a 'professor', though Alicia did learn later that almost every university-affiliated academic in America is labelled 'professor'. And Greta? A squarely-built German Hausfrau, for sure.

Alicia went through to the sitting-room, checking in the hallway mirror, en route, that she was at least a presentable mouse for such boring company, if mouse she had to be.

She heard the guests' voices in the hallway. *He*, John Wrexford-Smith, sounded very English. Very English and quite self-opinionated. *She*, Greta, sounded surprisingly American, with no trace of a German accent. Even more surprising was her entry into the sitting-room, for Greta turned out to be a page three clone with clothes on, but her clothes, a tight-fitting, nearly-transparent blouse, and a short, pale blue skirt displaying a visible panty line, seemed to reveal rather than hide the woman's gorgeous figure. Her long, blonde hair was beautifully styled, and Alicia immediately hated the woman who cat-walked across the carpet in dangerously high heels to greet her.

"Well, hi there, Alicia. I'm just so pleased to meet you," she said effusively, holding her timid hostess at arm's length before offering a heavily-scented and made-up cheek for an overtly-unwanted kiss. The very shape and size of the woman's bosom made Alicia feel inferior and sexless, and her see-through blouse left little for the imagination. The sort of figure that great painters and sculptors of nude females from the past might well have fought to the death over, though Alicia just thought 'page three!'

Then Tayler introduced her to his friend, John. How wrong her image of this man had been. She stepped forwards to shake his hand feeling acutely shy, for here was a man straight out of some Hollywood movie. A perfectly-proportioned heroes' hero with finely-chiselled features, a keen gaze that made all other men, including her husband, look like wimps, and a warmth in his smile that rubberized Alicia's knees.

"Alicia!" John exclaimed. His hostess's face turned red. "I do hope you've not gone to too much trouble for our sakes! Tayler's always said what a good cook you are, though."

A sideways glance in the direction of his page three wife informed Alicia that Greta was *not* a good cook.

"Well, honey, I just spend as little time as I can in the kitchen. You know that," announced Greta. The woman pouted in mock offence at her husband's insinuating expression, pushing her impossibly-voluptuous bosom out even further as if to imply that she had better things to offer this film star husband of hers than mere good cooking. "What *would* we do without that microwave, honey?" she added as she sat down in the arm-chair that Tayler had just offered her 39-24-38 figure, proudly showing off her curvaceous legs to above mid-thigh.

Alicia disliked the woman even more for those beautiful legs. Feeling flustered, and embarrassed by her blush, she awkwardly excused herself and returned to the safety of her kitchen, leaving Tayler to offer pre-dinner drinks and nibbles and enjoy the experience of Greta's company. Or rather, her legs.

So bloody unfair, thought Alicia. She looked down at her own cleavage and breasts. *Hers are three times the size! And those flipping legs! They stretch half-way across the sitting room. Obviously doesn't need to be a good cook with a body like that.* She gazed sorrowfully at the wonderful, glazed apple tart she had made for dessert, then smiled to herself. "I can *make* a tart, but she *is* a tart!" she muttered.

She immediately felt bad about being so antagonistic towards her female guest. As she stirred the soup, she realized her own feelings of inadequacy had nothing to do with this German-American page three Venus, although in the proximity of the 'film star' husband, the woman made her feel even mousier than mouse. What she had failed to appreciate was that this sense of inferiority was not really about her looks, or lack of them. It was to do with her husband. Tayler had never once paid her any meaningful compliment about her appearance, although she had always tried so hard to dress well and to use make-up pleasingly. He had failed to make her feel like a woman.

Also, having no job and no children, after four years of marriage, had sapped her self-confidence. She had never completed her teacher training, and when Tayler said that she had no need to go out to work, for his IT business was earning quite enough for both of them, she felt quite positive about being a 'lady of leisure' until they could start a family. In truth, her shyness meant that she was not really cut out to be a teacher.

But the children never came. After two years they sought advice from a doctor who said, 'wait another year'. They waited another year and went back to the doctor. Tests were run, and nothing abnormal showed up. 'Be patient', they were told, but they were still childless after a further year of being patient. Tayler was working harder and harder and became less and less interested in sex. Alicia, who began to feel she had been reduced to being just a 'good cook', even wondered whether there might be another woman, but her husband showed no signs of this being the case. Only permanent exhaustion from overwork.

Meanwhile, whilst they were awaiting an appointment to see an infertility specialist, Alicia, who now regretted that she had not completed her teacher training, spent most of the time feeling bored. All these things convinced her she was mousy and unattractive. *So unfair*, she thought, *that Greta should already have had two children and be a page three look-alike*. No, she did not really hate Greta. She was simply envious.

Alicia took the tray with the bowls of soup through to the dining-room.

"Ready when you are, darling," she said to Tayler.

To which John responded:

"Well, I'm certainly ready for your wife's wonderful cooking. And Tayler, you bad man, you never told me your wife was so beautiful!"

On hearing this, she nearly spilled one of the soup bowls over the table. She went an even deeper shade of crimson and had to scuttle back into the kitchen before they noticed. She fanned her face with a frying pan and looked once more into her small hand mirror. Her features were regular, even pretty. Her eyes were large, although often sad-looking. Her figure was neatly feminine. But she had only ever thought of herself as mousy. Even at her all-girls school there had been embryonic page three girls like Greta who had made the shy little Alicia feel very unattractive. *Beautiful?* Did that Hollywood heart-throb of a man mean what he said? Did he really think that? She looked again in the mirror. Thankfully, the blush was fading. She smiled. Perhaps she really was pretty. Could a mouse ever be pretty?

Alicia returned to the dining-room. The others were already seated, and there was a vacant space opposite John Wrexford-Smith. *Her* space. The man looked up from his soup.

"Tayler, please tell your gorgeous wife to sit down. I can't possibly enjoy a meal without a lovely woman to look at." He smiled again at Alicia and once more she felt her knees go weak. She sat down.

"This soup really is delicious, Alicia. I do wish my wife could cook like you!"

Alicia blushed for the third time.

"Carrot and coriander," she said quietly.

"It's lovely," John said. "Perfect! Like the cook!"

And the look he gave Alicia informed her he was enjoying more than the soup. He turned to his old friend.

"Tayler, I really had forgotten how beautiful English women are."

"And what about German women?" Greta interjected, pouting again.

"Darling, of course you're beautiful too," acquiesced John, winking at Tayler—but the banter was lost on Alicia's poor husband. He was now so shaped by boardroom politics that this sort of talk was like a foreign language to him. His wife, however, felt more than excited to be called 'beautiful' by the Hollywood hero opposite.

"Tayler told me that you were a trainee teacher but never finished. Is that right?"

John was addressing her. She felt flustered.

"Yes, well we got married, and—"

He smiled again. Thank goodness she was seated, otherwise her knees might have given way altogether.

"I understand. Even lecturing at university can take it out of you. Facing a mob of unruly and unwilling children who'd rather be anywhere other than a classroom must be pretty intimidating. Particularly when you're hardly allowed to say a single cross word without some damn parent lodging a formal complaint!"

The way John spoke put Alicia her ease. She started to open up, speaking freely about all manner of things, something totally outside her usual comfort zone. Tayler, meanwhile, was giving Page Three a dull dissertation about his IT business and the pitfalls of the computer industry. Page Three's boredom showed in her eyes. They now resembled those of a dead codfish.

Alicia got up to clear away the empty soup bowls, placing these on a tray. She did this as slowly as possible, for she was aware of John looking at her and she enjoyed being looked at by a man. A *real* man! John stood and gallantly opened the door for her. She smiled as sweetly as she could. Alone in the kitchen, she was still smiling. She smiled as she took the fish out of the oven and removed the foil from the top of the dish. She smiled as she put the potatoes and the vegetables into separate bowls and then she adjusted her neckline so that more of her cleavage showed. She was still smiling when she brought all the dishes through into the dining-room.

They were discussing Greta's job. Page Three had been the fashion editor for a New York journal. Half-an-hour earlier that very fact would have depressed Alicia, but when John looked at her again, as a man looks at a woman, she felt curiously buoyant and not the least bit depressed. Tayler served the wine as Alicia started to dish out helpings of fish onto her guests' plates, watched all the while by the

Hollywood should-be. She asked both guests to serve themselves to potatoes and vegetables whilst she put fish onto her husband's, then her plate.

"Do start, please," she said, eyeing Mr Hollywood. "Physics, Tayler told me. Your subject at university. He says you're a professor of physics. Sounds so high-powered!"

Alicia sipped from her wine glass feeling bold and buoyant.

"Well, sort of physics, but more engineering really. And 'professor'? Not *really*. Back here I'd be but a humble senior lecturer!"

"Too bloody humble," Page Three echoed caustically. "And do you know, I earn more than he does?"

John frowned.

"I do what I love to do, darling," he protested.

"Oh, you always do that all right!" continued Page Three, picking at the fish.

"This is simply delicious, Alicia," said John ignoring his wife to compliment his hostess. "Just wonderful. We have fish so rarely and I absolutely love it." He turned to his wife. "See, I don't always get what I love, do I?"

"Well, dear," said Page Three, "you can get all those microwaveable meals here in England, so there's nothing to stop you just filling up on fish all the time."

As alcohol began to mix and flow with the blood in everyone's veins, the conversation became even less inhibited and the crossfire between John and Page Three increasingly aggressive. Alicia noted that it was always Greta who seemed to be on the attack, although John's quick wit usually got the better of her. Tayler merely got duller and duller as the evening wore on, whilst John looked and acted increasingly like a Hollywood heart-throb. His frequent glances at Alicia across the table, together with the wine, began to make her feel not only attractive but like a much sought-after movie heroine.

John addressed his old chum who seemed to have difficulty in constructing sentences that had nothing to do with computers:

"I hope you don't mind me asking, but what does your lovely wife do with herself all day on her own?"

Alicia blushed for the fourth time.

"Oh, she finds plenty to do, don't you darling?" Tayler replied, glancing at his wife. Alicia raised her eyebrows but said nothing. She raised her eyebrows for John. John smiled back. Alicia felt happy. Happy and, for once, completely confident in herself, for she knew exactly why her husband's old friend had asked that question.

"Just that. On my own. All day long," Alicia affirmed. But there was no sadness in her voice. It was a statement of fact. For John's ears.

"Well, *I've* already found work with one of your English magazines," Greta boasted. "Have to get enough money somehow to pay for the children's nursery care. John's getting paid even less over here than he was in San Francisco."

John shot his wife a disapproving look. He knew how upset his friend had been about not having a child, and they had agreed beforehand that neither of them would talk about the children. There was a short, though embarrassing, period of silence. Then Alicia noticed that John had finished his fish. She stood up and reached back for the fish dish standing on a hotplate on the sideboard.

John noticed how appealing her youthful breasts were when she turned sideways with her back arched. She quickly leaned forwards with the dish, for it was hotter than she expected, and placed it on the mat between them. Everything about this pretty woman fascinated John. She was so feminine, so unlike Greta. Greta was beautiful, voluptuously so, but her total preoccupation with her own beauty and her appearance gave her a harshness that somehow accentuated the soft attractiveness of the modest young woman across the table. How fed up he had become with Greta and how he now yearned for a woman like Alicia. And how was it that his old friend just did not appear to realize his young wife was so lovely? As Alicia reached forward, with the heavy dish in her hands, John could not help noticing her cleavage and the soft whiteness of her breasts part-exposed by her loose blouse dropping forwards.

So soft, so white, he thought to himself. *Perhaps—oh, just maybe—?*

"More fish?" Alicia asked, picking up the serving spoon.

"So soft, so white," John said dreamily, still staring straight ahead at his hostess's cleavage.

"Cod, actually," Alicia said, grinning. "Would you like some more?" Her eyes met John's when he looked up.

"Oh, yes please!" replied John. "It's, erm, so soft—and white—and, erm, lovely. Simply lovely. Yes please."

He offered up his plate for more fish.

"No thank you," said Greta without being asked, blocking access to her plate with an over-manicured hand.

More fish. More wine. Then dessert. An exquisite, glazed apple tart. *What a wonderful meal it's been,* thought John, his head swimming. *But Alicia! God, what a woman! A real woman. You lucky bastard, Tayler!*

"What a lucky man you are to have a wife like Alicia," he said. "What a *very* lucky man!" What he *almost* said, with all that wine on board, was 'and please, *please* let me take her to bed!'

Alicia looked across at him; a shy, fairy-tale princess peering at her prince as he circled, on verbal horseback, the castle in which a fairy tale ogre had imprisoned her. God, the wine had gone to both their heads! Alicia floated like a magnificent rainbow-coloured bubble in an alcohol-scented cloud whereas John's addled brain went into testosterone-driven free-fall:

Delightful, charming and lovely. And alone all day every day! Bloody disgrace! But that look that she gave me. No doubt about it. None whatsoever! It's gotta happen!

"Well I think the evening went really well," said Tayler when the guests had finally left. "John loved your cooking. And Greta—she's quite a looker, isn't she?"

"Is she?" queried Alicia. Her own thoughts were elsewhere.

A year later, Tayler e-mailed his old friend, John Wrexford-Smith, to let him know the wonderful news. John and Greta were now separated and in the throes of a divorce. John had custody of the children and had returned to the United States, having been appointed to a prestigious post in Boston. Tayler told his old friend about John, their son, now four months old. He apologized for not e-mailing sooner, but he and Alicia were so busy with the baby they had barely a moment to spare. He said he hoped the other man did not mind that they had chosen the name 'John', but Alicia apparently thought he looked like a 'John' when the little fellow was born. Tayler told his friend that he had never been so happy in all his life. Before dispatching the e-mail, Tayler added: *P.S. Alicia sends her love.*

Alicia had only ever really known one John before her son was born: John Wrexford-Smith, with whom the baby shared striking blue eyes and blond hair.

The Christmas Dance

'Come and Enjoy our Christmas Dance!' beckoned the poster in the waiting area. *'Help to raise money for a new cancer scanner.'*

Enjoy? No joy there, the thin man thought. *My last Christmas ever and I can't dance. A musician who can't dance. How bloody silly!*

"This way, Mr Howard. Dr Stanley won't be long." The nurse showed him to a chair.

"Like a naughty boy waiting to see the headteacher, huh?"

The nurse forced a weak smile. "The doctor's just having a look through your case file. He'll call you in when he's ready." She scurried off leaving Kenny Howard sitting on the chair. As staff and other patients passed by, he felt like an exhibit of rapidly-diminishing bodily substance for the world to gawp at. Of course, he already knew. From the girl's expression. She would have seen his case file where it would be written down for eyes that understood such things. He reckoned he could always tell what eyes had seen and read from the look in them. Eyes never lie. This was why she had disappeared in such a hurry.

She doesn't want to be the one to tell me I'm dying.

It was his niece, Denise, who had insisted he should see the doctor.

"You're ridiculously thin. A skeleton! You've gotta do something about it!" she demanded when she came around one evening.

"It's nothing, sweetheart. Been so busy. Recital tours back to back. Then that flipping orchestra lost their lead violin, and—well I couldn't refuse, could I?"

"Dad!" He'd looked after Denise since she was six, when both her parents had been killed in a car crash. He was not merely her surrogate 'Dad', he was her *only* close relative. Strange how history repeats itself, for he had also played 'father' to his younger sister when their widowed mother died. It seemed so natural at the time to do the same for his sister's daughter.

"What?" Kenny always became evasive over matters of his health, but Denise's concern troubled him.

"You don't turn into a skeleton by being busy!" she insisted.

"Okay! You win. I'll see a quack. I promise. Cross my heart I will." Denise usually won in the end.

He had never married, what with his work and a bright and ambitious child in tow. Now twenty-two, Denise, the only woman in his life, and an able musician herself, kept an ever-watchful eye over the uncle she so adored. She did try to persuade him to get himself a partner who could look after him when she went on to college, but she did not win that one. He had excuses. The girl knew the real reason, of course. At least she thought she did. Behind a jokey exterior he was impossibly shy.

But something was revealed at the inquest that Kenny had never told his little niece, and it haunted him for the rest of his life. How could he ever forgive himself for insisting his sister tell her husband the truth about her affair when she came to him, tearful, after it had ended? Of course, he had never expected her to tell his brother-in-law whilst the man was driving their car that very same day, but still he blamed himself. It turned out that Denise's father found out there and then. A friend had called Denise's mum, whose phone was linked to the car, and she asked whether *'she'd told him'*. "Told me what?" the father was overheard asking when it was played back at the coroner's inquest. From the shock of hearing his wife's answer he must have lost control of the vehicle. Death was inevitable for both parents after hitting a tree at sixty miles an hour.

Kenny blamed lust, as well as himself, and he swore that he would never allow this most vile of human attributes to fracture the child's life again. He avoided close relationships with women and he never danced. Only in his dreams would he allow himself such carnal pleasures: closeness to a woman and dancing.

Now it's all too late, he realized after seeing the poster about the Christmas Dance in aid of a new scanner for the hospital.

"Mr Howard?"

"Howard'ya like to be *me* just now? Ha-ha!" The stocky doctor standing in the doorway frowned rather than smiled. "Or should I have said, I haven't seen him for a while, that Mr Howard! Trying to avoid mirrors 'cause he's getting too thin to see, right?" Kenny explained, chuckling.

"Would you like to come in?"

You stupid bugger, Kenny! Don't take it out on the poor doc, he thought as he followed the man into the consulting room. *He's only doing his job!*

Kenny sat and watched the other man flick through his case file.

"Wouldn't fancy your job!" he said. The doctor ignored the remark.

"Did your general practitioner tell you the result of the scan, Mr Howard?"

"Kenny, please. I prefer Kenny. No, he's a one-way revolving door, my GP. Stuff goes in, but nothing comes out. Ha-ha!"

"Well, there are things here we'll need to talk about—after I've—erm—"

"It's okay. I'm not driving home." Another puzzled look appeared on the exhausted doctor's face. "I won't crash my car if you tell me the truth!"

"Shadows," the doctor said. "There are shadows on your scan."

Over the following month, Kenny lived with those shadows. The shadows got larger and he got smaller, for these were the shadows of death. The biopsy told them. Cancer. As Christmas drew closer, he became weaker, and as he became weaker he felt the welling up of yet more guilt.

He had always been too over-protective with Denise. Having failed her mother, he had wanted to make sure the same thing never happened to the girl he now thought off as his daughter. Denise hardly ever went out, had no steady boyfriends, and she certainly did not know how to dance. Yet another musician unable to dance. Ridiculous! He had to make amends, however late in the day.

"I *insist* you go to that Christmas Dance, Denise. The one I saw advertised at the hospital. They're raising money for a new scanner."

"Couldn't possibly do that, Dad," she said.

"A dying man's wish?"

"Dad! Please don't!" Tears filled the girl's eyes.

"Tell you what, Tulip." He had called her 'Tulip' after, as a child, she said 'two lips' instead of 'tulips'. "You're worried about me being on my own, now. Right? So, I've the perfect solution. We'll have a little Christmas treat. A weekend together at the five-star hotel where they're holding the dance. We'll be in the same place, and I can go to bed early, and you, my girl, will go to that dance and stun all those young men with your beauty!"

"But Dad, I can't dance!"

"I gave in to you over the doc thing, Tulip, so I'm afraid you're gonna have to back down on this one." Kenny winked at his niece. "Please?" he added.

He needed a wheelchair from the taxi to the hotel room which he never left. Denise brought him up food on a tray. He thanked her but had not the heart to tell her he would be unable to take even one mouthful.

"Get along with you to the dance," he urged. "Don't deny those young men your love and your looks! And Denise—"

"Dad?"

"I'm sorry I never insisted before. About you going to dances and stuff."

"You will be all right, won't you?"

"I won't be if you don't go now, Tulip!"

Denise kissed him on the forehead and squeezed his hand.

"Phone down to reception if you need anything!" she said.

Kenny nodded and smiled. *She is so beautiful*, he told himself as she left the room, *and beautiful people can always dance.*

Tired and drained, Kenny drifted off to sleep. He awoke with a start when someone shook his arm. He expected it to be Denise checking on him, seeing whether he was still alive. Instead it was a hotel porter.

"She's waiting for you," the man said. Kenny rubbed his eyes. The man was still there. Not just an apparition.

"Who?" he asked. "What are you talking about?"

"Can't keep a lady waiting!" the porter said. "Follow me."

Kenny had never kept a lady waiting. Never been in a position to. Slowly, he eased his stork legs to the ground. He thought he would fall over, but he did not. His legs felt strong and supported him as he followed the man out of the room, along the dark corridor, into the lift and down to the ground floor. It was bright in the hotel lobby, and he had to shade his eyes. The porter disappeared along another corridor, and Kenny ran to catch up.

Ran?

I can't run, he thought. *I'm dying from cancer. You don't run when you're dying from cancer.*

But he was running.

The corridor was even brighter than the lobby, and on turning the corner, round which he had seen the porter disappear, he became dazzled by the intensity of light. The porter was there in the doorway of a ballroom, and beside him was a young woman with long, blonde hair. It was difficult to make out her clothes since she was silhouetted against the brightness beyond, but he could tell from her figure she was stunning. Strangely, he felt young again. Not just a breathing corpse.

"She's waiting for you to take her to the dance, sir," the hotel porter said.

"But I can't dance," Kenny insisted, staring at the hour-glass figure of the young woman ahead.

"They all say that."

"Besides, I'm only wearing—" Kenny aborted his sentence on looking down at himself. Instead of pyjamas, he was in a dinner jacket with a white shirt and bow tie, and in place of bedroom slippers he had on a pair of shiny, black dance shoes.

The woman stepped forwards and offered her hand. He saw her face. A true Fra Angelico angel. At first, he seemed uncertain whether he should kiss her hand, shake or hold it. He did all three and, holding hands, they walked on into the brilliance of the dance hall.

The band was already playing old-fashioned dance music. Kenny was pleased about this, for, whether he could dance or not, it meant he could hold the woman close and feel her body up against his. There *was* something odd, however: no other couples. None that he could see, although the light was so blinding he had to squint at the face of the woman to take in her lovely features.

Although Kenny had never 'had' a woman—not in the sense expected of a man—he had always felt there was something mystical about feminine beauty. It had been an unreachable landscape in his life, but as this mysterious woman pulled him towards her, entwined her slender arms with his, he felt something he had never before allowed himself to feel because of his young niece:

Passion!

Whether or not Kenny could dance, he danced. His feet moved with hers and soon they were swept along by the rhythm of the music. Quickstep, foxtrot, tango—these all happened in that dance hall as he twirled the woman, feeling the swish of her dress against his legs, the flick of her long hair across his check, and—oh, how wonderful it was— the soft touch of her lips against his.

They spoke not a word for there was no need for words. Speech was there in those deep blue eyes and in the warmth of her smile. And as they swung and stepped to the music, and as the music grew fainter and the light became brighter, Kenny Howard knew this was to be his last and only dance. A dance with the Angel of Death.

*****

Denise loved the Christmas Dance. She was discovered by a kind, shy, young doctor who laughed when she said she had no idea where her feet should go. She, too, laughed, and they talked, and they danced anyhow, and they kissed and he asked her where she'd been all his life up until then, and she said she'd been waiting—waiting to meet up with him—and they danced again, and kissed and later, when the dance was over, they made love in her room, for she knew this was the man... the man for whom she had been waiting so long.

"I have to check on Dad," Denise said, after disentangling herself from a passionate embrace. She donned her dressing-gown and slippers and went and knocked on the door of her uncle's room. Silence. She knocked again. More silence. She had the other key in her hand, and, trembling, she entered the room and switched on the light.

She did not scream. Besides, she was half-expecting what she saw: her uncle dead in bed. She was saddened, though. At first, she felt guilt for the pleasure she had had with the man whom she knew she would always love, until she got close to the bed.

Her uncle's eyes were open and staring and very dead, but his face was happy. It bore a smile such as she had never seen before on him. With tears streaming, she closed his eyes. Leaving the smile at peace, she stepped backwards towards the door, turned and went for help.

The Letter

"Clamp, nurse!"

The surgeon's gloved right hand shot forward whilst its owner peered down at the bruised, pink brain framed by bloodied green drapes.

"Goddamnit! I'm not operating on a bloody horse! Smaller!" More irritable of late, since finding out, he dabbed at the brain with a gauze swab. The doe-eyed scrub-nurse retrieved the wrong clamp, replacing it with a smaller one.

"Hmmph!" grunted the surgeon, glancing up at the girl. Turning away from his gaze, she wondered how a man, normally so gentle and considerate, could turn into such an ogre whilst operating.

The surgeon stared at the injured brain. It was far worse than the scan had led him to believe. Had he known the true extent of the damage he would never have operated. Having got this far, he felt obliged to attempt evacuation of the clot and removal of the damaged tissue. He looked at the anaesthetist whose nod told him to get on with it.

*****

The man glanced at his watch. He could not understand why time hadn't changed since boarding the train. He held the watch to his ear. It still ticked.

I must get to a phone, the man thought. *Tell Jean I'll be late. That I've been delayed.*

He had left the car behind. It had stalled and would not start up again. He had tried calling the AA, then Jean, but his mobile phone didn't work. The man encountered a similar problem with the station telephone. He decided to try again when the train arrived. Then he would explain everything. Jean could pick him up from the station. He felt quite reassured.

*****

"This is bad, bad, bad!" muttered the surgeon, wiping away the blood to get a better view.

"Pressure's dropping, Jim" warned the anaesthetist.

"What?" grumped the surgeon.

"Blood pressure, Jim. It's falling. Just thought—"

"Okay, okay! Won't be in here much longer!"

*****

The man stared from the train window at the haze outside.

How strange, he thought, as fields, trees and solitary buildings slowly appeared out of the mist, gathered speed then flashed past never to be seen again. Everything he looked at seemed uniquely significant until gone. Then, in an instant, it became nothing. The man shivered as he wondered whether his own life could ever be like that. Like those approaching trees, so uniquely special, would *he*, one day, be gone forever in a flash? He looked again at his watch. Unchanged but ticking.

The thickening mist troubled the man. How would Jean be able to drive to the station in it? The trees and the farm buildings were barely visible. He began to wonder whether he only imagined their fuzzy outlines. Was he merely looking at swirls of fog? What really began to alarm the man, though, was the change in the rhythmic sound of the wheels on the track and in the jerking and the juddering of the train...

*****

A sudden gush of blood caused the scrub nurse to gasp.

"My God!" exclaimed the surgeon. "Another clamp, nurse. Quick!" A clamp slapped into his open palm whilst a hand reached across to mop the beads of sweat peppering his brow.

"Doesn't look good, Jim," said the anaesthetist as he twiddled and fiddled with the knobs on his machine.

"Bloody awful!" snapped the surgeon, struggling to control the bleeding.

"Married, I understand," the anaesthetist continued. "Two children. A businessman."

"Hmm—what?"

"He's a businessman. Says so in his case notes."

"Was!" emphasised the surgeon. "Won't be doing much business with this brain, I can tell you!"

262

An alarm sounded. The anaesthetist looked up at the monitor.

*****

The man reached into his jacket pocket and pulled out the letter that had puzzled him so much. How it got there, he had no idea and, although he understood the individual words, he could make no real sense of what these said.

"I must ask Jean," he murmured, stuffing the letter back into his pocket. It seemed to involve her.

He looked again out of the window. The reason why everything appeared so strange hit him like a punch in the stomach. Through the mist he saw only water and waves.

The man stood up. The carriage, which had previously appeared half full, was empty. The rhythmic sound of the train wheels had been replaced by the drone of an engine. He had to hold on to the edge of his seat to remain upright, for the carriage was now pitching and rolling in an extraordinary fashion. His eyes searched, in panic, for some explanation. There was only one: he was on the lounge deck of a boat. Overcome with terror, he made his way to a stairway at the far end of the lounge.

"This can't be! I'm on a train. I need to get home. And Jean? How can she meet me now?"

Clinging to the banister, he pulled himself up the steps to emerge onto the open deck of a large ferryboat.

"No, no, no! This is all wrong!" he yelled. "Where's the train gone?"

He looked around for someone to question but there was no one.

The boat leaned abruptly to one side, causing the man to take a series of small running steps until he fell against the railing which he grabbed and held on to. The water was grey-green and appeared almost alive as large wave humps slunk towards the side of the ferry where they merged with an arc of foaming surf that trailed from her bow. The waves kept on coming out of the mist. There seemed to be no end to them as they journeyed homewards from an invisible horizon.

For the first time, the man felt fear. How come he was on a ferryboat when he had boarded a train? Who could give him answers? Using the rail, he pulled himself along as the boat tilted first to one side, pulling him down, down, down, then, in the swell, up, up, up.

Crew! A cabin, another deck, somewhere? I must find a crew member. I must—

He stopped short with a sudden jolt.

*****

"Cardiac arrest!" called the operating theatre technician assisting the anaesthetist. The surgeon stood back, allowing the flurry of activity to continue, a blood-soaked swab covering the brain on which he had been working.

"Adrenaline!" then "stand back!"

*****

"My God! What the—?" gasped the man, clutching at the breast of his jacket inside which was concealed the letter. It felt as though he had been kicked by a horse.

A plaintive shriek called out from the mist. Feeling very unwell, he looked up. His eyes struggled to focus but were able to make out two—no *three*—seagulls appearing out of and disappearing back into the mist. Red spots daubed their beaks.

"Blood!" he whispered.

The gulls soared, hovered and swooped, their graceful movements in perfect harmony with the constant motion of the grey water. They were so incredibly beautiful and in some strange way supremely significant, like the trees seen from the window of the train that had approached like ghosts out of the mist. The white surf as well. That had to be important too, he thought, before being swallowed by the dark water and, as with the trees, vanishing forever. The emptiness left behind seemed so total, so meaningless.

One of the gulls cried out again and the man saw that it was looking at him. Then he knew why. It was his beautiful daughter. No doubt about it. He shouted to her, but the wind blew his words back at him. Then all three gulls cried out.

So sad. And so far away.

"Jean!" the man shouted. "I'm on my way home but the car wouldn't start, and the phone wasn't working. Please meet me... please... *please... please...*"

*****

"Cardiac arrest again! Asystole!"

The anaesthetist looked at the surgeon. The surgeon looked at the scrub-nurse then at the theatre sister. He glanced at the bloody swab covering the small square window in the green drapery. The blood had congealed. He shook his head.

"There's nothing more we can do for this man," he sighed. "Call it a day."

"I agree, Jim," replied the anaesthetist. Together, they stared at the monitor as it displayed the last electrical flickers of a folding life.

Before leaving the operating theatre, a nurse told the surgeon that the nurse in resuscitation wanted him to phone her back.

"Yes?" he asked tersely over the phone. Failure always weighed him down.

"We found a letter in his jacket," the nurse replied. "Difficult to understand but it seems his wife might have been having an affair."

"You mean—?"

"May not have been an accident."

"So... he wouldn't have thanked me."

As the surgeon sat in the changing room, his moistening eyes fixed on his booted feet to avoid the stares of others. No one must know the real reason for his tears: the anonymous letter he had received about his young wife and his colleague. Was this a premonition?

The Shop Window

Ever been to Hasselt in Belgium? If you have, you will know why it is sometimes called the fashion capital of Flanders, for in the main street almost every other shop is a designer clothes shop or a stylish shoe shop. Quite extraordinary for such a small city. And early in the morning, in those empty streets, you would be perfectly justified to wonder how the shopkeepers make a living with so much competition. But wander around the pedestrianized area in the afternoon, and you soon realize how they do. The streets teem with fashionable, shoe-conscious men and women of all ages.

It was on one such afternoon that Pieter Thywissen wandered down Demer Straat and into a shoe shop so posh that there were only two shoes in the window. To the right, a stiletto-heeled, pastel pink lady's shoe with an elegantly-pointed toe, carefully placed just in front of a small leather bag of precisely the same colour. To the left was a man's shoe. Lime green, with white stripes. It stood alone, and together these three items, none of which bore any indication of price, defined a space in the centre. It was mid-spring, and this space had been used for a small display heralding the season: a few sprays of artificial pink blossom and a square of artificial pale green grass on which had been placed an open picnic hamper with a bottle of champagne and two tall champagne glasses, both empty.

There were many more shoes arranged neatly along shelves inside the shop, but Pieter Thywissen had no interest in these. It was the shop window that had caught his eye, and that is where he was heading for. No one seemed to pay him any attention as he stepped over the stiletto-heeled pink shoe into an area behind the artificial blossoms and the picnic hamper with its champagne. No one appeared to see him as he set up his easel, upon which he rested a large oil painting. The shop assistants remained oblivious of the smaller paintings and drawings that Pieter Thywissen had spread out on the floor in front of the picnic hamper and the shoes. He had also brought with him a small stool and placed this beside the easel. He sat on the stool and looked out at the people looking in, hoping, desperately hoping, that someone—just one person, maybe—might notice his painting. Not only notice it but actually *look* at it. Pieter Thywissen was an artist. That is all he was... now.

The painting on the easel was more than mere communication of beauty from one person to another. It was a baring of his soul, and, as he sat and looked back at those gazing shoppers, he wondered whether there was anyone amongst them who would wish to see into the soul of another. He thought of all those great Flemish masters. They had done it. They had bared their souls, and, long after they had died, people came to see their soul-paintings— even paid money to gaze at works by those grand masters of the past. Now, at last, Pieter Thywissen, hitherto unknown in this world, had his own space, his own gallery. Surely someone would care to look at his soul. And for free.

Many came to the shop window and looked at the pink shoes and pink bag and the ridiculous green and white stripy shoes, and some of them laughed. Not at him, but at the shoes. They appeared not to see him or his paintings. But he continued to hope. He sat there, looked out at the street and he hoped and he waited.

The painting depicted a woman, a man, a child and a dog, and for Pieter it somehow mirrored his soul so perfectly. It was his best ever work. Of course, his soul also mirrored the souls of people he had known—people, just like those who stood and stared at those garish shoes. Surely they would see their own feelings reflected in his work? he thought, as he sat and waited. And if this were to happen, they would want to tell others, and they, too, would come to the shop window to look at his soul and see their inner feelings mirrored there. People would come not only from Hasselt, but from all over Belgium. From other countries in Europe, and from America and Japan. They would come not to see the pink shoe and the green shoe with white stripes. They would come to see the work of Pieter Thywissen.

Meanwhile, he sat and he waited and people came and stood and looked. At the shoes. Some entered the shop and browsed the shelves full of other fashionable shoes, some shook their heads, grinning, and walked on to the clothes shop next door. Those that did not headed in the opposite direction for the chocolate shop on the other side of the shoe shop.

Days passed, and Pieter Thywissen was still there, sitting in the shop window beside the easel bearing his large oil painting. Hundreds—no, thousands—of shoppers must have stopped and peered into the shop window and looked, but had any of them seen his soul? Had any even noticed his painting? He was patient, though, for time was on his side. It imposed no restriction on him as he sat, and he watched, and he waited whilst shoppers peered at the shoes and the bag and nothing else, and the glamorous shop assistants went about their business taking no notice whatsoever of the man sitting in their shop window.

One day he left. Of course, he could have remained there for all eternity staring back at the staring shoppers, but for the sake of his bared soul he could take no more of it, and he left. He left behind his painting, his soul, for it no longer seemed important. He stood up, stepped over the pink stiletto shoe and the hamper and the bottle of champagne, and he left the shop straight through the window and through the staring, visionless people. He continued down Demer Straat, passing through others on the way, and on towards the old cemetery where he shrank back into nothing, beneath a crumbling grey tombstone. And he never knew about the little girl.

"Mummy!" cried a little girl as her elegant young mother stared at the pink stiletto shoe in the shop window. "Look at that girl in the picture, Mummy. She looks like me! But why is she dressed funny? And why is she looking at me like that?"

The girl's mother was far too absorbed with her own inner *should I or shouldn't I?* debate to hear what her small daughter was saying.

"I think Mummy should get her shoes here, darling," the woman said to the girl.

"Mummy, can we get a dog like the one in the picture? Please?"

"Come on, sweetheart. I'll try them on. I won't be long."

"The dog, Mummy? Are you going to buy the dog in the picture? I love it!"

"No dog dear. Mummy just wants to try on those shoes. Look, there's a chair inside. You can sit and read your book."

"But Mummy, I only want to look at the picture. I want to look at the little girl and the dog. She really *is* me!"

Her mother was not listening, and, reluctantly, the child stopped looking at the painting and followed her mother into the shoe shop, but she never did forget the image of the young girl with her parents and a dog in that shop window... and in a world that she had once inhabited.

Whatever Happened to Harry Plant?

"Remember poor Harry?"

"Harry Plant?"

"Yeah! Buddy Boy, we used to call him!"

"Do I remember? Livened up the worst years of my life, taking the piss out of Buddy Boy. Whatever happened to him, I wonder? Harry Plant, eh! What a name!"

"And what an arsehole! Got himself into one of these, I guess!"

John, an actor so famous that he was a household name, patted the soft, purple, cuboid poof upon which he was squatting. Danny, his old school chum whom he had not seen for over twenty years, looked puzzled.

"Furniture design?"

John collapsed into laughter. When recovered, he reached across and slapped the other man on the back.

"Can see why you're a lowly insurance salesman, Danny. Like to put my feet up on him when watching the telly!"

Him?

A tall blonde, still as shapely as when she was a teenage temptress, fixed her diamond-hard gaze on John.

"So, what makes you so certain Harry was gay, huh?" she asked.

"Do us a favour, Sally! Harry Plant? As queer as a three-pound-note! Hey, Danny—d'you still remember the Harry Plant chant?"

The two men, locked together in a recall of malice, recited in unison:

"Harry Plant, Harry Plant
Loves to wank when told 'you shan't!'
Yes, I can! Oh no, you can't,
Or we'll go and tell your flipping aunt!"

And like a couple of oversized schoolboys, they giggled themselves helpless. The woman cut into their mirth with a

tongue curiously sharpened since her classroom dumb-
blonde pin-up days.

"You never answered my question!" she snapped.

"Oh, come off it! Harry Plant? Didn't need poof proof
with Buddy Boy!"

"How come? Did you sleep with him, then?"

Before John could answer, Sally vanished into the Class
of '95 Reunion gathering, her muttered "arsehole!" of
disgust drowned by the ear-destroying blare of 80s Glam
Metal music.

"Not such a great idea perhaps, this get together!"
suggested Danny. "Wasn't it Sally's anyway?" John nodded.
"And at your place? Why?"

"Sally again. She's the one who hunted down the
rabble—then twisted my arm to hold it here. One of the
penalties of being famous, ay? The only bastard with a place
big enough, I guess."

"What's *she* do with herself these days? Sally? Bit past
it for modelling—though mind you, I wouldn't mind a bit
of—you know—with her! Would have to soften her up first
with a few G&Ts, I guess!"

Two quite different men sniggered about a shared past.

"Buggered if I care what she does with herself!" said
John. "But what *do* you think became of Buddy Boy?" he
asked after a pause.

"Harry? A professor, of course! What else? Always top
in bloody everything. Probably stuck in a lab somewhere
like an experimental rat working his arse off. Expect they
wheel him out for the odd university function or two, then
wheel him back and let him get on with his miserable little
life."

"Professor? No! No people skills. Students would skin
him alive. What about banking—or—" John's eyes lit up.
"Got it! Not furniture design, but fashion stuff. Like that
bloke on the telly."

"The one with the earrings, a neat little butt and an
'ain't I cute' haircut?" offered Danny. "Into cooking too, that
bloke is."

"Can't you just see Buddy Boy poncing around with big, dangly earrings? Perfectly safe with those scantily-dressed dolly birds, ay?"

Danny shook his head.

"No, I can't. Can't imagine him anywhere near a girl. Too much of a nerd. But Sally standing up for him? That's a bit much! She used to do the Harry Plant chant better than any of us! Had a good voice too, did Sally!"

"Pure bloody guilt! Oh, let's forget Harry! There's someone I want you to meet again. The only one of us I kept in touch with till today. Conky!"

"Conky Tim? You're joking, mate! Weren't he and Sally—?"

"He and Sally no longer, the fortunate bugger."

"But—didn't he—you know—?"

"Do time? Sure. But he's reformed. Sort of."

"And *she* contacted him?"

"Nope! I did. Told her, of course."

"To which she said—?"

"'Delighted!' E-mailed, at least. The bloody hypocrite! Come along. Don't be scared. Conky doesn't bite. Not in public, anyway. Bit more subtle than he used to be."

John stood up and Danny followed him to the other end of the spacious room.

"You know, I did look him up on Facebook," announced John as he searched half-familiar faces for Conky Tim.

"Conky?"

"No! Harry Plant!"

"And?"

"Nothing!"

"Should've tried Bum-book!"

"Hmmm!" grunted John as Danny chuckled at his own humour. Even at school his jokes always fell flat.

"What about Google?"

"Tried it. Only horticultural stuff. Hey—Conky! Remember Danny here?"

John tapped the shoulder of a tubby forty-something with a horseshoe of creamed-down black hair and a high gloss pate. The man turned, and Danny's heart did a somersault as his eyes met the eyes of Conky Tim O'Hara.

They were as evil now as they were when a long-haired Conky ran a high school protection racket that made the Kray brothers look like a couple of amateurs and had boys trembling in their trainers. Neither Danny, nor John, ever let on how much they used to pay into Conky's 'benevolence fund'. The only boy who refused to cough up was Harry Plant, for which he got beaten to a pulp one evening after school. And Sally was the only girl in their year brave enough to sleep with Conky—or so Tim O'Hara claimed.

"Of course, Danny my boy! Good to see you again. Don't look a day older!"

"Same for you, C—C—erm—Tim—"

Conky held out his hand whilst Danny wondered how he should now address the one-time scourge of his school.

"Still the same old Conky, if you please."

Damn you, thought Danny grimacing as the other man's vice-like grip squeezed the blood from his hand.

"So, erm, what are you doing with yourself these days, Conky?"

Conky and John exchanged a 'shall-we-tell-him?' look whilst Danny played with the empty beer glass in his hand.

Stupid bloody question. He's bound to have a gun in his back pocket.

"Helps people with stress," offered John who had noticed his one-time friend glance at Conky's tightening fist with recalled respect. Danny, awaiting further explanation that never came, fidgeted nervously.

"So kind of you to invite me, John," announced Conky. "Great opportunity for re-establishing old contacts, ay, Danny boy?"

Danny nodded.

"We're all set up, Conky," replied John. "Huge house like this? No bother! None at all. Call it the old boys' network' if you like."

Conky squinted at John.

"I don't do favours, pal. You should know that by now!"

"Remember Harry Plant, Conky?" asked Danny, trying to alter the course of the conversation. "What a wanker, ay? Whatever happened to him, John and I were just wondering!"

"Last guy who asked me that got fished out of the river." Danny stopped fidgeting. Conky slapped his thigh with amusement and gave Danny a 'playful' punch in the side. Danny held his breath against the pain of its 'playfulness'. "Always were too serious, Danny. But you weren't like Harry, I'll give you that!"

"Married," said Danny quickly. "Erm—with three kids."

"You need relaxing then. All that stress! What do you do apart from the daddying stuff? Shelving at Tesco's?" Danny laughed. At least he remembered to laugh at Conky's humour.

"Insurance salesman," he replied.

"There you go, then! Said to myself as soon as I saw you again—'Conky,' I said, 'here's a man you *can* do a favour for. Just look at him. Worn down by overwork.'"

"Not too bad, really. Just a bit—" Conky was right. It had been bloody awful since the recession. No one had money to waste on insurance.

"Usual room, John?" interrupted Conky, ignoring Danny's attempt at protestation.

Soon, Danny found himself being led by John along a corridor to join a line of men, some recognizable, most not, leading up to a bedroom door.

"Counselling," whispered John. "It's what Conky does now and he's fantastic. Helped me no end. Most of us top actors are into it!"

"Are you also married, John?" asked Danny. The décor and wall paintings—even the purple poof (*particularly* the purple poof)—had a bachelor feel about them. The door obviously opened into a bedroom. But he never got an answer because Conky appeared and John froze.

"See you later, Danny. And stress-free, ay?" his one-time friend added before disappearing beyond the door with Conky.

Danny was left standing stupidly in line. He asked the others, "Whatever happened to Harry Plant?" but was answered only by a row of silent stares. Danny shrugged his shoulders and waited his turn. Was this a joke? Nope! Conky never did jokes unless they involved stuffing other kids' heads into recently used, unflushed toilets.

Slowly, the line got shorter as every few minutes someone would exit the room and the next in line would disappear into it. Those about to enter appeared to fumble in their pockets. Those leaving that room seemed to fumble with their minds. Danny, his own mind filled with Conky-tinged memories, did not dare to question any of this.

It happened when he was at the very head of the line. A loud bang, followed by the sound of breaking glass, mingled with screams. Three black-helmeted police officers appeared at the far end of the corridor. With automatic weapons raised, wearing bullet-proof jackets, they ran towards Danny and the two others still in line. The first officer kicked open the bedroom door then shouted:

"Police! Freeze!"

Another officer handcuffed Danny and his old classmates, but before he got yanked away he caught a glimpse of the bedroom through the open doorway. Conky was at the window, having decided at the last moment against diving through the glass onto the ground twenty feet below. His accomplice, and the fellow who had been ahead of him in line, were seated on the bed in front of a small table. On the table were a candle, a spoon and a polythene bag full of white powder.

They all met up again at the police station. Sally was there as well, the only one not handcuffed.

"Good one, Sally," congratulated one of the armed officers. "Pulled it off again, ay?"

"Sally? With the police? Bloody hell!" swore John.

"DS Plant to you!" corrected the officer on overhearing him.

"What? Sally *Plant*? As in Harry?"

Sally came up close to John. *Very* close. Never before, thought Danny, had she looked so beautiful.

"I'll tell you what happened to Harry Plant. I married him. And in a few minutes, you can see him yourself. As my boss, DI Harry Plant. We've been planning this sting for months. Tell you the truth, we didn't think it would be this easy. But your kind, you're just so bloody predictable, aren't you?"

Danny glanced sideways at John.

"Your kind? What's she mean, John?"

"Oh John, you bad boy! Forgot to tell your old friend, did you?"

She left Danny staring open-mouthed at his old school friend. At the door, she turned around and called out in a voice meant for all to hear:

"John and Conky are an item, Danny. Always have been!"

The Last Ski Station

Two thousand and sixty-four. The year of the monkey. *Always a bad year, the year of the monkey*, thought Jake, as he sat in the Everest ski station canteen. Using his chopsticks, he glumly prodded the limp vegetables floating on the surface of the bowl of soup noodles that they had given him in exchange for a lunch voucher. He was not feeling particularly hungry. He pushed an unappetizing-looking lump of cabbage below the surface of the lukewarm fluid. *If it floats back up, things will get better in the year of the cockerel after next month,* he conjectured. *If it sinks, they'll go from bad to worse.*

It sank.

His daughter had died from bone cancer the previous year. The doctors blamed her cancer on persisting radioactivity in the soil from the fall-out after India lobbed nuclear war-heads at China, all those years back, when India's huge neighbour to the east strengthened her hold on the 'liberated territories'. They said it would last for centuries. Australia had already become a dying continent, due to the unexpectedly rapid acceleration in global warming, when he was a child in Melbourne. Jake and his wife were amongst the last Australians to be 'repatriated' during the evacuations. Later, he found out that the refugee camp in the beautiful mountainous region of Yunan province in China, where Janine was born, was one of the most radioactive areas in the country. There were other things that Jake had learned from those illicit books he obtained with such difficulty and with so much danger: that China had already wiped out New Delhi, Calcutta and Mumbai with nuclear strikes before India struck back, unsuccessfully, and that Europe and North America, economically crippled after China took control of the oil flow in the Middle East, had been forced to relinquish their independence and accept the sovereignty of the Chinese World Authority—the CWA. The United States of America, as a part of North America used to be called, had never truly recovered from the massive tsunami that obliterated its large eastern seaboard population in the late twenties. Like all of Africa, and much of Asia, the southern part of North America had become uninhabitable. Those books also spoke of isolated pockets resistance to the CWA in the Rockies, in New England and in the Appalachians. Small communities of folk, as hard as the ground they worked, who would dispatch unwelcome intruders in the blink of an eye. No such communities existed in an Asia subjected to rule by the Grand Alliance after the Great Sino-Indian War.

Officially an alliance between China, Japan, Korea and India, the 'Grand Alliance' had really been a front for the Chinese Peoples' Party to gain world dominance. After this happened, the party conveniently renamed itself the CWA. It was difficult for Jake to believe, as illicit books informed him, that Europe and North America had once been more advanced than China.

Jake worried about his wife's health. Linda had been profoundly depressed since the Janine's death, but she had to continue to work. Depression was not on the list of illnesses for which treatment might be sought. Any absence from work through depression would result in 're-education'. This meant that the offending individual got sent thousands of miles to one of the CWA re-education camps, usually never to be seen again. More commonly, the depressed person would commit suicide, an action favoured, almost encouraged, by the CWA. Since everything tangible belonged to the CWA, all personal items were then returned to the authorities after death. Such people were quickly forgotten by the world. Jake could not bear the thought of this happening to his beloved Linda.

He also worried about the effect that continuing climate change might have on both his and Linda's jobs at the Everest Ski Centre. He had worked for fifteen years in ski stations and now held a highly sought-after position as chief engineer at one of the last two remaining stations. He had heard from a reliable source that the Mount McKinlay

Ski Centre was under threat of closure due to poor snow conditions over three successive winters. The high altitude of the Everest Ski Centre would ensure good conditions for a few years yet, but the chief engineer at Mount McKinlay was a Han Chinese. Jake knew that there was a high probability this man could displace him if Mount McKinlay were to close down for good.

The CWA had been quick to counter fears of continued environmental collapse by broadcasting figures that showed how effective their measures to reduce hydrocarbon and other harmful emissions had been, and how the ozone layer was returning, but experts knew this was far from the truth. The Earth was slowly turning into a fireball and Jake feared that soon the Everest Ski Centre would be the last and only place on the planet where high-ranking Chinese officials could continue to enjoy their favourite pastime: skiing. If either Jake or Linda were to lose their jobs at Everest, their futures would be entirely in the hands of the faceless CWA. Without a doubt, they would become separated with little chance of ever seeing each other again. Only CWA officials, their friends or family, were permitted to travel for distances greater than a hundred kilometres. If separated, Jake and Linda might find themselves at opposite sides of the globe. The only thing in Jake's favour was his ability. He was exceptionally good at his job. Better than anyone else. There had been accidents due to equipment failure at Mount McKinlay, but never at Everest, despite the complicated operating system and, at times, unreliable electricity supply. The authorities knew this was because of Jake's competence. Even a Han Chinese replacement could lose not only his privileges but also his life should anything untoward happen to the President, or to a member of his family, whilst skiing at the Everest Ski Centre. The President and his family had only ever skied at Everest, and Jake knew that the authorities would take no risks when the President's life was at stake. This was why he held onto his position.

Jake was trying to cheer himself up by thinking positively when he was joined in the canteen by a bright young ethnic European called Dave. Dave, who only spoke Mandarin, had come from China a month back and he was a conscientious worker. However, although eminently sensible with work-related matters, when it came to his personal life Dave was less than sensible. In contrast to Jake's measured caution when dealing with the Chinese authorities, Dave's bravado seemed reckless. Particularly where women were concerned. His background had perhaps allowed him a dangerous level of self-confidence. He had been orphaned at the age of three following an explosion in an industrial plant in Hubei province where his parents worked with many other Europeans. The orphanage consisted almost entirely of Han Chinese children and Mandarin was the only language that Dave knew.

"So, it's the big day today!" said Dave, pulling a chair up beside Jake. "President Leung and his daughter coming to the Everest Centre for three days." He nudged the older man with his elbow. "They say his daughter is a real dish! I'm so fed up with all those sharp-nosed foreign girls who work here! Can't wait to see a bit of real female beauty!"

Although Dave's nose was every bit as sharp as those 'foreign girls' noses', he saw himself as different from other Europeans. Jake, however, knew that the Chinese officials still regarded Dave as a second-class citizen, despite his fluent Mandarin, but he had great difficulty in getting this across to Dave. And he did not want to see the younger man come to harm through some miscalculated remark or stupid indiscretion.

"Dave, don't even think of *looking* at the President's daughter, let alone trying to strike up any kind of relationship with her," warned Jake, turning to face his colleague. "Are you completely mad?"

"Oh, you are a miserable old sod at times! Those Han women just love us men of European descent." He paused a moment, then added, "But then *you* wouldn't know, would you? Faithful to that Australian wife of yours. I can tell you, when it comes to a bit of 'you know what' they'd choose us lot any time! Han men don't stand a chance in that field!" Dave started to twirl his soup noodles with his chopsticks. "Of course, you have that funny accent, too," he continued through mouthfuls of noodles and cabbage. "Could turn them off! See, I can really woo those Han Chinese girls. Mandarin is such a wonderful language. We have this thing called poetry and the girls love it, you know. Really turns them on. Nothing like that in the English language, is there?"

The older man knew otherwise from books, but he remained silent. He had learned to be careful about sharing his knowledge with others. Now that Janine was dead, Linda was the only person with whom he could discuss such things.

"Just think, Dave!" Jake cautioned. "The President's daughter, for God's sake—his own bloody daughter! She could be the most beautiful woman in the world for all I care, but to make only a glance in her direction could be suicide. And it doesn't matter whether you're Han Chinese, Indian or European. Plus be careful with what you say, too. Even I have no idea who the informers are here. Could be one of those sharp-nosed European women serving in the canteen for all I know. One way for us non-Chinese to get privileges. Why, just the other day an English guy shopped a Han fellow for borrowing a pair of skis for his friend without a permission slip. The guy got off lightly, mind you. Only ten years of re-education. But no one would have suspected that Englishman. Be sensible, Dave!"

Jake raised his soup bowl to his mouth and slurped the remaining noodles and chunks of cabbage. He had tried his best. He had warned his brash young colleague, he reassured himself as he left the canteen to continue with the preparations for the President's visit.

The President and his daughter would arrive by cable car at two o'clock. All systems were suspended whilst every working part of the machinery was checked and rechecked.

This took the whole morning under Jake's personal supervision. Yes, he was particularly good at his job. Nothing slipped past him unnoticed. He reassured himself that a Han Chinese chief engineer would really have to prove his worth before they would dare to replace him. If the Everest Ski Centre were to close during a Presidential visit, then the lives of the Han officials in charge would no longer be worth living. They owed him a lot, Jake reckoned as he made a final check on the dials, the meters, the cables and the computer settings. Everything appeared to be in order and he phoned down to the base station. The cable jerked and came alive. The President and his daughter were on their way up.

Jake, Dave, and a few other important workers, had joined the end of the line of Chinese officials who stood to attention at the top station when the President and his daughter stepped out of the cable car helped by two female attendants. Jake kept his head respectfully bowed all the time. As he stared at his own shoes, he was aware of the shiny shoes of important people walking past just in front of him. He had no idea which of these belonged to the President, to his daughter, or to the numerous officials and attendants. He did not care, either. He simply remained dutifully stooped and still until the Presidential entourage was safely inside the building, taking President Leung and his daughter to the Presidential suite. Then Jake could disappear into the control room and stay there for three days until the end of the President's visit. On these occasions he trusted no one else. He even slept in the control room, although he did venture out to the canteen for meals.

Jake was cold, and exhausted, when he returned to the canteen that evening. The outside temperature had dropped to minus fifteen, and much of the energy required for heating had been diverted to the Presidential Suite, even during the day whilst President Leung and his daughter were out enjoying themselves on the ski slopes. He had already seen Dave earlier on when the young engineer had paid him a brief visit in the control room. Dave had only come to brag about the President's daughter.

"The stupid bugger," muttered Jake, as he sat down with his tray on which had been placed a bowl of barely-warm rice and a small dish of cooked vegetable stalks and fatty pork. That afternoon, Dave had shoved his face over Jake's shoulder whilst the older man was scanning his monitor screen, and had whispered smugly into his ear:

"What a lovely girl! Oh, what a beauty! You should have seen the smile she gave me, too. You just wait, Jake! I'll put that smile to good use, ay?"

Jake had not even bothered to acknowledge Dave's presence at the time. Now, as he looked around the canteen and failed to see Dave, he became worried. Despite the young buck's annoying conceit, he was not a bad man, and he was a good worker. Jake could rely on him. Turning, he tapped the shoulder of one of Dave's colleagues seated behind him.

"Dave?" Jake asked. "Where is he this evening? Not like him to be this late. Held up perhaps? No problem with the lift mechanism, I hope?"

The other man looked around furtively, leaned backwards and whispered in English.

"Gone. Reported to the Peoples' Police." The man immediately resumed eating.

Jake heard no more about Dave. There was no communication from the officials, no correspondence. The following day Dave's name no longer showed in the computer files. It was as though the man had never existed.

In less than a week Dave's replacement appeared. Han Chinese, transferred from the Mount McKinlay Ski Centre...

Whispers of Death

"It's happened again, hasn't it?"

Gertie sat forwards in her armchair, her C-shaped spine turning her body into a human question mark, forcing her face to stare at the floral-patterned dress hiding her swollen, arthritic knees. She half-turned her head sideways, as far as her neck would allow, and fixed a bloodshot eye on the smiling face of John, the nursing home care assistant.

"Don't fret yourself," he said before helping the old lady out of the chair and over to the Zimmer frame. "Mashed potatoes, mashed peas and mince for lunch," he added whilst supporting her with a helping hand as she prepared to set off for the door that led to the dining room. Her slipper-shod feet, with holes cut out for bunions, slid slowly forwards like a wind-up child's toy in need of a rewind.

"You don't believe me, do you? About the walls? I tell you, I hear them all the time. Whispering things." She stopped. "They tell me when it happens. Can't keep any secrets from the walls. They never lie, these walls."

"You love mince and mash, Gertie. I know you do."

The old lady grunted her frustration before continuing her determined, soft shuffle towards the door.

"It happened again this morning. The whispers told me," she muttered.

John smiled down at her. "And jelly and ice cream," he said.

"Pff!" exclaimed Gertie. "One day you'll hear them yourself, I'm telling you. Then you'll understand—but it'll be too late!"

"And custard. Bird's Eye. You'll feel so much better after lunch, Gertie."

Gertie's feet halted, rooted firmly to the floor. "*Too* late! Can't you see that? When you hear the whispers it's already too late." She pushed her walking frame forwards a few inches before easing her frail body into the safe space it enclosed.

"We'll be late for lunch, Gertie. They're all waiting for you."

John's gentle hand guided the old lady through the door and on into the dining room.

"No, they're not," she snapped, tilting her head up in an attempt to take in more than just the floor around her feet. "There's one missing!"

Eight old people sat around three old tables, eating in slow motion. There were four empty chairs. John held on to Gertie's arm as she lowered herself from her walking frame into one of these.

"Where's Hermione?" she asked sharply, blinking at the empty chair beside her.

"Don't worry yourself, Gertie. I'll get your lunch for you. The mince is particularly tasty, ay Mr Jackson?"

"Like shit!" The old man sprayed out globs of white, green and brown from a mouthful of food as he spoke.

"She's dead, and you're not telling me. But the walls know, so you can't hide it from me. They whispered it. But where do you people—?" But John had already left the dining room, still smiling.

"Tastes like shit, I promise you," repeated old Mr Jackson, decorating Gertie's place setting with yet more bits of his meal from his overfull mouth.

"Have *you* seen Hermione today?" Gertie asked the watery-eyed Reverend Cooper seated next to Mr Jackson. The old cleric had one eye trained on Gertie whilst the other peered vacantly at the untouched food on his plate.

"No point in asking the reverend here," said Mr Jackson, scooping up another forkful of mash and mince. "Can't remember a thing from one minute to the next. Doesn't know who he is or where he is."

"Thought he might have an answer. Being a vicar. She's dead. I know she is. Those whispers are never wrong. Remember Mrs. Fairley last week? The whispers were right about her."

John returned with a steaming plate displaying a patchwork mound of mud-brown, pea-green and off-white.

"Where do they go when they die?" asked Gertie. "Where do you people put them all?"

"Eat up, reverend," John said, ignoring Gertie's interrogation and looking at the frozen figure across the table who still eyed his plate and Gertie at the same time. "Food's getting cold."

"There's no point in trying to find out from him. Or the reverend," Mr Jackson chipped in. "Can't tell the difference between beef bourguignon and horse shit, that one."

The Reverend Cooper pawed at his fork, as though half-remembering something hidden somewhere in his brain.

"You'll like it," encouraged John.

"Like hell he will!" mumbled Mr Jackson through another mouthful.

The cleric picked up the fork and stabbed it into the mash. "Watch him," the other old man said as he scraped up the last remaining particles of food from his own plate. "Just plays with it. Hasn't a clue why it's there."

"Let me help you," offered John, abandoning Gertie to attend to the reverend.

"You don't care, do you? None of you cares what happens when our place goes empty," she complained.

Old Gertie felt cross. One by one they were all disappearing, and no one talked about it, no one listened to her. It was as if it wasn't happening, but the walls knew. They whispered to her. About death. But those whispers of death gave no answers to her questions.

That night, in bed, Gertie heard them again. No words. No voices. Only whispers. She knew they came from the walls, for that's all there was in her room. The walls were bare. No photos, no pictures and no treasures from her past to remind her of a life that once was. Just walls, and when they whispered to her it was like wind gusting through the trees, cutting across telephone lines, whirling into chimney pots, but without the sound. They were soundless whispers. They spoke only of death and of dying, telling her whenever one of them was to be swept aside by Father Time who waited, patiently, for the next in line. She wanted to speak about these things, but the walls had no answers to her questions, gave no soothing for her fears. The walls could not weep. And the others, John, Mr Jackson and poor old Reverend Cooper, they *would not* weep—or even listen to her.

Old Gertie closed her mind on death and slept.

"Bloody scrambled egg again!" complained Mr Jackson as he began to tuck into his breakfast the following day.

"And baked beans," added John. "Cook says there's nothing healthier than baked beans!"

"There's always horse shit," grumbled Mr Jackson, a baked bean stuck to his food-smeared lower lip that moved up and down as he spoke. "That's healthier than *these* baked beans."

"Let me get you started, Reverend," said John kindly, lifting an egg-laden fork to the old cleric's quivering mouth.

"Oh, just scrape *his* crap onto *my* plate," suggested Mr Jackson. "Can't go wasting the stuff."

After John left the dining room, Mr Jackson reached sideways and helped himself to what remained on the Reverend Cooper's plate. Then the two old men sat in silence. There was no one else at their table.

The Fiftieth Audi

A droplet of sweat trickled from Timmy's right temple and came to a halt on his grimy cheek. He swept the back of his hand across his wet brow then rubbed at the teasing droplet, working in the dirt and the grit. His other hand gripped the warm handle of the pick.

The road drill started upon again, hammering at his senses. It was another sweltering day, and he was thankful he was not doing road drill. His hands went tingly whenever he used the drill and the heat would make the tingling a thousand times worse. The unbearable would become—well, a thousand times worse than unbearable. What word, Timmy wondered, might describe this?

"Alf!" With the steel-jawed foreman facing the other way, his mate Alf was also taking a momentary break. "Alf, why the heck are we digging this ruddy hole?"

"Not a hole, Timmy. A bloody trench!"

"Hole, trench! All the same to me. What are we digging it for? Seemed a perfectly good road five days ago when we came here. Before we began chopping it up."

"Buggered if I know or care, Timmy," replied Alf, leaning on his shovel. "If they pay me to dig, that's okay by me!"

"Yeah, but what's the bloody point? Just digging a trench for the sake of it?"

"Point is, mate, you're working for Damien Black Road Maintenance and if they got the contract to dig a ruddy trench here you bloody well dig it."

Alf lifted his shovel and stabbed it into the rubble at his feet. Timmy, still leaning on his pick, stared intently at the passing cars streaming along the single traffic lane.

"There goes number twenty-three," he said.

Alf looked up.

"Twenty-three bloody what?" he asked his mate.

The steel-faced foremen swivelled round and stared at Timmy who quickly grabbed his pick and swung it into the dark grey ground.

"Audi," Timmy muttered under his breath. "Twenty-third flipping Audi just went past. I've been counting 'em. That's the twenty-third one gone past since we began digging this bleeding trench five days ago." Timmy paused again as Alf continued to shovel away. "And you know what, Alf? When I get to fifty, I'm calling it a day. Fifty, and I'm jacking it in. Downing my tools and leaving this shit hole!"

"It's a trench, Timmy. Not a hole! I keep telling you."

"Walk free and buy one of those Audis for myself. That's what I'll do when I've counted fifty."

Alf looked up.

"You've lost it, mate!"

"Got it all worked out, Alf," the other man continued before smashing his pick into a slab of tarmac broken off by the road drill. "Second hand one. Pre-used, as they say in the States. Good deals in the local rag, Alf. Seen 'em under classifieds. Then—" Timmy took another determined swing with the pick whilst Alf shovelled. "Then I'll bleeding-well be offski. I'll wave to you as I drive past in my Audi. And you know what else, Alf?"

"What?" Exasperated, Alf wiped sweat from his own brow. The heat was getting to him as well. "Tell me!"

"I'm gonna go beyond the traffic light, Alf. To where I won't have to ask any more questions. That's where I'll be going. Beyond that bleeding traffic light!"

"It's the sun, Timmy. Must be melting your bloody brain."

"What else is there, Alf? More digging? Another hole—trench—whatever? I'll be free of it!"

That day, when the temperature touched thirty-five Celcius, and when the sweat had soaked through Timmy's vest and had stained his shirt, he counted a further six Audis. The following day was another scorcher. Timmy thanked God again that he was not on road drill. It was not just the bone shake and the tingling that Timmy hated. It was the drill that had started the senseless carving up of a perfectly good road. It was the drill that attacked and split the unblemished tarmac, sending clouds of dust into the stifling air that hung over the sun-seared road. And it was the noise of the drill that drove the men mad. That day, as he cursed the road drill, he counted a further eight Audis. The next, when a light breeze cooled the men's faces and the sun came and went, there were ten more. Three to go—

On the morning of the eighth day of digging, Timmy felt almost happy, despite the rain. The rain was as bad as the sun. Sweltering heat had been replaced by a penetrating damp, and asphyxiating dust by the cloying squelch of mud. After working for two hours in the drenching rain, Timmy and some others complained to the foreman.

"We can't work in this," they said.

"You bloody will!" the foremen snarled. "Got a trench to dig here. You'll get it dug, like it or not. Even if it's pissing down cat puke and dog shit!"

Timmy and Alfie sploshed and dug and shovelled in the mud under the unforgiving gaze of the foreman. That afternoon, like others who had complained that day, Timmy was doing road drill. *But,* he told himself, *what do I care?* He had just counted the forty-ninth Audi as it glided majestically past.

Only one more!

Just as Timmy slammed into the tarmac with the drill, another car came into view. Another Audi.

"That's it," Timmy called out, laying the drill on its side. "The fiftieth Audi just went past. Packing it in. That's me offski now!"

Under the cattle-herd stares of his bewildered workmates, Timmy left the trench and walked down the road for a mile to the small village where he caught a bus home. All the time, he thought about that Audi advertised in the local paper. 'R' registration. M.O.T. tested. £597. Back home, he dialled the number and bought the car.

Only twenty-five quid left in the bank, but what the hell? he thought afterwards. After all, he had an Audi, so no more senseless holes—trenches—whatever!

The following morning, Timmy drove his Audi along the very same road. He slowed as he approached the 'Road Works Ahead' sign, then halted at the end of a line of cars in front of the traffic light. Although this was red, nothing came from the opposite direction. *How odd!*

It had not occurred to Timmy, whilst working away with his pick, shovel and road drill, that the unidirectional flow of traffic was weird. All those fifty Audis had been going in the same direction as he was, now. But Timmy's thoughts were with his newly-found freedom and the feel of the Audi's response to the turn of the steering-wheel and the pressure of his foot on the accelerator.

The light turned green. The Audi yielded to the will of its new master. He was now its foreman and it moved forwards at his command.

With a cracked exhaust pipe, the car sounded like a racing Maserati. Timmy liked this. It made him feel important, and Alfie and the others would hear the noise, turn and look up. Then he, the proud owner of an Audi, could wave like a general in a Jeep whilst driving past.

Alfie and his mates looked up. He waved, but they did nothing. It was not supposed to be like that. They should have at least saluted him. He felt let down. Their envy would have been his triumph over the futility of it all. Engrossed with the annoyance of this, he ignored another team of workmen filling in and re-tarmacking the same trench further along the road.

Disappointment was still gnawing at his brain when, just around a bend, his right foot slammed the brake. An eye-to-foot reflex had by-passed his consciousness, but when the nerve cells kicked in a fraction of a second later he was aware of a police car parked diagonally across the road. Its blue light flashed. Timmy was still gripping the steering wheel as a burly police officer sauntered towards him. The man lent on his forearms across the car roof and peered down at Timmy.

"This your vehicle, sir?"

Sir? No one bloody calls me 'sir'. "Yes, officer," Timmy replied with pride. A large open hand appeared through the car window. It smelt of the law.

"Vehicle registration and test certificate, please." Tommy's own hand, shaking, fumbled in the dash-board and pulled out the registration document and the M.O.T. certificate. He placed these in the hand of the law.

"Licence?" The hand reappeared, empty, as though it had swallowed up the other documents and was hungry for more.

Timmy reached into his pocket and pulled out his wallet from which he extracted a frayed driving license. The officer examined all documents thoroughly and handed them back before making two menacing circuits of the Audi, stopping to inspect the tyres and lights. He returned to his original position beside the driver's window.

"That way, please, sir!"

With a wave of his hand he indicated a narrow track leading away from the road.

"But where the f—?" began Timmy, checking himself before the rest of the 'f' word could escape. "I've not done any—"

"Over there, please," insisted the officer: "Follow the track. An Audi with a registration number starting with a letter between M and W, and that's where you have to go. Sir!"

"Why?" Somehow Timmy found the courage to ask. Things were not going according to plan. He had been forced to ask "why?" He had left the road-works to escape from the 'why?' Why dig a trench in a perfectly good road? And now this!

"No why about it, sir. Audis with those registration numbers have no authorization to continue along this road."

Timmy was sorely tempted to say 'f--- you!' to the police officer and drive on, but, he was a law-abiding citizen. Instead he shrugged his shoulders, started up the engine, and steered the Audi off the road and along the dirt track.

The rain had stopped, but the sky was still heavy with cloud as the car bumped and shook its way over the loose gravel. He caught up with a 'P' registration blue Audi at the tail end of a convoy of Audis. They slowed to a crawl before coming to a standstill. Beyond this was a large, lifeless, grey building—a sort of giant warehouse. Every few minutes the blue vehicle in front of Timmy's edged forwards, car length by car length. Gradually, his Audi edged closer to the grey building. If it had not been for a large notice with red lettering on a white board, Timmy would have got out of his car and tried to find out what it was all about, but the notice was clear:

All Drivers Are Forbidden to Leave Their Vehicles.

Only two more vehicles ahead of him! Perhaps, Timmy wondered, there was some sort of mechanical fault with Audis bearing those registration numbers? If so, maybe they were offering a free service inside the grey building. He knew how amazing Audis were, even second-hand ones. So here he was, in line, and about to get his car fixed for free.

Not bad, huh?

Ten minutes later his Audi was at the head of the queue. He decided to tell them what great cars Audis are. A bit of flattery and they might give him a free car radio too.

The mechanical steel doors clanked open. A speaker to the side of the door commanded him:

"Move forward, please!"

Timmy slipped the Audi into gear and eased it through the open doorway. He found himself in a large dimly-lit shed. The door snapped shut behind his car and his smile vanished. Just ten metres ahead, a huge circular magnet had swung down and attached itself to a large cube of crushed blue metal. Flattened wheels that stuck out at right angles informed Timmy's brain that this had once been a car: a blue Audi. The vehicle in front of his? A steel cable tautened, and what remained of the compressed car was lifted into the air. It hovered, motionless, for a second or two before swinging sideways where it was dropped like industrial dung onto a heap of similarly crushed car cubes.

Timmy became aware of four walls and a ceiling moving inwards. He tried to open the car door, but nothing happened. It was jammed. He tried to climb out through the car window, but the space was too small.

"What the—?" he screamed.

As the metal tomb encasing him groaned and cracked from the relentless pressure of incoming walls, and as the car roof pressed down onto his shrinking brain, Timmy desperately tried to make sense of it all until the 'why' was squeezed out his brain. He never got to read the bold inscription on the giant magnet:

'DAMIEN BLACK RECYCLING'

The shell cracked open. Dazed, he crawled out onto the sweet-smelling grass. A woman peered down at him.

"Mother?"

"You should have been like the others, Timmy. Accepted without asking why."

"But you always told me to ask."

"To question your motives, son. Not the same. You'll have to go back, I'm afraid. Try again."

"Wh—?" He checked himself. "So, you think I just wanted to be better than them?"

Without answering, his mother turned and walked away.

Cissy

"It's all right," said Steven. "She's going to be a princess now."

Steven's mother was kneeling beside her son. Next to him was the dead cat, cast aside in the gutter, its head split open by the impact of the car. They had heard the screech of rubber on tarmac as the car braked. When they arrived at the scene, blood and pink stuff was oozing from Cissy's broken head. Her limbs were twitching but the jerks slowed until she finally lay still. Steven stroked her battered body. Steven's mother rested her arm across the boy's shoulders. She knew how much Steven loved his cat.

Steven and Cissy were the same age. Cissy, the kitten, came to join the family two months after Steven was born. A friend's cat had had a litter of three kittens, then just eight weeks old, for which the friend was desperate to find new homes before she moved house. At first Steven's parents were hesitant, but on seeing Cissy they made up their minds. She was smoky grey with black ears and beautiful orange-brown eyes. Very unusual, they thought, although it was not so much her appearance as her gentle nature that endeared her to them. Cissy stood apart from the rough and tumble play of the other kittens, padding her tiny paws on the carpet and looking shyly up at Steven's parents with inquisitive eyes. They fell in love with her.

"Yes, Steven. She *can* be a princess now," said Steven's mother, giving the little boy a hug. She was proud of her son for taking it so well, knowing how he had doted on Cissy. The cat would follow Steven everywhere, like a little shadow. Steven's mother remembered how upset he had been when he was told that Cissy was not allowed to sleep on his bed because of his asthma, and how they reached a compromise by buying a wicker basket, with a cushion, which was placed beside Steven's bed just for Cissy. Whenever they went out as a family, they always had to wait for young Steven to check on Cissy before they were allowed to go. Now Cissy was dead, killed by a car, and Steven appeared to be totally calm about it all. She liked the idea of Cissy turning into a princess, though. This would be his childish, fairytale way of coping, she thought, and she went along with it.

Cissy remained in a cardboard box overnight. The following morning was a Saturday. Steven's father would be at home all day, and after breakfast he suggested to Steven that they dig a hole in the garden for Cissy. In this way she could have a proper burial, he told the boy.

"No, Daddy," said Steven. "We have to cremate Cissy."

Steven's father was more than a little worried about this, not least because of the smell the burning cat flesh might emit and the concern that this could spark off amongst their neighbours. He spoke with Steven's mother who thought it would be no worse than the smell of a barbecue, and that if this were Steven's wish it might help him with his grief. She did, however, express surprise that Steven was taking it so well.

"It's strange, but it's almost as though Steven was happy that Cissy died yesterday," she said. "Sometimes I simply don't understand that little boy."

In the afternoon, Steven and his father made a fire. There was plenty of brushwood for them to use in the yard. Also, in the garage, an old cabinet which they could break up and burn. Steven's father put some coals on the fire to retain the heat, and later that afternoon he and his little son placed the cardboard box, with Cissy inside, onto the smouldering embers. Together they watched the smoke escape from the edges of the box as it crinkled and buckled in lively response to the heat before suddenly erupting into a burst of orange flame. The skin and hair of the cat sizzled.

Steven's father was thinking how remiss he had been for not having made up a little prayer for Steven to recite over Cissy's funeral pyre, when Steven did something quite extraordinary. He held his small hands together in a *Namaste* greeting, just as his father had seen people do in those temples when he and the boy's mother had taken a holiday in Thailand before their son was born, then spoke in a strange, deep voice, as though chanting. It was completely unintelligible. This went on for at least five minutes, during which time the boy's father simply stared at the boy. He could not believe what he was witnessing. Quite abruptly, Steven stopped his chant, took a step back and bowed towards the fire. After this he turned around and, without looking at his father said, "We can go now."

*****

Ravi and his younger sister, Radha, lived in a wooden hovel at the edge of a tiny village that nestled in a deep valley cutting through the foothills of the Himalayas in North-East India. The hovel also housed the children's parents, grandmother, and a widowed aunt. The sleeping area was separated from the living area by an old worn sheet that hung from the makeshift roof. Wooden planks, swept away during the previous year's floods, had been replaced by bundles of sticks filled in with mud.

Despite the family's poverty, Ravi and Radha were happy children. They ran and played barefoot around the village, they listened eagerly to their grandmother's stories and they would often venture together into the forest to hear the birds, the animals and the spirits of the forest. There, Radha would sit and listen to her elder brother tell convoluted stories about the gods as she fixed him with questioning eyes, hugging her folded legs with little arms and resting her head sideways on her knees. Sometimes her long, straggly, black hair would fall over her face and she would flick it to one side in order to see her brother better.

Radha was always plying the boy with questions. Ravi usually did not know the answers, but so as not to disappoint his little sister he would invent something and say it in a way that made her happy. Radha's big brother was her fountain of knowledge.

The hovel belonged to Ravi's grandmother. There had been a time when her son, Ravi's father, earned a reasonable wage as a skilled worker in a factory in the city where the family used to live in a small apartment. Then the

297

factory closed down, following a scandal involving the managers, and never re-opened. It proved impossible for Ravi's father to find employment locally, so they were forced to stay with his mother in the hills until he was able to secure another job. He would be away for weeks on end earning whatever he could, always hoping to find something permanent to enable him to properly support his family. This had gone on for over two years. The children's mother earned a little by helping out in the village shop and, although desperately poor, they did not starve.

One day, in the forest, the children talked about re-birth. This was something that they both accepted must happen to all living creatures. The discussion started when Ravi explained to his little sister how the goddess Radha had once been a bird.

"I don't think I want to be a bird, but I really do wish I could be a princess," said Radha. "A princess living in a grand palace, with gold and jewels."

Ravi laughed at his little sister. "Well, to become a princess you have to be good in this life. Come. We must go home and help our mother get Granny's food prepared, and *then* you can think about being a princess."

Radha looked upset. "Ravi, do you remember that old man at the other end of the village last year?" she asked. "The one who said I'd come back as the lowest of animals when I took a mango that had fallen from his tree. Will it come true, what he said?"

Ravi offered his hand to help his little sister up. "No, Radha!" Ravi said with confidence. "You, my little sister, will become a princess."

"I don't want to be something really horrid. Like a snake or a rat!" Radha said emphatically as they walked home together through the wood. That evening, Radha tried so hard to be helpful for her mother.

Every year, things were bad in the monsoon season. The roof leaked and there was no way that they could stay dry. Worst of all, food became sparse. Previously, they had always just about coped, but this year was different. It rained non-stop for weeks on end. Ravi's father, who was unable to find any work in the monsoon season, spent most of his time trying to keep their home from falling apart. Then, one evening, it happened.

There was no warning. The family sat huddled together in the sleeping area, the driest part of their home, trying to remain cheerful whilst Ravi's grandmother was telling a long-winded story about something that occurred one monsoon season many years before, when they were startled by a deep rumbling. *Like a giant gargling,* thought Radha. Rapidly, this grew louder until it became deafening. Terrified, the whole family, apart from the old lady, rushed outside into the wind and the driving rain. Almost instantly they were met by a towering wall of water as it thundered into the valley from the mountains, smashing their village into fragments. They had no time to speak with one another, no time to embrace or to say farewells. Together with the shattered remnants of their hovel, surrounding houses and uprooted trees, they were carried away like puppets to be dashed against rocks, buildings, abandoned vehicles and anything else that got in the way of the swirling, brown torrent. As Ravi felt the anger of the flood water tear away his life, his only thought was for his sister, Radha: their little princess.

*****

The following day, Sunday, Steven awoke early and went to play outside in the yard. His father loved to laze in bed on Sunday mornings but on that particular Sunday the man felt he ought to get up and check that his son was all right after the previous day's events. He slipped on his dressing gown and, after stepping into his shoes beside the back door, he went out to find Steven crouched beside a heap of grey ashes where the fire had burned. The boy stuck a piece of wood into the ash-covered ground and again pressed his hands together. On the wood was something written in childish handwriting. Quietly, his father retraced his steps and, moments later, returned with his wife. He pointed at

299

the piece of wood sticking into the ground. Steven's mother read the words aloud: 'Radha can be a princess now'.

Ryanair Aphrodite

David fastened his seat belt and looked up. He could scarcely believe how beautiful she was. The young flight attendant in the blue uniform was walking down the aisle towards him, checking on her passengers, first to one side, then the other. He blinked, but the image did not go away.

It's her, he thought. Although her long copper red hair was neatly tied back, as a flight attendant's should be, and it had never before been red, he knew it was her. David's heart quickened when she approached.

"Everything all right, sir?" she enquired in a soft Irish accent, smiling cheerfully. As always when they met, he felt strangely warm inside.

"Fine," he said. "Just fine."

The Ryanair jet taking him and the other passengers from Edinburgh to Dublin was a small plane. Seated at the back, he had a full view of the aisle down the centre of the aircraft, and throughout the short flight he found it impossible not to look at the flight attendant as she went about her business. The ways in which she turned her head, moved her hands, and spoke with her passengers, showed him that he had to be right. It *was* her. He felt almost disappointed when their imminent arrival at Dublin airport was announced. Once again, she passed by and smiled at him as she checked on her passengers' seatbelts. He smelt her perfume. *Mountain flowers*, he thought. *Flowers from Mount Olympus, fragrant with the morning dew.*

The plane landed smoothly, taxied off the runway and came to a halt. David waited until most of the other passengers had disembarked. *Just another minute,* he kept saying to himself. Then she came slowly down the aisle to where he was seated.

"Let me help you," she said, reaching up to open the overhead locker. Even a flight attendant's uniform could not conceal the beauty of her figure as she stretched up.

"Thank you so much," said the middle-aged woman sitting beside David. "I can do everything else, but I can't lift things down. It's my back, you see. Osteoporosis!"

"That's quite all right, Madam," said the flight attendant, taking down a small bag and a walking stick. David took the stick from her and, with the woman supporting him from behind and the flight attendant holding his arm, he managed to stay upright whilst slowly manoeuvring himself into the aisle.

"He's not bad for eighty-five!" the woman said as she took the bag from the flight attendant.

"Can I help you take him down the steps?" the younger woman asked.

"Thanks so much," the other said, "but I can manage fine from here."

Professor David Rawlings and the woman, his daughter, made their way slowly through the airport, the professor periodically stopping to lean on his walking stick to catch his breath. At the arrivals gate stood a young woman pushing and pulling a child's buggy forwards and backwards. In the seat of the buggy a little girl was fast asleep, her head lolled to one side. The young woman waved excitedly at the professor and his daughter.

"Hi Mum! Hi Gramps!" she called out.

David gave his granddaughter a hug and a kiss.

"So good to see you, Louise," the older woman said to her daughter. "And just look at little Sarah!" she added, bending stiffly forwards to look at the child. Sarah opened her sleepy eyes, looked at her grandmother, and immediately struggled to get out of the buggy, waving her arms at the woman.

"Hold me! Hold me!" she cried out, bouncing up and down.

Louise laughed, lifted her daughter out of the buggy and, to Sarah's delight, handed the lively bundle to her mother.

"She just *had* to come with me," said Louise. "Give Gramps a kiss as well, Sarah," she said, stroking the child's blonde hair. Louise locked her hands around David's arm whilst her mother sat Sarah on the luggage trolley where she remained like a princess in her royal carriage as they all set off for the car park.

"Flight okay, Gramps?" Louise asked, holding onto the professor and supporting him at the same time.

"Wonderful!" he replied. "So comfortable, and—" He was going to say how kind the cabin crew were when his daughter butted in:

"Rather fancied the dishy flight attendant, he did," she said loudly. Louise laughed again, then tugged at the old man's arm.

"Gramps," she said, "you're incorrigible! Don't tell me you saw *her* again!"

The old professor and his granddaughter held back for a few moments to let his daughter pass by as she pushed the luggage trolley with little Sarah, on top, chattering away to her from her suitcase throne.

"I just *don't* want to know!" David Rawling's daughter haughtily informed him without turning. "Come on Sarah, let's find the car."

When Professor Rawlings was sure his daughter was out of ear shot, he spoke to his granddaughter.

"It annoys your mum," he said, "but yes, it *was* her. I'm certain of it."

"Tell me," asked Louise, "are you old classics professors all the same? Do all of you see bits of Greek mythology around you all the time?"

"I can't answer for others," said David. "I only know what I see myself."

"Do tell me about the times you've seen Aphrodite, Gramps. You know how I love to hear these things over and over again."

David spoke with a quiet voice: "Well, don't let your mother know," he said, grinning. "She'd be livid, and she certainly wouldn't want Sarah to hear!"

"Little Sara knows all about Greek mythology already, Gramps. She just loves to listen to the stories you used to tell me. Now where was it the first time? Florence?"

"Yes, Louise my dear, Florence it was. Before the second world war when I was even younger than you are. On a bus in Via Cavour, just passing the Convento di San Marco, the place with the Fra Angelico frescoes, when I first saw her. Dark-haired, that time. Eyes that made your heart melt. She was getting off the bus, but that glimpse I got was enough to know."

"A lot of lovely women in Italy, Gramps! They can't all be Aphrodite!"

Louise enjoyed teasing her learned old grandfather and he rather enjoyed being teased.

"She was different, my dear, That's all I can say. Different!"

"And the next time?" Louise asked, pulling lovingly at the old man's arm. "America, wasn't it?"

"Yes, dear," agreed the professor, evidently delighting in the opportunity to relate for the hundredth time his previous encounters with the goddess of love. "It *was*. Vermont. When I had a sabbatical there after the war. Just walking casually across the campus, she was. It was a cold New England day in late winter and she wore a blue coat. Blonde hair halfway down her back. No, more of a gold, I'd say. And that was the first time she spoke to me."

"Hi there?" suggested Louise, knowing this to be what Aphrodite had said to her grandfather in New England. "Not even, 'have a good day'?"

"Yes," acknowledged Professor Rawlings, "she just said 'Hi there!' That's all. *And* she smiled. At me. What a smile! Imagine being smiled at by Aphrodite!" He grinned at Louise.

"Not bad, huh?" chuckled Louise. "And then she went oriental, didn't she, Gramps?"

"Of course! The most beautiful women in the world are in China, but still she stood out. On the ferry to Lantau Island in Hong Kong. There she was! Exquisite!"

"And now on a Ryanair flight!" Louise continued. "Pretty good for a budget airline!"

"Indeed," laughed the professor. "And *now* we had better catch up with your mother, or we'll both get a telling off."

As David Rawlings and his granddaughter caught up with his daughter and his chattering great granddaughter, Louise asked the old man a question:

"Why does she always look different, Gramps? I never really asked you that before."

"Simple," answered the old man. "She's a goddess. Not like us mortals. She can look however she wishes to look like. But Aphrodite always looks beautiful. After all, love itself stems from her, and what can be more beautiful than love?"

"Gramps, thank heavens you never married one of those Aphrodites. If you had, none of us three ladies would be here today!" Louise, now serious, looked at her mother and daughter conversing so happily.

"Oh, but I did," insisted David Rawlings. "I married your Granny for love and for nothing else. Love is Aphrodite, you see. You're all here *because* of Aphrodite, not despite her."

Louise gave her grandfather another hug when they reached the others. Just at that moment a bolt of lightning shot from a darkening sky, followed by a rumble of thunder. David and Louise shared the same thought: that Zeus was calling Aphrodite back to Mount Olympus. The old classics professor and his granddaughter kept the thought to themselves.

Old Annie and her Last Chicken

Old Annie's yard was silent. The silence unnerved Sean. He halted halfway up the path. Without the usual comforting cluck-cluck-cluck of Old Annie's hens, his courage wavered. It was not that he was scared of Old Annie. No one could ever be scared of the old woman, dotty though she seemed to be. It was age that frightened him, and without the soothing sound of Old Annie's 'chicken' (as in 'children'), the yard appeared ancient and worn-out. Not only was age scary but it also seemed pointless to young Sean—as was everything about growing old: the change from smooth and soft to hard and wrinkled, the greying of things, the sadness, the stooping—and the sticks.

The tap-tap-tap of Old Annie's two sticks on the pitted wooden floor of the cottage *did* scare Sean. It reminded him of bones and bones meant death, like the silence of the yard without the clucking of hens.

Clutching the cloth-covered tray of buns his mum had asked him to deliver to Old Annie in exchange for a dozen eggs (she always refused money), Sean walked slowly and cautiously through that silence to the back door. The cottage was dark, but this was not unusual. Old Annie never had any lights on.

"Seen it all before, I have," she once said when he told her how dark it was in her house. "Ain't no need for no lights!"

Now, in that creepy silence, it was as if the cottage itself had given up on life, its carcass partly shrouded by the rampant shrubs scaling its walls, its door threatened by a tangled rose bush that had long-since forgotten how to make roses. And there was the wheel-less wheelbarrow and the broken garden fork; all these things, so familiar to Sean, now seemed full of menace. Before knocking on the door, he turned again to look. His frightened gaze searched the still yard. No 'chicken' in sight.

"Well now, young Sean! What a pleasure it be to see you round here."

Sean fair jumped out of his skin. He spun round and forced his lips into a smile for the old lady.

"I sees you coming up yon path and I says to myself, 'he'll be bringing them buns and I ain't got no eggs for him this time.'" Sean's smile faded as he stared at Old Annie. "'But I'll have 'em anyways, them buns,' I says, ''cause young Sean here, he won't want to be telling his mum the sad story of it all. He be a good lad, young Sean, and not the type to go upsetting his mum like that.' So I says to myself, 'let's just see what Virginia can do, and all by herself.'"

Old Annie winked at Sean, which gave him courage, but he had no idea what she on about. He only knew that Virginia was the woman's favourite hen.

"Oh, there's me yakking on and you'll not be knowing what the old bird's talking about!" Old Annie chuckled. "Be a darling and bring them buns into my kitchen for me. Then I'll tell you why there ain't no clucking and scratching going on in my yard no more."

Sean, gripping the tray tightly for fear that an invisible ghost hand might reach out from the wall and grab it, followed the tap-tap-tapping into a musty, grey room at the back of the cottage—the one she called her 'kitchen' and that always smelt of cooked cabbage. He put the tray carefully down on the top of the sloping wooden table.

Re-discovering courage, Sean said, "Mum says there's no hurry about the tray. Any time will do, she says."

"She be a right angel, that mum of yours." Sean grinned. He agreed with Old Annie. "Now you sit yourself down there, my lad, and I'll tell you a secret story that'll fair chill your young bones!"

Sean felt certain his bones did not need further chilling as he sat politely on one of the chairs by the table. Old Annie sat on the other.

"You be comfortable, Sean?" she asked. Sean nodded. He did like the idea of being in on the old woman's secret as long as it was not *too* scary.

"It were early this morning, before the sun came up and before the postman came pushing all them love letters through Old Annie's door—" The woman winked again and chuckled. "—And whilst Virginia was still dreaming about that chicken heaven up there."

Sean gripped the edge of his seat for he was certain the story had to involve a ghost.

"I heard this sound coming from the yard. It were like some spirit was out there seeking out a new soul to gather in. Brushing the trees and the bushes with long, cold fingers. Feeling, searching, always searching..."

Sean felt himself go shivery inside, but he hung on to his courage, determined not to show any fear. He studied Old Annie's moles and wrinkles for they were familiar to him. Familiarity helped to smother his fear.

"And the sound of that spirit, it came closer, Sean. Ah, it be so close that Old Annie, she could feel the breath of it coming through her window. And still not a peep from my chicken out there. But I knows there's something in that yard and I goes to the window, see, and I looks out—" Old Annie paused. Sean's eyes widened, begging her to go on. "Nothing! I looks out and sees nothing!"

She smiled at Sean and her smile told him there *had* been something out there, in that yard alive with dead spirits and demons. It was that sort of a smile. *Go on, Old Annie, please go on*, his eyes urged—cautiously.

"But I knows better, didn't I!" She tapped the floor with one of her sticks and Sean shuddered, ever so slightly. "And I be right all along!" Old Annie nodded, and Sean nodded too, not taking his eyes off the old woman. "See, I went back to bed, but these old ears, they stays awake. Ain't nothing that can fool an old set of ears like mine!"

Sean slowly shook his head.

"No sooner did my old ears hit that pillow than it started up again. All that brushing and scraping—and them lost souls a-stirring—"

Sean began to count the moles on Old Annie's chin. It helped to take his mind off the fear.

"Then—"

Six! Six moles. No, seven! That's one too—I think.

"—See, before it happens it always grows quiet. Quieter than Death himself."

Or is it? Perhaps it's not a real mole, that one. Different colour. But what else could it be?

Sean fixed his gaze on that thing on the old woman's chin, his hands sore from gripping the chair.

A stain—perhaps? Could it just be a sort of stain there?

BANG!

Old Annie struck her stick on the floor, shaking the dust and sending a shock-wave down Sean's spine.

"Six... no... seven!" the boy gasped. "I'm not sure!" The old woman frowned then continued.

"Oh, the noise of it! The screeching and the hollering and the panic! Yes, Sean, it were the sound of panic coming from Hell, I can tell you!"

"Yes!" Sean went rigid. His fingers ached from gripping the chair.

"Killed the lot but for my Virginia. Know why?" Old Annie laughed. Sean shook his head. "We be friends, me and Virginia, that's why!" Sean only stared at the old woman. Perhaps she was even dottier than he'd thought. "And you knows what we does with friends in Old Annie's house, ay?" Sean shook his head again. "Like my young friend, Sean, here?" Sean shook his head even more vigorously and made a mental note of the distance between his chair and the door. "We lets 'em in, see. Virginia, she always sleeps in my bedroom. Can't have a friend sleeping out there, can I?" Sean grinned and froze at the same time. He had no idea where this was leading. But Old Annie, she just looked sadly at the tray with the buns. "So we mustn't go upsetting your mum by telling her that a sly old fox went and killed all Old Annie's chicken, right? All, that is, except for Virginia!"

Sean's relief showed on his face. A fox! That's all this was about. A stupid fox.

"So, we'll just have to ask poor old Virginia to make up for the loss, ay? Think she can lay ten times as many eggs, Sean?" Still smiling, Sean shook his head again. "Well, if I ask her very nicely—like she'd be doing my friend Sean here a really big favour—then maybe she'll have made you half a dozen of her eggs for your mum by next week! How's that, Sean? You just say to her, Old Annie will ask her chicken to do her best. Her *last* chicken. Her *very* last, 'cause Old Annie, she won't be wanting to feed that old devil fox no more chicken, and there ain't no room in my little house for more than Virginia and me!" The old woman struggled back onto her feet. Sean, too, stood up. "Now you be sure you thanks that dear mum of yours for them buns, ay? And come back next week for my last chicken's eggs. *Extra* special eggs, they'll be. Virginia will see to that!"

Sean listened to the tap-tap-tap of Old Annie's stick on the ground as she followed him to the door. Now he found the sound comforting but felt saddened that it would have to replace the sound of the clucking of hens in the yard as a source of comfort.

Exactly one week later, Sean returned to the cottage. The silent front yard no longer harboured fear. There were no ghosts or ghouls lurking behind the untidy bushes and trees. He walked boldly round to the back door and knocked loudly. Whilst waiting for the old woman to appear, he tried to imagine the size of Virginia's eggs. They were sure to be simply huge to make up for the loss of her dead fowl friends.

No sound.

He knocked and knocked. Still nothing. He walked round to the window in the front and peered into the darkness. He could just about make out the shape of the old woman's armchair but there was no sign of Old Annie. He returned to the back of the cottage and to Old Annie's bedroom window. The curtain was closed. Old Annie never slept during the day. Sean tapped at the window, but the curtain remained drawn.

Sean did not see Old Annie again. After he came home without Virginia's eggs, his mum went around to the cottage. She was away for ages, and the noise of an ambulance siren told Sean something was very wrong. When his mum finally returned, he sensed her sadness.

"What's wrong, Mum?" the boy asked. "Is Old Annie okay?" At first, she said nothing. "Is she okay?" he repeated. "And Virginia? Did she lay those extra special eggs? Like Old Annie said she would?"

"She's passed on," Sean's mum said at last. "Old Annie's left us."

"You mean she's dead?" questioned Sean. He became aware of his eyes moistening. "Like her chickens after that fox came?"

"There'll be no more eggs," his mum said quietly.

"But Virginia? Old Annie's last chicken. Couldn't she stay with *us* now, Mum? Dad could make a run for her in the garden. One that'll keep her safe from that fox." Sean's mum came over to the boy and stroked his hair.

"She'll not be laying any more eggs, Sean. They found her in Annie's bedroom. Maybe the old bird saw no point in carrying on with Old Annie lying there, dead in her bed. Virginia was on the floor beside the bed. She, too, was dead."

The boy realized that neither Old Annie nor her last chicken could have continued to live on in the cottage without the comfort of the clucking and scratching of the other 'chicken' in her yard. But one question continued to niggle his mind. Had it been the Devil himself, disguised as a fox, who had visited Old Annie's yard that night?

Fallen Angel

Sooner or later, greed brings payback for all who fall prey to its power. There are no exceptions. Not even for Danilo Taddei, the illustrious jewel thief of Poggibonsi in Tuscany.

For some of us, greed is, of necessity, rooted in poverty and circumstance, but with Danilo it was pure greed. He had never known poverty and there was no necessity for the jewellery thefts. Every stolen stone he kept for himself to feed an insatiable passion for jewellery. He loved the patterns of light he saw in the gems hoarded in his spacious Poggibonsi apartment, the feel of the cut diamonds as he traced his nimble fingers over their multi-faceted surfaces— and he would imagine that he was Danilo the King proudly revelling in the magnificence of his wealth. And yet this was never enough. He always had to add to his priceless collection, not once considering the feelings of those women who had lost their precious jewels to his thieving. Nor did the man give a jot for those poor *Capi della Polizia* who had been demoted, or sacked, for failing to catch the infamous jewel thief of Poggibonsi. The ongoing thefts had become a national scandal and insurance companies had taken the unprecedented step of clubbing together and offering a huge reward for information leading to the capture of the culprit. Of course, the downside of such a reward was a disincentive for Danilo to sell on any of his gems, for a receiver would have invariably pocketed a greater fortune by shopping Danilo than through onward sale of the stolen jewels. Besides, Danilo made quite enough to live off through income-generating pursuits: theft of cash, credit cards, cameras and mobile phones. The jewels were his hobby, like coin or stamp collecting.

Danilo inherited his thieving skills from his mother. His love of jewellery too. Sadly, his dear mother disappeared one day, never to return. Danilo, forever the loyal and dutiful Italian son, was devastated. Why or how she disappeared, he never found out, but he feared she must have got rather too drunk on Chianti that evening (she was forever in the bar) and had been run-over on her way home as cockroach.

He had often warned her about the dangers of being a cockroach, but she would never listen to him. Nevertheless, the image of her as a sticky brown patch on the road somewhere between the bar and their palatial apartment haunted him like crazy during sadder moments. With her gone, his jewellery collection became his single purpose in life.

Danilo was so thankful to his mother for having taught him how to transform into any creature he wished to be, for without that ability he could never have reached the lofty status of the 'Great Jewel Thief of Poggibonsi'. "I'm *not* a witch!" she would reassure him during his training years. "It's a gift, passed on through the generations—just like the jewels in our collection will be." His ability soon surpassed that of his mother, much to her annoyance, but she always insisted her cockroach was better than his. Her ultimate undoing!

Danilo should have been happy in his bejewelled solitude, but there was still something missing. Something he simply had to have. He had seen it on many occasions in newspapers whenever La Contessa had been photographed at an important function: her exquisite diamond and sapphire necklace.

It was beautiful beyond compare, and his longing to feel it, gaze at it without La Contessa's scrawny neck spoiling the enjoyment, became overpowering. A special stand for the necklace, purchased at a pricey antiques shop, already occupied prime place in his collection. How wonderful it would look there. How gloriously happy he would be to possess it.

His plan was clever. He had done his homework and he knew that La Contessa always had coffee and a cake, with her husband, at the Casa del Belvedere coffee house mid-morning every Thursday. Whatever the weather, she would wear a brown cashmere scarf around her ageing neck, and this would be removed inside the Casa where the waiter would carefully hang it on the rack near the entrance. The necklace would then be revealed in its full glory. As a spider, he could hide in the neck scarf. There were many spiders of a colour similar to that of the good lady's scarf. He had a book about spiders of the world. He decided on a species from Borneo. Less likely to meet a female of the same species in Italy (he knew that some female spiders ate their males). He would then wait patiently in the sumptuous residence of La Contessa, locate the necklace in the dead of night then transform into a marmoset. A marmoset would be perfect to accomplish the theft and escape from the elderly couple's stately home. He had never done marmoset before, but he had read up about them and reckoned for size, stealth, agility and brains it would best fit the bill.

Thus, one bright, sunny Thursday morning in May, Danilo Taddei found himself sipping coffee in the Casa del Belvedere at a table near the entrance. He even treated himself to a cake. He merely glanced at La Contessa and her husband when they entered, but he did make careful note of where the waiter hung the cashmere scarf. He paid the waiter, and, feeling peculiarly generous that morning, left the man a generous tip. He turned briefly, on opening the door, catching a glimpse of the most wonderful piece of jewellery he had ever seen, soon to be his. He allowed the door to swing closed. In front of him, for he was still in the Casa del Belvedere but as a Bornean spider scuttling across the floor towards the oak coat rack. The spider easily crawled up its smoothly-polished wood, over an elegant, curved hook and onto the soft scarf where he remained safely hidden from view inside a dark fold of material. Danilo had no difficulty clinging on to the cashmere wool, particularly when his anchorage was helped by silken strands of spider web that shot from his bottom. *What wonderful stuff spider silk is*, he thought. *As strong as steel, they say.*

In the spacious villa of La Contessa, he crawled out from his hiding place and up onto the good lady's brown walnut dressing table. Perfect camouflage for a brown Bornean spider. He hid behind a framed photo of La Contessa's lovely granddaughter. Perhaps, he thought, he might one day acquire a wife as beautiful as her and allow the good lady to wear the diamond and sapphire necklace, although only for him to admire in the privacy of their home.

From his hiding place, he could see, through composite eyes, where La Contessa kept it. In a box, inches from where he sat crouched on eight legs. It was something a marmoset would be able to open without any difficulty, and it was not even locked.

The sun sank, and the room grew dark. At last La Contessa entered the bedroom and switched on the light. She undressed, slipped into an elegant nightdress, and retired to bed. No Count! Perhaps he, or she, snored, thus explaining separate bedrooms. Wonderful! Danilo's risk of being discovered was reduced by fifty percent.

Soon, aristocratic snores resonated in the plush bedroom. La Contessa was fast asleep. A small grey-brown monkey, with tufts of white fur tipping its ears, sat on La Contessa's dressing table and carefully raised the lid of a lacquered Japanese jewellery box. The animal could barely contain its excitement as it extracted the awesome necklace. It made 'Ooh-ooh-ooh' sounds, jumping around and swinging the necklace to-and-fro with tiny, clawed hands. La Contessa stirred in her sleep, smiled and rolled over. In her dream, perhaps, she was once again Jane to the Count's Tarzan as they enjoyed a jungle ball serenaded by real monkey calls and imagined lion roars. Meanwhile, Danilo the marmoset leapt to the floor, climbed the curtain, jumped up to catch the frame of a half-open top window, which allowed a pleasant, cooling breeze to enter La Contessa's bed chamber, and slipped out onto the balcony. The small monkey sat on an empty window box to admire the latest possession about to be added to his already massive collection of jewels: the fabulous diamond and sapphire necklace of La Contessa di Poggibonsi.

There was a full moon, and millions of celestial diamonds winked mischievously at him in the cold white moonlight, but the gleaming sapphire in the necklace seemed only to taunt him from its smoothly-faceted face of deep Mediterranean blue:

"You'll never have *me*, monkey thief," it seemed to warn.

"But I've got you already," the white-tufted marmoset whispered back, tightly gripping the necklace with greedy little fingers.

Up the front of the villa, and onto a pergola, a few feet below the balcony window box, snaked a creeping vine.

Easy, thought Danilo. *One jump, and I'm away. I'll slip it around my neck, turn into a fox, for nobody chases or shoots foxes in the middle of the night, and as a fox I'll dart home before enjoying the rest of the night as Danilo Taddei, the greatest jewel thief of all time—and the proud owner of the most exquisite piece of jewellery in the whole of La Toscana.*

Marmosets are jungle creatures, not designed for the open spaces of aristocratic Tuscan gardens. Danilo's white ear tufts, so cute for little children who joyfully look at these animals in the zoo, stood out like beacons in the bright moonlight. A large owl in the cypress tree beyond the pergola had noticed them, and had been studying Danilo's every move, although the marmoset was oblivious to the avian harbinger of death staring down at him. He did not even hear the swish of the great bird's wings as it swooped from its branch when he leapt to the top of the pergola with necklace in hand. But he certainly felt it when those cruelly-clawed feet gripped his body and lifted him, helpless, up and up towards the top of the cypress tree.

Split second decision making. We all do it, don't we? When there is no time to weigh out the pros and the cons, the 'should I or shouldn't I?', and the 'what if, but supposing?' You will know only too well the sort of mental 'cha-cha-cha' that rules most of our lives for much of the time, but you'll also be aware of those occasional moments, infinitesimally brief, and with no more than a hint of conscious control, when actions are unaccountable. Such was the case when Danilo the white-tufted marmoset found himself involuntarily heading for the top of a pencil-thin cypress, kicking his little monkey legs and flicking a useless monkey tail.

Owl meat or transform, up in the sky, into my default mode, Danilo Taddei, Italy's greatest ever jewel thief?

In that split second of unconscious thought-processing, the owl option seemed just too awful. Besides, on his way to the ground he might just have time to escape death by transforming into a large bird (*condor... not done that before?*) before hitting *terra firma*.

La Contessa heard a muffled thud and a sort of yelp. That was all. It was enough to awaken her, but she soon drifted off to sleep again. The next time she awoke it was to the excited jabber of voices. She recognized the maid's coarse Sicilian, and the melodic Tuscan of the gardener. There were other voices too. Her husband's uninspiring drawl, and the sharp authoritarian voice of the new *Capo della Polizia*.

It gave La Contessa quite a shock to see a sprawled-out body there on the path below her bedroom balcony. She had never seen a dead body before. Not a real one in the raw, so to speak. Only in movies, or, when she was younger, the occasional dead aunt or uncle lying peacefully in an open coffin, dressed up to the nines with hands folded and eyes closed. The body made her shudder. The unseeing eyes were still open and there was blood everywhere. She could stand it no longer, and, feeling faint, went back inside to sit down. Soon, the *Capo della Polizia* entered her room and sat beside her.

"Signora La Contessa, I want to thank you. It worked, although I didn't expect it to be quite like this."

He reached into his pocket and pulled out the diamond and sapphire necklace, offering it to the old lady.

"Keep it," she said with disgust, brushing away the item with the back of her hand. "It would make me feel ill to touch it."

The *Capo della Polizia* returned the necklace to his pocket.

"A remarkably good fake!" he continued. "I must congratulate Benvenuto for making it. And now, honourable Contessa, you may retrieve the original from the vault of the Banca Toscana without any fear of having it stolen."

"And thank *you*, too," insisted La Contessa. "I was so upset when you told me I should no longer wear my precious necklace. Wearing it has always meant so much to me. And to my husband on seeing me wear it. That fake, yes it was a good fake, but people could tell, and I felt so cheapened having to wear the thing. Keep it for your museum of difficult crimes. If you have one! But your idea was brilliant. It worked, and now, thanks to you, we're all quite safe." She smiled benignly at the stiffly-polite senior police officer.

"Thank you kindly, Signora. Oh, there is one other thing," the man added as he stood to take his leave. "The young man—the thief—he had wings, you know. Very odd! Maybe you didn't see them. They were a bit crumpled. Two large wings on his back, just like Icarus. The pathologist who's going to do the autopsy is quite excited about it. Says he's never had one with wings before. If it hadn't been for what the young man was up to, one could have been forgiven for thinking he was a fallen angel!"

La Contessa called after the *Capo della Polizia* as he left the room:

"Perhaps he was!"

"What, Signora?" asked the *Capo*, turning to look at the old woman.

"A fallen angel!" she replied. "Perhaps, if it wasn't for his greed, he could have *been* an angel. Even without the wings."

The *Capo della Polizia* shrugged his shoulders and left the room.

Singularly Beautiful

One hour to kill before she was to pick up her dress. One week before the wedding, the one day of her life with the one man in her life. 'One' was such a special number for Val. Soon she and Allan would be 'one'. They would have one home, one family—one, one... one!

Life is singularly beautiful, she thought as she slipped into a café on the corner for a quick coffee before the bridal shop re-opened after lunch. There was only one other customer. *Great!* Until Val realized that with her that made two, and until she saw the other person, a girl of no more than fifteen, was crying.

Val, eager to play mother hen, took her coffee over to the same table.

"Hey now!" she said to the girl. "I'm getting married next week! Can't have all this sadness just before my wedding."

The girl stared at the Diet Coke in front of her. The closest she got to acknowledging Val was to circle the rim of her glass with the tips of her fingers before nudging it to one side.

"I'm a good listener, you know," persisted Val. "I mean, we all have our ups and downs and at your age I was very down at times. Thought the whole world was against me. Convinced no one cared. I was sure—" The girl wiped the back of her hand across her mouth and nose.

If she only could give me eye contact, Val thought. *Such a pretty wee thing—little more than a child—and thinks the weight of all the miseries of the world have been heaped upon her young shoulders.*

"Boyfriend trouble?" she tried. "My first boyfriend dumped me for my best friend. I thought I'd murder her when I found out, but a month later I realized he was about the most selfish bastard you could ever imagine." No response. *Too young for boyfriends? A family dispute, perhaps? Has the girl been threatened with a grounding for some trifling little thing? All girls go through a rebellious phase.* How on earth her own mother coped when Val used to do the theatrical grand huff, she had no idea. She had been a right little pouting Meryl Streep at that age. "My family—I used to think they really gave me a tough time. Particularly my mum."

The girl with a Botticelli face remained as motionless as a weeping statue of the Holy Virgin. *This café could become a place of pilgrimage!* Val reckoned.

"I felt my mum always wanted me to be someone else, you see," she continued, feeling obliged to finish what she had begun. "Wouldn't accept me for who I was. Sometimes I couldn't wait to get away. In fact—"

On the run perhaps?

But there was no tell-tale holdall. Only the girl, her untouched Diet Coke and her tears.

"I did think about running away from home once. Had an older cousin down south I thought would put me up. But—"

You stupid woman, scolded Val's inner voice. *Of course the girl's not on the run! Wouldn't make herself so conspicuous. Think again, Miss-soon-to-be-Mrs Clever Dick!*

"It's awful all the bullying that goes on at schools nowadays. Bad enough when I was a girl, but now—Pff! Something really should be done about it. It's often pretty girls like you who get targeted, too. If you don't fall in line with the cat-pack, if you're at all sensitive, you're considered good prey by those bitchy pack leaders. Mostly jealousy, I guess. And, you know, those girls don't have any real power. They're not super-girls. Scrape the surface and you'll find a frightened child inside all of them!"

The girl reached out and took hold of the glass. For a moment Val thought its contents were about to be flung at her as she saw the child's fingers tighten then relax. Instead, the girl just took a quick sip of Coke and returned her hand to her lap. The tears had stopped but her gaze remained fixed on the table.

I'm not doing at all well here, thought Val. She began to feel guilty for being sorry for the girl. *What the hell! Heavens above, there are so many people in the world far more deserving of pity than a moping teenager.*

She glanced at her watch. Thank God, the bridal shop would soon be open.

"Is there no one you can talk to?" she asked, forcing a smile. The girl shook her head, only just detectably but Val felt pleased with herself. A response at last. "A teacher—someone at school who might listen?" she asked. The girl shook her head again. "Grandparent?" Another shake.

There had to be someone the girl could talk to, and it was bound to be something blown out of all proportion. She knew all about teenagers and their so-called problems.

"Brother—sister? My big brother was a great sounding board for me."

"Don't have any!" the girl said in a voice so soft that Val could barely make out the words.

"Only one of you? But one's wonderful! Singularly beautiful, you are! What about—?"

Val froze. The girl looked straight into her eyes and the pain in the girl's eyes seemed to bore through to the very centre of Val's soul. She had never experienced anything like it before. Her own voice continued, disconnected, as if trying to protect her from that pain.

"Your family doctor? There are counsellors and people who are trained to—you know, who can help to—erm—"

But the girl's eyes were telling her that she was totally out of her depth. No words of her own would get even close to what was really going on in that young mind. She became aware that the girl's vision was focused on something behind her. Val turned. A man had entered the café. He appeared to be injured for he was carrying two crutches.

"Sorry I took so long, Sarah!" he called out. The girl stared blankly at him. She said nothing, but tears began to stream again. The man walked over to the table. He frowned at Val who, at first, avoided his gaze. Something felt horribly wrong. The man reached across and grabbed the girl's arm. He seemed annoyed.

My God! thought Val. *White slavery—child prostitution! The poor wee thing. Probably East European. I should've guessed. Why, the bastard's gonna—!*

"Look, do you mind—?" she began, her temper swelling, but she got no further with her sentence. After being handed one of the crutches, Sarah raised herself up, leaning heavily on the table and allowing the man to assist her as she hopped sideways. She was given the other crutch and the man released his hold. She swayed slightly for a few moments whilst she repositioned the crutches. Val tried hard not to look.

"Just out of hospital this morning," Sarah explained. "Only it didn't work. I didn't take enough bloody tablets. Know anyone who could help me out? Someone who could really understand why my life's not worth living? Do the job properly for me?"

"Okay, Sarah! That's enough! We must get going." The man walked slowly towards the door beside his daughter who, balanced on the two crutches, painfully swung her single leg forwards with each step. Halfway to the door they stopped. The man half-turned.

"Riding accident," he explained. "Horse crushed her leg. She was the European under sixteen show jumping champion last year. Her one and only international trophy. It's so very hard for her."

Val watched stupefied as the girl, too, turned her head.

"'Only one life,' that shrink at the hospital said! And only one leg! Yeah, one's great, huh? Like you said!" Her pretty blue eyes appeared to focus on something on the ground yet there was nothing there. "Well—what if that one life happens to be crap?" she asked. "What then, ay?"

"Sarah, please! It's not her fault!"

"He won't leave me alone with my crutches, now! Not after what I did."

"Sarah!"

The girl looked away and, step by step, supported by her father, swung her single leg out of the café. Val, too, left. Never before had she felt so stupid. The bridal shop was open and she went in. Like an automaton, she tried on her wedding dress and stood in front of the mirror. A solitary figure stared back at her.

One, one, one?

"Excuse me!" she said suddenly and, to the shop assistant's surprise, rushed out in her wedding dress and with bare feet. It flapped like a shroud as she ran.

You stupid, stupid woman! It's not one that's great, it's sharing! It's all about sharing. I've just got to share my wedding with that poor child. She'll be my chief bridesmaid! The others will understand.

She knew they could not have gone far and there was only one car park in the vicinity. She ignored the puzzled looks of passers-by as she ran along the gutter. A car, out of control, was coming straight for her. She recognized the face of the girl in the passenger seat. She saw the girl's hand grab the steering wheel from her father. The car swerved. There was a loud bang as the vehicle hit a stationary truck. Silence, a pause between breaths, then screams. Her own.

Sarah, whose seatbelt was undone, would have died instantly. The father was unscathed. Val, a key witness at the inquest, sat there with her husband. Could not face being on her own. Learned that the girl's father was a widower and that the child had meant everything to him. "Death by misadventure", they said. There was no mention of the girl grabbing the steering wheel and Val said nothing.

At least I can do that for her. Stay silent for a change, Val thought, her eyes swollen with tears. *Oh, if only I'd shut up and looked under the table!*

"Just look at this, dear!"

No response. Arthur put the magazine down, on the coffee table, and glanced at his wife.

"Heather?"

Nothing. He could tell from the woman's vacant stare that she had lapsed into another of her black moods. He sighed as he struggled to his feet. Every movement caused a thousand pains to stab at all the joints in his deformed body. Arthur reached for his stick then hobbled slowly over to Heather who sat like a frozen waterfall, her right hand capping a cold mug of coffee and her left cupped over her mouth as if trying to cover up the sadness. Tears hung at the corners of her eyes.

"Dearest, you'll be all right. You always are, after it passes." Arthur wished he could believe his words as he painfully rested an arm across his wife's motionless back. "We'll double up on the pills."

The doctor's remedy for all their ills. Whenever Arthur's arthritis turned him into a statue of agony, it was "double up on your pills," and when Heather dipped into deeper depression, the same thing: "double up on the medication!"

But doubling up never worked. Arthur had bad days and extremely bad days. The rheumatoid arthritis was winning the battle and slowly turning him into a useless puppet. As for Heather, depression rarely relaxed its grip. Life for both Arthur and Heather had become existence without meaning.

Arthur shuffled sideways and lowered himself onto a chair beside his wife, coaxing her hand away from her face.

"If only I had a normal body like yours and you, my dearest, an untroubled mind. Then we'd get our happiness back. Live again, huh? Remember how we used to run free together in Richmond Park? Free in body and mind."

Arthur's mind switched to the magazine lying on the coffee table. *Frog therapy?* How could holding a frog in his deformed hand cure his crippling arthritis? And how could the same frog, held in Heather's sorrowful hand, pull her back from the depths of despair? Sheer nonsense, like many things he saw and read about. *Wasting money on the National Lottery, for instance?* This also had to be nonsense—but then there was always someone, somewhere, who would win the jackpot, shower friends with gifts, party all night and fly off to Barbados in the morning. Praying was nonsense, but surely there had been a few people, at some moment during the world's tortured history, whose prayers were answered? Statistics informed Arthur that miracles happen. Perhaps a blind baby in ancient Greece once recovered its sight; maybe a Tang dynasty Chinese farmer, whose crops had failed, awoke one day, after praying all night to the Buddha, to discover a bumper yield of rice in his paddy fields. No one would pray if a prayer had never, in the chronicles of mankind, been answered.

He watched a tear trickle timidly down Heather's cheek. Why shouldn't they spend their money on a lottery prayer for his body and for Heather's mind? A two-page spread in the magazine on 'Frog Therapy' had rekindled his hope:

'Guaranteed success for most conditions of the body and mind.'

Most?

'Money refunded if no response within one week.'

Nothing to lose?

'Body or mind restored to normality for one day minimum. Occasional long-lasting cure.'

One day of their old life back? One more day of happiness?

"What do you think, Heather? For one day, and who knows, it might last. Says so here. Occasional long-lasting cure."

Heather heard but was not listening. She heard Arthur dial, heard him talk over the phone but said nothing for his words were mere sounds. Nothing had meaning in that dark tunnel in which she had become trapped.

"No waiting list, you say?" Arthur's face betrayed excitement whilst that of his wife displayed only misery. "And chances of side effects only one in five million? Like the National Lottery in reverse, huh?"

Arthur paused. He asked himself inside his head: *What side effects could you possibly get from just holding a frog for five minutes? I could never win the lottery, anyway. Oh, for one day of freedom from this nightmare!*

"Yes, ten o'clock tomorrow would suit us fine," he continued into the phone. "Conditions? Yes, we'll accept those. And no, we don't have any cats or dogs."

"Cats or dogs indeed!" muttered Arthur on putting down the phone. "Why on earth should they make a difference?"

For the rest of the day Arthur's useless limbs struggled to care for his fit, inanimate wife. They fed her what little food she would take, gave her water, toileted and put her to bed—fully-clothed, for removing her clothes would have been impossible. Too exhausted to change into pyjamas, Arthur was also fully-clothed when he finally climbed into bed beside Heather.

He awoke to a cloudless morning and prayed that the weather would be the same for their day without pain or sadness. A day they could cherish forever. At ten o'clock sharp, the doorbell rang. By three minutes past, Arthur had reached the front door.

"Not to worry!" said the tall young man from Frog Therapy Ltd. after Arthur had apologized profusely for taking so long. The man held a green box.

"It's why we need this therapy," Arthur explained. He showed the man his deformed hands. "And my wife's in one of her dark moods."

"Oh, I'm used to waiting," the man said, stepping inside. "All part of the service. As the week passes the waiting gets shorter. Day seven and we'll have you running to the door!"

Arthur forced a weak smile as he followed the young man to the kitchen. Heather sat in front of her untouched breakfast.

"Particularly effective for depression," explained the man. "And no need to ask your own problem, sir. Great for arthritis, too." Arthur glanced doubtfully at the little green box. "One week, maybe sooner," the salesman continued, "and we'll have you both skipping around, happy as lambs. Perhaps... (he paused and looked mischievously at the older man) perhaps even a bit of the old kiss 'n' cuddle in the back row of the cinema again, huh?"

Wounded by the man's words, Arthur avoided his gaze. It had been years since he and Heather last made love.

"The good lady first?" The man questioned. "With the frog, I mean?"

"Yes! Of course."

The man from Frog Therapy Ltd. carefully lifted the green lid, put his hand inside the box and withdrew a half-closed fist. Slowly, long fingers unfurled. Arthur gawped at the tiny green frog squatting on the man's outstretched palm, with its oversized orange and black eyes staring up at him.

"That it?" enquired Arthur. There was a hint of accusation in his voice.

"Sure is!" replied the salesman. "Difficult to believe, right? What it says in that magazine is all true, though. All those testimonies and the occasional permanent cure." He placed the frog on the table in front of Heather and took a pad from his pocket. "Before we start, sir, could I ask you to sign here? An indemnity waiver. In case of side effects. Wouldn't want you suing Frog Therapy Ltd, right?" He chuckled.

"One in five million? Not much chance," agreed Arthur, signing. "By the way, what—?"

"As you say, sir, little chance of being the unlucky one in five million. Not a jackpot winner myself, either. But one of you might be the lucky devil who gets the cure! Odds are far better." Arthur could barely conceal his excitement on hearing the word 'cure'. "Shall we get started, then? Hold both hands out. Like this, madam."

Heather sat staring into space. Arthur lifted one of his wife's hands up off the table, opened out her fingers then did the same with the other hand. The man from Frog Therapy Ltd. placed the small green amphibian with orange and black eyes into the cup of her hands and started a small stop-clock.

"Five minutes precisely! Not one second less or one second more."

The green frog looked up at Arthur as the clock ticked. It shifted its body through 90°, then looked at Heather. Her face remained expressionless as she gazed at the live thing in her cupped hands. Arthur began to have doubts.

Just before the stop-clock alarm sounded, the little frog gave a croak, as if to announce that his first patient's time was up.

Arthur's turn...

Make me better! Come on, you little green bastard, take the pain out of my joints. Make me run and jump again!

Inside his head, Arthur willed the frog to cure him. The creature looked up with those orange and black eyes that seemed to say: *'Patience, Arthur!'* But five minutes holding a frog can feel like a long time when you're racked with arthritis. Arthur was relieved when the alarm finally sounded, and the frog was returned to its box.

"Same time tomorrow?"

"What?" Arthur's thoughts were elsewhere—running free. What if this were to work? A whole day together as they used to be? Already, his brain was making plans.

"Shall I come back the same time tomorrow?" the man repeated.

"Oh—yes. Same time," agreed Arthur before seeing him to the door.

That evening, Arthur's joints were so excruciating that he had difficulty in getting off to sleep. He did the usual—doubled up on the pills—then cursed all frogs. Heather, too, seemed worse. Tears about nothing streamed down her waxwork cheeks.

"We'll try once more," Arthur said that night, in the dark. "Give it one more shot, but if we're worse again that does it!"

*****

"Coffee?"

Arthur blinked. A spear of morning sunlight thrust through a small gap in the curtain, touching an apparition. Or was that actually Heather standing beside the bed?

"Would you like a cup of coffee?" she asked.

Arthur blinked again. *Heather, not an apparition!* He eased himself up before realizing that there was no need to be so cautious for he felt barely a twinge of pain. He stretched both arms sideways, reached forwards then raised them up in the air. He could not remember when he had last done such things.

"Well, I can't wait all day for an answer!" taunted Heather.

"But Heather, what about—?"

"Must get going, Arthur. Lots to do today."

"Yes, lots," agreed Arthur swinging his legs out of bed. "And I'd *love* a cup of coffee, dear!"

Can this be real? Arthur asked himself. *Heather making coffee? Must be the tablets. How could a little frog—?*

At ten o'clock, the man from Frog Therapy Ltd. rang the bell. Heather reached the door before Arthur who was still a little stiff. Behind the salesman, the neighbour's black cat slunk past. Arthur said nothing.

Perhaps the frog's just frightened of cats and dogs, that's all.

Another dose of frog therapy for each and the following morning there were further improvements in Heather's mood and Arthur's joints. Heather was able to smile and Arthur could reach the Corn Flakes on the top shelf without a step ladder. The next day he was able to walk around the bungalow without a stick. The passing of each day of frog therapy was like the peeling back of another layer of misery from his life, but most of all he delighted in hearing his wife laugh again. It was a most wonderful thing. And they started to make plans for 'the day'.

It had been so long since they had last truly done anything together that Arthur felt more like a teenager planning his first date. Only two days of therapy remained, and he had already booked a rental car. He had not driven for years and could hardly wait to feel the vehicle respond to his liberated joints and sense the power of the engine on pressing the accelerator with a pain-free foot. They would drive down to Richmond Park where they used to ramble as young lovers thirty years back, and walk once more arm-in-arm, smell the grass and the bracken and breathe in the fresh park air.

Heather giggled like a schoolgirl during most of her final session of frog therapy. She said the little green animal tickled her. As soon as the man and his frog were gone, Arthur fetched the car and they were off.

Richmond Park was just as Arthur remembered it. *How odd that nothing's changed*, he thought, but then realized that things like grass, bracken, trees and the deer do not change. Only people change. How wonderful to be given that chance to change back again on such a perfect spring day. In his memory, it had always been a perfect spring day in Richmond Park whenever they walked there together and whatever the time of year.

The deer herds lazed in the distance—always in the distance—and he and Heather ran towards the deer, holding hands again. Heather laughed, and Arthur smiled to hear his wife's happiness. They sat on the grass and looked at the deer and the trees as they stared into a distance that they could never reach, then lay back on the ground, still holding hands, and stared up at the sky and the clouds, both now dwelling in a past long gone.

The sun was low when Arthur drove the rental car back home. That evening, he took Heather to a local Italian restaurant where they had *sopa di funghi* and *cotaletta*

Milanese di vitello and a half-bottle of *Frascati Bianco,* and they ate and drank and laughed again and forgot all about arthritis and depression and the sadness... and the little green frog.

Later, Heather complained of feeling very tired. Arthur thought, *why shouldn't she?* After slipping effortlessly into his pyjamas, he, too, felt he had squeezed half a life into a day. Only a few stabs troubled his joints as he snuggled up against Heather. Nothing to complain about. They kissed goodnight and Arthur prayed that the following day, and the day after that, would be the same. He prayed for a cure for Heather, not himself.

In the morning, when Arthur opened his eyes, there was an empty space beside him. A good sign! He smiled. He turned this way and he turned that way—not even a twinge of pain and, remarkably, his joints no longer appeared deformed. His smile broadened.

"Heather!" he called, springing out of bed.

No reply. Only a loud thud from the kitchen as if a sack of potatoes had been flung across the room. Arthur hurriedly donned his dressing gown. Another thud, as he walked along the corridor, was followed by a crash of breaking glass and crockery. He ran.

"Heather?" Arthur shouted.

The only response was a deep croak. He burst into the kitchen. The floor was wet and slimy. He slipped and fell awkwardly, banging his head. He was in agony. Not from his head, but one of his hips. He was looking up at the ceiling, clutching his injured hip, when that loud croaking again started up.

"Gribbit! Gribbit!"

Slowly, Arthur eased himself round, supporting the hip with both hands. In the corner of one eye he spotted an enormous green frog, the size of an arm-chair, its huge orange and black eyes fixing him with intense amphibian suspicion.

'Gribbit! Gribbit!"

Its cheeks ballooned with each croak. Then a long, thick, pink tongue shot from its mouth like an uncoiled rope, missing Arthur by inches.

"Heather!" he screamed.

Paradise Lost & the Helmsman

The man whom they called 'The Fox' fastened a heavy belt firmly around his waist. Four white packages were attached to it. The belt's pressure on his belly was a reminder that this would be his last trip on Earth, and the start of a journey to Paradise. Of this, he was in no doubt. They had told him, and they knew so much. Beautiful women, palaces filled with gold, exotic gardens. All these had been promised, and it was to be so soon. The women would find him even more handsome now that he had grown a beard.

He felt excitement well up inside him when the diesel engine jerked alive. Turning to check for passing vehicles caused a twinge of discomfort when the tight belt dug into his flesh, but he had no fear of the pain to come. This would be but a transient annoyance on the path to Paradise... they said. He alone had the power to activate the mechanism by flicking a switch and his only concern was of premature detonation. But they had reassured him that the mechanism was infallible. He had no need to fear. He trusted them as they had trusted in him.

Driving slowly along the narrow streets, The Fox glanced at his watch.

That watch! Accurate to the nearest hundredth of a second, and it was his. *They* had given it to him, and he wore it with pride for they had selected him out of so many who had come forward. The watch reassured him that the bus was on its way to the target location, a pull-in bus stop three blocks ahead. The bus was never late. They told him that, and they knew everything. As he drove, he thought what a grand job they had done on the van and he smiled to himself. Re-sprayed, it really did look like a water authority vehicle.

He pulled the van into the roadside opposite the bus stop where a line of children stood, waiting and chattering. The bus, already crowded with other schoolchildren, appeared on cue from around a bend and came to a halt. The children who had been waiting, mounted. The Fox, with his head bent, mumbled a short prayer then looked up. The van's engine was still running. He glanced at the bus and at its driver. Something was horribly wrong. The driver's gaze was fixed on him whilst a small boy also stared at the van.

The two men acted in unison as if choreographed... The Fox to secure a place in Paradise, the bus driver to save the lives of his young charges. The van's engine roared when The Fox slammed the accelerator pedal. The bus lurched forward as the van swung round in an arc, but it was too cumbersome. When the van caught the rear of the larger vehicle, The Fox flicked a switch.

The explosion rocked the city. A brilliant flash, then whole buildings shook. The air shimmered with fragments of shattered glass as a blanket of choking yellow smoke unfurled into dirty, rubble-strewn streets. An eerie silence followed, broken, after what seemed like an eternity, by shrill screams. These filled the thick yellow air. They were the screams of a child. A man's voice called out. The words said nothing but meant everything: horror—panic—loss—anger.

The Fox looked down at his hands but there were no hands. He moved his non-hands up to his face, but there was no face. He tried to cover his ears to stop the screams, but there were no ears to cover. His non-hands moved across his non-head and passed through each other. He was not sure where he was. He tried to run but there was no movement in his legs. It felt as if his feet were locked into wheel clamps. He looked down. No feet, no legs. He tried hard to remember but could only recall a promise. Something to do with a place called Paradise. It was *they* who had made the promise—but who were they? In fact, he was not sure what Paradise meant, but he knew it must be something other than this awful screaming. He had to get away, but how? Imagining that he had feet, he started to run, feeling joy, for surely he must be moving. Yes, he was moving. *To Paradise?* Oh, what a wonderful place it would be...

But the faster The Fox ran, the faster he was pulled backwards as if by a huge elastic band. Back to the memory of it. Faster and faster, back and back, until with a sudden jolt the man they called 'The Fox' found that he was sitting in the seat of a bus. A comfortable seat. *The bus to Paradise?* He had no fear, no doubts. He looked down. Wow, his hands and his feet were there! He peered around. The bus was full of children. Like himself.

What self?

Strangely he remembered a man—a man with a new beard—one whom the women would love. He felt exhilarated, for the word 'Paradise' conjured thoughts of gardens, wonderful food—and, of course, beautiful women.

He felt his face. What on earth had happened to that beard? He examined his small body. Far too young for facial hair. But what about the beautiful women? Surely they would prefer a man with a beard to a little boy?

"And what did you think of that last goal?" The Fox was nudged by the boy sitting beside him. "What a header!" the boy exclaimed, laughing and theatrically jerking his head.

The Fox, too, laughed. *Why? And do I know this boy,* he wondered? He understood the boy's language, and yet it seemed strange. The Fox looked out of the bus window. A water authority van was parked on the opposite side of the road. He saw the driver of the van. A man with a beard. How odd! *Also trying for Paradise? He should also be on this bus full of children!*

Something happened. The bus driver shouted:

"Down, children!"

As he and the boy beside him followed the bus driver's instructions, the bus jerked forwards. The seat hit him in the back, there was a sickening metallic crunch, the bus swivelled and swerved then everything seemed momentarily suspended as he was blinded by a dazzling white flash. The pain was intense, and there *was* only pain. Pain and silence. The Fox peered down, but all he could see was a dirty grey-yellow. No hands! Could not even feel them. Then the screaming began. Legless, he ran. Nothing happened. He tried to shield his ears from those awful screams, but where were his hands... where were his ears?

A thought entered his mind. *Paradise? Of course!* That is where he was heading. That is what the bus was about. But where was the bus—and what was Paradise anyway? He could not remember. Only that they had told him, and they knew everything—but the pain—did they know about the pain? It was unbearable, as was the screaming that prevented him from working things out in his mind. Had they told him about these things? Pain and screaming? He tried to remember.

He ran without legs. All the while, as he ran, he was being pulled ever backwards. Then silence...

The Fox was sitting in a bus. The same bus? The one that would be taking him to a place called Paradise? *Sure it will!* He felt proud. Beautiful women, palaces, gardens of flowers. As he sat musing, the silence was broken.

"And what did you think of that last goal?" a voice beside him enquired. He knew that voice. Knew it so very well. He felt a nudge. "What a header!" said the excited small boy beside him.

The Fox wondered why he was sitting next to a little boy on this bus when he should be on his way to Paradise. They had told him nothing about the boy although they knew everything.

Who were they? Where were they?

The Fox felt fear for the first time. He saw a van parked on the opposite side of the road. One of those water authority vans. Why did its bearded driver seem so significant to him? He could make no sense of it. Perhaps this man, not the bus, would lead him to Paradise. There was shouting, the bus jerked and threw him back. A loud crash, a sudden jolt, then pure unblemished whiteness followed by silence. The white dimmed and turned a foul, dull yellow. He tried to breathe, but as he breathed all that entered his body was a sound emerging from the silence. A plaintive and terrifying sound—the sound of a screaming child. The air was thick with shards of splintered glass. He felt he was being pulled backwards by an unimaginably powerful elastic force as his mind filled with awful shrieks and squeals. Now he knew. The screams were crying out for a place called Paradise. A place he could never reach. And he knew it that was he who was screaming and that the screams would never, never, *never* stop...

*****

Beyond the sliding door was a grey concrete quayside. Through the cold mist, a vast, wooden barque bobbed lazily as if in no hurry to leave. The solitary figure of the helmsman stood in the stern, his hand resting easily on the steering arm of the rudder. His face appeared pale against the dark oak planks of the boat, his eyes were fathomless and when he turned his gaze towards the front of the vessel, his sharp nose seemed like a pointer towards something beyond the grey swirls that engulfed the bow. This was all that could be seen from the doorway.

The silence was broken by a whirring. The automatic door slid open, then snapped shut after disgorging an elderly woman. With her head stooped, and her knees deformed by arthritis, she moved slowly towards the barque until her white hair merged with the mist. She was heading for a narrow gang-plank that connected the quayside with the barque, shuffling along on old, bent legs. When she was half-way there, the door opened again. She did not stop to look at the bearded young man who emerged from the building but merely continued her resolute journey as the man swung round and attempted, unsuccessfully, to return through the closed door. Just before he reached it, he appeared to be yanked backwards. He turned and ran off along the quay, directionless, disappearing into the mist before reappearing like a puppet on a string. He span around, then shot off in another direction, only to be pulled back again. Whilst the old woman slowly made her way towards the gang-plank, the man, consumed by terror, continued to dart this way and that. He would disappear into the mist then return even more terrified, for in the mist he must have seen something unimaginably awful. Thus began the bearded man's eternal Brownian dance with the Devil...

The door whirred open again, allowing an orderly crocodile of children to pass through. They looked as if they had just dismounted from a school bus and remained huddled in silence outside the door. No sooner had the door closed than it reopened, and a uniformed man stepped calmly out onto the quay. On seeing the children, he joined them, took the hands of the two at the head of the crocodile and, following the old woman, walked with the children towards the barque. Meanwhile, the boat continued to bob, and the pale figure of the helmsman bobbed with it. The door onto the quayside opened and closed, again and again, and each time it did so more figures emerged, mostly solitary but occasionally in twos or in small groups. They were all silent. Some headed purposefully towards the barque whilst others, like the bearded man, would immediately start to spin about in a frantic, directionless atom-dance.

The column of children and the uniformed man, who had overtaken the old lady, approached the gang-plank. The first to step onto it was a little boy. His features lit up when the helmsman turned to face him. He climbed the gang-plank, and others followed, including the man with the uniform.

The bearded man suddenly reappeared out of the mist, then got flicked backwards by the invisible elastic that controlled him. He tried, again, to run towards the barque and did not seem to see the old lady when he rushed past her. Like a blind man, he flipped over the edge into the mist that occupied the bottomless space between the wooden side of the barque and concrete of the quayside. As he did so, it became apparent that the quayside was not truly silent, for beyond the silence of the mist was an awful screaming—millions upon millions of voices screaming. The bearded man vanished beyond the quayside into that mist. There was no splash. Only muffled screams that blended with the screams of others who danced for eternity with the Devil.

The small boy reached the deck of the barque. One by one, those that followed him did so too. He walked over to the helmsman, beaming, and the helmsman leaned forward and gently touched the side of the child's cheek. The boy and his friends moved on to the fore of the barque where they vanished into the mist. And from there, from across the silence of the mist, came the sound of voices. Voices of men and women. Welcoming voices. Happy voices.

The last onto the deck of the barque was the white-haired old lady. She, too, smiled as the helmsman touched her wrinkled cheek. And she also made her way to the fore of the boat. As she did so she became less bent, more upright—young again.

The helmsman pulled up the gang-plank and released the barque from her moorings. The ship moved away from the quayside, and gradually, *so* gradually, she slipped forwards on the invisible water and soon became swallowed by the mist. When the barque was gone there was only the grey quayside, the mist, the silence of the mist—and the screams beyond that silence.

Our Lake

I went there again last week. To the lake. First time for nearly twenty years. I followed the same path that winds through the dense wood, and there it was. A stagnant pond that smelt of dead things and decay.

We never called it a pond. Back then. To us it was a lake. *Our* Lake. So much more romantic sounding, don't you agree? Think of clear mountain lakes ringed by alpine flowers, mirror lakes that trap the moon, stars and the faces of young lovers. Then there is the English Lake District. Can you imagine 'The English Pond District'? And what about Swan Lake? There are duck ponds and horse ponds, into which horses shit, but I know of no 'swan ponds'. How could a magical ballet ever happen around a 'pond'? No, lakes are places of poetry and of mystery. The Lady of the Lake, her arm reaching up into the ethereal mist to retrieve Excalibur, would have cringed at the thought of being labelled 'The Lady of the Pond', and it was to a wondrous lake that the three mysterious crane maidens of Chinese mythology would fly, as birds, and, divested of their white feather garments, transform into three young women of legendary beauty. That could never have happened in a pond.

But what about death? Hedgehogs, newts, worms and other crawly things die in *ponds,* but surely not in lakes, whereas Donald Campbell, in his bid to become the fastest man on water of all time, died on a lake, and lovely young maidens wishing to end it all, Ophelia-like, by drowning should only perish in lakes. Not in ponds. For God's sake, never in ponds...

Every evening, after school, we took that same path all those years ago. And beside the 'lake' we talked and talked and talked. We talked about what lay beyond the tangle of bushes on the other side of our 'lake' and about the secret path that we believed would lead us to a future together—to our happiness. And when the words ran out, we kissed, and I would let her soft lips drive me crazy for her heavenly body, but we never got beyond the fondling and the caressing—and the tears.

I was too young to understand those tears. Too young to know what love can and cannot do. Too young to prevent it from happening.

It was my father who told me about the body in the pond. *Her* body. The old swine called it a pond—*and* he shouted at me:

"I told you to f------ leave her alone, you stupid little sod! A Muslim girl, for Christ's sake! And now look what she has gone and done. Why couldn't you bloody-well listen to me, huh?"

Of course, Rahana's father had shouted at *my* father down the phone, but even so I could not forgive the man for calling it a pond. And when I heard his words it was as if a trap door had opened beneath me and my soul had slipped through, leaving behind a shell. My father's words hit that shell and shattered into sharp splinters of sound... falling daggers that pierced my trapped soul. Whilst my soul, racked by guilt, tried to understand, the shell lived on. It ate, slept and went to school—*her* school—and when time had moved on it had a career. It married.

Of course, I have never had a religion. Only dreams. I was too young then to understand how she must have felt. She loved me as I loved her, I knew that, but she also loved her parents and her two elder brothers. They were a part of her, like her religion, and when her father told her she would go to Pakistan for the first time in her life, after her sixteenth birthday, to marry an older man whom she had never met, the poor girl was torn apart. She would never disobey her father and yet she had not the strength to destroy our love. She pleaded with me, beside our lake, to stop loving her, to let her go and forget her. But I could not, and I told her she couldn't, and I kissed her through her tears and she kissed me back. I had told her so many times that nothing could destroy our love. In the end, without any warning, she destroyed her life.

My soul never recovered from the guilt and the awfulness of not being there for her. How alone she must have felt lying in the 'lake' after taking all those tablets, waiting for the black shadow of death to smother her. How tortured her young mind must have been to prevent her from picking herself up and staggering off for help. And how I wished I had listened to her and at least tried to know how she felt. Killing off my own adolescent love would surely have been a thousand times easier than having to live on after the girl I loved so much had died. Because of me.

Many a time, afterwards, I had arrived there, in my mind, beside our 'lake', just in time to rescue her and carry her, alive in my arms, through the undergrowth to that path—the one that should have taken us to our happiness. Ever since the day I lost my soul, that fantasy has played over and over and over in my mind like a faded vinyl record when the needle gets stuck in a groove. But when I stared at the pond last week—my father was right, it is only a pond—I knew that there is no path on the other side. Only darkness. Darkness and death.

My wife screamed at me: "There's another woman, isn't there? I know it!"

"No. A girl—" I began. "A girl called Rahana. At school. She—"

"A girl? At school? Why, you filthy dog!" she yelled. "You dirty, filthy old dog!"

I'm a teacher, you see. But I cannot blame my wife. She only has my shell, not my soul, and, sooner or later, every shell, broken or not, must be thrown away. I left without bothering to explain. The truth is I *couldn't* explain. Still grieving, so many years after a childhood romance that went seriously wrong, it made no sense, but it's how it was, and I left. I found a cheap lodging house and I got hold of a gun. Surprising how easy it can be to get hold of a gun, even in Britain. Without batting an eyelid, the man showed me how to use it. Put the gun in my hand, helped me snap in the bullets and unclick the safety switch. He showed me how to aim it, supporting my wrist. Didn't ask whom or what I was going to shoot. I never had to tell him that I was going to a 'lake' to shoot a pain that wouldn't go away. Kill a forbidden love that should never have happened.

Holding the loaded gun, I stood at the edge of the 'lake'. I'll call it a lake again, for we are talking tragedy here, not the demise of a wandering hedgehog or a sick frog. And I looked at the icy water and at the bare winter trees. Then I saw him: a silent, black-cloaked figure, leaning on his scythe, his hood empty where a face should have been. I knew that he was waiting for me. I looked again into the water and I saw her face, as it used to be when we stood there together, smiling and looking back at me. She hadn't changed at all, and neither had I. After so many years my love for her was as strong as it had always been.

"I still have her in my memory," I screamed at the static figure. "You thought that was it, killing her off like that, didn't you? And you've been waiting to get me ever since, but she's still here inside me—what's left of me—and you're not getting her again. Not a second time!"

The splash of the gun hitting the water cut through the cold winter air, and I watched the spreading rings of ripples until they merged with the stillness of the 'lake'. Then I returned to the shell of my life.

Automatic Door

There was no reason for Art to be anything other than proud. A job worth two hundred thousand dollars a year, in line for position of CEO, a Cadillac, a swimming pool and a beautiful wife—he had everything! In fact, he was thinking about diamond earrings for Arlene's fortieth when the security guard grabbed him by the elbow after he had passed through the automatic door:

Diamond earrings—must be diamond—Jesus, I love that woman!

"Mr. Forsman—"

"Hey—Doyle—thanks, but it's okay. I've learnt to stand up on my own. You've no need to hold on to me!"

Doyle avoided eye contact.

"Mr. Forsman—I'll accompany you to your office to collect any personal items. Then I'll see you straight back here. To the door. Afterwards you'll have no right to re-enter the building uninvited. Do I make myself clear?"

"Good one, Doyle! You in training for Hollywood? Mr. Forsman indeed! Always been Art and Doyle, us two, right? Look—my arm—do you mind—it *is* me, you know—your old pal, Art."

The large African-American guard relaxed his grip. "I know who you are, Mr. Forsman. And this ain't no joke. Order came through this mornin'."

Art rubbed his arm where the guard's hand had squeezed a little too tightly.

"Order?"

"No longer an employee of Mercer's Incorporated, Mr. Forsman."

"But—just a minute—"

"Follow me—sir!"

Sir? I ain't no 'sir'. I'm Art!

A hole opened somewhere beneath Art and his pride, the bit that mattered for Arlene and his two daughters, fell into it. His body walked away from the automatic door in the wake of the broad security guard whilst he struggled in that hole—struggled to make sense of the other man's automatic words—struggled to even try to understand what it really meant for him...

Fired! No job? Can't be! Things like this never happen to successful guys like Art Forsman. See, I own a cadillac, have a swimming pool, a beautiful wife and two lovely teenage daughters both in private education. Fired people don't have kids in private schools. This is simply nonsense! How can I pay the school fees without a job? All Arlene does is charity stuff.

Doyle opened the door to an office that was no longer Art's and remained in the corridor, impatient and embarrassed. It seemed as if he wished that Art no longer existed. Feeling shaky at the knees, Art stepped into the room, and into a past where pride was a matter of course. A past now gone.

'Possessions', the security guard, his one-time pal, had said. What possessions? He looked around the office. At the shiny desk, the computer, the cabinets, the trash can and the silent, turning ceiling fan. He stared at things he had always taken for granted as 'his' but which now had nothing to do with him. Then he remembered—the photo in the desk drawer. He glanced back at Doyle and pointed to the desk, unable to articulate a single word.

"The desk? Sure! Remove anything of yours, Mr. Forsman. Any of your property left behind will be destroyed."

Destroyed? Hell, they've just bloody destroyed my life, you jerk!

That was as close as Art got to anger. He approached the desk. He had to pull at the drawer a few times before it would open. A missing roller, for sure. For weeks he had meant to get someone to fix it. Now the sticking drawer would be someone else's problem.

Maintenance? Art Forsman here. Look, I'm sure sorry to trouble you like this, but there's this drawer in my desk— keeps on sticking—'course I ain't no handyman myself, but

I reckon it's missing one of those roller things. Like a tricky big dipper in a fairground, huh? Ha-ha! Big dipper. Ups and downs of life, man. Ups and downs!' Jesus, I'm down. Down and done for. Ain't no jobs for a fired forty-five something.

The desk drawer had only ever contained one item: a small, framed photo of Arlene. Why hadn't he kept it in full view on top of the desk?

God, I love you, Arlene. The thought of other men stopping and looking at you—on my desk—your picture— their dirty dog desires. Couldn't handle that, Arlene. All that pride, and I couldn't handle that small thing: jealousy. Jesus, who cares now? I'll not blame you, girl, if you choose to leave me. Who wants to be saddled with an out-of-work bum till the end of her time on earth?

Art slipped the photo into his pocket. Then he saw an envelope. Odd that he had not noticed it before, purposefully placed at the far corner of the desk, away from the comfortably-upholstered swivel-chair, as if telling him not to sit down for the chair no longer belonged to him. His brain must have refused to see it, for he already knew its contents.

'Art Forsman' was neatly hand-printed on the front.

Who'd have done that, huh? Written my name on my execution warrant, 'cause that's what it is. An execution warrant. I'm gonna be cut away from the life I led. Without a job, I'm as good as dead.

Doyle began to tap his feet. "Ain't got all day, Mr. Forsman!"

Art snatched up the envelope and flung it in the trash can.

"Sure thing, Doyle! Not your fault. I understand. No hard feelings, huh?" he said. He brushed past his expressionless old chum. It seemed of no consequence to Doyle whether or not Art harboured ill-feelings.

Art's body walked back along a familiar corridor of the past, descended in the elevator, crossed the lobby and reached the automatic door.

Arlene? What will I say to her? And the girls? Next semester, and they'll have to go to a public school. God— it's Arlene's birthday tomorrow, too. Diamond earrings, ay? Earrings from a dead man?

The door slid open. The big man—the one he used to call Doyle—blocked his return. Art never looked back. He said nothing when he crossed the threshold into an empty future. The past snapped shut behind him, like that automatic door, as he hit the silence of the car park.

An empty future should remain forever silent. But not yet, Arlene! Those earrings! Goddamnit, I'll go get you those earrings, my love. Go downtown to that jeweller in the mall. The one who helped us decorate our past. Remember our diamonds of happiness, Arlene? Those things we did together? Ain't no one who can take them from us, Arlene. They can take away my pride but not our past!

Art, an automaton, walked to the Cadillac, still his, parked in what used to be his car space.

Well, old girl, won't ever be filling you with gas again, that's for sure!

The diamonds of his past still sparkled in his mind when a tree hit the Cadillac doing ninety-five miles per hour. A loud bang, a flash and another automatic door closed with a snap, shutting out the bright diamonds of Arlene's and Art's life. All that remained was a charred wreck and the scorched number plate. That is how they identified the charcoaled body of Art Forsman.

Arlene Forsman never knew that her husband had been fired.

The Girl on the Bench

Feeling suddenly older, that day he took the path beside the ponds rather than the steep one that climbed the hill overlooking London. Why this was called Parliament Hill he had no idea, for he could never see the Houses of Parliament from it. Perhaps its origin came from 'talking'? After all, isn't that what 'parliament' means? *Talking? Men and women talking?*

Would that they had talked more, but God gave them so little time together. As for his walks on Parliament Hill Fields, he never talked to himself. He often saw old people walking alone and talking to no one, but he was not one of those. He was a silent old person. Silent and sad. Sad to have been on his own for so long.

And he was silent, that day, as he took the pond path for his daily exercise stroll across the 'fields'. There was something strange about the path, which is why he usually avoided it, but being the anniversary of her death, he felt drawn towards the ponds. She had always said how special they were. Also, he was beginning to find the hill climb too strenuous.

His legs were already tiring as he approached the second pond. There was a bench there, but to his annoyance someone was sitting on it. A schoolgirl with an old-fashioned brown paper bag on her lap (why not polythene?) and she was eating a sandwich. He was about to trudge on to the next bench when the girl looked up. He recognized her immediately.

"Chrissy?"

She gave him an odd look. Did she truly not recognize him?

"How do you know my name?" she asked, with her sandwich on hold halfway between lap and mouth. He frowned. Was his memory playing tricks?

"You are Chrissy, aren't you?"

"Yes, but you haven't answered my question. How do you know my name? You're not one of those old pervies, are you?"

Chrissy had put the sandwich back onto her lap and fixed him with bright, young eyes.

"Oh!" he exclaimed after a pause. He felt confused. It had been so long. "Your parents. I knew—erm—I *know* your mother."

Suspicion entered the girl's eyes as she stared at him.

"What's Mum's name, then?"

"Susan," he replied immediately. How could he forget? "Her name's Susan. Look, may I sit please? My legs are very tired, and I always take a rest half-way through my walk."

The girl shrugged her shoulders.

"Suit yourself. Guess I can run faster than you, anyway," she answered.

He sat beside Chrissy who continued to eat her sandwich whilst he searched his brain for the words he might say to her. His head felt empty. He heard a duck quack then beat the water with its wings. He stared at the chasing ripples that spread outwards from where the duck had been. Why couldn't he say anything? Why did he feel so embarrassed?

"So, what do you make of her?" the girl asked.

"Who?" he asked, turning to face Chrissy. It pained him to look at her. With a quack, the duck landed on the pond again.

"My mother, of course!"

"Oh—well, a fine woman. Very fine." Which was true.

"Pff! Then you don't really know her!"

Perhaps it was understandable that the girl didn't recognize him. After all, it had been such a long time.

"A truly remarkable woman, your mother."

"Hey, are we talking about the same person?" questioned Chrissy before taking an apple from her brown paper bag. She took a bite then grinned mischievously at him. That grin had not changed.

"Susan? Why, yes! A wonderful person. She—"

"Well, me and Mum aren't on speaking terms. Not today, anyway." Chrissy had stopped grinning, but she continued to munch her apple as she studied the old man. "Can you keep a secret?" she asked after a brief period of silence. He smiled. She, of all people, should have known the answer. He nodded. Chrissy threw the apple core in the vague direction of the duck who skidded across the water to inspect the offering. "Do they eat apples?" He laughed without answering. "It's about Dave," Chrissy continued.

Dave? Their son was called Dave.

"If it wasn't for Dave, I'd have run away. We usually meet here during lunch-break. His school is next to mine. My rubbish school! Something must have kept him back today because he's always here before me. Mum doesn't like me seeing Dave, but she simply doesn't understand. Anyway, it's too late." Chrissy looked at him. Those eyes! No doubt about it, but all this talk about Dave? Their son wasn't even alive back then. Before he met her.

"What do you mean, 'it's too late'?"

"You *can* keep a secret? Truly?"

"Truly," he replied, weakly.

"We're lovers," Chrissy announced proudly. He looked away. It felt as if he'd been hit by a ten-ton truck. "Honestly, we are. Lovers. But Mum doesn't know."

"Your father?" He knew the answer. He only said that to keep up the pretence.

"Haven't got one. He died when I was little. Surely you knew that!"

"Oh—of course! Sorry!" he exclaimed, pretending he had just remembered.

"He's going to take me to Italy one day. Dave, that is. We're both into art, see. Going to go to art college together. That's the thing that's niggling Mum. If she only knew what Dave's really like, but she'll never understand because she doesn't want to."

He looked at the duck which had now lost interest in the floating apple core and was slowly swimming away. Chrissy sprang from the bench. Her eyes positively glowed.

"There he is!" she said excitedly, looking into the distance. She momentarily fixed the old man with those incredible eyes. Her pretty, young face was ecstatic. "Dave!" she shouted before running off up the path. She ran into the arms of a youth in a black school blazer. The old man looked away. He could not bear to see the two young lovers kiss. When he finally summoned enough courage to glance in their direction they were gone.

That was the last time he ever saw Chrissy. She cannot have been much younger than when he had married her. He knew she had been on the rebound back then. 'A schoolgirl romance gone wrong,' she told him. The boy had won some sort of scholarship and disappeared off to Italy and they had fallen out over this—or so she said. She never told him the boy's name.

Chrissy was an art student at the time, less than half his age. He owned a book shop and he fell in love with her as soon she walked into his shop to ask for a book on Giotto. He did not have one, but he put in an order for her then asked her out. He could not believe his ears when she said "yes"—and twenty years his junior! But they did not have long together. She died in childbirth. Their son, Dave, survived. She had insisted on the name 'Dave' if it turned out to be a boy.

Nine months earlier, Chrissy had gone to Florence by herself. He could not leave the shop, but he understood how much it meant to Chrissy to see those Giottos and Masaccios and Piero Della Francescas. She was sublimely happy when she came back from Italy. He never forgot her radiant smile on her return for which, mistakenly it now seemed, he had thanked Giotto.

Over forty-five years had passed, and that smile remained imprinted on his brain, but now there was another image to haunt him. The image of a schoolboy with darkly-handsome features identical to those of his beloved son, David.

The Soul Sweeper

Ever wondered what happens when it is all over? Wondered whether you just crawl unseen from that grave and start looking for a sign-post that reads *'To the Pearly Gates'*; whether you will mysteriously grow luminous white wings and soar above the clouds to lands that grow brighter, not darker, the higher you go; or whether, after all, there is just one big, long and boring nothing. Of course you have! You will have wondered, and none of what filtered back to you would have made any sense. Anyway, here is the truth, for what it is worth...

A guy with a brush comes along and sweeps us up.

As simple as that. No ordinary guy, mind you, and no ordinary brush.

When it is over, all that is left is the soul. The body—the part that talks, walks, sleeps, and eats—is, by then, neatly tucked away under the ground or stored as dull-grey ash in a dull-looking urn in a dull place of repose.

Repose? For what?

The soul, the bit that matters, is somewhere else—waiting. We never see waiting souls because there is no substance to them, but they are there. And a fear of the soul sweeper lies dormant within each and every one of us. After the soul is cruelly disengaged from the body it grows to love so dearly on earth, freed from thoughts of work and love and anger, and when memories of what happened before death have grown dim, all that's left is the cold, universal fear of the sweeper of souls. The waiting soul has no legs or arms. It cannot wriggle its undefined existence like some spiritual slug at the start of an eternal journey or beam itself up onto a higher plane. It's just there, wherever the person it was gave up the ghost, awaiting the soul sweeper, amorphous, invisible and afraid.

We do not see the souls and we do not see the soul sweeper as he glides silently through streets, graveyards, across fields of battle, into houses, always searching and sniffing for souls. And all he can see is released souls, for that is his only purpose. To clean up the spiritual detritus of the world.

It may be minutes, months or many years before a released soul feels the approach of the soul sweeper. Feels, not hears, for the soul has no ears, and no one, no soul, has ever seen the soul sweeper. But the silent swish of the brush will trigger a replay of memories for the frightened soul; flashbacks of things done and undone, words spoken—or unspoken—but the soul knows, and he knows, and nothing, nothing on earth that is, could be as terrible as the fear the soul feels just before the final swish of that brush. This way, heaven, that way, hell—leaving behind neat dead-leaf piles of the good and the damned. The soul sweeper decides. It's his job.

The world is a big place for just one sweeper of souls, but eternity is a long time and he is in no hurry. He knows where they are, those souls without bodies, and he never misses one out because it is all he does, moving across the land, the seas, with his brush at the ready. In his wake he leaves only wormholes for heaven and wormholes for hell. No free souls are left behind.

Hawai'i

It appeared out of a soft, blue haze that shimmered beneath the sun. At first, I was only aware of an indefinite shape, a sort of stretched-out triangle hovering on the horizon as if left behind by ancient gods after a geometry lesson. I soon realized I was looking at the bulk of a huge mountain mass emerging from a seemingly limitless sea. Big Island, Hawai'i.

Excited, I fumbled with my compact camera, eager to capture something of the majesty of the vast volcano, and it was then that my elbow brushed against the arm of an elderly gentleman in the seat beside me. I thought this odd since it was unoccupied when the plane left Honolulu but assumed the old fellow must have changed seats to get a better view.

"Aloha!" the man said when I turned around. His face, brown and wizened, reminded me of the bark of an ageless tree. His hair was a coarse, white mat, and there was white stubble on his chin. He was unusually thin for a Polynesian.

"Erm—hello!" I replied. I lowered my camera. Besides, the sun was too bright. I looked again at the changing shape of the volcano.

"She's dead, that one," said the old man.

"What?" I asked, turning again to face my travelling companion.

"Dead!" he repeated. "Well, ain't that *she's* really dead, see. Kinda moved on, like." His accent was strange. American, but clipped and foreign sounding. "Moved on to Mauna Loa, she did, millions of years back."

I had read my guidebooks and knew he was referring to that aeon-paced southerly march of volcanic activity that created a string of geological jewels in the timeless Pacific.

"American?" he queried. His voice resembled the hum of a half-heard distant beehive.

"No," I replied. "Scottish."

"Sure, thing," he said. "England! Used to be our friends, you English. Have your flag on ours, too."

"No," I frowned. "Scottish!"

"Ain't where you come from that matters—it's where you're going to that counts."

The wrinkled face stretched itself around a toothless grin. The old man just stared at me, so I turned to glance again at the bulk of Mauna Kea wearing her skirt of black lava fringed with pearl-white surf as she lay sandwiched between the blue of the sea and the blue of the sky.

"*Akua!*" he announced to the back of my head, forcing me to swivel and face him again.

"What?"

"*Akua!* Like *her. Pele.*"

"Oh!" I said, not knowing of whom or what he spoke.

"Tallest mountain on Earth," the old man remarked, nodding at the window. I frowned again.

"What about Everest?" I asked, boastful of my superior knowledge, but the old man continued as if addressing a child:

"Everest? She starts in the clouds. That one—" he peered at the ancient volcano, "—that one, she starts way down under the sea."

"Oh!" I remarked, unconvinced that the part of the mountain below the sea should be used to elevate its status to the world's tallest.

"See," the old man went on, "you carry on goin' down, keep walkin' down over there—" He raised his skinny arm and pointed a stick-like finger towards the window. "—And goin' on down and down and you gonna feel like you've gotten ten thousand laden trucks across them shoulders of yours."

"Quite," I politely agreed, distinctly uneasy about his mental status.

"Brain squeezed to a pinpoint. And still goin' down and down. So goddamn dark down there can't even see your hand to wipe your arse!"

The man grinned again. It was then that I noticed for the first time his extraordinary eyes. It would be an understatement to say they 'twinkled', and certainly wrong to use the term 'shone'. It was something to do with their depth. Not a physical depth, more a depth of meaning, of understanding, which made the old guy seem as ageless as the mountain we were discussing. He stared at me again, still smiling. After looking straight into his eyes for a while, a sensation that no words can describe slammed into me. I felt compelled to turn and gaze out of the window.

Mauna Kea was now close enough for me to see a cluster of white buildings perched on her head, picked out by the sun (I knew these belonged to the famous observatory), and there were patches of green decorating the lower flanks of the volcano, but otherwise it was all black volcanic stone that swept with dignity, not menace, down towards the sea.

"Hell!" he said.

Once more I turned to engage with the strange old fellow.

"Hell!" he repeated. "That's where you gets to if you keeps on goin' down and down out there. Hell! And it ain't hot either. No man, ain't no hot place, *that* hell! So, you see, she's givin' you a chance to escape."

The conversation was not what I wanted to hear at the start of a week's sojourn on a paradise island. I had different images of Hawai'i imprinted upon my mind: holiday brochure pictures of curling breakers, incandescent blue in the sunlight, bearing ecstatic surfers towards untold happiness; photographs of rainbow-coloured, tropical fish and languid sea turtles, and of slender palm trees lazily yielding to a caressing sea breeze. I had no place in my brain for pictures of a dark and heavy hell at the bottom of the Pacific Ocean. Nope! *My* holiday was going to be in that other place, the brochure paradise.

"See—" persisted the old man, "I met a guy once. He figured out that if you reach hell by just walkin' down and down, why, if you just keep on goin' up and up, then you gonna get to some whole place else!"

My fellow traveller both irritated and fascinated me. Had he just read my mind after that talk of hell? The airplane banked steeply. I glanced out of the window again and caught a fleeting glimpse of another mountain mass beyond Mauna Kea. Less of a mountain than an enormous smoking black dome.

"And *she* there, she's the biggest goddamn mountain on Earth."

"I thought you just said—" I began.

"Biggest, not tallest," he corrected.

"Oh!" I exclaimed, nodding and feeling somewhat like a small child who had been taught a truly basic fact. I looked out again as the aircraft banked the other way. The tallest and the biggest mountains on Earth drifted out of view. For a few giddying moments the horizon was replaced by a wall of indigo sea, terrifyingly close and alive with curling strips of white surf which appeared and disappeared like the whitened eyebrows of fleeting spectral faces.

"Keep on walkin' up," the old guy said, "up and up on *her*, that other one, and instead of gettin' heavier you gets lighter." He was talking to the back of my head again. "Up and up and up and all that darkness inside of you, weighin' you down, just disappears. Everythin' goes bright. And that fella he says this too—says you can't stop, see. Not even when you gets to where *she* lives, at *Halema'uma'u*. 'Cos you're so filled with *Mana*."

I wanted to call the flight attendant for help, but something prevented me. Perhaps it was the old man's eyes when I turned to look again; that strange feeling of depth, of long-forgotten knowledge and a pull towards the timeless dimension of ancient Polynesian gods.

"Mountain climbing?" I suggested stupidly. "Never really been keen on it, myself. Prefer to brave the sharks with snorkelling." I knew I was being trite, but the old man had unnerved me.

"Ain't like that," he continued. "This ain't no mountain climb, what that man said. No sir, not when *she's* there. See, where *she*, the goddess Pele, lives, up there, you is only just startin' when you gets to the mouth of that crater. And I tell you another thing. You don't wanna be upsettin' her, 'cos she can get kinda touchy. Keep on the right side of her and you have to keep on goin'. Pulled on up, you are. Light as a feather off a chicken's hiney." His gnarled hands emphasised the upward migration of a feather-light searching soul whilst the vast shape of Mauna Loa, now closer, appeared once more in the window and the airplane continued its final descent towards Kona airport. "And you'll no longer need them legs to carry you. You just keep on goin' up. So light. So bright. *She* takes over, see, like the blackness and the thousand-truck weight takes over down there that other way. And then she breathes a whole new life into you with that fire of hers."

I was beginning to wish the aircraft would land there and then—anywhere! I tried to avoid looking again into the old man's eyes, but something pulled me back into them. A light, perhaps? I could swear I saw a glimpse, just a glimpse mind you, of a 'light' the like of which I had never seen before. Not a light in the visual sense of the word. His pupils were as black as coal, but 'light' is the closest description that I can offer. The sensation of this 'light' disturbed my sense of reality. The reality of who and where I was. I talked in a matter-of-fact kind of way to keep a hold on sanity, particularly as the old man never stopped smiling.

"What happened to this man?" I asked.

"Like I said, just keep goin' up and *she* takes over," he failed to answer. "And that lightness—well, it kinda becomes everythin'. Know what I mean? *Every*thin'! *Mana!*"

I avoided his gaze and looked again out of the window, relieved to see that we were close to land. I made out the coastal road and the 'toy' cars and trucks down there, the white buildings stark against the bleak, black lava, and clusters of incongruous, green palm trees braving the strange landscape. All this, together with the waves, the turtles and the colourful fish, would be my paradise over the week to follow.

"Beautiful! Just look at those breakers," I said, pointing to the rim of white surf marking out the limit of the silver-sanded beach. I turned to face my travelling companion, but the seat was empty. I looked up and down the aisle. Nothing. Several seats were hidden from view. Perhaps he'd returned to another seat or merely availed himself of the toilet before landing.

We arrived at Kona airport a few minutes later. The airplane taxied off the runway and came to a standstill. The engine whine dwindled to silence and a hundred or more passengers jumped up like released Jack-in-a-Boxes. I searched the bobbing heads for the old man but could not see him. Had the poor fellow collapsed in the toilet? I hurriedly grabbed my luggage from the overhead locker and rudely pushed forward to the front of the plane where three cabin crew staff stood in the galley. I was aware of causing annoyance to other passengers whilst I tried to explain to the flight attendants that the old man who had been sitting beside me might have collapsed in the toilet. One of the attendants frowned.

"What old man?" she asked. "The seat beside you was unoccupied throughout the flight, sir."

"I know—" I began as I manoeuvred my hand-luggage to one side to let a dangerously-irritated woman squeeze past. "I know the seat was empty when we took off, but this old guy came and sat beside me for a chat before we came in to land. He had white hair, and—" I was about to describe the guy but was interrupted by the flight attendant:

"I'm sorry sir, but we have a lot of passengers to disembark and we do have a very tight schedule. May I suggest you take this up with the ground staff. Thank you, sir."

Her companion, a dark-skinned Polynesian girl, of whom the older woman seemed unaware, stared in my direction with an expression that informed me I was not completely mad. She knew exactly what I was talking about.

"*Aloha!*" the Polynesian girl said in a voice of scented flowers and clear, rippling water. She had a beautiful smile. Our eyes met for a brief instant only, but this was enough for me to recognise once more that very same and extraordinary 'light'.

The Goddess Pele?

The Visitor

The town was dead. Dead as the air-con in my beat-up old Buick. In the Alabama heat, it seemed my brain was about to swell and burst out of my hot skull, so I pulled up at a fast-food joint near the edge of the small town and got me an iced Coke to put out the fire in my head. An old black guy, seated at the next table, must have noticed the sweat glistening my brow and soaking my tee-shirt. He grinned at me and winked.

"You could just about melt out there, huh? Melt and hope you'd evaporate, 'cos ain't no one in this goddamn hole would sweep up the mess if you didn't."

Holding the glass of iced Coke against my cheek, I grinned but said nothing.

"You a visitor or you just passin' through?" he asked.

"Passing through," I echoed.

"You know, we had ourselves a visitor once."

I put the glass down. He wanted to talk, and I was in no hurry. I scraped my chair around to face him.

"No one really knew exactly when he moved into a run-down ole shack the other end of town. Just that people kinda noticed him around. Ain't no one knew his real name, either. 'Him', he gotten called.

"And a funny ole town this is 'cos she ain't got no soul. See, she kinda lost her soul after it happened. Long before he arrived. 'Course, I was just another black boy back then. A black boy in a town split in two like all them other Alabama towns was. And we blacks were doin' all right 'cos we'd gotten our rightful dignity back after that Dr Martin Luther King shared his dream. When he done that, we finds we can do just about anythin' them white guys can do and sometimes better. We'd gotten ourselves teachers and lawyers and doctors, but we kept ourselves to ourselves back then. Didn't go mixin' any. Yeah, before it happened, she was split down the middle. Black and white.

"Then it happened, and when he arrived, all those years later, our small town had lost her soul because of it. You could even be forgiven for wonderin' why they'd ever gone and built the dang place, for afterwards it was like she was hangin' there in that heat, on them crossroads, just like she'd been crucified. Only there wasn't no Jesus in her! No sir!

"'Course, that visitor he knew nothin' of what had happened when he came. Ain't many folks around now that remembers it either. Even them white folks, and they were the cause of it all. Me, I was only a kid back then, but ain't nothin' happens in this town and not everyone knows about it. Now some, they blamed everythin' on that war in the Nam, but me, I knows different. It was people, not the war, done that thing.

"See, first it seemed like the war would finally make one community out of us, for black boys and white boys, they were sent to the Nam to fight together side by side. Whites saved blacks, blacks saved whites. And the letters that came back from the Nam, they were all mixed up together, those from the black boys and those from the white boys. And the bags the bodies came back in, they looked the same till you opened 'em up. Then you'd find some were white inside and some were black, and some were neither white nor black for you'd find you was just starin' at charcoal and bones and wonderin'. Yeah, if anythin' that goddamn war almost brought our two communities together. Until it happened.

"His name was Chuck. Chuck's daddy, he was kinda rich. Owned a real estate business and a Cadillac convertible. And that daddy. he allowed his boy to drive the Cadillac, and the boy sure was proud to be seen drivin' his sweetheart, Mary-Lou, to drive-in movies. They would sit there and kiss and cuddle like there wasn't no one else in the whole goddamn world.

"Chuck and Mary-Lou had been sweet on each other ever since junior high school, see, and it seemed there wasn't nothin' could separate 'em. Not even the war in Vietnam. When Chuck gotten signed up he must've been all of nineteen years of age. Thought he was a man, he did, but I knows now he was only a kid. His and Mary-Lou's partin' brought tears to everyone's eyes. Us blacks, too. They all said their love was like that white man's book, Romeo and Juliet.

"Mary-Lou, she was the prettiest girl y'ever did see and some folks said the sadness in her blue eyes after Chuck gotten sent to the Nam made them even prettier. At first the girls and the mommas, they would say no news was good news if the mail man put nothin' in their mailboxes, but even us boys knew that was a cover up for fear. The fear inside of every woman: fear that the man they'd kissed goodbye to, the man who looked so strong in that fine uniform, that same man was lyin' dead and dirtied in a paddy field with nothin' to cover his bullet-ridden body other than the rain and the mud. And that was what they feared when they said those brave words over and over, and the fear it ate into their souls and it changed 'em like the fightin' changed the men.

"And so it was with Mary-Lou. She'd gotten one letter from Chuck, after three weeks, sayin' how he swore his undyin' love, and they said she went around with the letter hidden under her blouse. Closer to her heart, they said. Then no more letters came. They kept saying to the girl 'no news is good news', but Mary-Lou, she knew different. After three months, even they stopped pretendin'. Chuck's daddy, he tried gettin' info' from the military, but they told him it was kinda messy out there and all he could do was to wait. Wait and hope. They said the boy might have gone MIA. Sounded kinda important, to go MIA, but that was just military talk for 'he ain't never gonna come back—not even in a body bag'.

"The next month Mary-Lou's momma, she told the girl to find another boy. 'Besides,' she said, 'you and Chuck weren't even betrothed.'

"Mary-Lou, she cried for two weeks. Shut herself in her bedroom and cried and wouldn't come out. Then one day she stopped cryin', like somethin' inside of her had died.

'Course, she was still as pretty as ever, and the boys in town that hadn't gone to the Nam, they were delighted, but it seemed like the girl no longer cared. Every evenin' she drank downtown. That's how she met Jason.

"Jason, he looked like a normal boy, strong and handsome, and he worked in the gas station, but he'd never gotten sent to the Nam on account of his asthma. On medications for it, he was, so he never gotten sent to be shot at by the Cong. We blacks thought Jason was a good boy, but after it happened the white folks just couldn't decide. Them that lived at the south end of town, where folks were poor, thought he was good, but them other white folks, the landowners and the lawyers at the north end, they said he was real bad.

"Whether he seduced her, or she seduced him, whether the girl loved Jason or her MIA childhood sweetheart, that seemed of little importance when it gotten known by all that she was three months' pregnant. Didn't show much then, but already the whole town was talkin' about it. Like I said, ain't nothin' ever happens here and not everyone knows. They were all expectin' Jason to propose to the girl, even though he was only a gas station attendant and she was a high school graduate hopin' to go on to college.

"Then Chuck returned. Came back with only one and a half legs. He'd been away for eleven months and Mary-Lou was five months pregnant and now it did show. Mary-Lou, she still looked beautiful, but her ole sweetheart had grown ugly lookin'. The boy whose charm and smile could have once turned a ravin' slayer into a saint, he now had a mean look about him. *Real* mean. They said his eyes had gone funny. Kinda hard, and if you looked into 'em long enough you'd see black clouds all heavy with rain, and the water in the paddy fields, just water everywhere, and the shells explodin', then you'd smell the stench of them shells and feel the touch of death. Folks said if you looked even harder into those eyes you could see the eyes of the Cong, keen and cold and starin' at you from the undergrowth, from gutted buildin's, all the time starin'. Said you might even see the fire of hell in that boy's eyes. And the eyes that showed these things, they saw that hump on Mary-Lou's belly. They saw her tears, too. But the small boy behind those eyes, he just didn't know what to do after he saw his sweetheart with child by another man. Mary-Lou, she pleaded with him. Near drowned her childhood lover with her tears when she told Chuck she still loved him, she did, and she begged him to forgive her. Said she'd died inside herself when they told her he must be dead. Said she no longer had any use for her body, bein' dead inside, when she gave it to that gas station attendant. But Chuck, he only saw a beautiful girl, his girl, and that girl had given herself to another man. Called her a cheap hooker and a bitch and a whore. She ran from him. She ran cryin' as the small boy watched her through those cold, hard eyes. He couldn't run after her on account of only havin' one and a half legs, but the small boy wouldn't have known what he was runnin' to, even if he could have, 'cos he never knew how much that girl really loved him.

"They found Mary-Lou swingin' from the branch of a dead tree down by the river. It was her Daddy who cut her body down. A broken man, he was.

"Now Chuck, he never understood nothin' 'cos inside he was just a small kid, like I said, but that small kid inside of that crippled demon they sent back from the Nam, he knew only hate and anger and revenge. No one will ever know what went on in the mind of that kid as he watched his other self, the demon soldier with only one-and-a-half legs, shoot that Jason boy in the head. No one will know, 'cos the demon just turned the gun on himself and shot the small kid in the head.

"Already, before the shootin's, whites were split between them that saw for Jason and them that saw for Chuck. It was like the dead girl was the prize that never really mattered, but them whites were still fightin' over it. After the slayin's, the split in the whites was as deep and wide as the Grand Canyon in Arizona. Whites livin' in the south end of town, they sided with the dead gas station attendant's family. For them, Jason was a good boy who'd been unlucky enough to fall in love with another boy's sweetheart, and they saw only the demon in Chuck. White folks at the other end, the north end, the rich ones with the big houses, they were all with the realtor. They saw only Chuck, the small boy who'd gotten sent to the Nam to fight for his country and came back missin' half a leg. Wouldn't have happened, they said, if the gas station attendant hadn't stolen the girl from him, and they blamed Jason's family. Should've controlled the 'dog' as they called him. And his family, they blamed Mary-Lou's folks for encouragin' her to lead him on. So, one war led to another. The whites of the north would drive in their posh Lincolns and their Plymouths all the way to the next town to fill up with gas. Kept on doin' that even when they'd forgotten why. The kids from the south end never sat with the kids from the north end in school, and in church the two lots of whites, they separated like oil from water. Until the visitor arrived...

"It was around the time of the relocation of them South Vietnamese who'd fled from the Cong who had made monkeys of our troops. And they came with their families and spoke no English, so they kinda stuck together. That visitor, he found a town split into four like a Thanksgivin' turkey.

"He wasn't much to look at, that guy whose name no one knew. Kinda shabby. But he spoke to people. Gentle voice, too. Spoke to anyone and everyone and our four-way split meant nothin' to him. They said the look in his eyes seemed to say, 'Hey, I sure would like to listen to you, hear what you have to say', and people kinda like folks who listen, shabby or not. He listened to darn near everyone in our town, but the funny thing was, never once did he ask them to listen to him. Folks only told him things—never asked him. That's how no one knew his name.

"After he came, things began to change. Blacks spoke to whites and whites from the north spoke to whites from the south, and the Vietnamese, when they learned English, they spoke to anyone. White doctors and lawyers, they showed up at the gas station, and boys from the north end would even hang out with girls from the south end.

"And another thing happened. Money came available at the public library for kids' activities. Activities that helped to bring all four communities together, and soon the children here played as one. There were dances, too, and no one asked who sponsored these, but whites from the north end danced and laughed with whites from the south end.

"So, our town, she gotten back her soul. For a time, the war, Mary-Lou and the whole goddamn sadness of the slayin's was all forgotten.

"Then he left. Never mentioned that he was leavin', and, 'course, no one thought to ask him how long he was stayin'.

"'Seen him today, Earl?'

"'Funny thing, that, Warren. No, I ain't. Not for two days.'

"'Me neither, Earl.'

"No one ever saw him again. The ole shack at the edge of town stayed empty, and soon it seemed like nobody had lived in it for years. Many stories went around. Stories about what had happened to him. Some said he'd gotten sick, and not wantin' to bother folks here he kinda just walked off. Others said he'd gotten called away on urgent business. There was even a story that he'd been kidnapped. Folks said he had big money and perhaps they took him for his money which he kept hidden away. Enough money to fill a bank vault twice over, some said. Now there was a few who kinda implied he'd never really existed at all. Not solid, like. Reckoned he was Jesus just visiting folks in their minds. Not me, I should add, for I sure knows what I sees, and I sees him all right, but that's what some folks was sayin'. Never could figure out why they said that.

"For a while our town she stayed alive. Kept her soul and stayed alive. Those dances and kids' activities, they carried on. And soon they forgot how it all came about, the bringing together of our four communities. They forgot about 'him' as they'd forgotten about the happenin'. Until..."

The old guy sighed.

"'Course, it was a white boy and a white girl again. He was a rich kid, just back from college, who took a fancy to a girl who was a waitress downtown. Trouble was, she was already married. Her husband used to fix them broken telephone lines, and they had a cosy little house at the south end of town. Too cosy for a girl on her own, she thought, and when her husband was away for lengthy periods, fixin' phone lines, she'd phone her lover-boy. Husband went ape-shit when he found out his cute little wife was lendin' her body on the side to one of them rich boys. Slapped her around, he did, and the next day she and lover-boy vanished. And so it started up all over again. The blame and the takin' of sides—and the warrin'.

"Like I says, it's all down to people. And the visitor? Man, you's lucky if you meets a guy like that who brings folks together just once in a life-time. Our town, she only got lucky the once."

The old black guy grinned again, displaying pink fleshy gums. I had stopped sweating, but my tee-shirt was still damp. I raised my glass to my lips for the first time. The ice had melted, and the Coke had gotten warm, but my brain, though reeling from the old man's story, was no longer on deep fry. I smiled at him and, without a word, paid up and left.

"Darn it!" I muttered as I opened the door of the Buick. I had forgotten to ask the old fellow about getting the air-con in my car fixed. The heat was already extracting beads of sweat from my forehead again as I retraced my steps into the fast food joint. It was empty of customers.

"That old black guy I was talking to just now—about the war in Vietnam. Do you know where he's gone?" I asked the man at the cash-desk.

He gave me a funny look.

"Heat must be gettin' to your brain, sir. Ain't seen no ole black guy in here today." He turned and spoke to the girl cooking French fries. "You seen an ole black guy, Polly?"

"Can't say I have, Mr Rocco!"

And the sweat travelled from my temples to my chin.

The Author

After Oliver Eade, a doctor, awoke one night with a ghost story in his head, he took to writing short stories, several winning prizes, and was seven times winner of the Wilfred Hopkins Prize for creative writing. During a visit to his Chinese wife's mother country in 2006, he became interested in Chinese mythology, thus inspiring his first middle grade readers' novel, *Moon Rabbit*. A winner of the Writers' and Artists' 2007 New Novel Competition, and long-listed for the Waterstones Children's Book Prize, 2008, this was followed by a sequel, *Monkey King's Revenge*, a children's section finalist for the People's Book Prize, plus another three young readers' novels. His debut adult novel, *A Single Petal*, a story of passionate love, family honour and political skulduggery, set in ancient China, won the 2012 Local Legend Spiritual Writing Competition. *Voices*, also for adults, was inspired by his childhood in London and his experience, from clinical practice, of covert child abuse within families. *The Terminus* is a time-travel, post-apocalyptic novel for young adults addressing friendship and first love. Further novels include a young adult trilogy, *From Beast to God* set in North America, a story of the trials of young love involving travel to the Americas of the distant past and inspired by First Nation North American and Mesoamerican beliefs and a blending of Christian and Native spirituality. Later, this was revised as a three-part novel, *Eyes of Fire*. In *The Kelpie's Eyes*, sisterly love wins through against the darker forces of

Scottish mythology. The novel won first prize in the 2018 *Words for the Wounded* Young Adult Novel Competition.

The author's experiences as a doctor help to illustrate advances in the history of medicine in *In the Blink of an Eye*.

Although not confined to any particular genre or style, Oliver feels most comfortable in that space between reality and fantasy; the space into and out of which children slip so easily in their play; the place of dreams, myths and legends deeply ingrained in diverse cultures across the globe; the magical realism of Latin American writers like Gabriel García Márquez and Isabel Allende in her young adult trilogy.

Oliver also writes plays. In 2018 his dark comedy take on the bizarreness of quantum reality, *The Other Cat*, was winner of the Segora International One Act Play competition, whilst his surreal play, *The Gap*, was inspired by being caught up in an earthquake in southwest China in 2008. Four of his plays have been performed, on tour, in Scotland, one in 2012 and three in 2019.

Having lived and worked as a doctor in England, Scotland and America, with family and friends in many countries across the world, he is inspired by the common thread of human experience across all cultures and societies. He is also a keen photographer and winner of the 2022 Amateur Photographer Readers' Portfolio Competition.

Website: *www.olivereadebooks.org*

For other Silver Quill Publishing books, please visit: *www.silverquillpublishing.com*